M000190892

Kiss the Stars

A.L. Jackson

NEW YORK TIMES BESTSELLING AUTHOR

Copyright © 2020 A.L. Jackson Books Inc.
First Edition

All rights reserved. Except as permitted under the U.S. Copyright Act
of 1976, no part of this publication may be reproduced, distributed,
transmitted in any form or by any means, or stored in a database or
retrieval system, without prior permission of the publisher. Please
protect this art form by not pirating.

A.L. Jackson
www.aljacksonauthor.com
Cover Design by Silver at Bitter Sage Designs
Editing by Susan Staudinger
Formatting by Mesquite Business Services

The characters and events in this book are fictitious. Names, characters,
places, and plots are a product of the author's imagination. Any
similarity to real persons, living or dead, is coincidental and not
intended by the author.

Print ISBN: 978-1-946420-75-6
eBook ISBN: 978-1-946420-44-2

Kiss the

Stars

More from A.L. Jackson

prologue

I raced out of the suite and down the hall. The wall of windows to my left overlooked the pool and yard just beyond.

A storm bared down. Gusts of wind that lashed through the trees. It sent them whipping and shivering and howling beneath the moon that burned through a thin break in the clouds.

My heart raced as I took in the man who was a shadow beneath it, his shoulders hitched high as he strode across the yard toward his little home.

If he even had one.

The man lost.

A wanderer who raged as he searched through the Earth for where he fit.

I wanted to carve out a place for him. Show him what it was like to belong. To be treasured and loved, the way he showed me without asking for a thing in return.

I burst through the door, pummeled by a squall of wind.

A fierce fury that blasted through the air.

"What if I don't want you to go?" I shouted above it. "What if I want you to stay, right here, with me?"

In the distance, he froze, as if he had been impaled by the plea. Staked to the spot.

Slowly, he turned. Rain began to pelt from the sky.

"I keep telling you that you don't want me. That you don't have the first clue what you're asking for."

I didn't.

I didn't have the first clue what he was going to do to me.

If he would love me or if he would wreck me.

Maybe I should have turned my back right then.

Taken heed of the warning that flashed across his gorgeous face.

But I stepped out into the rain.

And I took the chance . . .

one

Mia

"Are you okay?" Lyrik asked just loud enough for me to hear over the din of live music that echoed through the air. A clatter of voices and laughter mingled with it, glasses clinking as the sounds of the extravagant party carried around us.

My older brother had hauled me into a deserted hallway where we were hidden from view of the rest of the guests who overflowed his mansion, the man holding tight to my elbow as he searched my face.

I got the sense he was worried it was the only way he could keep me from floating away.

"Lyrik, I'm fine." As fine as I could be with my heart a jackhammer in my chest.

Nerves rattled.

Breaths jagged and shallow and exposing everything I wanted

to keep hidden from my brother.

You know, the straight up lie I was spouting.

But sometimes telling them were the only way to get by.

Lyrik caught it. Did I expect anything else? He'd always read me better than anyone.

Dark eyes flared as he glowered down at me. "Bullshit."

"I don't know what you want me to say. That I freaked out? That I overreacted? Or that I really was scared?"

All of the above.

I didn't know how to fix it short of locking myself in a room forever and never coming out.

Lyrik would probably think that was a fantastic idea.

"Honestly, if it was my choice, I wouldn't let you out of my sight."

A mix between affection and disbelief rumbled in my chest.

I knew him, too. Knew him inside and out and back again. And that meant I knew he was hurting almost as badly as me.

Worried.

Aching for a way to take it away, to make it better, and realizing it didn't matter how much fame had come his way or how many zeroes he had sitting in his bank accounts, he had no power over this.

What was done was already done.

Buried six feet underground.

"That is ridiculous and impossible and you're being overbearing again," I tried to reason, to calm him down. I was riddled with enough anxiety for the two of us.

"I'll show you ridiculous," he warned, glancing around like the monster would suddenly make himself known in the middle of one of the biggest galas of the year. "Told you the lengths I'd go, Mia. Wasn't joking."

"And you know I would never ask that of you. This isn't your responsibility. You've already done enough."

Lyrik scowled.

I swore, the man appeared nothing less than a demon in the shadows of the private hall, towering over me while I tried to remain standing and not break down from the accidental brush of

a stranger's hand.

Lately, crowds and I hadn't been friends.

Problem was, being alone was worse.

"Who was it? Just point him out, and he's out on his ass. No questions. Not gonna tolerate that kind of bullshit going down under my roof. Asshole should know better."

"That's not necessary, Lyrik." My head shook as I gathered myself. "He . . . caught me off guard, that's all. He didn't even mean to touch me. I'm sorry that I made you worry."

There'd just been something in the stranger's seedy eyes that had sent my mind spiraling back to what had happened at my gallery three weeks ago. Something that had sent me running out of the room, close to suffering a full-blown panic attack.

A reel of dark, cruel images hitting me.

Frame after frame.

In that second, the only thing my mind could process was the memory of the evil glaring out from under that mask.

Lyrik stared down at me with stark brotherly concern.

All black hair and even darker eyes.

"Don't you dare apologize, Mia. There isn't one goddamn thing for you to be sorry for. None of this is your fault." His brow drew tight in emphasis, like he'd somehow taken on some of the blame.

A self-conscious breath huffed from between my lips. "Are you joking, Lyrik? I've become nothing but a burden to you and Tamar. You're constantly on edge, and I know you haven't been sleeping."

His expression darkened. "Yeah, well that bastard is still out there. Loose. Not gonna rest until he's behind bars. Or dead."

Grief grasped me by the throat.

This sticky, heavy sensation that made it close to impossible to breathe.

"And you know the detective has concluded it was random. A botched robbery. I'm not in any danger," I choked out around the clot of devastation.

Wishing there was some way to accept that conclusion. To find peace that wouldn't seem to come. I didn't know if it ever would.

"Not a chance I'm willing to take," he grunted, gritting his jaw.

My big brother was tall and thin. Wiry, even. Oh, but he left no illusion that he was one to be toyed with.

He was nothing but rippling, lean, packed muscle. Exuding a vibe that promised he'd strike faster than any ill-intention someone might have.

I'd seen it plenty of times.

Lyrik West wasn't talk. He was straight—I-will-fuck-you-up-and-I-won't-apologize-later—action.

He'd ridded himself of his tux jacket and rolled up the sleeves. Every inch of skin it revealed was covered in the gruesome designs he'd permanently etched on his flesh. I knew he'd done it because he thought he needed the reminder of the evil that lived within.

Only I knew better.

He had angel's wings hiding under all that brash, hard exterior.

And it wasn't like I could hold his looks against him. If it weren't for the handful of years separating us, we probably could have passed as fraternal twins.

"And I'm staying here with you. Just like you asked me to." In emphasis, I touched his arm. "So you need to rest in that. Tonight is supposed to be fun. Your entire band is here. Your *best* friends. Your *brothers*. And the only thing you're doing is worrying about me."

"You think I care about the party?" he demanded, his face angling down close to mine. "You think I give a flying fuck about any of these pricks roaming around here like they are better than the rest of the world? Only thing I care about is my crew. My family. Tamar and Brendon and Adia. You and Penny and Greyson. Rest can burn. So, don't give me this bullshit that you're some kind of burden, yeah? Because I would gladly die before I let someone get to you."

Lyrik edged back, shoved his hands in his pockets, and smirked. "But that won't be necessary. I will raze the whole fuckin' city before anyone gets between me and you or my family. You understand what I'm sayin'?"

A quirk of a smile edged my mouth. "Yeah, yeah, yeah. You're a badass. I get it," I teased.

Only thing it did was cause his smirk to expand. "Hey. Everyone needs a badass on their side."

"Like I said—ridiculous." I tried to shove off the rush of emotions. My heart expanding with the love I had for him.

Lyrik had always taken the time to make sure I knew I was something important in the middle of his great big world.

I forced some levity into my tone. "And newsflash, Lyrik. I don't need you to go around thinking you need to protect me the way you used to do. I'm not a little girl anymore."

So maybe he'd tried to chase off every boyfriend I'd ever had.

He touched my cheek. "Yeah, well you'll always be my baby sister. Get used to it."

"I'm going to survive this, you know." It came out a whisper.

Chest trembling with grief and the hope I refused to let go.

His smile was soft. "You're the strongest person I know. Most wouldn't be standing here right now. You're going to be okay, Mia. I promise you that."

"I have too much good to fight for not to be." A fresh round of emotion crawled my throat.

I beat it down, refusing to feel it.

I felt desperate for a reprieve.

To forget.

Just for tonight.

I forced a bright smile to my face. It was a wonder that it was only half-faked. "Let's just forget about it all right now. Okay? You have important people here to entertain."

My attention drifted to the right, to the main room of his gorgeous Hollywood Hills home. It was crawling with guests for the fundraiser he and his wife, Tamar, hosted each year.

You couldn't turn a corner without running face-first into an A-list celebrity.

The most loved musicians and the most sought-out actors.

Directors and managers and producers.

There were the up and coming and others that couldn't step out on the street without being recognized.

Of course, there were some no-names like me, wide-eyed and unsure and hovering on the fringes in hopes they'd remain unnoticed, while others were clearly waiting for an opportunity to reach out and sink in their claws, salivating for a taste of the fame and fortune you could feel oozing from the bodies that overflowed the space.

"Fuck 'em."

So Lyrik.

I rolled my eyes. "Um . . . your wife put a lot of work into this whole thing, and you're raising money for a good cause."

"You're my good cause."

"Lyrik." It was nothing but exasperation.

"What?" he deadpanned.

A heavy sigh pilfered free. "I love you. Adore you. I'm pretty sure you're the most wonderful man on the planet."

Men like him were rare.

Hell, I was beginning to think they had become obsolete.

Loneliness swelled.

With everything, it shouldn't even be a consideration or thought.

But it didn't matter that I knew better. There were just times . . . times when I wished I had someone to turn to the same way as they could turn to me. Someone who wrapped me up in their arms at night and whispered that everything would be okay.

"Go. Be with your wife. Your friends. Enjoy tonight. Just . . . let me try to do the same. Please."

Not possible.

But at least I could give him an out.

And I was trying.

Trying to act normal. To put on a good show. If the rest of his guests who were parading around in all their diamonds and exaggerated smiles could do it, no cares in sight, then I could do it, too, right?

"I mean, seriously . . . this is ridiculous, Lyrik. You have *Dreams Don't Die* playing on *your freaking patio.*" I lowered my voice like it was some kind of secret.

Believe me, it was a big freaking deal. I'd had to stifle a squeal when I'd gone into the kitchen earlier and found Sean Layne digging around in the refrigerator.

Fangirl (almost) down.

It wouldn't have been pretty.

And let's be clear, I was so not into musicians. I'd sworn off that kind of heartbreak a long time ago.

I'd witnessed enough through Lyrik and his friends.

They were too passionate.

Too volatile.

Too much trouble.

I did not have the time nor the heart for that kind of stress in my life.

But still . . . Sean Layne.

Lyrik hiked a casual shrug. "We own them."

Right.

Of course, they did.

My big brother was the lead guitarist of Sunder, one of the most popular bands in the world, a band that now owned their own record label, spearheaded by their original lead singer, Sebastian Stone.

Lyrik? He was a rockstar, and I wasn't talking the *someday I'll be famous* kind..

He was a guy who stopped traffic when he walked down the street. Someone who couldn't walk into a store without being accosted for his picture and his signature and half the time his freaking shirt.

But he was so much more than that.

He was a man who'd made horrible mistakes and paid for them dearly. A man I'd watched struggle with addiction and suffer with the regrets of it.

A man who'd stumbled time and time again.

He was also a man who'd clawed his way out of the self-destruction to become something great. A man who'd found the girl of his dreams and made the family he'd believed he'd never have.

But the thing about him becoming great was that he'd always been *great* to me.

It didn't matter the sins he'd amassed or the wrongs he'd committed.

He'd always been my hero, and the last thing I wanted was to drag him down tonight.

"So go show them they were a worthy acquisition." My brows lifted with the prod.

He hesitated. "You sure you're fine? Saw your face, Mia. Didn't like it. Will call this whole damn thing off if it makes you more comfortable. Just say the word, night's over."

"No. That's the last thing I want."

I looked back out to the great room. It was open to the lofts that circled above from the second floor. A massive wall of windows at the far end that overlooked Los Angeles had been drawn open, letting the warm California air invade the space.

Just beyond the doors and next to the negative-edge pool that overlooked Los Angeles, Dreams Don't Die played on a makeshift stage. The sultry indie song they played vibrated the house and rumbled along the polished wooden floors.

Strains of music flooded the rooms, the walls throbbing with depth and sensuality.

The crush of bodies and the volume of voices and laughter trying to rise above it gave the atmosphere a vibe of barely-controlled chaos.

As if we were climbing toward the peak of something magnificent.

Or maybe something horrible.

But Lyrik didn't need to be concerned with that.

"Go be with your wife. She is looking awful sexy tonight."

There.

Temptation.

One I knew he couldn't resist.

No dog could resist a bone. And Tamar West had this bad boy collared.

Lyrik cut an eager glance to the side where she was in a small circle. She was cracking up where she chatted with her best friends, Shea Stone and Willow Evans, both wives of Sunder members.

My sister-in-law, who I adored and loved like she was my own blood, was wearing this black clingy dress that hugged every inch of her abundant curves, the dress super long and hitting the floor

with slits riding up the front of the skirt and diving down her cleavage.

Ink covered most of her skin, too.

She wore five-inch heels and a gleam in her blue eyes.

My brother was head-over-heels for her. Steel turned to putty that she held in the palms of her hands.

I'd never thought he'd love again until the day he'd shown up at our parents' humble house with her in tow.

It was clear he'd been long gone before he'd even known it himself.

But sometimes love took us hostage before we even realized we'd been captured.

Lyrik looked back at me, mouth quirking at the side. "My wife is always sexy. She's just a little . . . extra tonight."

"Extra is always good."

"Oh, don't worry, I'll be giving her plenty extra," he drew out.

With the back of my hand, I smacked him on the chest. Apparently, I'd given him the green light to take it too far. With Lyrik, all roads were always wide open. "Eww. I can do without the innuendo, thank you very much. It's bad enough I have to watch you slobbering all over her every day."

He rumbled a chuckle, way too pleased with himself. "Hey, just tellin' it like it is."

Laughing under my breath, I gestured in the direction of the raving crowd. Softness infiltrated my words. "Would you get out of here and stop worrying about me? I will be just fine."

He hesitated. "You're sure?"

"One-hundred-percent."

Okay, like . . . two percent.

"Besides, you have more security here than Fort Knox."

Still facing me, he took a couple steps backward. "That's because what I'm guarding is more important."

He swiveled on his heel and started for the mass of people crushed in his house. Right before he got to the end of the hall, he turned back to face me.

Something severe had etched itself into his expression. "Every single person here is my guest, Mia."

My head shook slightly, unsure, not understanding the flip that had just been made.

His expression darkened. "But that doesn't mean they're good. That they can be trusted. You get what I'm telling you?"

There was no mirth in the warning.

No tease.

Just the truth of what he said.

I swallowed around the lump that had made itself home at the base of my throat for the last three weeks, gave him a tight nod. "I know that."

Like I hadn't stumbled on my fair share of scumbags.

He dipped a nod. "Good. Then be careful."

"I will. I promise."

I wondered if I'd already known it was a lie when I said it.

Mia

*L*yrik was right.

Not all of his guests could be trusted.

My pulse raced wild.

A frantic boom, boom, boom that I could feel thundering in the middle of my chest.

Panic raced, my throat closing off and my sight going blurry.

I tried to free myself from the hold of the man who was breathing his vileness all over me. Before I could even make sense that he'd been waiting for me when I'd left the restroom, he'd backed me into a wall at the base of the curved staircase.

His stench stung my nostrils. Sweat drenched in depravation.

His breath a toxic blend of alcohol and sex and corruption.

He edged me farther against the wall, as if his admission to this party had purchased him any evil.

"I said to get out of my way," I forced out under my breath, teeth gritting in the hope that it might keep the terror that was streaking through my veins from seeping out of my pores.

The last thing I wanted was this asshole to sense my fear.

A monster scenting its prey.

"Come now. Don't be like that," he slurred, pressing his nose to my throat. "I just wanted to say hi. Introduce myself. You look awful pretty wandering around here all by yourself."

I cringed. "I'm not alone. Now let me go."

He tsked like my statement was absurd. "I should have known Lyrik West would invite the prettiest girls to his party. He always has the best *entertainment*."

I would have laughed if vomit hadn't already risen to my throat, vocal cords chained in alarm and dread.

This jerk had no idea my brother would gladly snap his neck. Gut him and leave him floating face-down in a river.

But right that second, my brother was nowhere to be found and neither was any of the security.

We were hidden by the curve of the stairs, tucked in the shadows and concealed by the din of music.

Voices and laughter echoed from the main room.

Nothing but taunts and jeers that pounded my ears.

Lyrik's warning screamed, and fear pressed down as the bastard covered me with his sweaty, meaty body.

There was a halo of it.

A dark, dense fog.

I struggled for a breath, sickened by the same man who had almost sent me to my knees two hours earlier.

Turns out, I should have trusted my instincts, after all.

"Your heart is beating so fast. Excited, love?"

Love?

This guy was seriously confused. Confused and deranged and disgusting, and I had the overwhelming compulsion to spit in his face.

I did.

Shouting a profanity, he gripped me by the jaw.

Hard.

"You fuckin' bitch," he gritted in his English accent, cinching down tighter. "You'll learn better than to cross me."

Something fake and desperate bled from his being. I wondered if he were half as desperate as me.

Urges hit, a storm of panic and survival.

Instinct kicking in.

Fight or flight.

I surged forward, taking the jerk by surprise.

My forehead connected with his.

Hard.

A white-hot splinter of pain cracked through my head at the connection, but at least I was prepared for it. I managed to keep my footing at the impact when he completely lost his and stumbled back.

Momentarily stunned.

I didn't give him time to recover.

I grabbed him by the shoulders, and I drew my knee up as hard as I could. The crunch vibrated up my leg when my knee made contact with his crotch.

The slit of my dress ripped at the same time.

His wail of agony was at one with the chaos, with the throbbing laughter and the beat of the drums and the pulse of the music that made it feel as if I'd stepped into a house of horrors.

Those crazy-ass mirrors surrounding me. Distorting everything. My brain rattled and my spirit shaking.

Adrenaline sloshed through my veins, bleeding out and draining free and leaving me gasping.

Visions rushed.

Taking me to another time. Another place.

Fast flickers of a nightmare that I would forever relive.

Frantic, desperate.

Lana on her knees.

The glint of silver.

A deafening ring.

Blood.

Blood.

So much blood.

I choked on the memory. The man in my gallery. Backing us into the corner. Pulling the trigger while I'd had to watch hopelessly.

I staggered backward while the dirtbag bent in two, struggling to get his breath.

Flight kicked in.

The desperate need to flee.

Hide.

Remove myself from the situation.

I raced upstairs, the torn skirt of my dress clutched in my trembling hands, holding it up so I wouldn't trip on the long white fabric. The second I hit the landing, I ran to the right, my high heels clicking on the wooden floor as I raced down the hall.

I bypassed the room I'd been staying in for the last three weeks and, instead, I rushed all the way to the end of the corridor where a second set of stairs led to the top floor.

It called to me like a beacon. Like *safety* was written in red, glaring lights.

Hand clinging to the railing, I fumbled up the steps to the third floor, and a harsh breath of relief gushed from my lungs when I caught sight of the closed double doors on the right.

I burst through them like my life depended on it.

I slammed the doors shut behind me and whirled around so I could lock them.

Hands shaking.

Spirit manic.

Nothing quite cooperating.

Metal scraped as the lock finally engaged, the sound of it like a gunshot reverberating through the dark, vacant room. I dropped my head to the ornate wood, hot air jerking in and out of my lungs as I tried to steady myself after the altercation.

Never before had I considered myself weak.

And now all it took was a jerk getting handsy and I was falling apart.

I should march back downstairs and tell my brother. Make a statement. Make him pay.

And the only thing I wanted to do?

Hide.

Remain concealed and protected behind the thick, solid doors.

Here, where the music was muted, nothing but a dull vibration that rumbled underfoot.

Voices distant.

It gave the illusion that I'd risen above it all.

Besides, the last thing I wanted was for my brother to get arrested for murder tonight.

Tomorrow I'd tell him. When enough time had passed. When rash, imprudent reactions were less likely to be made.

For tonight, I'd wait here.

When my heaving breaths began to slow, I finally peeled myself from the door and swiveled around to face the duskiness of the room.

The massive library that Lyrik had attempted to turn into an art studio.

It was where my spirit had immediately been called to in turmoil, as if it heard the melody of this place, even though it no longer knew how to sing.

Like all the beauty had been ripped from it that horrible night.

I had no idea if I would ever get it back.

My eyes scanned the lapping shadows of the rambling space.

A muted sheen of silvery moonlight flooded through the huge circular window that was made of white and black translucent stained glass. It faced out upon the front of the luxurious home, distorted the view in a gorgeous sheen of sparkling crystal and cast the rich, plush furniture and tapestries in shadows.

The floors were covered in thick, woven rugs.

Shelves of books lined the towering walls, all the way to the severe pitch of the cathedral ceiling.

My gaze moved to the far corner.

Drawn to where easels of partially-painted pictures stood like half-bared secrets.

The obscured faces painted on the canvases veiled in mystery.

Blowing out a haggard breath, I eased deeper into the room, and I let my fingertips gently flutter over a picture.

The man's face misshapen.

Haunted eyes stared out into the nothingness.

I moved to the next, stood at where the small child crouched at the edge of a gurgling stream, staring at her reflection in the glistening water, her angelic face contorted.

Sadness crested and rose, crashing like a tsunami of broken dreams.

Hopes shattered in one careless, senseless act.

I traced my fingertips over the image, wishing it could somehow seep into my soul, breathe its life back into me.

I thought I felt a flicker of it.

Energy.

A depth that had been missing that billowed and blew. A soft whisper that breezed through the room.

Chills flashed, and the fine hairs on my arms and neck lifted in a whoosh of awareness.

I froze, throat closing off as that sensation twisted and cut into me with a stab of fear. As I realized I was not alone.

Ever so slowly, I shifted around.

One-part terror.

One-part curiosity.

My eyes narrowed as I struggled to peer farther into the hushed shadows at the far end of the room where I felt the crash of energy emanating from.

A brewing of intensity.

My heart shivered in my chest as a dark figure sitting on an oversized chair slowly came into view.

At the sight of him, a scream gurgled in my throat, though it got locked in the barbs of tightness.

My stomach twisted into a thousand knots.

I should run. No doubt. Just get the hell out of there and pretend like I hadn't even noticed a man lurking in the far corner.

But I was frozen.

Slammed by another bolt of that severity.

Bound by shockwave after shockwave of energy that surged and rocked, gluing my feet to the ground.

He just sat there, not making a move, eyes clearly watching me even though I couldn't make them out through the darkness.

"Oh my god, you scared me," I finally managed to force out. My gaze darted to the door, searching for the closest emergency exit and not knowing whether I should use it or not.

Oh, I should.

I knew I should.

But I just stood there, robbed of the sense of *flight*, stammering, "Wh-wha-what are you doing in here?" at the faceless silhouette.

The outline of him was nothing but wide shoulders and hard body, legs stretched out in front of him so casually.

Like he couldn't feel that his presence was singlehandedly tilting the earth on its side.

The man emitting his own gravity.

He barely shifted, the rocks glass he rested on the arm of the chair glinting in a ray of light as he rolled the base in a slow circle.

"Seems to me the exact same thing as you." His voice was gravel, controlled with a razor-sharp edge.

Intrigue billowed, wrapping me in bindings.

I'd always considered myself decently intelligent. Graduated salutatorian of my high school class. Earned a full ride scholarship even though finishing my degree had been rough considering my circumstances, but I had done it and I'd done it well.

Had started my own business.

And there I was, struck dumb.

Senseless.

Fascination taking me over like it was the only wisdom I knew.

"What's that?" I asked instead of rushing out the door where my common sense had clearly already fled without me.

"Hiding." The word was a deep drone. He sat forward. The air stirred. I sucked in a breath as heat gathered in the atmosphere and covered my flesh in a flashfire of anticipation.

What the hell?

"Though I doubt we're doin' it for the same reasons," he said.

I could feel the flit of his gaze racing over me.

Assessing.

Calculating.

"You don't know anything about me." It came out a shaky defense. I didn't even know why I was offering it. Why I was even humoring this conversation.

Although there didn't seem to be anything humorous about it.

This feeling that had become all too real and potent.

Instant.

Urgent.

He slowly stood to his full, towering height.

Oh God. Chills streaked and sped, and I was standing there on shaking knees.

"No. But I'd say you're pretty easy to read." His words were gruff.

"And what is it you think you're seein'?" My voice trembled, and God, I needed to shut my mouth and get the hell out of there. Red flags were getting thrown all over the place.

Out of bounds.

My feet carrying me in a direction I definitely did not need to be traveling.

Because Lyrik was right.

Not all of his guests could be trusted. Not all of them were good.

And this guy screamed danger.

Trouble.

But on an entirely different level than the jerk downstairs.

Because I was feeling compelled. Drawn into the darkness swarming the space. Rushing and crashing.

Somehow, I got the sense that if I got any closer, I was going to get swallowed.

"Fear." His arrogant statement rippled the air.

I gulped.

Maybe I'd had it all wrong. Maybe he was the hunter who was scenting his prey. That he could smell the way I was drawn. Helpless to whatever the hell this attraction was—something I'd never once in all my life experienced before.

A dark lure.

I took a step backward like I could possibly get away from it.

He took one forward.

It brought him into a stream of light.

My mouth dropped open and my belly bottomed out.

I couldn't tell if he was terrifying or beautiful.

Terrifyingly beautiful.

Yes, yes, that was it.

Tall and lean. Different than my brother, though.

Shoulders wide. Corded muscle visible, arms rippling with strength. The guy wearing a tee and tattered jeans and Vans to a gala in the Hills.

His jaw was clenched, a perfectly carved stone held so tight that I feared it might shatter and crack.

His nose straight and his brow defined. Plush lips set in a firm, hard line.

His eyes were the only part of him that could have even hinted at softness. The color of brown sugar. The edges the hardest, deepest black. Like maybe he'd witnessed too many horrible things and the grief and hatred had crystallized into slate.

And I was standing there gawking and flustered and trying to get my legs to cooperate. To knock some sense into myself because I was locked in a dark room with a stranger.

But I couldn't move.

Stuck in a quicksand I could feel pulling me under.

His eyes traced me.

Blatantly.

Bluntly.

Something that sounded like a growl crawled up his throat when his attention fixated on where my dress was ripped at the seam. Realizing it was gaping open, I rushed to gather up the material that was split so high it was threatening to reveal my panties.

His massive hands curled at his sides.

"What happened to your dress?" His question came out sounding like a threat.

"Nothing . . . it's fine." It flew from my mouth at warp speed.

He surged forward, and I gasped.

He touched my chin.

A gentle prod that angled my face up into the light. He let his fingertips trace up the side of my face until his thumb was running softly over the knot that had already risen on my forehead.

Tremors rolled and I was having a hard time making sense of anything right then.

"Liar," he grunted.

"I'm fine."

"Don't look so fine to me."

Those warm, sugar eyes traveled to where my hand was fisted in the skirt, his jaw ticking as he angled his face toward mine, his presence invading.

The words scraped across my cheek as he issued them. "I'm probably not the only man here who would gladly rip this dress off you, gorgeous, but it doesn't look to me like you agreed."

Turbulence rolled like thunder in the room.

The man too bold.

Too crass.

Too forward.

And I knew I wasn't alone in this crazy attraction that fired and pulsed and covered me like a wicked dream.

I should run from it. No question, something that powerful was dangerous.

But I wanted it.

To feel it.

To feel alive and whole.

To stoke this spark that suddenly came to life inside me. One I'd thought had forever gone dim.

The fantasy flashed of him actually doing it. Him pushing me against the wall, hands finding my flesh under the frayed fabric, pushing it over my hips.

The clink of his belt as he freed himself.

As he took me.

Touched me and kissed me and owned me until the only thing I felt was him. Until the pain had been chased away.

What the hell was wrong with me?

I was just asking for it, wasn't I?

Bad judgement and all of that.

I blamed it on the PTSD.

Looking for something to make me feel good in the middle of the grief, but I knew those rugged, masculine hands weren't going to help a thing. No doubt, it wouldn't take more than a brush of them to leave a scar.

Knowing myself, I'd be worse off than where I'd started.

"I handled it."

A rough, disbelieving chuckle left him. "By running in here scared? Locking yourself behind a door? Hiding? Is that what you call handling it? Because I could think of plenty better ways of *handling* it."

Tension bound the room, the stark violence that oozed from this man.

Something intense and protective rising up and taking over.

Urges slammed me on all sides.

Coaxing me to slip into it.

Get lost.

Maybe see if it was powerful enough to make me forget.

I swore, the man had me intoxicated.

Enraptured.

"I thought you said you were doing the exact same thing?" I challenged on a whisper, his lips so close to mine, my eyes tracing every line of his face.

Looking for something.

Trouble.

That's what it was.

It took about all the strength I had, but I edged back an inch, desperate to put some space between us before I did something I was going to regret.

Like it knocked him out of the daze, he took a step back, too. Frustrated, he dragged his fingers through the wayward, unruly locks of his brown-hair, the longer pieces on top hinting at a disaster but the sides trimmed around his ears. "Don't like parties much. Especially the kind going on downstairs."

Even though I knew better, my eyes went exploring, taking him in through the lapping shadows. The strength of his arms that peeked out beneath his rolled sleeves, wiry and vibrating.

Like his demons were crawling his flesh.

All his wrongs written in the jerks and tics of his packed, bristling muscle.

Everything about him was brutal.

No pretenses and zero fucks to give.

Exactly the kind of guy I'd sworn off years ago.

I tore my attention back to his face, doing my best to claw my way back to solid ground.

Only that wasn't a safe place, either. One glance across those lips and up to his eyes and my stomach was clamping in a needy fist. "Then why are you here?"

He angled his head with a rumble of low, seductive laughter. "I've been asking that question myself."

"Did you figure it out yet?" The words came out a breath.

The slowest grin pulled across his sexy mouth. "Starting to get an idea." He reached up and fiddled with a lock of my black hair, eyeing me as he did, the world unsettled and vibrating around us. "How about you, gorgeous? You don't strike me as the type who begged someone to get through that door. Don't seem like you belong in a place like this."

Defensiveness blustered through my being. "And what kind of place is that?"

He laughed a scornful sound. "Don't tell me you don't feel it. The greed and the gluttony running rampant downstairs. Every prick showing off what he's got. Desperate for more. To elevate himself. Not caring who the fuck he tramples to get himself there. Money and fame fucks with your head. Or maybe they were all already fucked, and that's what got them here in the first place."

"And you and I somehow don't count?" It was disbelief. Maybe disappointment. Because I was so not about lumping people into a group and labeling them.

"Didn't say that," he grated.

My family's faces flashed through my mind. The rest of the band and their wives and their children. All these amazing people who had knitted themselves so intricately into my life that they'd become a permanent part of me.

Family.

"Not everyone is looking for an opportunity to take advantage of someone else. Not everyone here is bad."

"Maybe not." Brown eyes glimmered in the rays of murky,

shimmering light. "But you sure seem to keep running into the worst of them."

It was a warning. One I heard loud and clear. This man was lumping himself into his own pile.

Bad.

Vile.

Destructive.

But it was the bare warmth hiding in the pools of his eyes that kept me pressing.

This man nothing but a raging contradiction.

Emphasis on the *raging*.

Energy came off him like a storm held in the horizon. Dark and ominous.

And there I was, itching to disappear into it so I could discover why it was.

"I think you're wrong. I bet I could ask you to hunt down the guy who got handsy with me and you'd do it without blinking. I bet you wouldn't even care or consider the consequences."

"I was right," he said with a coarse chuckle, eyes skating my face.

Confusion pulled a frown to my brow. "About what?"

He was back to fiddling with that strand of my hair.

Winding me up.

"That you don't belong here. You came running in here just as lost as me. Except you don't have the first clue when you're running straight for danger. You don't make people earn your trust—you trust first and regret it later. You dig around to find the good when there is no good to be found. Sound about right?"

Air wheezed into my lungs, the room spinning with the blunt force of his words.

"Wow. You're kind of an asshole."

He laughed. A low roll of scorn. "You say it like I'm not already fully aware of who I am."

It felt like he'd called me out on my every deficiency. Accused me of being weak for the sake of being kind.

But the truth was, I was begging him to give me a reason to trust. Praying that this seed of bitterness wouldn't take hold and invade every element of my life. I didn't want the last grains of hope I was holding to bleed through my fingers.

Gone forever.

And the scariest part was I could feel it slipping away.

On top of that, I was left asking the question—why him? Why was I always drawn to what would clearly hurt me?

He edged in so close that our noses brushed, the scent of him invading my senses.

Clove and whiskey. Warmth and sex.

Dizziness spun.

"So yeah, you want me to go after whatever prick messed with you?" he rumbled, head angled low. "Make him pay the hard way? You're right. I'd do it in a heartbeat. Say the word, and it's done. I'm really good at destroying whatever I come into contact with. Whatever I touch."

He reached out and ran a fingertip down the side of my face.

Chills tumbled down my spine.

"Question is, is it gonna be him or is it gonna be you?"

Leif

$\mathcal{D}$o you believe in fate?

In destiny?

In that fairytale bullshit that everything happens for a reason?

Living each day thinkin' every event, conversation, and person that passes through our lives has been set on that path long before we even know what direction we're headed?

Carved in some proverbial stone eons before we were born?

All comin' together for the greater good?

Fuck that.

If you asked me, our lives were nothing but a pile of rubble. Debris made up of the mistakes that we had made.

Every horrible choice another piece that carved and morphed us into something more and more appalling.

You disagree?

I had proof.

It was right there in the fact that I was going toe-to-toe with this girl who obviously came stumbling in here, nothing but a lost-fucking-soul desperate for reprieve.

Seeking sanctuary close to the clouds.

Way up close to the stars.

And she had the grave misfortune of running into me.

She blinked up at me with these intense, sable eyes. I didn't know if it was the destitute belief shining in them or her fucking tight, sexy body that had gotten me hard the second I'd seen her fumble through the door.

Girl coming in here floating through these crazy-ass paintings that filled the room like some kind of gorgeous, fading vapor, wearing this whimsical white dress that had the power to leave me weak in the knees.

Wonder in her being and something sweetly seductive oozing from her soul.

I'd instantly wanted her.

To take her.

And I was really fuckin' good at taking what wasn't mine.

She'd let me. I knew that she would. Could feel her almost trembling with the kind of sorrow that could only be assuaged by letting go.

By completely getting lost.

But there was something about her that was stopping me.

She stared up at me, unsure, maybe disappointed.

"Is that what you want?" she demanded in that wispy voice. "To hurt me? I guess maybe I did stumble into the wrong room." Her sweet brow curled in disgust, and her words whispered like regret through the dense air.

The chains that would forever bind me only cinched down tighter.

A warning.

Didn't matter.

My arm was looping around her waist, tucking her close. Clearly, I wanted the pain.

Hers or mine, I didn't know.

The bare skin of her back exposed by the drape in her dress scorched my arm.

It sent a shock of lust running rampant through my veins.

"Problem is all the things I'm wanting to do to you," I murmured down at her. Straight up. Because I was betting this girl deserved the truth. "Pretty fuckin' sure it would scar us both."

Greed flash-fired.

A thunderbolt that struck in the middle of us.

Hot enough to torch this fucking ridiculous house. Leave it nothin' but ash.

"And there's no fucking good that could come of it."

"Because you don't want it or because you don't deserve it?"

"Because I will ruin you." The words were hard. Angry in their truth.

Sable eyes narrowed like she didn't have the first clue what to make of me. "Why would you say that?"

"Because I'm already ruined, baby."

We were swaying, swept up in this unstoppable dance that I never saw coming.

I hadn't felt anything similar in three years.

Guilt clotted the flow of air to my too-tight lungs.

That realization right there should have been enough to send me hauling ass out those doors.

"I should walk away, shouldn't I?" she whispered.

I gave her a tight nod.

She touched my chest.

Motherfucking flames.

"So what is this feeling that's begging me to stay?"

"No doubt, it's the exact same thing that is going to make me push you away."

Otherwise I was going to have her pinned against the wall and ripping that dress the rest of the way from her body.

Using her up.

Feeding from all the soft sweetness I could smell radiating from her flesh.

Revulsion clenched my stomach.

No.

I'd never wanted to become who I had.

Had never wanted to be revered and respected in a way only brought about by brutality.

Had never wanted to be feared.

Had never wanted to be the *bad guy*.

Maybe the reality was that I'd never known how to be anything else.

Fated. Vile from the get go.

Depravity written in my DNA.

This elusive feeling pounded around us. A song that started low.

A melody ushering in what was to come.

Dark and mesmerizing and sexy as fuck.

"What if I don't want you to push me away? What if we were meant to be right here? Even if it is only for tonight?" She blinked hard, her teeth raking her plump bottom lip, making it glisten and my mouth water. "Do you feel it? Whatever this is?"

Rough laughter broke free, and I couldn't even answer that question. Because if I did, I knew there would be no stopping the direction this would go.

"You don't have the first clue what you're asking for, gorgeous," I told her instead.

Didn't even know why it mattered. Why I cared. Clearly, this party was all about *excess*. Over-indulging. And taking of this girl would be nothing but gluttony.

"You're right. I don't. But what if I want to know you? Maybe I stumbled in here and found exactly what I've been looking for." Vulnerability flashed across her striking face. Nothing weak about it.

I was getting the feeling that maybe for the first time in a long time, she was feeling brave. Pushing herself to take a step that she should know better than taking.

"And maybe you're looking in all the wrong places," I tossed back, voice grit, and still I was tucking her closer. Her unforgettable face pinched in confusion, girl so damned pretty she was hard to look at.

Stoic and soft.

Determined and pliable.

In contemplation, she pursed her lips, that mouth painted in this lust-inducing red, a stark contrast to the pure-white of her dress.

Her head slowly shook.

I saw it for what it was.

Regret.

Disappointment.

Acceptance.

Neither of us owed the other anything.

Yet somehow, it felt like I did.

I owed her this—walking away.

I knew better than to dip my fingers into places where real beauty lived.

She wound herself out of my tight grip.

"I guess I usually do find myself in the wrong places," she said, words thick.

I had the urge to apologize.

For me. For who I was. For who I wasn't ever going to be.

And I didn't even know her goddamn name.

Realized in that second that I was in more danger than she was.

That I was the one with more to lose.

That this angel had me enraptured.

Taken in a heartbeat.

My phone dinged and vibrated in my pocket. Sound of it jolted us both from the cocoon.

I dug it free and took a quick glance at the message.

Lyrik West: Where are you, asshole? Been looking for you the last thirty minutes. Meeting in downstairs office in five.

Could almost hear the smirk in the dude's voice. Had known him for all of forever. Since *all the way back to who I'd been,* and he'd still invited me here. Up until three days ago, I'd thought there wasn't a thing in the world that could tempt me into returning to this fuckin' wasteland of a city. Was stupid as shit, relenting.

31

Coming here nothing but reckless.

A death wish.

Yet here I was.

I glanced back at the girl who stood there fidgeting, that dress hugging her slim curves that I was itching to memorize, face so damned pretty I was having a hell of a time looking away.

She was nothing but temptation.

Sweet motherfucking temptation.

I tucked my phone back into my pocket. "Have to go."

Her eyes squeezed close for a beat as she said, "I get it."

"No, you don't."

Thing was, I didn't want her to. Because this girl was looking at me like she might actually be able to see through all of the bullshit, and that was not a place I could let her go.

I moved for the door. Energy stretched tight, a connection I didn't anticipate flying frantic around the room. The hollowness carved out at the center of me teased and taunted.

Another penalty.

Fact it was always gonna be there and there was no way to make amends.

No way to fill it.

At the double doors, I twisted the lock. Halfway out, I paused and looked back at her from over my shoulder.

Her arms were crossed over her chest, girl standing beneath the massive stained-glass window with her face tipped up to the sky. Moonlight streamed in and covered her in a silvery hue.

A black river of hair cascaded down her back, brushing over her skin that was close to white in the halo of murky light.

Angel.

But I didn't get a savior.

Not when I was the devil.

She cut those sable eyes my direction.

"Wish I was him," I told her, words grating up my throat, unable to stop the betrayal before it was out.

But if it were a different lifetime, if this past didn't exist, I'd want to be him.

The kind of guy who could ask her for her name and her

number like a normal-fucking-human being.

Maybe date her. Kiss her and hold her and treat her the way she clearly deserved to be.

Way she wanted to be.

No.

I didn't know her.

But like I'd told her, she was easy to read.

She cast a gentle smile. "I guess it makes me a fool that I wish you were, too."

I gave a tight nod. "Lock this door behind me."

Because God knew I wasn't the only monster roaming this place.

Leif

"Holy shit, it's *the* Leif Godwin, in the flesh." Ash Evans, Sunder's bassist, pulled me in for a tight hug the second I walked through the door.

The office was tucked at the end of a cavernous hall, the walls made up of ornate dark woods and the ceilings adorned with heavy crown molding where it cut through a private wing on the first floor. Sounds of the party echoed through the thick walls and vibrated the floors, strains of music filtering to our ears.

Shocks of laughter spiked through the middle of it.

Vibe was different here than when I'd been hiding out upstairs, though.

Up in that attic, it was like I hadn't been a part of the chaos roaring through the house.

Like I'd gotten lost and had fallen into a dream.

Hallucinating.

Had to have been.

That girl's stunning face strobed through my mind, the feel of her tight, sweet body against mine still lingering on my flesh, the scent of her still overwhelming and flooding my senses.

Cocoa and cream.

Fuck. I had to have been dreaming. Losing my mind. Losing my grip on reality.

Ash clapped me on the shoulder before he edged back, but he only stepped far enough away so he could grab me by the upper arms, like some kind of old aunt who hadn't seen their nephew in twenty years and was wanting to get a good look.

If I wasn't careful, asshole was liable to pinch my cheeks.

"Dude, how the hell have you been?" he asked. "Haven't seen you in years."

"Can't complain," I told him, fighting the rush of unease.

Fuck, what was I thinking, coming here? Could feel two worlds getting ready to collide.

"It's been too damned long." Could see the undercurrent of amusement riding through his expression, like he was all the way back to those days when our paths had first crossed. Back when Sunder hadn't yet been discovered, and I was still banging away with a heavy metal band in the slums of L.A.

Wishing I was different then, too. Faking a life. Pretending to be someone I was not. I hadn't known them all that well considering I never allowed myself to get too close.

Too involved.

A philosophy I'd applied to everything.

Until I'd fucked up worse than ever before.

Taken what never should have been mine.

Selfish.

Disgust swilled and warbled, and I pinned on a fake smile, convincing myself to sit tight and not bolt out the door.

Apparently, being in Los Angeles was fucking with my brain.

"Years," I told him.

"You haven't aged a day." He patted my cheek, grinning like an asshole, sarcasm riding free.

35

"Fuck you, old man," I said with a laugh. "Last I checked, you were older than me."

Truth was, he looked better than he had back in the day. Healthier. Happier. Whole ton sappier, too. Guessed that was what love and marriage and all that bullshit did to you.

Didn't negate the fact the guy was a badass.

A legend.

I mean, fuck, I was in a room full of them.

I let my gaze slide across the faces filling the posh office. Room decorated with oversized, dark furniture. The entirety of Sunder had gathered there and were waiting for me while the party raged in the main rooms of the house.

Sebastian Stone, or Baz, like everyone called him, and his younger brother, Austin.

Ash Evans.

Zachary Kennedy.

Last but not least, Lyrik West. My chest tightened when my attention landed on the guy, wondering what this was and what I'd gotten myself into.

I lifted my chin in a casual gesture. "What's up?"

Lyrik pushed to standing from where he was sitting on the edge of the desk. "Glad you could make it on such short notice."

He shook my hand and pulled me in for a clap to the shoulder. "It's good to see you."

"You, too. So, what was so important that you needed to get me out to L.A.?"

Couldn't imagine my invite to this party came without ulterior motives. Not to mention the fact they'd sent a private jet to South Carolina to get me and had a chauffeur waiting to pick me up at the airport.

Pretty damned sure they wanted something out of this.

Lyrik angled his head to an empty chair. I took it, started drumming my fingers on the top of my thigh because I didn't know much of anything else.

Sunder's drummer, Zachary, better known as Zee, stood up from where he was hunkered in the corner. "Saw you playing with your band back in Savannah a couple months ago."

I itched, glancing around, nothing but eyes on me. Whole point of taking up as the drummer of an unknown country band that only played dives in the south was the fact that no one would *notice* me. That I'd be an ocean away from those who might recognize me.

But then Carolina George had begun its rise.

"Have to say, your performance blew my mind. Not a whole lot of people can drum like you. Lyrik said he knew you, so we were able to track you down to bring you here. Truth is, drummers tend to take a backseat, blend in and just become a part of the background, and you might as well have been set up at the front of the stage."

Unease churned through my being. Dude thought he was complimenting me when he wasn't being anything but the bearer of bad news.

"Thanks," I forced out.

Because what the fuck?

Sure, I knew most of the guys from way back when.

But we'd been little more than acquaintances.

Running the same circles.

The same backstage parties.

Bodies riddled with the garbage we pumped in our veins and snorted up our noses.

Then Sunder had hit it big. Their backstage parties no longer hosted in the dank, disgusting holes I'd been assigned.

When I'd fled Los Angeles three years ago, I'd never thought I'd see any of them again. Had nearly shit myself when I'd caught Lyrik's eye in that small bar that night six months ago, and I'd been gone before he had the chance to track me down.

Like I could just pretend that he was hallucinating.

Making that shit up. Guessed Zee had noticed me at the same time.

I never should have gone to that audition. Never should have answered that fucking ad for a drummer. Thinking it would be cool. A cover. An outlet. One place to exorcise my demons. Or maybe where I could just let them come out to play.

Richard, the lead of Carolina George, had been all over the fact that I had a heavy metal background.

Loved my style.

Loved the vicious way I attacked the drums. Said he was searching for a drummer who could bring a different element to his band, and he thought that guy was me.

He had a vision of meshing country and rock in a way that had never been done before.

I should have known better.

But if I didn't have music, I didn't have anything, so what the fuck did I have to lose when I'd already lost it all?

A disturbance rumbled through the middle of me.

Truth of what I did have to lose.

What was on the line.

"So why am I here?" I finally asked, cutting a glance around at each of them, calculating just how quickly I could bolt.

Zee gave me a slight nod. "We're slated to hit the studio next week."

I edged back, defenses coming up. "And what's that got to do with me?"

"Would like you to stand in for me," Zee said.

Disbelief had my brow shooting to the sky. "You want me to step in for you? Got my own band, man. Things are moving for us. Not about to do something that will threaten that."

And the last thing I needed was something that would expose me.

Put me in the limelight.

Was already balancing a quickly fraying tightrope.

Zee tossed a glance at Lyrik, but it was Ash who was piping in. "Now don't go and worry yourself about that. My boy Lyrik here gets all kinds of raw and bitter when broaching the subject of poaching, don't you, dude?" he asked, sidling up to Lyrik's side and slinging a casual arm around his neck. Ash squeezed him. "You remember it, Lyrik? Those hacks who thought they could actually lure you away from us? Could you imagine? Like you'd ever step away from all this greatness."

Ash held his arms out at the sides. "We make magic, baby. Nothing can touch us. Nothing ever will."

Lyrik scoffed with the tug of a smile, and he crossed his tattooed arms over his chest. "If you can't be loyal to your crew, who the hell are you going to be loyal to?"

My head shook, agitation eating me alive. "Then why am I sitting here?"

"Wearing jeans and a tee in the middle of the damn fanciest party I've ever been to, mind you? How is this fair?" Ash tugged at the bowtie of his tux, tossing the razzing out, nothing but a joke. Like he could feel the tension radiating from me and he was doing everything to rid the room of it. "Asshole gets to wear what he wants and you made me put on this shit?"

He gestured at me.

If I possessed the ability, I would have laughed.

Dude had always been a nut.

Anxiously, I drummed my fingers on my thigh, feeling naked without the drumsticks that I took everywhere I went.

"Sorry. Last minute, like you said. Didn't have time to rent something more appropriate," I told him.

Not that I would have, anyway. Not exactly my style.

Lyrik pushed out a heavy sigh. "Listen, man. This is coming out wrong. It's really not a big deal. Zee here has no intention of leaving the band. His son Liam is some kind of soccer prodigy and has the chance to play this summer for this big-ass kids' league, and he wants to be there for the games, which means there's a scheduling conflict. You're the only one we know who is good enough to take his place on the tracks. Simple as that. And you'll still have the time to meet all your obligations with your own band. Know you don't have any shows for a handful of weeks, and we were hoping you'd be willing to spend those weeks in the studio with us."

"That's it," Sebastian added from where he was sitting behind the desk, arms tucked behind his head and rocked back in the chair.

Sebastian Stone was Sunder's original lead singer. He'd relinquished the mic a handful of years back to be closer to his family, and he'd started a recording label of his own, Stone Industries.

Now his baby brother, Austin, had taken the lead, though it seemed Baz hadn't really taken that far of a step back from the band.

You hardly saw a picture in the tabloids or music mags without all five of them together.

"Honestly not a big deal, but there's a ton of money in it for you." Baz cocked a wry grin.

"Probably could have just shot me a text rather than dragging me out to L.A. to ask me." I eyed them, defenses lowering, but still, this was over-the top.

Zee shook his head. "Nah. Needed to invite you face-to-face. Let you know what it will mean to me, considering you're the only person who can do it, and I need to be there for my son."

"Sorry, you could have saved yourself some time because I can't stay in L.A. Plan on getting the hell out of here tonight."

Never should have come in the first place.

Had no clue what that compulsion had been.

The fiery blaze that had me tapping out an acceptance.

Like coming here might bring me closer to vindication.

But I had to chill the fuck out. Wait. Bide my time. Do it right.

Baz rocked forward in the chair and tapped his fingers on the desk. "Not going down in L.A. We'll be recording at my studio near Savannah, Georgia out on Tybee Island. Puts you in a good spot to go back and forth when your band needs you since you're predominantly in the south."

"You aren't going to catch my ass hanging out in L.A. for any length of time, either." Ash added. "Most of us are raising our families back in Savannah. Only one of us who even has a place here any longer is Lyrik. This fucker is the only reason any of us dragged our asses across the country in the first place."

Lyrik grunted. "I share custody with my son's mother," he clarified, like I needed to know all the intricacies that made up their lives. Like they needed to lay it all out to gain my trust. "Brendon will be spending the entire summer with us in Savannah, so it works out."

I hesitated. Only good thing I'd ever learned from my pile-of-shit mother was if something seemed too good to be true, it probably was.

And why the hell did I want this, anyway?

But it was there . . . the thirst to play.

The thing I'd kept for myself.

My one love when the rest of it had been ripped from me.

I bounced my knee. "How long do you plan on being in the studio?"

Sebastian rubbed his hand over his face, contemplating. "Six weeks . . . two months tops."

"And we all have places there . . . you're welcome to stay with any one of us." Austin Stone seemed to be the most reserved of the group. Something deeply thoughtful about him. "Or we can put you up in your own apartment if you're more comfortable with that. I mean, basically whatever it takes for you to agree." There was the tug of a smile from him at that.

Lyric stretched his long legs out in front of him and rocked farther back against the desk. "My wife and I actually have a guest house on our property. At the risk of soundin' cocky, it's pretty damn sick. Yours if you want it."

"You? Cocky? Never." Ash smacked him on the back. Probably a little harder than necessary.

"Fuck off, dude, you want me to take you out?" Lyric threw an aimless punch at him. Ash jumped back and returned the favor, laughing hard. "Try it, fucker."

Two were acting like they were thirteen and hanging at a graffitied skate park rather than in a multi-million-dollar mansion.

"So that's it? Play some music with you, and then I go on my merry way? No questions? No attachments?"

"That's it," Baz said, elbows on the desk, angling my direction. "It's great exposure. Know Carolina George has been in talks with Mylton Records about a possible deal. This can only help you."

Disbelief pulled at my brow as a chuckle ripped free. "Last time I checked, you and the CEO of Mylton records weren't exactly friends."

Their band had almost fallen apart because of the pressure from their old label, which was the reason Sebastian had started his own.

Didn't necessarily like the head of Mylton Records myself. Karl Fitzgerald was a fucking scumbag. But that didn't mean he couldn't do great things for our band.

"How much?" I asked.

"Thirty K a week . . . plus royalties." Sebastian lifted his chin.

Like he was daring me to pass it up.

Holy shit.

That was a lot of change, and I couldn't help but think that might finally get me where I needed to be.

Enough cash to make it happen.

To pay and swindle and bribe myself in through the back door.

That prick unaware before it was too late.

"I've got one requirement."

"What's that?"

"Need you to use my stage name. Don't want anyone tying me back to the old days."

Didn't that sound pretentious as fuck?

They didn't need to know the actual reason.

He shrugged. "No biggie. Tons of people do. Par for the course in this game."

"My band needs me? I go," I added.

If I was going to do this, they needed to know Carolina George had to be my first priority.

"Not a problem." Lyrik gave a tight nod. Relief pulsed through his demeanor, right before his expression hardened. "One more thing you need to know before we all agree to this."

"Yeah?"

He looked around at his friends before pinning me with his dark stare. Eyes so dark they were almost black.

Something familiar rocked through me.

That girl slammed into my mind.

I roughed my fingers through my hair.

Fuck.

I needed to scrape her from my being.

Forget it.

Because she was something I couldn't have. One encounter, and she was haunting me.

"Just need to make it clear that we walk a straight line. All of us have families. All the bullshit we were into in the past is exactly that—in the past."

Knew exactly what Lyrik was telling me. He was right back to the days that Ash had been referring to when I'd walked through the door.

The depravity and the wickedness and the evil.

Thing was, Lyrik didn't know the first of it. If he did, there was no chance in hell he would be inviting me to his place.

"Haven't touched that shit in years," I told him.

Didn't mean I wasn't still a prisoner.

"Good. Because I protect my family at any cost. We all do. They will always come first."

It was a point-blank warning.

"As you should."

It was the only thing any of us had. Fighting for our families.

"Good."

"So, you're in?" Zee asked, more eager than he probably wanted to let on.

I roughed a hand through my hair. This was crazy.

But just like when the SOS had come in, asking me to be here, I couldn't find it in myself to say no.

"Yeah, count me in."

He blew out a sigh. "Thanks, man. That's a huge relief. Don't want to let down the band, but I *can't* let down my kid. Hard balancing, you know? But family has to come first."

Grief constricted my throat. I shoved it down, let it feed the fury.

"Glad I can be of help."

"More than you know. I'm in your debt."

"I think I'm being plenty well-compensated."

Zee grinned. "No. Money ain't bad."

I glanced around Lyrik's extravagant house. "Obviously."

Lyrik nodded. "I need to get back out to the party. Plane will be waiting for you, like you requested, unless you want to stick around and hang with us?"

"Think I better get back."

Away from this place.

I pushed to standing.

"I'll have someone get in contact with you to make arrangements to get you and your things out to Savannah. Plan on being there Wednesday."

Lyrik put his hand out.

I shook it.

Sealed the deal.

Couldn't help but feel like I was signing my name in blood.

"I'll be there."

"Excited about this," Lyrik said with a nod. "Feel good things coming from it. Know you write. Never hurts to have a fresh ear on the mix."

I felt a stir from deep within.

Something powerful.

Stronger than the most depraved parts of me.

Music was my one good.

The one contribution I could make.

"It'll be cool, yeah." I glanced around the room. "Guess I'll see you all later this week."

I shook hands with everyone, accepting their welcomes into their world while hoping beyond hope that I wasn't making a huge mistake.

Considering I'd lost all hope years ago, it didn't do a whole lot to reassure me.

I stepped back out into the clamor that echoed down the hall. Nothing but a rush of voices and music and energy. I waded into the middle of it, letting it fuel the fervor. The heat and the need and the greed.

I cut right through the crowd without slowing and out the front door toward the car that was waiting.

I needed to get the fuck out of this city. Flee from the ghosts that forever ran these streets. Thing was, it didn't matter how far or how fast I went, they would always be right there, hunting me down.

Waiting in the darkness.

I strode down the walkway, getting ready to slip into the

backseat when the driver opened the door, only to pause to look over my shoulder toward the house.

Gaze drawn.

Lifted.

Right to the shadow outlined in the towering stained-glass window.

She was watching down on me.

An angel in the attic.

Heat clawed across my flesh, clashing with the cold.

That vacancy howled.

I gave myself over to it for one moment, for one fleeting second, before I ripped myself from her stare and slipped into the backseat of the car.

Because it didn't matter where I went or who I pretended to become.

I could never escape the reminder of the penalty that was left to pay.

five

Mia

*F*rom where I sat at the island in the kitchen, I stared out the

windows that overlooked Los Angeles as the sun slowly rose above the horizon. It tossed a kaleidoscope of colors across the city.

Pinks and oranges and bursting blues.

I sipped at my coffee while I relished in the sight.

There was always a quiet peace that radiated with the breaking day.

As if we were being offered a second chance. A new story. Our spirits renewed.

I guessed I wasn't surprised when I was hit with a surge of sadness.

It wafted and curled and saturated. Its own entity. I reached out, welcomed it, held it close to my heart.

I allowed the grief to consume me for the briefest moment. My mother had taught me that sometimes the most important part of healing was allowing ourselves to feel. That we had to allow ourselves to truly *feel* it without trying to minimize its pain, before we could possibly expect it to not hurt so bad.

And God . . . it hurt so bad it was physical.

An ache that wasn't close to being dull.

Sharp and biting and as raw as could be.

"I'm so sorry," I whispered beneath my breath, my eyes pressed closed as if she might be able to hear.

Praying that she could. That there was somewhere so much bigger than this life out there.

I jerked out of the daze when I heard a stampede of footsteps thundering from the opposite side of the house.

My aching spirit soared. Lifted like I'd been tossed a life raft.

The one thing in this ugly world that could truly save.

It grew louder and louder. A riot that came closer with every beat.

Two seconds later, the swinging door burst open. A whole herd of children crashed into the kitchen.

Jostling and vying to get in front of the other. Nothing but flailing arms and shrieking voices and laughter that could go on for days.

A soft smile edged my mouth when I took in the tangle. They didn't even notice I was there considering they were far too busy trying to outdo the other.

Kallie and Connor, who were Baz and Shea's kids.

Liam, Zee and Alexis' son, who was seven.

Colton, the three-year-old wild child who belonged to Ash and Willow. Nothing but a ham, just like his daddy.

Sadie, who belonged to Austin and Edie, was right on his tail.

Brendon and Adia, Lyrik and Tamar's children—my niece and nephew.

It was no secret the Sunder boys had been busy the last few years.

"I'm first!" Kallie shouted as she pushed Brendon to get in front of him, her blonde hair flying around her as she made a last-ditch effort to get in front of the pack.

Brendon threw out his arm.

My breath locked in worry because he just about clothes-lined her to keep her from rounding to the front.

Last thing we needed was her head cracked open on the marble tile.

Oh, but Kallie was on her toes, expecting his retaliation, the child diving to her knees so she could slide right under his barricade. The second she did, she jumped to her feet and slammed her hands down on the countertop. "Ha! I was first! Fair and square."

"Uh, not a chance, Kallie. I was definitely in front of you." Brendon raked her arms off the island and slammed his down in her place. "See!"

"No way. You're a cheater, Brendon West." Kallie propped her hand on her hip, giving him all her sass. "I touched it first!"

"Kallie won, Kallie won," Adia sang, shoving at her big brother like the four-year-old spitfire had enough strength to shove him out of the race.

"Nice . . . pick her side instead of mine, Adia. That's what's called a betrayal. How could you do this to me? I'm your big brother." He slapped a hand onto his chest.

Nothing but dramatic.

I swore, that boy was bound to be a heartbreaker.

Setting my cup of coffee on the breakfast nook, I stood and started to wander their direction. I wound around the large island just as Kristina, Tamar and Lyrik's trusted babysitter, came through the door.

She was carrying Greyson.

A rush of adoration spilled into my veins, my heart squeezing tight.

Talk about a heartbreaker.

Elation filled his face, and he pointed at me with his chubby finger. "Momma! I see you! I see you! Wook! Momma in the kitchen," he told Kristina with one of his emphatic nods, like she didn't notice me standing right there.

Love rushed. So fast and hard it nearly knocked me from my

feet.

"I see you, too, sweet boy," I murmured, pointing back.

I moved to them, all too eager to take my two-year-old son into my arms. The second I did, I bounced him, pressed a kiss to his forehead, breathed him in.

Joy.

Completeness.

Fulfillment.

"I missed you. Did you have so much fun last night?" I sang on a whisper.

Excitement widened his brown eyes. "I watched the dwagons!"

He said it like it was some kind of secret.

"You did, did you?"

"I *wuv* the dwagons."

"How was he?" I asked, glancing at Kristina.

She and a friend of hers had watched the kids last night over in the second wing of the house. We'd all wanted them to be close by but tucked safely away from the craziness.

It wasn't so hard to lure them with a movie-themed sleepover, Slurpie machine and all.

It wasn't like Lyrik was gonna skimp out on the good stuff.

It was a little harder to get me to agree. After everything, it was difficult to let my kids out of my sight, let alone for an entire night.

But I'd wanted to be there for Tamar and Lyrik. Support what they were doing.

Maybe even feel normal for a little while.

All it took was a single thought of him to send tingles streaking across my skin. Hairs lifting on end as I was hit with the remnants of the intensity I'd been prisoner to last night.

The man in the attic.

A dark storm.

A white light.

A coalescence of energy that had quietly seethed.

If I was being rational, I knew that intense encounter should mean nothing. I should have already forgotten it. Yet somehow, it had marked me. Left me tossing and turning all night, then had me up long before the sun, unable to find sleep.

No.

It wasn't insta-love.

It was insta-intrigue.

Insta-attraction.

And it'd left me *insta-crushed.*

Left with this little spec of *what-if* mangled inside me.

What if he would have stayed a little longer? What if I'd have asked a few more questions? What if I had pushed him a little harder—would it have led us somewhere we were meant to go?

What if he would have kissed me?

That roll of tingles turned into a flashfire.

What if he would have—

I gulped, unable to even bring myself to imagine it. Those hands and that body and that brooding heart.

He would have done me in.

No question.

What I'd done was dodged a speeding bullet.

A whole arsenal.

Hell, I'd probably avoided a landmine or two.

That man was written in mayhem. Tattooed in trouble. And I'd had plenty enough of that to last me a lifetime.

"Our Greyson here was a saint, weren't you?" Kristina fussed, singing to my son, snapping me out of the daze.

My brows lifted in disbelief. "A saint, huh? Why is it I don't believe you?"

Greyson might be the cutest thing on earth, but the child was a handful. So full of energy it was hard to keep up.

"Well, you should believe it. This one stole my heart. Even though he might have woken up twice in the middle of the night, didn't you, stinker boy?" She tapped his nose. "But I'll forgive you."

She sent me a small wink while he was giving her one of his smiles, the kind that was all chubby cheeks and tiny teeth and *I bet I can get away with anything* adorableness.

"Hey, I thought it was me who stole your heart?" Brendon called from the other side of the kitchen.

He was all smirks and black hair and dark eyes, just like his daddy.

Nothing but a flirt.

Kristina barked a laugh. "Oh, you think so, huh, Brendon?"

"Now don't go breakin' my heart, Miss Kristina."

It was hard to believe he was just shy of thirteen. The threat of his teenaged years was becoming more and more apparent with each day that passed.

As sweet and charming as could be, but there was no missing the flare in his eyes.

Something wild and unruly.

My ears perked up when another set of footsteps came trudging down the hall, slower than the rest, just like I expected them to be.

I looked that direction as the door swung open again.

Penny.

That overwhelming love slammed me anew.

Penny was my oldest child. Dark haired and brown-eyed. Stoic and willowy.

All things wonderful.

My sweet miracle because I was sure it was this little girl who had saved me when she was born. She'd given me something good and right to live for.

A purpose.

Set me on a different path than the one I'd been heading.

She shuffled down the hall long behind everyone else with her nose stuck in a book.

Surprise, surprise.

"Hey, Mom," she mumbled, barely acknowledging me as she moved for the table without pulling her face from the book.

"Missed you, too," I called as she passed.

She tossed an arm in the air in a *whatever* gesture.

So yeah, her teenaged years were lurking, too.

She and Kallie were both eleven. Thicker than thieves. Best of friends even though they lived on opposite sides of the country.

These gorgeous little girls who were getting ready to become bombshells.

The thought of that absolutely terrified me.

I wanted to gather up both my children and protect them from any heartache that might come their way.

From every misfortune and all their mistakes.

Keep them small and innocent and sweet.

But there was no way to stop the passage of time and the experiences that would come with it.

And truly, I wanted to embrace each phase.

Let them stumble and pick themselves back up again as they chased down their dreams.

Some days that was easier said than done because I knew that meant they were bound to go through all kinds of hard lessons to get there.

No one ever said *momming* was easy, and doing it alone was a whole ton harder.

Greyson smacked my face to get my attention. "I ready eat, Momma!" he shouted above the mayhem that was going down in the kitchen.

Connor and Liam had found themselves on the floor in a wrestling match, the rest of the children making a circle around them as they fought it out to see who would come out on top.

"Hey, don't you make me go wake up Uncle Lyrik to break up a fight. You know how that'll go down," I warned, trying to hold back my amusement.

Brendon cracked up. "Watch it, she's gonna get my dad, then you're all in for it."

"No way, I bet he'll give me five bucks if I pin Connor." Liam was gasping as he said it, flailing like crazy, both of them laughing so hard I doubted there was a chance either of them were going to get in a win.

A smile tugged at the corner of my mouth, relishing the feel. The joy and the love and happiness.

A stark reminder there wasn't only evil left in the world.

That I could do this.

"All right, let's feed you, my sweet boy," I sang to Greyson as I hiked him higher on my hip and started for the refrigerator.

That was right when Tamar came fumbling down a set of side stairs that led from the second floor into the kitchen. She tugged the belt of a silky leopard-print robe tighter around her waist as she took in the scene. "What in the world is going on in here?"

"Got ten bucks on Liam, Momma Blue. He might be tiny, but he is mighty." Brendon grinned triumphantly as she stepped down into the kitchen.

She frowned. "Um . . . what have we said about gambling, Brendon?"

"Not gambling when you know you're gonna win."

I laughed. Couldn't help it. I shook my head at his step-mother as she looked over at me in exasperation.

She might not have birthed Brendon, but she loved him with all her might. Treated him like he was her own. Respected his birth mother, coming alongside her to make sure Brendon was raised the best as he could be considering he was being raised in two separate homes.

It was never easy. Never perfect. But the truth was, families never were. But love truly living there was what made them completely right.

She ruffled her fingers through his hair and dropped a kiss to the top of his head. "You are nothin' but a troublemaker, do you know that?"

"That's why you love me."

She sighed again, holding back a giggle, adoration filling her expression.

Adia made a beeline for her. "Hi, Mommmmmy!"

She threw her little arms around Tamar's middle, and Tamar hugged her close.

"What are you doing up already?" Kristina asked Tamar, biting back laughter when Tamar looked in desperation at the coffee pot. "I didn't think we'd see you at least until noon."

She rolled her eyes over her daughter's head. "Seriously . . . I think I could sleep for a straight week. But my littles were calling to me, so Momma got her tail out of bed. I figured everyone was going to be hungry."

"I hungry!" Greyson's hand shot into the air, a worthy volunteer.

"I would have been happy to feed them," Kristina said.

Tamar waved her off. "It's fine."

I jolted when the side door banged open from behind us.

I could almost feel it.

The way the levity drained from the air and aggression flooded in to take its place.

A cold dread that lifted the hairs at the nape of my neck and twisted my stomach in an instant knot of worry.

I guessed everyone else felt it, too, because Kristina stopped what she was saying and all the kids went silent.

From my vantage, I watched the deepest frown set into Tamar's expression.

Warily, I turned to look over my shoulder to find Lyrik raging in the doorway, wearing tattered jeans and an even older tee and hatred on his face.

"Lyrik. What's wrong?" Tamar managed, her voice quivering with a shock of dread.

Hands curling around the doorframe, he swallowed hard, the tattoo on his throat bobbing as his eyes skated the room, instinctively moving to land on me. He glanced back at Tamar. "Need to talk to my sister. In private."

Chills skated down my spine.

A slick of ice.

Freezing me to the spot.

"Please," he grated, clearly not wanting to make a scene in front of the kids.

I forced myself to snap out of the stupor. I gave a jerky nod.

"Sure." I attempted to play it off. To act like it was no big deal when Penny finally pulled her attention from the book and shifted it to me.

Like she could feel all of this, too.

Worry etching her sweet, sweet face.

Shakily, I moved for Tamar. "Can you watch him for a second?"

"Of course," she said, taking him from me and hugging him close while continuing to stare at Lyrik with a million questions playing through her eyes.

He didn't say anything when he ducked back out. Feet heavy,

I followed him into the muted light of the morning.

"I didn't think you'd be up yet. I needed to talk to you, too," I rambled at his back as he headed to the edge of the patio, doing my best to break the tension. Terrified of what could have him so upset.

To pretend like this wasn't a big deal when I could feel the severity of it banging through the atmosphere.

The air colder than it should be.

A frigid warning that scraped my skin in jagged pricks.

There was no missing the fact that Lyrik was doing his best to keep his cool and losing his battle with it, his hands curling into fists, something vicious and dark and cruel radiating from his being.

When we were fully hidden from view of the kitchen window, he finally whirled around.

The outright horror curling his face made me stumble to a stop, breaths going shallow and hard, alarm slowing my pulse to a ragged thud.

"What's going on, Lyrik? You're scaring me."

His eyes pinched for a beat, and he roughed a hand through his hair as he looked away, like he was trying to gather himself, keep it together, but there was no use in it because I could already feel myself falling apart in front of him.

"Got a call from security this morning," he grunted. He warred, clearly not wanting to continue, his voice cracking as he forced out the words. "Said they had an issue with one of the guest's cars. They didn't discover it until this morning. I went out to the lot to check it out. Mia . . . all your tires . . . they'd been slashed. Fifteen fucking other cars had been out there last night, and yours was the only one that had been touched."

Terror squeezed my heart in a vice grip.

Anxiety clawed at my flesh.

Deep and biting.

Freeing the fear that I'd been trying to outrun for the last three weeks.

But it couldn't be. It just . . . couldn't. There had to be another explanation.

My head shook in refusal, not even wanting to contemplate the possibilities. "What do you mean . . . I thought . . . I thought there was security?"

"There was . . . but apparently not enough. Bastard got through."

Dizziness whirled.

Faster and faster.

The grief I'd been suppressing for weeks rose to the surface, no longer able to be subdued. I tried to break through it, to find air above the dark waters that lapped and churned and fought to suck me under.

My mind raced. It finally came around to settle on the asshole who had gotten handsy.

"I-it had to be that guy last night," I barely managed to stammer. "The one who'd freaked me out."

My tongue darted out to wet my dried lips, and I fidgeted and ran my hands through my hair like it might have the chance to calm me down. "He . . . he backed me into a corner after you and I talked. Acted like I was there as part of the entertainment or something. Like he could just have me."

Lyrik gripped two handfuls of hair. He turned a livid circle.

A complete three-sixty that only poured fire on the flames.

Hatred rushing free, hurt bleeding from his mouth.

Lyrik style.

"What the fuck, Mia? Why didn't you tell me? Come find me? With all this shit goin' down? God damn it." The last dripped from his mouth like he was the one to blame.

My head shook. "I took care of it."

"And how did you do that?" Lyrik looked like he was going to completely come out of his skin. What really terrified me was what peeling that back might actually reveal.

"I fought him off. Spit in his face and kneed him in the dick. I didn't wait around to see how pissed he was, but from his yelping and crying, I'm sure he was plenty offended."

"God damn it, Mia."

There was almost the hint of a smile on his mouth.

Like he was proud.

Proud and so very pissed.

"Asshole is lucky he only got kneed in the balls, and I wasn't there to cut them off. In front of everyone. Might finally teach the prick a lesson. I bet I know exactly who you're talking about."

"Which is exactly the reason I didn't come looking for you. I wanted time between what happened and when I told you so we could report him. I had every intention of it, Lyrik. I was just waiting for you to wake up. But this is something that needs to be reported to the cops, and not for you to go hunting him down to make him pay for it. You know that's not going to do either of us any good."

"Bet I know exactly who it is, too. Dick is always sloshed, touching things he shouldn't, thinking he's the shit." He rambled the words, grunting and ranting.

I didn't even have to describe the guy.

Apparently, his reputation preceded him.

What a creep.

"It had to be him," I said, nodding, doing my best to convince myself.

Because something didn't sit right.

Because my car . . . how would he have known? The guy didn't know a thing about me. And if I had a million bucks to bet, I would put it on my car being the crappiest out there. Unnoticeable among all the rest.

Like Brendon had said, it wasn't gambling when you knew you were going to win.

All the fancy sports cars and over-the-top luxury sedans that had pulled up to the valet stand last night. The cars the rest of the band and their families kept for when they were in the city.

And there was my five-year-old Accord sitting in the middle of them.

I wondered if Lyrik was thinking the exact same thing because his focus had drifted out over the city, the man working his jaw hard and his vision narrowed at the nothingness.

I jumped about fifteen feet in the air when his phone suddenly rang from his pocket, the shrill tone slicing into the silence.

He dug it out, glanced at the ID, quick to accept the call when

57

he saw whoever it was. "What do you have?" he demanded the second he put it to his ear.

He watched me as he listened to the voice on the other end of the line. His expression morphed and churned and darkened.

I could feel it.

That shattering of energy that flared and pulsed.

The way his entire being morphed with his own fear.

A buzz of horror.

Teeth gritted, he pulled his phone away to look at something on the screen.

It was a video his security team had sent through. He watched it twice, his muscles twitching as he did, violence growing stronger with each pass.

While I stood there trying to pretend like this wasn't another moment in my life that was going to change everything.

Finally, he held it out for me to watch it, like he hated to do it but had no other choice because there was no protecting me from the reality of this.

Warily, I watched the scene play out on the screen.

Fifteen seconds of horror.

That was all the time it took for nausea to hit me, full force, so fast and fierce that I didn't make it all the way to the edge of the patio before I threw up in a planter.

Retching in terror and sickness and cutting grief.

On the video was a man, dressed in all black and wearing a ski mask, waving a knife at the camera like he wanted it to capture everything.

Like he was issuing a threat.

I was one-hundred-percent sure he was the same man that had been in my gallery that night.

The same man the detective was certain had been a random.

The same man who had found a way into my brother's compound.

The very same man who had murdered my best friend.

58

"What the hell, Mia?" Nixon hissed at me from under his breath where I stood outside the doorway of his shop, hugging my arms over my chest in an attempt to hold myself together. "You can't just up and leave to Savannah. Are you crazy?"

Disbelief pulsed through his being, his surprise injected with a shot of anger, his eyes hard and filled with the cruelness I knew he could mete with the flick of his wrist. His hair was close to white and cut short, his face all blunt lines and harsh expressions.

Even though he'd cleaned up his life, he still looked every bit as menacing as he had since the day I'd met him.

Trouble.

Apparently, I had a type.

His harsh gaze went for a hostile ride over his shoulder, searching the street as if he were wondering if I'd been followed. If he was going to have to beat someone down right there.

Just the thought of it made me want to puke.

The idea that someone was after me.

Every question of *why* coming at me at warp speed.

Ill-at-ease, I shifted on my feet, no longer comfortable in my skin or in my world or in my city. "I would be crazy to stay here, Nix. You have to understand that. After everything?"

"Exactly. Mia. After everything. You need to be here. With me. You can't just take off with my kids."

Disbelief narrowed my eyes. "And you want me to keep them here? While some psychopath is out there, after me for God knows what? You know I won't . . . that I can't . . . put my children at risk like that."

Faster than I could make sense of it, he gripped me by the elbow, tugging me closer, desperation in his voice. "Then stay with me. Let me take care of you. You know I can protect you. Stay with me, Mia. Be with me. I'll fix whatever the fuck has gone wrong here. I promise you I won't let anything happen to you or the kids."

God. Were we doing this again?

Sadness shook my head. "You know that's not going to happen, Nix."

Our relationship had been tumultuous.

Off and on and off again.

He'd been the guy who'd stolen my eye when he'd gone riding by on his motorcycle, bad and mean and every-single-thing I should never want.

I didn't really know how *bad* he was until a few months in, when I realized his line of work wasn't exactly legal.

That I was getting caught up in something that I shouldn't.

That was right about the time I'd found out I was pregnant with Penny. I'd given him an ultimatum—me and the baby or that life.

He'd walked.

I should have chalked it up to being a blessing, but when he'd cleaned up his life, turned himself around, and had shown up at my door wanting to take his position as Penny's dad, I'd given him the benefit of the doubt.

Problem was, the man was a whirlwind, sweeping in, turning everything upside-down with a flick of his hand.

A few months later, I was pregnant with Greyson, and we were right back in the same position.

No more.

Not ever again.

I'd learned my lesson the hard way.

Twice.

I wouldn't be repeating it.

The problem was, he'd been trying to convince me all that time to come back to him. That we could make it work when there was no chance that we could.

There was too much hurt and garbage and distrust littered between us.

But even then, he'd been there to support us. Being the best father to the kids that he could be. He'd even come alongside me when I'd been chasing down a dream of opening my own gallery, investing time and money and effort into the little shop.

My insides clutched at the thought of that building. At the memory.

At the vision of the walls and the floor where she'd lain.

Blood.

So much blood.

"Why not, Mia? Hasn't enough time gone by? Haven't I done enough?" he pushed.

My brow drew tight. "And you told me you were doing that because you care about me as a friend. Because you want the best life for our children."

It was never supposed to come at a price.

He roughed a frustrated hand through his hair, angling away, before he was back to staring me down. "I did it because I love you. Because I always have. Because I love them. Because I want us to be a family."

I blinked hard, fighting the emotion I could feel welling in my throat. "I'm sorry, Nix. But I can't stay here."

Dread filled the hard lines of his expression. "How am I supposed to take care of you when you're not here? You need to stick close, Mia, until we find out what is happening. And besides . . . you're just . . . going to walk away from the gallery? You need it."

Chills crawled up my arms, a slow-slide of anguish and mourning. My hands chased it, like it might be enough to warm the cold spot carved out in the middle of me. "You know I can never step foot in that place again."

His eyes pinched closed. "Then we'll find another space."

I backed up, looking for some space of my own.

"I'm sorry, Nix. But I'm going. Just for the summer. Penny loves it there, anyway. She'll be with Kallie. You know what that will mean to her. It's for the best."

"And what about me?" Disappointment flooded his tone, his normal arrogant posture dampening in the rejection.

Taking another step backward, I gave him the most honest answer that I could. "It was never about you."

Leif

"Dude, if you even think about bailing on us, I will hunt you down and personally drag your ass back to South Carolina." The tease Rhys sent me through the phone was delivered with the undercurrent of a threat.

Carolina George's bassist was loud and crass, his big, bleeding heart worn on his sleeve with a scrap of barbed-wire around it to protect it.

My gaze drifted out the back window of the luxury SUV as I traveled deeper into the Historic District of Savannah. Carolina George had played downtown along River Street enough times in this small city that everything felt familiar.

Homes that hailed from more than a century before. Grand and pretentious.

Spindly age-old oaks grew up on each side of the narrow roads,

and flares of sunlight struck down through the breaks in the leaves, the moss-covered branches stretched overhead like passages that led into a brand-new world.

A place removed.

Another time.

Like you'd stepped back into a different era and no one even noticed you were there.

Whimsical and quaint and ripe with history.

Unease shivered through my senses.

Could almost hear the ghosts howling, haunting the streets, flitting through the highest branches of the trees as they searched for what had been lost.

Somethin' eerie all mixed up with a vibe that billowed peace.

I itched, knee bouncing out of control, my fingers drumming my thigh even faster. Trying to calm myself the fuck down, but unable to stop the anxiety that was crawling over me like a bad dream.

A bad omen.

Got the premonition that I was driving toward destruction, and I didn't have a clue why. All except for the fact I'd always known Los Angeles would one day catch up to me. I could almost sense it now, right there, hunting, so close I was only a single misstep from it taking me down.

Wasn't a chance in hell I was going to let that happen.

Not until retribution had been paid.

Revenge had been served.

I had to keep it together, bide my time until *time* had come to fruition.

"I'm serious about this shit, Banger," Rhys said through a rough chuckle. I could almost see him flexing his ridiculous biceps from across the line, like the brawny motherfucker actually thought he could kick my ass. "Would give my left nut for us to get that contract signed. Em's thrown enough wrenches in the deal. Last thing we need is you givin' it a good twist."

"You have so little faith in me?" I asked.

He huffed, and I could hear the heels of his cowboy boots thudding onto the top of a table as he undoubtedly rocked back in a chair. Boy was about as southern as they came. A bull in a china shop. Always ready to jump into the saddle.

"Opposite, man. Opposite. If I didn't trust you, I wouldn't even have let you get on that plane to Los Angeles in the first place. I mean, shit, them wining and dining you with a goddamn private jet? That is some fancy-pants shit, bro. Now you're going to be chilling at *the* Lyrik West's Savannah pad—which I'd bet my left nut is probs as ritzy as his place in the Hills—for two months? For free? Plus all that dough? All for the sake of you laying down a few drum tracks on their next album? Sounds fishy. Smells fishy, too."

A dark chuckle filtered free. "You think I'm so good they would want to poach me? And you can't bet your left nut. You already promised it to get the band signed."

Rhys cracked up. "Balls are big enough to bet on 'em a few times. Plenty enough reserve to go around."

"You wish, asshole," I told him, chuckling under my breath.

The guy was cocky to the core.

Arrogance inbred.

But he didn't do it without reason.

He was a fucking superstar on the bass. Talented beyond measure. Didn't hurt matters in the least that women lost their goddamn minds every time he took to the stage.

Dude also liked to imagine Carolina George was the *actual* best band on earth.

Okay.

We were good.

Really fucking good. Guilt clawed. Hated using them as a cover. As a reprieve. First time I heard them, I should have known they were going places. That this unknown band was going to become something great.

Now I just had to pray that I could stick around long enough to help get them there.

Not fuck them over right in the middle of this chance that was being given.

"Do I think you're good enough for them to want to snatch you up?" Rhys scoffed, and I could feel the force of his smug grin.

Guy's personality was so big you didn't even have to be in the same state for him to be playing out in vivid Technicolor.

"Only reason we even put up with your brooding ass is the fact you are so good," he ribbed.

Fighting the quirk of a smile, I rested my head back on the headrest. Flickers of sunlight slanted through the windows, the area growing more upscale by the second as the driver drew us closer to our destination.

My home for the next two months.

Like Lyrik had said—it really shouldn't be a big deal. I was simply standing in. Making life easier for a friend and earning a whole shit-ton of money while doing it. But I couldn't silence the warning blaring inside me that I should have just said no.

That mixing L.A. and business was about the worst thing I could do.

I had a plan. It'd do me well to stick to it.

Veering to the left wasn't going to help things.

"You never know, Rhys," I drew out, playing like none of this mattered. Like I wasn't close to coming apart. "I just might get cozy here and decide playing with Sunder is really where I belong. Can't imagine it would be all that hard to get used to."

The car made a right into a neighborhood that screamed old-world luxury. We rolled to a stop in front of what had to be the most over-the-top, palatial house I'd ever seen.

Lyrik's house in the Hills had nothing on this.

Yeah.

Getting used to hanging out around here shouldn't be all that hard to do.

I must have been gawking for too long because Rhys suddenly demanded below his breath, "Dude . . . it's *that* good, isn't it? Shit. I knew it. We're screwed."

"Nah, man, it's a hovel."

"Liar," he shouted in feigned affront.

The estate was secured between two tree-lined streets, taking up the entire end of an upscale neighborhood block. A black wrought-iron and red-bricked fence encased the entire property. Marble stairs led up to the walkway from off the street, that was if you had an invitation to make it through the security gate.

A sign wasn't necessary for it to read *keep the fuck out.*

Place was fronted by five huge steps that led up to the soaring columns of the portico, double doors waiting with a quaint welcome that belied the grandeur of the rest of the house.

It gave way to three stories of shuttered windows, columned porches stretching around the north side to the backyard that was enclosed by a high wall, inhibiting passersby from sneaking a peek.

"Yeah, you're right, I'm totally lying. Place is out of control. This is the way the other half lives, man."

"Stop rubbing it in, Banger," Rhys grumbled through the line. "I know you, and I know your ass still has heavy metal pumping through your veins. Last thing we need is for you to try to ditch us once you get another taste of it. Things are finally happening with Carolina George. Happening fast, too. Just like I told you they would. Knew people couldn't ignore our badassery forever. Don't you dare walk in that house and decide that is where you're supposed to be."

"So you're saying you need me now?"

He huffed through his amusement. "Barely."

"Come on, man, tell me you love me. Tell me the band is nothing without me."

"Fuck off," he said through a laugh.

"Have it your way," I told him, keeping the razzing alive as I clicked open the door. There was nothing more entertaining than fucking with Rhys.

"Fine. Fuckin' fine," he rushed. "Before you go inside that house, you gotta know the band would be an absolute shit-show without you. Not that we aren't all bad asses. But we are bad asses together. Bad asses united. Bad asses to eternity. Do ya hear me?"

The last he sang in his country drawl like he was trying to rally a squad of downtrodden troops, like he had a hand fisted in the air for solidarity.

Yeah.

Eternity wasn't in the cards for me.

But maybe if I played it right, I could help get them where they needed to go. Set them up before I folded.

"Unfortunately, I do hear you," I said, keeping my tone as light as I could.

"Bastard." Could feel his smile.

Figured I'd better put him out of his misery. "Don't worry, brother. I'm in and out. No one will even know I'm here."

"Oh, I bet Lyrik West's wife will notice you're there. Have you seen pictures of her? Fuck," he groaned. "I bet you met her this last weekend, didn't you? She is h.o.t. With a capital H. Hell, with a capital everything."

"Pretty sure if Lyrik West heard you say that, he would cut off both your nuts. No more betting for you."

"Like you're going to out me. Your best friend? Come on, Banger."

"Hey man, Lyrik and I go way back. You never know. And that's Head Banger to you."

"See . . . heavy metal. This is a goddamn nightmare," he whimpered in nothing but faked outrage.

I was chuckling low when I said, "I've got to go."

Driver was staring me down through the rearview mirror, biting his tongue, the poor bastard.

Rhys hesitated, then cleared his throat. "Seriously, Leif. This is cool. Proud of you. No one better to fill Zee Kennedy's shoes than the likes of you. I hope you know I truly believe that."

"Thanks, Rhys."

"Be good."

"Always."

I didn't bother to call my own bullshit.

I slipped out of the car and onto the sidewalk that was shaded by the towering oaks. The driver was already there, grabbing my single suitcase from the trunk, glad to kick me to the curb.

"Thanks." I shook his hand and slipped him a hundred.

Figured it was the least I could do considering all of my expenses were being covered for the next two months.

Wheeling the suitcase behind me, I headed up the walk. The gate buzzed before I made it all the way there. No doubt, Lyrik was anticipating my arrival.

I pushed through the unlocked gate and moved the rest of the way up the walkway. The front door whipped open as I climbed the steps.

"Leif. You made it. Glad you're here." Lyrik stepped onto the porch.

"Glad to be here." I glanced up at the soaring porch ceiling. "Nice place."

He chuckled a wry sound and rubbed his chin. "Don't judge. House hunting list of musts was we had to be within a mile of Shea and Baz's place and Ash and Willow's that is a mile in the other direction. Tamar's rules."

"And this was the only one that was for sale?"

"Only one that was within our price range." Asshole actually winked, hand flying out to smack me on the outside of my arm.

"Hard life, man. Hard life."

He was all grins, and he angled his head toward the door. "Come on in. Want you to make yourself at home, and I mean that. No fucking tiptoeing. You need something, you say it. You want to kick off your shoes, you do it. You want something from the fridge, you grab it. This place is family—comfort—no matter what it looks like from the outside."

My brow lifted when I stepped through the doorway because the inside looked like a goddamn museum.

Paintings covered every wall.

What got me most was a bunch of them were just like the eerie, mystical ones that had filled his attic back in Los Angeles. Distorted, obscured faces. Twisted in some kind of beautiful agony as they stared into the nothingness. Lost and seeking a way to be found.

To be understood.

Like maybe it was only the artist who actually could.

A shock of intrigue slammed me in the chest. A punch of that insanity I'd felt this last weekend. That overpowering lust that I'd had a bitch of a time forgetting.

Girl sinking in her claws without even gifting me with her name.

It crawled over me like the innuendo of a dream.

A vague, vapor of a memory.

Problem was, I couldn't tell if it was a nightmare I wanted to shun or an idea I wanted to wake up to and beg it to become my truth.

Materialize.

I tore my attention from one of the pictures that was hanging on the far wall, floating halfway up to the soaring ceiling. Room was decked out in massive arches and crown molding, giving it form and shape. A curved staircase ascended to the second floor, breaking off into two sections halfway up.

"This way." Lyrik moved through the foyer and living room that I was pretty sure you weren't actually supposed to *live* in.

"Ash's wife, Willow?" he hedged.

I gave a small nod to let him know that I knew who he was referring to.

"She refurbishes old furniture," he explained. "Pieces she picks up that are completely dilapidated and broken to shit. Half the time, she digs them out of a dumpster. Brings them back to life. Every piece in here is a piece of her."

Ah. Made sense.

Lyrik didn't exactly seem like the antique type.

"Beautiful stuff," I told him, making conversation because I just didn't relate to the whole 'making a house a home' bullshit.

Not when I'd burned mine to the ground.

"Yeah. She's super talented. Tamar has even helped her with a couple pieces. Weird how things become more treasured when you have a hand in their making."

Lyrik ducked through the next doorway at the end of the hall. It led into an enormous great room.

One-part kitchen.

One-part playground.

My eyes widened a bit at the mess.

Place was completely at odds with the area we'd just walked through. Pillows had been tossed from the overstuffed sectional couch that faced a TV the size of a football stadium, toys strewn everywhere, socks and shoes discarded on the floor.

"This is where we all pretty much chill. Warning, kids get nuts in here. You don't like the littles, you're going to have to hide out in your shack."

He grinned.

Sourness climbed my throat. I swallowed it down. Pasted on a smile. "Kids don't bother me."

Didn't plan on spending much of any time in here or around Lyrik's family. Like he'd warned me, they were his main priority. What he would fight for and live for and die for. I didn't have any business hanging around any of them.

Would make myself scarce.

Play when the band needed me and hide out when they didn't.

He laughed. A little harder than prudent. "Yeah, well, between me and my crew, we have a whole goddamn mob of them. Have a couple extras spending the summer here at the house, too. Place promises to be a fuckin' zoo." He stretched out his tattooed arms. "Welcome to the Wild, Wild West. No place better to be."

He smirked.

I chuckled. So it turned out the big, bad Lyrik West was kinda a sap. "Not a problem. Just here to play some music and mind my business. You won't even notice I'm here."

"You're going to be right out here." He gestured toward the bank of windows that opened up to the walled-in backyard. "Code to the door is 98564. We keep the main house locked, inside and out, to keep the kids away from the pool if they're not supervised. You're welcome to come and go . . . just make sure this shit remains locked."

Another warning. And I was starting to wonder why the fuck I had agreed to stay here. Maybe I just was wanting to torture myself.

"Got it."

I glanced through the windows.

Backyard, my ass.

It was some kind of oasis in the middle of downtown Savannah.

Fucking paradise.

Eden.

Fountains spouted from the four corners of the yard, and each was surrounded by lush, pink flowering bushes. A luxurious pool

sat right at the center of it, surrounded by an intricate brick patio and cool deck.

A long wing of the house extended along the right side, that portion one-story.

At the very back of the lot was a miniature replica of the main house. Two small columns framed the front door and small porch, the one story made to look like it was two.

"That's you. Hope it meets your standards."

"Looks to me like I'll be just fine."

He started to open the door, only to pause when a clatter of footsteps suddenly came pounding down a set of stairs that dumped out in the great room.

A riot of shrieks and laughter and shouting voices flooded the space.

You'd think an entire daycare was on a field trip.

Nope.

The chaos was summoned by three kids.

"Whoa, guys, watch yourselves. We've got company."

Kid at the helm put on the brakes, nothing but wild black hair and dark, dark eyes.

"You the drummer?" He was all eager grins and easy smiles as he came toward me like we were gonna be the best of friends.

Would put down bets this kid belonged to Lyrik, and I wouldn't need Rhys' nuts for collateral.

"Sure am."

His eyes moved over me. He nodded like he was giving his approval. "Cool."

Lyrik ran a tattooed hand over the top of the boy's head. "This is my son, Brendon."

I lifted my chin at him. "Great to meet you, Brendon."

"And this is my baby girl, Adia."

Tried not to puke right there when Lyrik hiked a little girl into his arms.

Probably three or four.

Gnashed my teeth together to keep from losing it. To keep from turning around and walking out the door.

Stupid.

Fucking stupid coming here.

Managed not to flinch when she squealed and threw her arms around his neck, wiggling in his hold and staring out at me with an overdose of cuteness.

Barely forced a wave at her. "Hey, there."

My attention got pulled to the corner of the room when I got smacked by an apprehensive aura that pulsed against the walls.

To the last of the children who'd come rambling down the steps.

This girl was probably a year or two younger than Brendon.

Wary and shy where she hung back at the base of the stairway.

Definitely one of Lyrik's brood. Long, black hair that she had in a ponytail, though her eyes were a different shade than the rest of his kids', like cups of black coffee had been swirled with a shot of caramel.

He sent a soft smile at her. "And this is my niece, Penny Pie. She's spending the summer with us. Penny, this is Leif. The drummer I told you was gonna be playing with us so Uncle Zee can tour with Liam."

Niece.

Not his kid.

I gave her a small wave.

The one she returned was leery.

Like she'd already seen straight through who I was and labeled me.

A bad guy.

Couldn't fault her for that.

"Nice to meet you, Penny."

Wow.

This was awkward as fuck.

Why Lyrik didn't point me in the direction of the guest house and bypass all of this bullshit, I didn't know. All of these introductions seemed entirely unnecessary considering I was about to split.

She nodded, seeming to contemplate what to say but stopped when someone from above called for her, "Hey, Penny. Have you seen Greyson's bear? I can't find it anywhere, and he needs it for

his nap. I swear to God, if I left that back home, we're all going to be in for it until Grandma can get it shipped to us."

I was slammed with what felt like a million things all at once.

A swell of energy.

Same as what I'd experienced last week.

Only this time, it came at me like a motherfucking tidal wave.

Footsteps echoed as they banged down the stairs, reverberating the floors, vibrating my legs and rocking me to the core.

Ears getting filled with a voice I'd chalked up to fantasy.

Eyes glutting on a face that nearly knocked me to my knees.

All of it damned near stopped my heart in my chest.

Seized.

A motherfucking stroke of horrible, terrible bad luck.

The angel in the attic.

The girl clamored down the stairs with a tiny boy fastened to her hip, not having the first clue that the devil had chased her to Savannah.

But I was pretty sure it was me who was in danger.

The girl a danger to my sanity. To my reality.

This girl had spun my mind in a way no one should have the ability to do.

In a way I couldn't allow.

When she realized there was someone standing in the middle of the room, she stumbled to a stop, clinging to the railing for support.

Or maybe she'd just sensed me the same way I sensed her. Had gotten swept up by a rogue wave that could bring nothing but destruction. That fucked-up connection I didn't want to feel stretched thin between us.

Simmering and shivering.

Crackling in the air.

Awareness pulled. A tug-of-war that demanded to be made known.

Silence descended, and that lush mouth dropped open at the same time as those sable eyes widened in shock when they landed on me.

Lust struck me.

A goddamn sledgehammer to the senses.

Clinging to the railing for support, she took me in like she was hallucinating.

If only that were the case.

I wanted to kick my own ass.

Irritation blazed through my being. One-hundred-percent of it was directed at myself.

Of course, this girl was Lyrik's sister. I mean, how the fuck hadn't I put two and two together? The woman who'd come stumbling into that room like an apparition, demanding to know what I was doing hiding away from the party, thousands of miles away from where I belonged, but acting like she had the right to be there? Like that was her sanctuary and I'd been the one to invade it?

And shit, Lyrik and this girl could be twins.

But I guessed I'd chalked her up to being nothin' but a figment. Too good to be true. Too perfect to be real.

Eliciting things inside me that should be impossible. Something I would *never* allow myself to feel.

And there she stood, gaping at me from twenty feet away.

She was wearing super tight skinny jeans and a thin sweatshirt that draped off one slender shoulder.

Delicious flesh that I wanted to devour.

Black hair a river of waves tumbling around her.

A slip of her stomach exposed.

My mouth watered, and my guts fisted in want.

Yeah, that compulsion had to die. Not a fucking chance would I touch her. Not even when my body was getting all kinds of wayward ideas that this was my second-chance, the guilt it evoked threatening to slam me up against a wall.

Knew this was a mistake.

Knew it.

And there I was, anyway.

A sucker just asking for it.

She swallowed hard, her delicate throat bobbing, the girl completely flustered. A shot of redness pinked up her cheeks, and her eyes were darting everywhere but on me. Finally, she forced a smile. "Oh, goodness . . . I'm sorry. I didn't realize you already had company, Lyrik."

She glanced at me, almost as wary as her . . . daughter.

I scraped a hand over my face like it might break me from the stupor, too.

Penny had to be her daughter.

If Lyrik could be her twin, the young girl was nothing but her mini-me. And the tiny boy in her arms? He was a mix of the two, caramel eyes, lighter hair, but his nose the same as his sister's and their mom's.

She was a mom.

Sweet and shy and bold and every-fucking-thing my fingers were itching to reach out and trace.

Touch.

Take and taste.

And I was so completely fucked.

So fucked as Lyrik looked between us, something like suspicion darkening his expression. "Leif . . . this is my baby sister, Mia. Penny and Greyson's mom. Three of them are staying here this summer."

I gulped around the jagged rock that was suddenly wedged at the base of my throat.

Painful and cutting off airflow.

If I listened hard enough, I could hear Karma kicked back in the lounger at the back of the room, laughing her ass off while she sipped at a frozen cocktail.

"Nice to meet you, Mia." Came out harder than it should.

Irritation buzzed through my being. The contract I'd signed with Sunder suddenly felt like a death sentence. Blood written on the motherfucking line.

Woman a temptation I didn't know how to bear.

If it was possible, her smile was even more faked than mine, her voice trembling when she said, "Nice to meet you, too, Leif."

Problem was, that voice came at me like a song. Something that had been haunting me for the last week.

Calm and peace.

But peace was not meant for me.

"Waif!" The little boy in her arms pointed at me with a grin that could singlehandedly decimate an ironhanded regime.

Awesome.

"Hey, there," I muttered, uneasiness riding free, and his mom was planting a kiss to the top of his head and then running her hand over the same spot like she was trying to get him to settle down, but I was pretty sure she wasn't doing anything but trying to settle her racing heart that I could feel pounding through the room.

Or maybe it was just mine stampeding out of control.

Wayward and hard.

Riding with a warning.

I glanced back at Lyrik. His displeased expression had kicked into a storm. He set his daughter to her feet. "We should get you settled."

"Sounds good."

Needed to get the hell out of this room before I suffocated.

I went for indifferent when I threw up a hand, though the words were harsh and low, "It was very nice to meet you all."

Lyrik punched the code into the door to open it, and I followed him out. It ran me smack into the heat, a wall of oppressive humidity instantly coating my skin in a slick of sweat.

Or maybe it was visceral.

This reaction that made me feel like I was gonna come right out of my skin. I had no fuckin' clue how I was supposed to spend the summer living on the same property as that woman.

Come to find out, *Eden* was actually hell.

Now that was what was called cruel and unjust.

But I guessed if the punishment fit.

In front of me, Lyrik stalked along the sidewalk that edged the left side of the pool.

The thick, stagnant air was full of the sound of the fountains gurgling and splashing into the carved stone reservoirs, birds chirping and flitting through the trees.

It felt like a complete contradiction to the drone of the city encircling the estate. Sirens and engines and the blare of horns.

Lyrik climbed the two steps to the guest-house porch and

swung open the door. "Here we go. Code is same as the house."

"Got it."

I angled inside, passing him and pulling my suitcase behind me. My attention bounced around, not that I really cared what my accommodations were going to be like. They could have put me up at a run-down hotel and I wouldn't have given two fucks.

But this?

It was warm. Comfortable. The living room in the front had every luxury you could ask for. Fluffy pillows adorned the plush couch, two sitting chairs set up on either side that faced the huge TV that hung on the wall. To the far side on the right was a high-topped bar that overlooked a small kitchen on the other side. I could only assume the short hall to the left of it led to a bedroom.

But what caught my attention was the drum-set and assortment of guitars and musical instruments that were set up in a cove on the left side of the living room.

"Figured you might want to play in your downtime," Lyrik said like it was no big deal.

"Probably going to need to practice a few new songs I don't know." I attempted to crack a joke, to lighten whatever this bullshit was I could feel clawing my skin, a million fire ants marching to a grim drumbeat across raw, bleeding flesh.

He just shrugged. "Don't have any worries that you won't catch on just fine."

There was an edge to him. A disquiet that I could feel radiating from his being.

Or maybe I was just projecting.

On a huff, he dragged his tattooed fingers through his hair. "Want you to know we are all grateful that you dropped everything to come help us out. Know Sunder has been playing together for a long time, but we don't want you to feel like you're just backup or a stand-in. This is you on this album. These songs will belong to you every bit as much as they belong to us. As long as you're playing with Sunder, you're a part of Sunder."

I gave a tight nod. "I appreciate that. And you know I'll give it my everything."

"Which is why you're the only one fit to stand here."

He edged back, glanced around before he said, "I'll let you get settled." A gleam lit in his dark eyes. "My wife is demanding that you join us for dinner tonight. She wants to make sure you feel welcome. We eat at seven."

I lifted a hand to reject the offer.

Because no.

Just fucking no.

He put up two. "Don't even try to argue, man. Know you don't know my wife, but take it from me—she invites you to dinner? You better accept the invitation."

I bit down on my tongue to stop the curse from dropping free. "Great. No problem. I'll be there."

"Good. Just holler if you need anything."

"Will do."

Guessed I really was projecting.

He turned and stepped up to the door, only to hesitate when he pulled it open. His back was to me, the guy holding onto the doorknob, clearly warring with reservation.

He looked at me from over his shoulder. "And what we talked about the other night? About the fact my family is my main priority? Their happiness and their safety my one concern?"

This time, my nod was tighter, so tight it was lucky my neck didn't snap in two.

"You need to know that applies to my sister. She's been to hell and back, and she's here to heal. So I can keep her safe. Last thing she needs is to be toyed with. If you catch my meaning?" His head cocked to the side. There was no mistaking the warning.

Stay the fuck away from my sister.

Got it because that shit was not a problem.

Still, my goddamn body physically jolted with the confirmation.

Knew it, that night. The girl had been running scared. Looking for a way to get lost. Swept away.

Now, I felt desperate to know the depths of it.

What the fuck he was actually implying.

Anger threatened to lay siege to my logic.

To raze my focus to the ground. I knew better. I didn't have

the time or the space or the *goodness* to care or to make it my problem.

I shoved it down in the pits of my corrupt spirit where it belonged.

It was no concern of mine.

Girl was fucking hot. My dick noticed. That was it. Nothing more.

Teeth grinding, I forced a smile. "No need to mention it twice. I got you. Wouldn't go there, anyway."

He studied me for a beat. No doubt, he hadn't missed whatever the hell that interaction was that had gone down between us in his family room. Whatever power had stopped both Mia and me in our tracks. Stole our breaths while something profound pounded through the atmosphere.

He was no fool.

But neither was I.

His nod was clipped. "Figured not."

I feigned an unaffected smile.

"See you at seven," he said, stepping out the door.

I itched, not sure how I was going to make it through this shit show. This mockery that was my life.

Motherfucking Karma.

She'd moved into my room and taken a seat at the bar, holding her glass in the air in a silent cheer.

She truly was a bitch.

"I'll be there."

Mia

*S*hit. Shit. Shit.

I shook out my hands where I paced the guest suite on the far wing of the house where I was staying with my children.

There was a living room in the middle with two bedrooms on either side. The entire place so warm and welcoming and perfect except for who was going to be shacking up in the house across the yard.

I shook my head, unable to believe my luck.

Life really did love to play cruel, sick jokes, didn't it?

I mean . . . seriously.

I'd all but begged that man to sleep with me, thinking it would be a single night. A single encounter. A single experience.

Desperate for a reprieve.

A balm for the pain.

But I should have known if I dipped my toes into the fire, I was gonna get burned.

Scorched.

And boy, oh boy, was I on fire.

I glanced at the mirror that hung over the dressing table, my cheeks beet red and my skin flushed a matching embarrassing color.

I touched the heated spot right over my heart.

Leif.

His name was Leif. Leif, the temporary drummer for my brother's band. Leif, the guy who was going to be staying in the guest house for the whole damned summer.

Leif, the man who had clearly not been thrilled to see me.

The way disgust and hatred had twisted his jaw in a fierce grimace was seared into my mind.

Massive hands curled into fists that he looked half a second from throwing through a wall.

I'd wanted to melt into a puddle on the floor.

Partly because of the potency of the need that instantly lit, a steady burn that didn't come close to being slow.

The other half? It'd wanted to disappear. Wilt into nothing. Hide the same way as I'd been doing that night.

But I guessed the problem with that was I kept running into *him.*

This terrifyingly beautiful man who left no question that he was bad, bad, bad.

Bad for my health and my heart and my sanity.

I jumped ten feet in the air when someone knocked on the door out in the hall.

God.

I really was going to lose it.

Flustered, I smoothed out my hair like it might settle the disorder that rattled through my nerves and rushed through the bedroom to the door in the living area.

I jerked it open.

Tamar was standing on the other side, smirking.

My eyes narrowed. "Why do you look like the cat who ate the

canary?"

A whole damned nest of 'em.

Probably baby ones, too.

Her smirk only widened as she waltzed in, her hips swaying side-to-side in her seductive way. I was pretty sure if I attempted it, I'd trip and faceplant into the ground. "I heard our guest arrived."

I swallowed down the turbulence and forced the words to come out as casual as could be. "Oh yeah. I guess it was about a half an hour ago."

Thirty-two minutes and seventeen seconds, to be precise.

But who was counting?

She moved into the bedroom where I was staying and flopped onto my bed, releasing a fluttery sigh.

I followed her, wondering what she was up to and knowing it couldn't be good.

She rolled over onto her side. Blue eyes ridged in perfectly done eyeliner twinkled in mischief. "So . . ." she drew out, scandal injected into the word.

My shoulders heaved in feigned confusion. "So what?"

She got to her knees, way too eager. "So, tell me about him."

"Um . . . his name is Leif and he's staying in the guest house and he's a drummer?" I formed it like a question, like that was all there was to him, nothing more.

Tamar huffed in disbelief, waving a dismissive hand in the air. "Yes, I know his name. Tell me about this whole, 'he stole your breath the second you saw him', thing."

I had to struggle to keep my mouth from dropping open in shock, almost as hard as I had to struggle to make the denial form on my tongue.

The lie.

Because the truth of the matter was he'd ripped the air right out of my lungs. Twice now. I was still finding it difficult to breathe.

"And who in the world told you that?" I asked, forcing the deepest, most innocent frown.

The last thing I needed was her hounding me on this.

Because that night? It was a mistake, and nothing had even happened.

Just five minutes of a man branding his being on me.

The slash of a tattoo in the passing of a hand.

Impossible but true.

"Um . . . my husband . . . aka your overprotective brother. He came into our room ranting and raving about how he wasn't going to let some drummer who was climbing for the stars to steal and then break his sister's heart." She giggled a wry sound. "He told me straight up, 'One look, and the asshole stole her breath. Not going to let him steal anything else'."

I almost rolled my eyes.

Tamar did it for me. "I think he thinks he's protecting your virtue. Poor boy acts like you're twelve and don't have two children."

"He's just looking out for me." Why I was sticking up for him in this case, I didn't really know. But him keeping me away from that man sounded like a pretty fine idea.

Distance.

It was bad enough I had to keep myself from going to the windows and peering out, hoping to catch a glimpse.

A chuckle fell from her sultry lips. "Yeah, and he forgets where we started. The fortresses we'd both had built up around ourselves. We didn't exactly have the best start. And look where we are now."

I let a grin pull at my mouth as I moved to the dressing table, taking a brush to run through my hair to give my shaking hands something to do. I looked at her through the mirror. "I'm pretty sure he remembers exactly how you two started."

She laughed. "I'm sure that is totally the problem. His little sister wouldn't dare do something so scandalous," she drawled.

Tossing the brush down, I swiveled around. "You're right. I wouldn't."

Couldn't.

Not after that feeling had chased me down for the last week.

Intrigue.

Fascination.

This sensation that I was missing something when I didn't have it in the first place.

There was no way my mangled heart could take it.

Not when I was looking for a way to fill up a hole when he would only dig it deeper.

Not when I had to spend the entire summer with him living on the other side of the pool.

Not when my mind was entertaining thoughts of more, more, more.

All those *what if's* from that morning had hit me from out of nowhere the second I'd seen him standing there, every bit as shocked at seeing me as I was him.

I got the feeling he'd gladly touch me. But there was no chance that bad boy would keep me. And even letting the thought of *keeping* slip into my mind was enough reason to pretend like he didn't exist.

My mother had always told me I was a sucker for heartbreak. She said it with love. With affection. Like it was a compliment. She said I was a fixer. A lover. A helper.

I was sure the only thing it really did was make me a fool.

Tamar's lips twisted into a pout. "And why not? I bet he's hot, isn't he?"

I shrugged an indifferent shoulder. "He's fine, I guess."

Wow did that lie burn coming off my tongue. He was hotter than a thousand blazing suns.

Yet somehow colder than the darkest hell.

A falling star.

One not sent as a wish, but rather a warning of what would soon burn out.

Laughing, Tamar swung her legs off to the side of the bed. "You are the worst liar I have ever met. You should see your face right now. You are actually blushing."

A pout pinched my mouth, and I glanced at the mirror at the evidence written on my face. I looked back at her. "Fine. He's gorgeous. And haven't you seen him before, anyway?"

She shook her head. "Nope. I've seen his band play a bunch of times back when I was working at Charlie's, but he took over for

their previous drummer about three years ago. I have never had the pleasure of meeting him." She pushed to her feet. "But I do have to say, I am very excited to welcome him to our home."

She fluttered her fingers over the top of my shoulder in some kind of tease as she passed by, heading back for the door.

"You say a word to him, Tamar," I said through a hiss, close to stamping my foot. The last thing I needed was her playing matchmaker.

She touched her chest. "Who me?"

I scowled at her. "You've been trying to set me up since the second you and Lyrik got together. I don't need your help. Besides, it's not like he'd want anything to do with me."

Was pretty sure he took one look at my kids and marked me as a foul line.

Do not cross at all costs.

Problem was, that was where I'd met him in the first place.

Out of bounds.

"You might not need my help, but you definitely need a little shove in the right direction." She softened, the ribbing vanishing from her features. "And are you kidding me? You are gorgeous, Mia. Wonderful and beautiful and one of the best people I know. You deserve to be happy. To have every single good thing this world has to offer."

I shook my head and headed to the closet where I was still unpacking my things. "Well, don't worry, you get a good look at him, and you'll see he is most definitely not the *right direction*."

He was an out of control street bike flying down a dead-end street.

"Besides, don't you think I have enough going on in my life that the last thing I should be doing is thinking about a man?"

I hadn't even had time to mourn. Not fully. Not with this lingering fear that something was coming that I couldn't perceive.

Her head tilted to the side. "I just . . . want to see you smile. See you truly happy. That's all. It's killing me that you're going through all of this, and there's nothing I can do."

My smile was somber, fueled by gratitude and dampened by grief. "You're wrong, Tamar. You already have. You've given us sanctuary. Safety and love. You have given us your home and your family."

They were the ones who were there when everything felt helpless.

Hope lost.

Sorrow the conqueror.

Sadness flitted across her face. "I just wish—"

Greyson started shouting from his crib that was set up in the other room, cutting her off, "Momma. Need you! I up!"

Penny came in from the hall through the main door at the same time, softly singing her little brother's name, as if she'd heard him calling, too.

My spirit throbbed.

Expanded and shifted.

And there was the fullness of my joy. The sound of my children. Because the truth was, I had no places left inside to be given or broken. No more risks to be taken.

They were my fulfillment.

My beginning and my completion.

And the only thing I should be focusing on right then was us.

On keeping my children safe.

Our family whole.

And once that bastard was caught, forever put behind bars, to finally focus on healing.

Tamar looked that way. "I love the sound of his little voice." She shifted back to me. "We truly are glad you are here, Mia. I hope you know that."

My wistful smile was real. "I do."

"All right then . . . we'll see you in a bit. I'm going to go finish up dinner. It should be ready at seven."

"Are you sure I can't help you?"

"Oh, I'm sure you'll be helping me plenty this summer. Finish unpacking. Relax. And don't forget we have a special guest joining us for dinner."

With that, she exited with a wicked, knowing wink.

And I was left wondering how I was gonna survive this.

Oh, I wasn't.

There was no way I was surviving this by any stretch of an overactive imagination.

I was going to succumb right there at the table.

Death by mortification.

Greyson cackled this riotous laugh while he banged the spoon that he'd used as a catapult to fling a wad of mashed potatoes and gravy across the formal dining table on the tray of his high chair.

It'd splatted on Leif's tragically gorgeous face.

"Waif! I got you! I got you!" he sang while I squeezed my eyes closed for a beat and prayed when I opened them, this would be nothing but a bad dream.

Too bad I'd heard it said it was the worst dreams that came true.

Finally, I snapped myself out of the stupor.

There was no hiding from this one.

"Oh, God, I am so sorry," I rushed.

Shocked annoyance blazed through Leif's expression.

A firebolt.

His eyes blinking a thousand times like he was trying to make sense of what'd just happened.

His hand came up to swipe a bit of the mess from his nose with his fingertips. He held it out to study it. It was probably a really bad time to be noticing how big his hands were.

Too late.

His mouth curled into a sneer of disbelief.

Greyson might as well have thrown a flaming bag of poop on his face. I guessed we could all be lucky it wasn't his diaper.

I reached out and pried the spoon from Greyson's chubby hand. "No, Greyson. Bad. That's very bad."

He scrunched up his adorable nose, snorting his little laugh. "I got him, Momma! I got him. *Kapow!*"

I could hear Tamar trying to subdue her laughter, but Lyrik just let it go. Cracking up from the belly like it was the funniest thing he'd ever seen. "Warned ya, man. Welcome to the Wild, Wild West. Saddle up, baby doll."

I glanced that way.

Leif had grabbed a napkin and was wiping the mess from his face.

Finally, I jumped into action, blazing out of the dining room to the powder room right across the hall. I grabbed a washcloth and ran it under the water, racing right back in while Leif was still trying to blot the glob from his face.

The only thing he was managing to do was drop little bits of it onto his lap.

"Here . . . let me help you." I was at his side, carefully trying to dab the mess from his face without inhaling the intoxicating aura of him.

Trying to fight the rush of dizziness I felt the second I got into his space.

Clove and whiskey with an undercurrent of sex.

The sweet, seductive smell of temptation.

All bristling with that same suggestion of disgust I'd seen written in his features when he'd seen us earlier today.

Part of me wanted to cry.

The more prominent wanted to shout at him that Greyson was just a baby. That he didn't know any better and I was doing my best as a mother to make sure he figured those things out.

But I didn't have time to do any one of those things because he was ripping the washcloth from my hands. "I've got it. It's fine."

He rubbed at the spot, cutting me a glance with the intent to demolish.

"You don't look fine," I retorted, teeth gritted as my inner momma bear threatened to join us at the dinner table.

She wasn't exactly friendly.

He glared. "I said I'm fine. Don't worry about it."

"He got you good, Leif!" Brendon shouted from where he sat between Leif and his dad. "Came this close to me!" He held his fingers together in a pinch. "Too bad you don't have mad reflexes like me. You woulda missed it."

Brown sugar eyes narrowed, though they were doing that soft thing again that I'd noticed that night, subdued warmth that was trying to make a break for it.

Or maybe he was just trying to break me.

Knock me down before I even had the chance of getting back on my feet.

"Hell yeah. My son's wicked fast." Lyrik grinned. Nothing but arrogant. "Sorry you got in the line of fire, man. Good job for dodging it, Brendon. Killer reflexes."

They fist-bumped like it'd been a challenge, Greyson the pitcher, Brendon sliding home, while Leif had been struck out.

Tamar chuckled under her breath. "Leave it to my men to throw our guest under the table."

"All's fair in love and war, Momma Blue. Don't you know that?" Brendon asked her.

"And this is a war?" Tamar's brow quirked in a show of disagreement.

"Uh . . . no. It's love. And I love my face. Have you seen me?" My nephew made a circle around his face. "Wasn't about to stand still and let it get mucked up. No thank you."

Penny giggled a shy sound, partially embarrassed and like maybe she wanted to hide under the table, too, but she wasn't about to miss out on the entertainment.

"I really am sorry," I said, a little harder, taking the cloth from him when he'd finally cleaned off his face. "He's two."

It was all a defense.

That strong brow twisted, the man so pretty I was having a hard time standing on solid ground. "Yeah. I know."

"Then don't be a jerk," I gritted, words low and barely heard as they ground from my tongue.

He laughed a low, menacing sound, angling up to look at me. "You think my sitting here and saying nothin' is being a jerk? You haven't been around much, have you, princess?"

I wanted to scream.

I couldn't help it, I inclined his direction, outrage taking hold of my senses as I spat the words, "I've been around plenty. Like I said, you don't know me at all."

Shit.

I was revealing my cards, not that I came close to having a good hand. I'd do best to fold.

Because with the tension that filled the room, there was no question it was becoming plenty clear that he and I weren't exactly strangers.

Tamar and the kids watched us.

Lyrik watched us *harder*.

Leif had the audacity to smirk, rocking back in his chair far too casually. "And like I said, you're easy to read."

I tossed the washcloth down onto the table, wondering why the hell I'd been attracted to this asshole in the first place. "Well, I'd suggest you find yourself another book."

Leif

I knocked back the amber liquid in the tumbler where I sat on a stool tucked up to the bar at Charlie's. Alcohol burned down my throat and landed in a flaming pool in my stomach.

Gasoline dumped on a pit of fire.

Hell hosting a goddamn party where the demons raged and rioted and tore stuff to shit.

Gulping hard, I squeezed my eyes shut, my chest tight and thoughts fuzzy. Could feel all the frayed ends wearing thin.

Getting ready to snap.

I drummed my fingers on the bar, fingers itching for the feel of my drumsticks, praying the beat might chase away the apprehension taking hold of my senses.

What the hell had I been thinking, agreeing to come here? Should have trusted my gut and refused to listen to the music I'd felt calling to me.

Dinner had been a motherfucking disaster.

Had proven how much I didn't belong.

An outcast.

Exiled.

A convict and a captive watching all the things he could never have from behind the bars of his cell.

Love had been so thick in that dining room that I had almost choked on it.

Knew it made me a prick that just watching Lyrik and Tamar together had left a bad taste on my tongue.

Bitterness.

Jealousy.

The adoration they had for their children had been too much to witness.

Add into the mix that woman who'd clawed herself into my every thought and desire, and then dump her kids in the middle of it?

Yeah.

That was not a good combination.

I'd wanted to disappear into the walls.

Fade into nothing.

I'd been two seconds from making an excuse and bolting when Mia's kid had to go and use me for target practice, drawing attention to the fact that I was even sitting there when the only thing I'd wanted to do was slip out the door.

She'd thought I was annoyed at her son. A jerk who didn't get the kid was just being a kid.

Let her think that.

It was for the better, anyway.

Hatred blistered beneath the surface of my skin. Old agony trying to bubble through where it festered and boiled.

Could hardly stand the way Mia made me feel.

The fact that she made me feel anything at all.

"Here you go." The bartender slid another drink across the gleaming bar.

"Thanks."

"Anything else I can get for you?" She stalled, eying me. No doubt, the girl was gorgeous, but she wasn't doing a thing for me.

"I'm good."

She hesitated. "You look familiar."

I would have laughed if I wouldn't have been cringing so hard. "Nope. Think I just have one of those faces."

Lie.

Clearly, she'd seen me on that stage six-months ago. But the last thing I wanted was to entertain and deflect and pretend if this girl went even medium-frequency fangirl on me.

Wasn't close to being up to it.

"Are you sure about that? I rarely forget a face, especially one that looks like yours."

"Yup."

"Hmm." Her brow drew together. "Well, let me know if there is anything else that I can get you, stranger."

She said it like I was going to bite onto the coy tease.

Finally, when I gave her nothing but a tight nod, she relented and left me there, moving on to other customers who were vying for her attention.

Bodies crushed and packed against the gleaming wood.

The place was packed.

Always was.

Charlie's was one of the most popular bars on the river walk. The vibe cool and somehow intense. Live music almost every night. Catering to anyone who walked through the door.

You didn't need to be a type.

You left your bullshit at the door? You were welcome.

Had become one of my favorite places to perform.

The bar was owned by Shea Stone's Uncle Charlie. A guy who'd apparently always been quick to welcome Carolina George to play, long before I'd come in and taken over on the drums.

I curled my hand around the glass as the din of the bar roared and boomed and blustered around me.

I drew the glass to my lips, taking a long pull, fighting off the barbs of sensation that wouldn't let me go.

Feeling that something was off.

Which was a goddamn joke because my whole life had been *off* since the moment I'd destroyed the one thing that mattered. Still, I couldn't shake the feeling, the air cloudy and buzzing with a darkness that consumed. Something sinister slicked across my flesh, and it didn't have a thing to do with the chick who continued to eye-fuck me from across the bar.

I shifted to look over my shoulder, gaze jumping through the faces in the raging crowd.

Couples two-stepped on the packed dancefloor at the foot of the stage, and groups gathered around high-top tables, tossing back beers and laughing too hard. My eyes searched into the murky shadows of the plush horseshoe-shaped booths that lined the far end of the space.

Nothing.

Didn't matter. I still felt it.

History creeping up on me before I had the chance to hunt it down first.

I let my attention rove across the sea of obscured faces one more time, finally deciding that I was losing it. Giving it up, I downed the entire contents of the glass.

I welcomed the reprieve.

The shock of dizziness that pounded through my brain as the alcohol finally hit my bloodstream.

The world going slightly off kilter, sight blurring at the edges. The way my limbs felt a little lighter, for a moment not weighed down with the burden.

By what was at stake.

I pushed to my feet and dug into my wallet, pulling out a hundred and tucking it under the empty before I began to stalk through the crowd. Pushing through the throbbing bodies, I felt a disturbance. With each footstep it only grew.

Walls enclosing.

Energy rushing.

Climbing and amplifying.

Becoming something massive.

Something fierce.

Too close.

Just out of reach.

This was it. I was finally going to lose my grip on the reality that I'd barely been clinging to.

I shouldered through the throng, ignoring the few glances I got.

I inhaled, lungs filling full of the need and lust that was palpable in the dense air. I should give into it. Take of it. Feed on it.

Let it fill me.

Take away the edge.

A distraction from the pain.

But I found I couldn't stay. Irritation pushed up from that dark place that howled from the deepest part of me. I broke through the mass, pushing through the door and out into the deep, deep night.

Music seeped through the walls and chased me out into the sticky, damp heat.

I started down the sidewalk in the direction of Lyrik's pad, place less than a mile away. At this hour, the streets were next to vacant. A few revelers stumbled out of the dives and pubs that lined the river walk, voices elevated and slurred, exorbitantly loud.

I edged by them, refusing to pay them attention.

When I made it to the end of the block, I took a right around a building. I shoved my hands in my pockets and dropped my head as I increased my pace.

I did my best to ignore the footsteps that I could hear getting louder and louder from behind.

Coming closer.

The irritation I'd been running from all night only grew.

Heightened in the stagnant humidity.

My skin hot, that fiery pit in my stomach lapping with flames.

Trees overhung the street, spindly branches stretching wide, a canopy that hid the stars in the endless sky. Tonight, the moon was missing, the night grim and oppressive.

Advancing in from all sides. Threatening to devour.

The sounds of the river walk faded as I moved deeper into the slumbering neighborhood. The only light was the few streetlamps that flickered and spilled their muted glow out onto the narrow sidewalk.

I took a right at the next street, shoulders hitched up high when the roll of footsteps behind me only increased.

Thud. Thud. Thud.

A war-beat that inched closer.

My heart rate sped. Battering at my ribs and flooding my veins.

Every sensation I possessed intensified as adrenaline lifted and rose.

Awareness tugged my chest into a knot.

The footsteps behind me got a beat closer just as a figure stepped out in front of me about twenty feet ahead.

I glanced behind me to see as some burly-ass dude encroached.

Motherfucker.

I was being hunted.

I swung back around to the guy who was waiting for me ahead. Two of them like wolves circling their kill.

Too bad they didn't realize their prey was rabid.

Foaming at the mouth and vengeance-minded.

Didn't contemplate or stall.

I flew for the prick, feet pounding the sidewalk through the vacant night.

Surprise knocked him back one step, and my fist connecting with his jaw knocked him the rest of the way to the ground.

Piece of shit howled as he skidded on the pavement. "Just wanna talk."

Right. Considering in the same second, the prick behind was on me, slamming me in the side. An elbow rammed me right at the top of my spine.

Fuckface had the full intent to bring me to my knees.

Pain splintered across my ribs. The only thing it did was fuel the fury. Chest shivering with greed. Mouth watering with the hunger for retribution.

I whirled around, left arm swinging, clipping him on the side of his head.

He swung at the same second.

His meaty fist caught me at the edge of my mouth.

Rage tore through me like a fever. A match that consumed an

entire building.

I threw two punches. He ducked and missed the first, but the second connected with his jaw.

He went down onto his knees, and my right fist connected with his opposite cheek.

His head rocked from side-to-side, and the next punch I threw landed on his nose.

I relished in the feel of the bone crushing, the blood that splattered onto the street. His hands went to his face in a vapid bid to protect himself.

I didn't hesitate. I delivered three more blows.

Crack. Crack. Crack.

Like a drumbeat.

A horrible, disgusting song that I was going to sing forever.

Apparently, they thirsted for the pain because the first guy I'd knocked on his ass climbed back onto his feet, stumbling my way like the moron actually thought he had a chance.

They wanted to take me down? They were going to have to do a whole ton better than showing up with fists.

I spun, throwing a kick before he even got within a foot of me. The sole of my boot hit him square in the chest. It blew him back, asshole stumbling before he lost his footing and fumbled back onto the ground.

Two pussies laying there in the middle of the road panting for a breath.

Unsuspecting.

I swiped at the single droplet of blood that ran down from the side of my mouth, glaring in disgust at the red from under the hazy, murky light.

I shook out my hands, knuckles busted and torn, probably more beat than the two bastards who were sitting there waiting for what was going to happen next.

Feeling the vibe.

The chaos that raged and hissed and seeped from my pores.

No fear.

Just the welcoming of pain.

"I'm guessing since you didn't come here with guns you came

to deliver a message." I spat the words at the pricks who sat there fucking shaking.

No doubt, they were brand new pledges into this seedy, sleazy world.

Uneasily, they glanced between each other.

"That's what I thought," I grated. "How about you deliver a message for me?"

Leif
Sixteen Years Old

I let loose a low whistle.

"Whoa, she is pretty, isn't she?" I asked through the awe as I let my hand flutter an inch over the gleaming bike. Brand new. Shining metal and perfect leather.

I was itching to caress it but I knew better than to actually touch.

The garage was dim, the only light getting in from the small windows that ran along the top.

"Happy birthday, Leif."

Confusion moved through me, and I spun to look over my shoulder at my step-father who stood ten feet away. Did my best to process what was happening when he tossed something into the air, metal glinting in the bare rays of sunlight that filtered down through the dusty glass.

I caught it.

A keyring.

For a beat, I just stared at the single key on the keychain that was the same design I'd seen before. A *P* with two slashing lines cutting through the middle of it. It was something my stepfather wore on his vest and had in the autobody shop that he owned.

I glanced over at Keeton.

Wary.

Guy was intimidating as fuck. Would kick my ass from here to the fucking moon if I even looked at him wrong. White beard and piercing eyes. Skin worn and thick.

But I respected him for the fact he'd gotten me out of that rat-infested apartment when he and my mom had gotten together two years ago. Our stomachs full and a roof over our heads. Treated her right. Made her happy, which meant she was no longer focusing her misery on me.

Other than that? I pretty much stayed out of his way.

"What's this?" I finally asked, dangling the key in front of me.

"Your birthday present."

Dude had to be punking me.

"You can't . . ." I swiveled to glance at the bike before I looked back at him. Excitement burned in my chest, all mixed up with the questions. "You can't be serious? This is for me?"

Guy wasn't about giving free rides. Ever since he'd come into our lives, he'd emphasized the fact that nothing came without a cost.

He pressed his hands together, rubbing them slow as he studied me. "You're one of us now."

A frown pulled my brow tight. "What's that mean?"

"Get on your bike, and I'll show you."

Ten

Leif

*A*nger burning through me, I swiped the drip of blood that oozed from the corner of my mouth and stormed in the direction of Lyrik's house. I glanced over my shoulder one more time before I pushed send on the message.

Me: Two pricks followed me out of a bar in Savannah. Got any word?

Didn't take but a minute for it to buzz back.

Braxton: Nothing solid. But Keeton has been asking around again. Pushing. You've been playing with fire since the second you joined that band. Warned you if you put yourself in that position things were gonna go south.

Rage singed my insides, fingertips pounding a little harder at the phone than necessary.

Me: That's because it's time for some things to burn.

Braxton: Yeah. And you were supposed to stay on the down-low until that time came to pass.

Years.
I'd waited for three fucking years.

Braxton: You didn't get a read on who they were?

Two pricks had run off into the night with their tails tucked between their legs.
Without saying a word.
Pussies.
Which meant they'd been expendable.
Sent as only a warning.
A reminder of what was unsettled.
Debt coming due.

Me: Two of them took off before I could get anything out of them.

Me: Whoever they are, seems we're running out of time.

Braxton: And neither of us can afford for that to happen until we are sure. We fuck this up? We're both dead.

Me: Price I'm willing to pay.

Owed it, anyway.

Braxton: Speak for yourself, asshole. You might relish the idea of getting cozy six-feet underground, but I

personally have plans on wreaking a little more havoc before I call it quits.

Could almost hear him chuckling from the other end of the earth. Braxton was a scary motherfucker. He never thought twice about smothering what needed to be extinguished.

But I also trusted him with my life. Two of us tied in this thing together before either of us had known what was happening.

Braxton: Patience, brother.

Me: Three years not enough?

Braxton: And that means you should be able to hold out a few more weeks. Don't do anything stupid. He's paranoid. Believe me when I say you're not the only one after him. His time is coming.

Braxton: Trust me to get a little more. I'll press Ridge. See if he has a lock on who might have pinned you in Savannah. Until then, sit tight and don't get stupid.

I hesitated, hating that I was at the wheel that was driving all of this. Riding too fucking fast when it felt like I'd been frozen still for half my life. What this could mean for Braxton and the rest of the people tied to me.

Me: Don't like that I have you so deep in the middle of this.

He didn't have to be standing next to me for me to hear his scoff.

Braxton: There was a reason I swore loyalty, Leif. Don't question it now.

Me: Thought you said you didn't relish the idea of going

to ground.

Braxton: One-hundred-percent. But it's not fucking going to come to that. Won't let it.

I blew out a heavy breath as I made it around to the back gate, the area fortified like I was entering a fucking palace.

Sounded about right.

Me: Okay. Keep me posted. Just . . .

I paused, trying to figure out how to put it into words. Fact I couldn't allow the mistakes I'd made—the life I'd chosen—to affect the people I cared about.

I glanced through the metal bars meant to keep monsters out, guts getting twisted up in painful knots when I thought of the people sleeping inside. Wondering how the fuck it was that I'd gotten so careless. Dragging more people into my lane.

Me: . . . Just find out who knows I'm here. Keep this shit in L.A. Can't afford for anyone to come sniffing this way.

Braxton: I'll handle it. Stay safe, brother.

A disorder blew around me, and I stuffed my phone into my pocket while I punched in the code with the other hand. The lock beeped, disengaged, and the gate popped open. I climbed the two steps through the entrance that led into another world.

I moved toward the guest house, slowing like some kind of fiend when I caught the wispy figure barely seen through the enormous windows across the yard. They could almost pass for mirrors in the shimmering, lapping night, my face some kind of hollow void in the reflection, overcasting the silhouette that stood facing away in front of a blank canvas.

Her delicate hand was poised with a brush, and her entire being tremored with expression. But her fingers were held, the ghosts I could almost see swirling around her leaving her with nothing to

say.

I scrubbed a palm over my face like it would break up the image.

Make it different.

But it was her. She was the artist.

Knew I had to get out of there before I let myself slip any farther.

Get gone before she noticed.

Too late.

Her spine stiffened and her shoulders tensed, her entire being coiling tight when she sensed my presence.

Slowly, she shifted around to peer out the windows into the night, the profile of her face sharp and bitterly sweet.

That ache in my gut tightened tenfold.

Remember, my conscience screamed, what little of it remained, only thing left the scraps of loyalty and gutting wrath.

That didn't seem to matter, though, because I took a step forward into a sliver of light shed from the porch above. Something inside me wanted to erase the fear I could see slithering across her flesh, same thing I'd felt that first night. All the while, I knew I couldn't do anything but add to it.

Her throat bobbed when those sable eyes traced me through the window, our faces over-laid in the glass.

What the fuck was I doing?

I needed to turn my ass around and head for the guest house. Lock myself inside. Pack my things and just go.

But no.

I was moving in the wrong fucking direction. To the door at the far left that led into the west wing of the house, fingers foolishly entering the code that was meant to protect but clearly had been bred for the sole-purpose of disaster.

But I couldn't stop myself.

Drawn.

Bound to this thing I couldn't put my damn finger on. Tension kinked my muscles. Coiled them with need.

I stepped into the billowing darkness of the large room, my eyes adjusting to take everything in.

It was some kind of play room that was doubling as an art studio.

A play area was on one side, and on the right side a couple of easels had been set up in a half circle, supplies in wheeled storage carts on each side of them.

Blank canvases leaned against that wall. Begging to be brought to life. To be assigned a meaning.

And there she was in the middle of it.

The angel in the attic.

Mia West.

Lyrik's baby sister.

Completely off limits and a straight up wet dream.

Wearing this flimsy pajama set, cropped pants and a strappy top. White, thin material. Close to transparent.

I itched. Dick hard. Throat dry.

I fisted my hands like it might give me the strength to hold it together.

Her chin quivered. "What are you doing in here?"

My lips pursed. "I . . ."

I warred with what to say, doing my best not to form a lie, but the truth was something that couldn't be spoken.

I can't stop thinkin' about you, and I don't know why.

You affect me in a way you can't.

Want to touch you.

Want to take from you whatever it is you don't have the strength to hold.

Want to kiss you. Hold you. Fuck you.

Yeah, that wasn't going to go over so well.

"Just . . . wanted to check on you. It's . . . late, and I saw that you were still up," I settled on.

Her eyes roved, widening when they passed over my mouth. "Are you hurt? What happened?" she demanded in worry, lurching forward a foot like she had the compulsion to take care of me before she came to a grinding stop.

Intuition kicking in, a warning not to get too close to me.

Smart girl.

I ran the pad of my thumb over the cut. "It's nothing," I grumbled.

She huffed out a disbelieving sound. "You've been in Savannah for one night, and you already managed to get into a fight? I guess you're easy to read, too, aren't you?"

Mia's head angled to the side in disappointment.

Doubted she knew how damned seductive it was.

The sharp angle of her jaw and cheeks, those full lips pulling into a pout, eyes keen yet sweet.

A glance and this girl could bring me to my knees.

"And what's it you're seeing?"

She took a step toward me. Felt like the girl was floating a foot off the ground. Vapors luring me into a dream.

"Trouble. I knew it the second I saw you."

"You wouldn't be wrong." It was a grunt. Deflection. A defense meant for her to pick up and use against me.

"Then why are you here?" she asked.

Lush hair rained down her back. A black, boundless river, weaving its way around the contour of her delicate shoulders as she edged my way.

Had the sudden urge to bury my face in it and drown.

"Why do you keep showing up in front of me like this is where you're supposed to be?" she pressed, those eyes so deep they could do me in.

"That's called temptation, Mia. A test. Not everything you want is good for you. Better to resist it now than to let it consume us later."

"So that's why you choose to act like a dick?"

A rumble of self-deprecating laughter left me, and I was inching her way, unable to stop. "No acting to it."

"Are you sure about that? Because it sure seems like you're covering for something to me."

Huffing, I shoved my hands into my pockets to keep myself from doing something stupid like reaching out and touching her. Would do well to keep my mouth shut, too, but no. I couldn't leave it at that.

Not with the hurt she'd worn at the dinner table so clearly emblazoned on my mind.

"I'm sorry if I came off like a prick at dinner tonight. I just . . .

can't afford to get involved."

Disbelief puffed from her nose, and those eyes were tracing me again.

"Who said I wanted you to get involved?" Girl was trying to mask her defense in a tease.

Casual.

When nothing about this felt casual at all.

I rumbled a hard sound that reverberated in my chest, and I was stalking forward, crossing so many goddamn lines as I rushed to get in front of her before I could stop myself.

My hand burned up the second I set it on her cheek. "You think I don't feel it, Mia, what's coming off you every time we get in the same room? I don't know what the fuck it is, but it's there."

And it was torturing me.

Shock filled her expression, and her tongue darted out to wet her plush lips at the same second her eyes were dropping to mine.

Fuck.

My hand curled tighter to her cheek, letting the guilt—my duty—become my restraint. "I don't even know you . . . but there's just something . . . something that got under my skin the second I saw you back in L.A. Know you feel it, too, Mia. But it doesn't matter that it's there. It doesn't change one fucking thing. It doesn't change who *I* am."

Mia's voice came at me like a song, low and intense and cutting to the quick. "I can't help but wonder why you're here. After that night, how could you be standing in front of me all the way across the country? I don't believe in a coincidence that big."

Rough laughter crawled up my throat. "Don't need to count it a coincidence. We have friends that run the same circles. Your brother asked for me. We were bound to meet again."

"And maybe there is a reason for that," she challenged.

"And maybe that only reason is for me to be reminded of what I can't have."

Fuck.

What the hell was I doing? Letting this shit spill from my mouth?

A scourge I would forever suffer.

She detangled herself from me, turning away, the girl little more than a silhouette and seduction. She moved back for the blank canvas, her hips swaying, whipping up a lust-inducing breeze.

Delicious.

Decadent.

My mouth watered, urges hitting me to lick her up and down.

She peeked at me from over her bare shoulder. "I think if you asked nicely enough, you could."

Motherfuck. I was right.

This girl was nothing but temptation.

Wicked, perfect sin.

"You don't even know what you're asking for, princess."

She let go of a soft, cynical laugh. "I'm no princess, Leif."

No rational thought remaining, I edged up behind her like I had some kind of right.

Pretending in that singular second that I wasn't committing a thousand wrongs.

Consequences be damned, I leaned in and murmured at her ear, "You're right. You're an angel. So sweet you're unreal."

My fingertips grazed her hip.

A shock raced up my arm.

Need and lust and gluttony.

I breathed her in.

Cocoa and cream.

She peeked back at me, everything in her demeanor shifting in a flash.

Sadness flooding in.

"Then why am I the one being condemned?"

Those eyes were wide. Flush with vulnerability.

Something ferocious clawed through my stomach, chest tightening as I was slammed with the same thing as I had been that first night.

Her fear.

My fingers found their way into the drape of her dark, dark hair. I weaved them all the way in to tickle along the crease of her neck.

She sighed a needy sound, her head dropping that way, like she was granting me the keys to a land that I could never conquer.

Still, I leaned in and inhaled deep. My words were a growl as unchained possessiveness singed my senses. "And who is condemning you? Who hurt you, Mia? Your brother said you'd been through hell and back."

Considering I was already headed there myself, I might as well take down a bastard or two on my way.

"I'm pretty sure the last thing you want to hear are my problems."

"Try me," I grunted.

Needed to know. This twisted protectiveness rising up. The feeling that I wanted to cover her whole.

"Why, so you can use it against me?"

"No. So, I can know what the fuck it was your brother was implying. Don't like being kept in the dark."

So, I could know exactly who was going to die. Just like I'd told her that night, I'd be glad to hunt the motherfucker down.

She laughed a disbelieving sound. "I'm not close to being your problem."

My mouth was at her ear. "You feel like a problem to me."

Awareness spun.

Need and possession. Muscles twitching with the demand to make her mine. To get lost in her skin and this body and those eyes.

Knew I wouldn't make it back if I did.

It didn't change a thing because I was pressing her. "Tell me."

She shivered.

"Tell me, princess, what's so bad in your life that your brother thinks he needs to lock you up in his castle?" The words came out like blades, like the anger didn't know where else to go.

She whirled on me.

Pissed.

I seemed to have that effect on people.

"Fine," she spat. "You want to know what happened? My best friend was murdered. And I had to stand there and watch it. Helpless. Horrified. The whole time wondering if he was going to turn that gun on me. That's what happened."

Fuck.

Rage grated my teeth. "Who? Tell me goddamn who. Just give me a name."

She blew out a cynical breath. "If I had a name, things would be a whole lot easier, wouldn't they? I wouldn't be running scared. Wouldn't lay awake at night terrified for the safety of my children. I wouldn't be jumping at every noise or having panic attacks when some jerk gets too close to me."

It would have been better if she had the same reaction to me.

If she stepped away when I curled my palm around the side of her neck.

But she just stood there with her pulse ravaging. Those eyes wild.

Vulnerable and resolute.

I had the overwhelming urge to wrap her up and hide her away.

Erase any threat.

Destroy any danger.

"Tell me," I demanded. "Tell me what the fuck happened to you."

I was a fool to think I had the right. A fool to think I could take on this responsibility. But there was no chance I could walk out of that room without knowing what she'd suffered.

Shivers raced across her flesh, and her throat trembled as she swallowed. "Her name was Lana. We had this little gallery. We'd dreamed of opening it since we were in college, bringing our two arts together. We'd had the best day. Sold three paintings and a sculpture."

Anguish flashed across Mia's face.

Stricken.

"We'd had a glass of champagne to celebrate in the back. We . . . we were locking up . . ."

Fury bloomed in my blood, and my hand twitched on her neck. "A man came in. He was wearing a mask. He demanded that I give him anything of value. I went behind the counter, and instead of getting out the cash, I pressed the panic button. I should have just done what he'd told me. I should have. If I could go back. God, if

I could go back, I would do it all over."

Moisture gathered in Mia's eyes. "He just . . . gave me this look when I did. Like he was happy I'd done it. Then he pulled the trigger."

Motherfucker.

"They said they thought it was random, Leif. A robbery gone bad. Her blood spilled for a few hundred dollars."

The last broke on a sob.

Fury raced, and every muscle in my body twitched for retribution. "Motherfucker needs to die."

Shivers raced across her flesh, a flashfire of horror. "He found me. The night of the gala. And I don't even know who he is or what he wants, but he found me. He was there."

Malice spiked in my blood, the words a curse as I realized what this had become. "And now you're here."

She sniffled, trying to hold it together while I stood there and interrogated her like she was the one to blame. "And now I'm here. Where you are." Her voice shifted in some kind of plea.

I couldn't stop the feeling that I was a second from coming unglued.

Disjointed, and there was a piece of me being regenerated in her.

"I wonder if the reason we feel this way around each other is because you know exactly what that feels like. Dying inside because you miss someone so much. Because you wish you could go back and change it and there isn't a damn thing you can do. I feel it coming off of you, Leif. I feel it. How is that possible that I can feel you this way?"

She curled her fingers in my shirt. "Tell me I'm wrong."

I wanted to push her back. Hold her close.

Fuck. This girl made me insane.

Old agony throbbed. An ache so intense I was sure I was getting ready to blow.

Combust.

"Or maybe you're so used to the pain, that's the only thing you know how to look for," I told her.

Clearly, she'd experienced more than her fair share. Girl

112

written in the strength exposed by her scars.

The corner of her mouth trembled. Rejection in what I'd said. What she didn't get was I was doing her a favor.

"Is that what you want, to hurt me?"

There she was, back to asking me the same question she'd demanded the first time our paths had crossed.

Problem was, Fate and Karma were old friends and they were laughing their asses off while they were frolicking around in the pool behind us.

"Only thing I know how to do, Mia."

"But I bet it would feel good, wouldn't it? If we let go? If I let myself fall, would you be there to catch me? Just for a little while?" Her hands cinched tighter.

A rumble of a laugh rolled around in my chest.

Wicked little angel.

This girl was disorder. Sweet to the bone and sexy to the core.

I bet if anyone asked anything from her, she'd give it. But she wasn't ashamed to ask for what she wanted for herself, either.

"Believe me, baby, a few minutes of bliss is never worth the pain that comes with the aftermath. And you obviously have too much to live for to be taking those kinds of chances on me."

Her eyes darted to the door that was cracked open an inch. No doubt, her kids were sleeping down the hall. That gaze came back to me. A pleading confession. "They're my world."

"As they should be, and I refuse to get in the middle of that."

Tried not to puke when the visions flashed.

Cruel, vile pictures of what I'd done. What I'd been responsible for. What I could never take back.

I needed to remember my purpose. The reason I still breathed.

Her disbelieving laughter was rough, laden with hurt and disgust. "So I'm a no go because I have the *horrible* complication of being a mother?"

It was an accusation.

Like she couldn't look at me for a second longer, she jerked away, turning to leave.

Panic belted me.

I grabbed her by the wrist because I couldn't let her walk away thinking something so wrong. She released a sharp gasp when I yanked her back around.

I leaned in close, the words gritted from between my teeth. "No. Because of the horrible complication of *who I am*. You want to know what I think about your kids?"

She blinked, unable to keep up.

"I think they're fucking amazing, and I think you're the luckiest damned woman to get to call them your own. That you get a love like that. But *I don't*." My teeth ground as I spat out the words.

She swayed, caught in a web. Not sure if she wanted to run or if she wanted to stay.

But I wasn't done, yet.

"You want to fuck, Mia? Fine. Let's do it. I'll gladly devour your sweet little body. I'll mark myself so deeply on you, you will never forget me. But you and I both know whatever *this* is? It's more than that. More than I can give. More than I can handle. And believe me, it is more than you *want*. And the last thing I want to do is leave another scar on who you are. I think you've had plenty enough."

Soft lips parted in surprise, in need, and fuck, I wanted to gorge on the sound. Her heart pounded in the bare space between us and those sable eyes darted all over my face.

"Is that what you think of yourself? That you're some awful human being?"

A dark chuckle rolled free. "You said it yourself. I'm nothing but trouble."

And that title wasn't some kind of cute nickname.

"I don't believe you."

"What you believe doesn't change who I am."

A tear slipped down her cheek. "And maybe you're the first beautiful thing I've seen since the last of the beauty was ripped from my life. I can't sleep. I can't dream. I can't *paint*. And then you came here . . ."

She trailed off. Unable to put a finger on what she felt or maybe not wanting to put a voice to it.

Agony clawed at my insides. That feeling overwhelming. This girl too fucking much.

My gaze moved to the blank canvas behind her. Slowly, I turned her back to face it. Taking her hand, I dipped it into the black paint.

Images of the paintings that hung in the house gusted through my mind, that haunting intuition that this girl held.

I clutched her by the wrist, and I set my lips against her cheek. "The only thing you see when you look at me is your beauty reflected back. You are the true definition of it, Mia. Beauty. You stole my breath the first time I saw you. You are the creator of it. I won't taint that."

Didn't matter if I knew her for a day or a month or a year.

Some people bled goodness. Kindness and hope.

Mia?

She gushed it.

The problem was, she was lost to a flood of goodwill.

All her broken, mangled pieces swept up in the torrent.

She slashed a single stroke down the length of the canvas. "And what happens when the beauty is gone? What happens when none of it is left inside?"

I pressed my front to her back, my hard up against her soft.

There was no way to mix it without something breaking.

My hand splayed across the pounding in her chest, my fingers tapping out the beat of a song that sought to be released. One that had possessed my spirit in an instant. Lyrics alive in my mind.

> *You came out of nowhere.*
> *A trainwreck.*
> *Paradise.*
> *Moved.*
> *Desolate.*
> *Would give it all up.*
> *If it would keep you from falling apart.*

My mouth moved to the shell of her ear. "You'll find it. You just have to look in the right places."

God knew, she wouldn't find it in me.

I forced myself to step back.

Felt like I was rending myself in two. Talk about fucked up. Didn't even know this girl, and she managed to make herself feel like something that had been missing all along.

Like she was essential.

Natural.

Fated.

The perfect torment.

What could never be.

Leif
Sixteen Years Old

Keeton held open the door at the back of his auto-repair shop.

One I'd chalked up to as storage but I was getting the drift real quick that it was used for undivulged purposes that I hadn't before been privy to.

"Go on in."

Wasn't even wary when I angled through the door, floating on this high from the bike ride over.

Didn't think I'd ever experienced anything that made me feel so powerful.

So free.

So *right*.

Like I'd just come into who I was supposed to be.

Vitality pumping in my blood, I stepped into the back room,

eyes taking in the space. A couple tables were set up in the middle, and there was a bar in the back.

The excitement I was drunk on only dipped for a single beat when I took in the men filling the space.

A couple faces I recognized.

Most that I didn't.

All of them rough like Keeton. Worn at the edges. Aggression and intimidation written in their bones. Didn't take a lot to surmise they did bad, bad things.

All those questions I'd had about my stepdad for the last couple years suddenly made perfect sense.

Every single one of them was looking at me.

Like they'd been waiting on my arrival.

Coming up to stand beside me, Keeton squeezed my shoulder. "Someone get this kid a drink. It's his birthday."

One of the guys behind the bar poured a tumbler full of golden liquid.

He slid it my way.

I glanced back at Keeton.

Again, wondering if I was bein' punked.

Set up.

Because this just wasn't right. Keeton nearly knocked out my teeth the one night he'd caught me stealing beers for me and a couple of my friends.

"Go on."

My brow lifted.

He chuckled a rough, commanding sound. "Grab your drink. Then sit down and listen."

My job was easy. There wasn't a whole lot I had to do. Sit in the front of the shop. Make it all look legit. Book appointments. Make sure the mechanics actually did their damned jobs so Keeton could do his.

Sit back and reap the benefits.

Money.

More cash than I could fucking count.

Not to mention damned near any girl I wanted would gladly take a seat on my dick.

It made me feel like some kind of god.

Flush with power.

All I had to do was ride my bike up the street, and the seas parted. Fear and respect synonymous with the name.

Pride of Petrus.

Except today.

Today it was different.

A layer of fear I hadn't felt in a long time palpitated under the surface of my skin.

I fought it. Lifted my chin. Got off my bike. Strode into the back of the club like I owned it.

Heavy metal screamed from the speakers. Place dank and dark. Seedy as fuck.

There were piles of coke on the table. Half-naked chicks running amok. Arrogant pricks leaning against the walls drinking beers like they were someone to be seen.

Every single one of them took notice of me.

I pushed into the back office.

Didn't even knock.

Did the deal.

And I strode back out feeling like a motherfucking king.

Mia

*W*hat was I doing?

My gaze followed the dark figure who moved toward the guest house on the opposite side of the yard.

A shadow.

A wraith.

Both soothing and terrifying.

Which made me question more why I couldn't stay away.

Why I was so intrigued.

Or maybe he had it right. Maybe the only thing I knew how to do was look for the pain.

Lately it felt like I didn't know anything else.

At the doorway to the guest house, he paused and shifted to stare back in my direction. From this distance in the muted lights, I doubted he could make me out through the windows. But still, he was gazing back at me like he could see me.

Like he got me.

Understood me.

Or maybe like he wished that he could.

Finally, he gave a harsh shake of his head, turned, and disappeared into the guest house.

It cut off the connection, jolting me back into reality.

I shook my head like I could shake myself from the trance. Rid myself of the attraction.

I really was looking for trouble, wasn't I?

Begging for it.

The man felt irresistible, which was kind of funny considering he was the one who was refusing to give himself to me.

One second, I was telling him to leave me alone, that I had no interest, and the next I was practically begging him to strip me of my clothes and put me out of my misery.

I got the horrible sense that he might be the only one who could do it. The only one who might be able to hold me tight enough that he could keep the ghosts at bay.

No, I had no illusions that he wouldn't crush me in the process.

But sometimes experiencing the pain was better than feeling nothing at all.

I looked back at the black streak I'd painted in a crooked slash across the canvas.

Feeling a flicker.

A spark.

Beauty.

I squeezed my eyes shut in a bid to cling to it, to claim it, but I felt it falter and fade.

Snuffed.

Blowing out a heavy sigh, I set the paintbrush aside and moved back through the shadows of the house. I tiptoed my way back into the suite, edging open the door that was left open a smidge and moving directly for the room on the left.

Where my children slept.

This was where the numbness abated. Where emotion rushed.

The issue was it was so acute that it nearly knocked me from my feet.

I moved across the room to the crib that sat on one side of the room. I leaned over the railing, peering through the dim light to where Greyson slept.

His chubby cheeks were pinked, his plush lips pursed and whispering in his dreams.

So peaceful in his rest.

My hand shook with the amount of adoration I felt as I ran my hand over the top of his head.

"I love you, sweet boy," I whispered, touching my fingers to my lips before I pressed them to his forehead. "I promise that we are going to be okay. I won't let anything happen to you. To us."

I murmured the hushed words to his sleeping body, praying he could feel their truth as I tucked his teddy bear closer to him.

I eased back. My heart lurched when I glanced to the side and saw Penny sitting up in her bed. She was clutching her patchwork teddy bear to her chest, watching me with her knowing eyes.

"Penny, sweetheart . . . what are you still doing awake?"

"I could ask you the same thing, couldn't I?"

Light laughter rolled out. Leave it to my eleven-year-old daughter to call me out.

Crossing the room, I sat down on the edge of her bed and brushed my fingers through her hair. "I couldn't sleep."

"Neither could I," she admitted in her quiet voice.

I searched through her expression, my words hushed in the night. "Did you have a bad dream?"

Penny shook her head, and she drew her legs up to her chest. "I guess it might as well be a bad dream." She blinked long, and my chest ached. "In the day it's easier . . . it's easier to pretend that everything is fine."

Her voice lowered in shame. "But sometimes when I close my eyes . . . I see her, Mom. I see Lana, and every time, her face changes into yours. I hate it, but I can't stop it."

She looked at me.

Hopeless and guilt-ridden and trembling with fear.

"I keep thinking about what it would have been like if it was you."

I kept brushing my fingers through the locks of her hair, trying to soothe her, trying to soothe myself.

Tears filled her eyes, and she peered up at me through the shadows. "Does it make me bad, Mom? Does it make me a bad person that I'm glad you're the one who is still here?"

"Oh, Penny, of course not, sweetheart. Never. You are wonderful and kind and full of love. It's only natural that we want to protect the ones who are closest to us."

"But she was like our family."

"I know. And I miss her so much. I know you miss her, too. What happened was horrible. Horrible in every way." I spread my hand over the side of her face, and my tone deepened with emphasis, "Don't you dare take on any blame or beat yourself up for anything you feel. We're all grieving. Handling it the best way that we can."

Guilt rippled and blew. How many times had I thought the same thing? What torment it might have caused my children if they were to have lost me?

My luck up against hers.

Was it wrong?

Was it selfish?

Tremors rolled down Penny's throat. "We're not here for vacation, are we?"

Grief tightened my chest in a vice.

I should have known my insightful child would realize packing up and leaving so quickly was more than an impromptu trip.

I ran my knuckles down her cheek that was thinning with her age, my little girl sitting at the verge of child and woman.

So innocent and wise.

Naïve and intelligent.

"You don't need to worry, Penny. We're here to heal. I would never let anything happen to you."

Her voice sounded smaller than it had in a long time. "Why would someone want to hurt us? Want to hurt Lana? It's not fair."

"Greed makes people do terrible things."

She blinked, her dark eyes pleading for a different answer. I wished with all of me that I could give her one. "Is that what that man wanted, all of her money?"

My nod was reluctant. "That's what the detective thinks right now."

That statement was beginning to feel like a lie, nothing making sense or adding up.

A frown pinched her brow. "But we're here, not that I'm mad or anything, because you know I love it here. It's my favorite place ever. But Mom, I know you're not telling me everything. I'm not a little girl anymore. You don't have to protect me."

There she was, acting an age older again.

"My only job in this world is protecting you, Penny."

"Is someone going to hurt us?"

Talons of agony sank into my spirit, and I cupped my hand tighter to her face. "No. We're safe here."

"Dad says we should be with him. He said no one would touch us if we were. Maybe we should go back to California and stay with him." Her whispered words started to fly, cramming closer and closer together as she suddenly launched into a plea.

I brushed my thumb along her jaw, tilting her face up to mine. "Your dad loves you, Penny. Very much. But it's best that we're on the other side of the country. The detective is working hard to arrest the man who hurt Lana, and until he does, we will be safest, far away from there."

I jolted upright to the alarm blaring through the house. I tossed off the covers, on my feet in a flash. I darted out my door, through the living area of the suite, and into my children's room.

Relief blasted through me when I found Greyson hadn't even budged. Penny rolled over on a long moan, lost to a deep, deep sleep.

The door to the suite blew open. Lyrik stood there, black hair wild, expression raging. "Are they okay?"

"Yes." I tried to keep the tremor from the words. "They're safe."

He gave a tight nod before he was flying back out. He raced the rest of the way down the hall and out the same door Leif had found me through earlier in the night.

Warily, I followed him.

Trepidation in every step.

Fear in every heartbeat.

A thunderous pound, pound, pound that blasted through my being. I thought it had to be louder than the alarms that blared through the house.

I slipped along the floor-to-ceiling windows that ran the hall and the big playroom. Through them, I watched as Lyrik darted out into the yard.

His head whipped from one direction to the other.

Every inch of his posture on guard.

The protector.

My eyes scanned, and I heaved out a breath when I saw a second man bolting across the yard.

Leif.

His posture was entirely different than my brother's.

An avenger.

A dark destroyer.

A demon that seethed in the night.

An aura of chaos swirled around him as he sprinted along the pool and headed toward the back of the lot.

Lyrik got in line behind him.

My pulse skidded and shook, fear taking me hostage as I watched the scene play out through the windows as if I were watching a movie playing out on the screen.

Leif scaled the wall. So fast it seemed inhuman.

A creature that had come to life.

Born of carnage.

Or maybe that was just what he threatened to bring.

He disappeared over the top, and Lyrik jogged right, following the back of the wall before he was climbing over it at the farthest end.

As if the two of them were boxing in their prey.

And I wondered who it was that was hunting who.

Warily, I eased out of the door.

The night was at its thickest.

Darkest.

Held just before the break of dawn.

Humid air scraped my flesh, and shivers rolled as I listened to the distant shouts.

All of them were familiar voices.

Lyrik.

Leif.

Lyrik again.

My gaze moved to the balcony that overhung the third floor of the main house. Tamar stood at the railing, clinging to it as she stared down.

Black hair whipped around her face that was held in morbid fear.

Our eyes met, and my mouth moved in whispered silence, "I'm sorry."

Her head shook.

No.

We were in this together.

Family.

But I was sure she and Lyrik had already endured enough pain.

I hugged myself over my middle like I could gather back up the pieces that I could feel finally slipping away.

I'd tried.

Tried so hard to pretend.

Tried to pretend that I wasn't going to crumble.

Tried to pretend it was all going to be okay.

That we were going to make it through this unscathed.

This was only a vacation, right?

What a joke.

Even my eleven-year-old child could see right through it.

Because there was no way to believe the lies you kept telling yourself when you had nothing left to support it.

Foundation cracked.

After what seemed like an eternity, the back gate buzzed and Lyrik came storming back through.

Agitation fizzed across the surface of his skin.

Immediately, his attention landed on me, tone gruff, "It was nothing. Probably a fuckin' cat set off the sensors or something."

The words left him like spite. Like he wanted to be sick for letting go of the greatest deception.

My lips trembled. "Are you sure?"

I didn't even know why I was asking it because I could feel the sick reality racing to catch up to me. Seeping in from under the fortified walls, clawing its way over the bricks.

His head shook, black hair whipping up a disorder. Frustrated, he brushed it out of his eyes. "We didn't find anything, Mia. It was a false alarm. Go back to bed. You should get some sleep."

With the way his eyes darted around the yard, I knew that wasn't going to be an option for him. He didn't come close to believing a thing that he was telling me.

"Is there footage?" I asked instead of agreeing.

"We'll see if anything was captured. But there's no one out there. There is no danger."

His words were hard. Angry. I wondered if he was trying to convince himself.

"Okay," I conceded, my hand curling in the neckline of the tank of my pajamas.

He moved toward me, watchfully, carefully, his dark eyes flaring. He didn't hesitate. He pulled me in for a tight hug, his breaths shallow, his muscles twitching with the residual of adrenaline. "It's okay. It's okay. Everyone is safe," he muttered again, clearly talking himself down from the ledge.

"Okay."

He pulled back, held me by the outsides of the shoulders. "I think we're all a little paranoid."

My nod was tight.

Was it paranoia if you were fighting for your life?

But why . . . why would anyone want to take it? Why would that sick, twisted bastard in that video track me down? What did he want?

Apprehension slithered beneath the surface of my skin. Something sticky and ugly that crawled my flesh in a slow-slide of dread.

Lyrik finally released me and stepped back. He stared at me for a long minute. "I won't let anyone get to you, Mia. Promise you."

"I know that." My acknowledgement was shaky at best.

With a clipped nod, he started back along the length of the huge pool, his eyes on his wife who was still staring down at the disturbance going down in the middle of their yard.

My attention slowly drifted to the right. Not lazily. But like maybe I was terrified to look that way.

It didn't matter.

I was hinged.

Chained.

Compelled to look where Leif was standing like a beast in the entryway of the gate, both arms stretched across the width and his fingers curled into the bricks.

Like he was holding himself back.

From what, I wasn't sure.

His wide chest heaved.

His gorgeous body coiled with aggression. At the ready to pounce.

Muscled arms rippling with strength, the few distinct tattoos on his arms twitching and jerking beneath his skin that was stretched taut.

Those brown-sugared eyes had hardened to stone. Carved of a rocky cliff that threatened to come crashing down.

The barest glow of the approaching day broke at the horizon, a murky gray that filled the sky with a shock of hope.

Staring at him, that was what I felt.

Obscene, obliterating hope.

Foolish girl.

But I trembled with it. Shivered with the impact as I remained there barely able to stand under the weight of his gaze.

"You should go back inside," he grated, his words panted with the exertion he'd just expelled.

I clutched tighter to the neckline of my pajamas' shirt. "Thank you," I managed to whisper.

"There is nothing to thank me for."

"I disagree. You are the one who just went running out into the night."

Reckless.

No care as to what he might be coming up against.

"I've done nothing but bring trouble to your door."

I wanted to fight him on it, but I was feeling too relieved to do anything but give him a tight nod, turn around, and head back through the door.

I guessed maybe it was an invitation. I didn't know. The only thing I was sure of was the way my heart ratcheted into a frenzy when I heard the gate swing shut and latch close before his heavy footsteps began to follow.

I felt it like a thunder in my soul, an erratic pounding that stampeded out of control.

Just as I pulled the door open, he was there, right behind me, holding it so I could enter. There was no shunning the weight of his eyes on me as I headed back through the large playroom, not sure whether to slow and face him or run away as fast as I could.

The light was muted yet dancing with the vow of a new day.

The alarm had long since been silenced.

The quiet stillness it left behind felt forged.

Counterfeit.

My footsteps were hushed. Trepid. Slowing with each step. Stopping at the head of the hall, I swiveled to look behind me.

He stood at the doorway.

Raging.

An ominous warrior.

The longer pieces of his hair tossed into his striking face. Concealing him like a shroud.

"Did you . . . see anything? Anyone? Or was this truly a false alarm?"

Leif grimaced. "I don't fuckin' know, Mia. I . . ." Helplessness seeped into his harsh tone. "When I came out of the guesthouse when I first heard the alarm, I thought . . . I thought I saw something at the far end of the yard. A shadow. A shape. Not sure because it all happened so fast. I went after it, but by the time I made it over the wall, there was nothing but air."

I gulped, trying to tame the terror I could feel tremoring through my being. Creeping deeper into my spirit.

Leif took a lurching step forward. "God damn it." His head dropped as he cursed toward the ground. "They might have been coming for me, Mia."

He lifted his gaze, meeting my eye, a torment so stark in the depths that it nearly knocked me back into the wall.

"Chances are, this bullshit has everything to do with me." Self-loathing oozed out with his words. "I won't pretend like I have the first clue what is going down in your life, Mia. What you're up against. The only thing you need to know is it doesn't matter if they're coming for me or for you. If anyone thinks about getting close to you? To your kids? Pray for them because I promise you, that will not end in their favor."

Rage spiraled through his body. Barely contained.

I blinked, my head shaking. "You don't owe me anything."

He laughed a bitter sound, and he took another step forward, his voice a growl. "Maybe not, but that doesn't mean you didn't just become my responsibility."

"What does that even mean?"

His head shook, his expression grim. "You don't know what vultures I might have just led to your doorstep. The bullshit I've been drowning in my whole life. If it followed me here? I'm out. But not before I'm certain there won't be any bastards who come sniffing this way."

I almost laughed. This was absurd. Absolute craziness. "I think we can be sure my life is a much bigger disaster than yours, and the last thing I can do is ask you to be my savior."

It was bad enough I was here staying with Lyrik and his family. One day, and I was already questioning that decision.

Leif huffed out a laugh, something menacing and twisted in the rumbling sound as he took another step my direction.

The space between us shivered.

God, he was beautiful.

Terrifyingly beautiful.

His head tipped to the side. "I'm no savior. You can be sure of that. But I'll gladly stand in the flames if it means keeping you from the fire."

"You don't even know me."

He was in my space.

Invading.

Plundering.

Wrecking me without even a brush of his hand.

Oh, but then he did touch me, and that plundering turned into an all-out ravaging.

His hand slipped to my neck. Palm stretched out as he ran the tip of his thumb along the length of my jaw. Warmth streaked. A flashfire. And I knew without a doubt that I was the one who was standing in the flames.

"Like I said, you're easy to read," Leif murmured.

"And what do you see?" My question was shaky.

"Hope." He edged in closer, intense eyes raking over me.

"Horror," he continued, that thumb caressing.

He inched in until our noses brushed. His aura all around. Intoxicating.

Clove and the vestiges of whiskey.

"Hunger." It was a grunt of need, his desire finally spilling free. "Tell me, what is it you are hungry for, Mia?"

There I was—right up against that crumbling ledge. I should scramble back. Rush for safety. But I stayed right there. At the mercy of his big, brutal hands.

"To feel something bigger than me. Something bigger than my circumstances. Something stronger than the grief and the hopelessness. You're right, Leif. I want to feel hope. I want to feel peace. I *want* to feel wanted."

He groaned, and his lips were on mine, no hesitation as he promptly pillaged my mouth.

His kiss was like candy. Crystallized brown sugar. Sharp as a knife.

His tongue tangled with mine in some war I didn't know either of us were fighting. He groaned louder at the contact, a dark rumble of lust in his chest, and we were an instant mess of desperate mouths and clashing teeth.

He pushed me up against the wall and pinned me with that

strong body.

Desire spiraled through every cell. So fierce I whimpered, and my fingers drove into his hair and raked down the sides of his neck before they sank into his shoulders.

Frantic to get him closer.

To quench this feeling that had infected me since the moment I'd seen him sitting in that corner. His draw a virus that had invaded my blood.

"Leif," I begged, trying to get my legs around his waist, needing to feel his hard length I could feel pulsing from his jeans. He pressed himself to me, to that achy place that throbbed and begged. "Please. Make it better. Can you make it better, just for tonight?"

I thought he might be the only one who could take it away.

He pressed himself against me, grinding his hard cock against my belly. "Fuck . . . Mia . . . what are you doing to me? What are you doing? I can't . . ."

Both of his hands found my waist the second he said it, and he tucked me against him in a forceful rock of need.

Desire slammed me in a rush of dizziness that I felt from head to toe. I shifted, begging for more. For reprieve. For him to erase our barriers. For him to fill me up and elevate me above it all.

To lift me to the stars.

His hand moved to cup my breast.

Pleasure shimmered and streaked.

He circled his thumb around my nipple.

I whimpered. "Leif. Why does it feel like I have known you my entire life? Like you're a piece that's been missing, and now that you're here, I'm whole?"

It was a stupid, stupid confession. I knew it. But I had never been about playing games.

He groaned. Only this time it was in restraint, his breaths short and rasping as he forced our mouths apart. His harsh pants scraped the vacant space between us, and our foreheads rocked together as we heaved for the nonexistent air.

"Leif." It was a plea.

He gave a sharp shake of his head as he curled his hands

around my shoulders to peel himself off of me. "Fuck."

"What's wrong?"

"I need to go."

"Please . . . don't leave."

He didn't meet my eye when he tore himself the rest of the way free and stumbled two feet back. "God damn it," he spat toward the floor as he quickly turned to face the opposite direction.

"Leif." I touched his back.

He jerked, shoving off my hand, and he whirled back around. The disgust that lanced through his expression did little to conceal the greed that blazed in his eyes.

A violent, sparking fire.

"We can't fucking do this, Mia. This can't happen." He jabbed his finger toward the ground.

"Why not?"

He laughed a bitter sound. "I already told you, Mia. Don't you fucking get it?" he bit out. "I don't have what you need. I see you. See right through you, and I am not that guy."

"You don't have any idea what I need." My voice quavered. God, I wanted to scream. Punch him. Beg him to stop playing this game.

"No. Maybe I don't. But one thing I do know? What you don't need is me."

Without saying anything else, he turned and stalked across the room and out the door, leaving me standing in the exact spot he had left me before.

My chest palpitated with a frenzy of convoluted emotions that careened through my body.

Need and anger and confusion.

This insane attraction that I was pretty sure was going to ruin me.

I couldn't be this reckless. Wrapped up in a man who didn't even want me.

Our intensity fire.

But where there was fire, there was ash.

Dust and debris.

And he was right.

The last thing I could afford was to be consumed.

Leif

"Here, here, assholes. You better be ready to make some magic because this boy can already feel it bleeding from his pores. It's about to go down."

Ash Evans grinned all his damned dimples while he plucked at his bass where he sat on a stool in the middle of the recording studio practice room. We were all down in the basement of the mansion Baz had purchased out on Tybee Island, about thirty minutes outside of Savannah.

The house had belonged to their manager before they decided it would be better suited to host the bands that Stone Industries produced.

House boasted an expansive living space—kitchen and great room and offices—plus there were two master suites on the main floor and six on the top. Not to be forgotten was the killer studio on the basement floor.

But what really made the place unforgettable? It was the view of the ocean out back.

I doubted it took a whole ton of convincing to get bands to spend a couple months in this place.

"This coming from the asshole who we were waiting on for the last thirty minutes." Lyrik tossed Ash a smirk as he hooked his guitar strap over his head and situated it on his shoulder. "Practice started at noon. Sharp."

"I was busy." Ash cracked a grin.

"Busy?" Lyrik was nothing but incredulous.

"Uh . . . I think you forget how hot my wife is. And I found myself in need of a little inspiration this morning. Don't judge me. You'll thank me later. Almost as profusely as I was thanking Willow. You wanted magic. Here it is." Ash winked, all kinds of smug.

I had to stop myself from busting out laughing. Was pretty sure it went against protocol to laugh about a man's girl, especially when I couldn't exactly consider myself tight with the band.

But still, there was no missing the closeness—the complete easiness—that radiated between them.

Lyrik chuckled a wry sound and scratched his index finger at his temple, flashing the words on his knuckles of that hand that were inked with the word *sing*. "And you think it's any easier for me to pry myself away from my wife? Sometimes we just gotta make the sacrifice."

"All of you are pathetic," Austin piped in from where he was flipping through a tattered pile of notebooks strewn across a grungy coffee table. "Won't be more than two or three hours before your girls come over for the barbeque. Think you can handle it."

Ash tossed a pick at him. Austin deflected it with a swat of his hand. "Dude. Are you for real right now? Your wife is in the room right next door, watching through the window on the couch. Talk about pathetic, man. She's got you wrapped tight."

"She's just making sure I'm on key. Here to offer advice if we need it." Austin shrugged in innocence.

"Liar!" Ash accused, pointing at him.

Lyrik laughed. "All right. All right. Can we just get this shit over with so we can get on with our day? Don't think any of us want to be in here any longer than we have to be. Have better things to do."

He raked his teeth over his bottom lip as he answered a text that was clearly from Tamar.

My eyes darted around to take in the three of them.

Just awesome.

I was surrounded by the love-fucked.

Was pretty sure they were split between the love of their music and the love of their wives. Loyalty pulling them in both directions, and they were balancing on a tightrope.

Understood it on a level that I wished I didn't.

Loyalty.

Being tugged in opposite directions.

Fighting for both and knowing you were going to fail because you knew full well you were never destined for harmony.

Wanted to refuse the vision that clamored through my mind. Black hair and sable eyes. The taste of the girl lingering on my tongue. My fingers itching to get another feel of Mia West.

My guts were still twisted in knots of lust that I doubted could be undone any time soon.

The door jerked open and Baz strode in. He glanced around. "Everyone good? Need anything?"

Lyrik nodded. "Yup. All's good. Want to run through a couple songs I've been working on getting down. Weave some shit in. Maybe we can test them out on a couple tracks in an hour or so?"

"Sounds good. Going to be upstairs on a call. Just holler when you're ready for me or if you need anything."

"We've got it," Austin told him.

"Know you do," Baz returned with a slight smile over his shoulder as he disappeared back out the door.

"Let's do this. We might do things a little unorthodox, Leif, but I'm sure you can keep up." Lyrik moved over to the sofa were Austin was sifting through the notebooks. He dug through, blindly pulling out one that was leather bound. "Been working on this one for a while. Like it . . . it's got an edge that I'm going for. But there's something missing. Something I can't put my finger on."

I glanced that way as he flipped it open to a page where a river of words had been scratched and slashed out and rewritten across the paper.

Incoherent.

A disjointed ramble that made no sense.

But I got that he knew. That he already recognized the words as his eyes dropped closed and he played a few chords.

The strains of a choppy melody filled the space.

Something seductive and dark.

Ash started to tap the toe of his Vans on the floor, head slowly bouncing in time before he started to pluck at the strings of his bass.

A new thread twined.

"You got a range on it, Austin?" Lyrik asked.

Austin began to hum, strumming quiet at the strings of his acoustic guitar. "Yeah. Think so."

My attention darted between the three of them as I let their process seep in. Getting it.

Realizing this was the way their magic was made.

There was a reason Sunder was one of the biggest bands in the world.

Their style setting a trend that had begun years before and had never found its end.

Powerful and gritty and raw.

The melody curled around me.

A perfect storm.

A beautiful nightmare.

I didn't know.

Only thing I knew was I felt it way down deep. Speaking directly to my spirit. I tapped my drumsticks against my thigh, letting the rhythm simmer and soak and become something fluid in my mind.

Couple of seconds later, Lyrik drove into a thrashing beat. Knocking us out of the quiet trance and catapulting us straight into the bedlam that was the music of Sunder.

Aggressive and hard and loud.

Austin climbed to his feet, his head thrashing as he found the rhythm. The lyrics choppy and sparse as he tried to make sense of them. As he tested the waters and brought them to life.

I caught onto it, let my sticks loose on the drums.

Got caught up in the raging beat.

Austin began to sing.

> *Are you lost?*
> *How did we end up here?*
> *I've been coming for a long time.*
> *Gone in your eternity.*
> *Now you've got me condemned in your sins.*
> *Do you want me on my knees?*
> *Now you're up and gone.*
> *Vanished without a trace,*
> *And you're still staring at my face.*
> *Don't know what to believe.*
> *Questioning everything.*

The song shifted from the screaming match that Austin was having with the mic, guy diving into the deep harmony, showing off the range of his voice.

> *Cause all you do is break me.*
> *Fake me.*
> *Bleed me.*
> *And I don't know what else I have to give.*
> *Break me.*
> *Fake me.*

Lyrik stopped abruptly, his hand clanking down on the strings, feedback flooding the space while the fierceness continued to resonate against the walls.

Huffing, he raked a hand through his hair before he pointed at Austin. "That, right there. Chorus is off. Way fuckin' off."

He paced a couple steps, his head toward the ground, like he was gathering up the energy of an earthquake. Harnessing it.

"Lyrics or key?" Austin asked as he scratched something out on the page and scribbled something more.

There was no missing the connection that banged between the three of them.

Between us.

Like I'd become partner to it.

Something brilliant. Feeling created out of nothing.

Enticed from the depths.

Pulled from memories and mishaps and miseries.

None here a stranger to them.

"Not sure," Lyrik mumbled.

"Chorus needs a contrast," I cut in. "She better be giving you something good if you're going to put yourself through that," I continued, letting a smirk ride free. Maybe I should keep my mouth shut, but I decided it wasn't time to give a fuck. They wanted me here and I was here. Was gonna offer my opinion.

Lyrik's attention swung my way. A grin pulled to the corner of the guy's mouth before he was grabbing the notebook and tossing it my way.

"Have a go at it then, brother."

I caught it against my chest with my left hand, snatching the pencil that came sailing at me with my right, somehow managing to keep hold of my sticks in the process.

I gave a tight nod, chewing at my bottom lip.

Contemplating.

Searching.

Catching the same vibe that Lyrik had been feeling when he'd penned these lyrics.

Resurrected from a reservoir that was an age old.

I tucked my sticks under my thigh, balanced the notebook on my forearm, pencil scratching across the page as I began to jot a twist in the words.

Cause all you do is break me.
Gut me.
Bleed me.

I'm cursed. Nothing left to give.
Spin my mind when you touch me.
Fill me.
Feed me.
I'm redeemed. All the reason left to live.

I tossed it back, and Lyrik glanced over it, smiling slow. "Ah, Leif here is a romantic."

Denial blew from my mouth on a pulse of air. "Hardly."

"Not to worry, man. I'm a firm believer you can't be a good songwriter unless you've fallen in love and then suffered its end."

My chest tightened. Painfully. In rejection. "They're just fuckin' words, man. Nothing more."

Too bad words were the power of meaning.

"Killed it, Leif. Knew you were going to fit in just fine." Ash clapped me on the shoulder as I wiped the sweat on my forehead with a hand towel. Skin drenched.

"Think I might be able to hack it." I grinned, body still on edge from the wild beat of adrenaline pulsing through my veins.

Ash slung his arm around my neck. "Now don't tell Zee I said this, but you nailed it. You're a rager. Full on beast. You should have seen the sweat flying off of you. Going to have to have someone come in here to mop up the mess. Epic. Seriously, you're playing with a country band? Don't fit, man. That shit's just weak," he razzed.

I shrugged him off with a slight chuckle. "Excuse me?"

"Nothing but wasted talent. Squandered. It's a damn travesty."

I tossed the towel into the bin. "You even listen to us?"

"Nah. Like I said . . . country."

I laughed. "You just keep telling yourself that. I bet you fall asleep listening to Carolina George."

He gasped. "Blasphemy."

Austin chuckled as he tossed his things into a bag. "Uh . . . Ash is the one who went nuts when Zee suggested we get in touch with you. Dude can lie through his teeth, but I'd lay down bets that if you looked up his most listened-to songs, Carolina George would be sitting at the top."

Ash lifted his hands in defense. "Hey . . . I just heard the word. Rumor spreads fast in these parts. Every time Carolina George comes into town, people lose their ever-lovin' minds. You'd think it was Sunder playing or something. Of course, that Emily girl might have a little something to do with it. She is somethin'."

I laughed under my breath. "That she is. Pretty sure she is the draw. She's an amazing girl."

Talented and gorgeous and sweet.

Truth was, the whole band was crazy talented.

"She deserves every bit of the limelight that is coming her way," I said. "All of them. They have worked their asses off to get where they are. I jumped on the train after they'd already paid the price. After they'd made every sacrifice. Can't take any of the credit, but what I can do is make sure they get where they're supposed to be."

Guilt pulsed. Just hoped I didn't fuck up before I helped to get them there.

Ash's smile turned soft. "Get it, Leif. They're your people. I'm just messing with you. Country might not be my thing, but there is no missing the fact Carolina George is stupid good. Great things are coming their way. After listening to you today? Can't wait to witness that for you."

More of that guilt.

This time suffocating.

"Thanks," I managed to mutter. Turning away before it ate me alive, I started to pack my shit because it was clear I needed to get the hell out of there.

I'd allowed myself to get too close to Rhys, Richard, and Emily. Something I'd promised myself I would never do. Refused to make that mistake again.

With these assholes, it would be easy to get wrapped up. All of them too damned likeable for their own good.

Ash's phone buzzed. He dug it out of his pocket, and a giant smile shot to his face. "Family's here. I gotta go." He bolted out the door.

Focusing on stuffing the rest of my things into my bag, I chuckled a disbelieving sound, wondering how the fuck I'd gotten myself here, the road I was supposed to be traveling getting twisted.

This band.

This city.

That *girl*.

Austin headed for the door. "See you upstairs. Don't know about you, but I'm fucking starving."

"Actually, I'm gonna take off," I mumbled.

Thank fuck my bike had shown up this morning. Band had seen to it that it and the rest of my things were shipped here from my condo in Charleston.

I sure as hell wasn't going to stick around for some kind of family gathering.

Austin stalled, his hair damp from sweat, his grey eyes kind when he looked back at me. "You sure?" he asked. "You're totally welcome. Think it'd be cool for everyone to get to know you."

"Need to work on some Carolina George songs."

"Ah, got you. No problem. See you at practice tomorrow."

"Sure thing."

The door shut behind him, and I breathed out a sigh of relief, only to tense when the voice hit me from the other side of the room.

"You played good today," Lyrik said, leaned up against the far wall with his arms crossed over his chest.

"Think we're going to jibe."

"Yeah," he agreed.

I kept stuffing nonexistent things into my bag. Didn't want to acknowledge the questions I could feel swirling through the air.

This guy's intensity fierce.

Loyal.

Savage.

Mix it with mine, and we'd bring the house down.

"About last night . . ."

Fuck.

I scraped a hand through my hair, blowing out a sigh. I chanced a glance his way, figuring I'd cut him off at the pass. "Heard the alarm go off and went to check it out. Thought I saw something."

"Did you?" he asked, straight up.

I hiked a shoulder. "Not sure. Gut tells me someone was there, but if there was? Fucker's a ghost. Was gone in a split."

"You didn't think too hard about chasing them down."

I didn't know if it was an accusation or not. Would take it, either way. Like I'd told Mia, if I dragged someone to their doorstep, I was going to be sure to drag them right back off.

Preferably in a body bag.

"Figure if I'm staying at your place, your place becomes my responsibility."

"A lot to take on."

I shrugged. "Life is what it is. You protect the ones you should. Hunt down the rest." I let a smirk crack my face.

Lyrik nodded, his voice rough. "Thought so. Guess you and I are alike that way."

"Doesn't surprise me."

"No. Doesn't surprise me, either."

I lifted my attention, intent clashing with his from across the room. "You want me to go? Just say it, man. I can find another place. No big deal."

It would be for the best, anyway.

Disbelief rumbled from Lyrik, his voice turning light. "Do I want you to leave? Fuck no. You run faster than me."

I gruffed out a cynical chuckle. "So, you didn't want a drummer. You wanted a security guard."

He laughed, low and dark. "Nah, dude, you're here to play. But it definitely doesn't hurt to have you around."

Didn't hurt?

Clearly, he had me pegged wrong.

Shifting, he pushed forward from the wall.

Warring.

Hesitating.

Like he was considering if he could really trust me.

144

Should do him the favor and tell him right then that he couldn't.

"Going to be straight with you. I'm not sure my sister is safe. Some really fucked up shit has gone down in her life. Brought her out here to protect her. Have to admit, any extra eyes on her won't be a bad thing."

Bitterness bled from me on a sigh. "You don't want me looking after her. I promise you that."

He lifted his chin in a challenge. "You've got your eyes on her, anyway. You might as well."

Wow.

Okay.

I scrubbed a hand over my face. "Already told you that I wouldn't touch her."

Yeah, and we saw how that went, didn't we?

That lie a thousand pounds on my chest.

The girl perfection under my hands.

He pushed the rest of the way from the wall. "Listen, know she's a grown woman. I mean, fuck, she has two kids. I can't stand in the way of her making her own choices. She's wicked smart. Strong and talented. I know I have to let her make decisions on her own. Doesn't mean I don't want to keep her from pain, and she's had more than anyone should have to shoulder. Just remember that, and we won't have a problem."

Denial blazed through my being. "You don't need to worry about it. Nothing is going on with us."

He took a step my way. "Guess that's what we all say when we're drowning, isn't it? So gone we have no idea that life is right there, waiting all around us. Love with a hand outstretched to rescue us."

"Don't believe in fairytales."

And if I did, mine were buried six feet underground.

Lyrik crossed the room, heading to the door. Right before he opened it, he paused. "Neither did I, man, neither did I. Funny how life turns out, though, isn't it? Now come and eat some chicken. Tamar insists."

The fucker winked. But it was me who was completely fucked.

fourteen

Leif

*C*limbing the stairs from the bottom floor, I hit the main level and quickly moved for the back door.

Like I thought I was all kinds of sneaky as I bypassed the kitchen that was packed with bodies preparing for a feast. Place filled with laughter and voices and clattering dishes.

It wasn't like I was going to escape meeting them.

But if I was going to endure this thing, I was going to need some fresh air and probably about fifteen beers.

The salty air hit me as I stepped out onto the large elevated deck that lined the entire back of the house. The view of the Atlantic struck me with a swift kick of awe.

Smoke curled from the built-in grill that took up the far end of the deck, the sweet aroma of honey-glazed chicken billowing with the air and mending with the scent of the sea.

Austin and his wife, Edie, who I'd met before practice, were down at the shore, their knees tucked to their chests.

"Ah. Tastes like summer, doesn't it?" Ash said where he manned the grill, dragging in an overexaggerated whiff.

I roughed a restless hand through my hair that whipped in the breeze. "Not exactly sure what summer tastes like, but that smells damned good."

Ash stretched out his hulking arms, tongs in one hand and a giant metal spatula in the other. Buffoon was actually wearing an apron that said *Kiss the Cook*. "Knew you couldn't resist this awesomeness. Welcome to a whole new brand of Ash-Magic. Griller extraordinaire."

"You mean bullshitter extraordinaire." The screen door slammed shut from behind just as the voice hit my ears. I spun around to find a tall, slender woman walking out, long, wavy dark-brown hair spilling around a face that appeared as innocent as could be.

"Darlin'. How could you wound me that way?" Ash asked, tone aghast and rippling with playful affection.

The woman tsked. "How could I what? Point out the fact that you are absolutely ridiculous?"

"Ahh, see, now I thought you liked it just fine when I got *ridiculous.*" There was nothing but suggestion in the words, and the woman was blushing as she walked toward him. Ash reached for her, tucking this shy girl into the curve of his side. She swatted his chest. "Like I said, ridiculous."

With a huge grin, he planted a kiss to the top of her head. "Leif, meet my Peaches. My wife. Most beautiful girl in the world. Lover of the *ridiculous.*" His voice dropped to a whisper on the last, and he nipped at her cheek.

She giggled a small sound and he groaned.

"Nice to meet you, Willow."

"We're really grateful you came. Our sweet Liam would have been devastated if Zee couldn't travel with him. It's kind of you to take time out from your own life to come and help us out."

I scratched at my temple, feeling like a total dick when I thought of the dollar signs that were currently going cha-ching as they popped into my bank account. But somehow, I had to accept it wasn't just about the money. I'd probably be here either way.

"Uh, glad to. Not a problem at all."

A clatter of movement burst from behind, and the door banged open again. This time, a stampede of kids came flying out.

Brendon was at the helm, the kid a complete wild child who clearly couldn't be contained, with about seven kids on his tail.

Only one I really noticed was Penny.

Penny.

She was there, emerging last, looking around, unsure.

My heart fisted in my chest.

What the fuck was that? This feeling that was too close to awareness. Knowing that her mom had to be near. This urge that made me feel like I needed to wrap this kid up, too.

Protect her.

Fight for her.

Her feet slowed just a bit when she saw me standing there, her brown eyes slanting my way.

Curious and shy.

A blonde girl who had to be about her age reached out and took her by the hand. "Come on, Penny. You're on my team. No way we're lettin' Brendon win this thing. His head's already big enough, don't ya think? He'll be rubbin' it in forever if we let him."

"My head is exactly the right size, thank you very much, Kallie!" Brendon hollered with a laugh over his shoulder as he bounded down the five deck steps to the boardwalk that led to the beach. "I think you're all just jealous I'm faster than you. Butterflies aren't exactly fast, now are they?"

Right, the blonde was Baz and Shea's oldest child.

"Um, you're older, that's why," she threw right back.

"And awesome. Don't forget that."

"Kallie *is* awesome," Penny defended.

Brendon grinned. "Oh, I know. I just want her to prove it to me."

They raced the rest of the way down the steps to the boardwalk. Austin and Edie stood to keep an eye on them as they tumbled into the sand.

Ash gave an amused shake of his head. "Hoodlums. All of them."

"Yeah, and let's just hope all those terrible crimes they are committing continue to consist of glasses of spilt milk and a few wrestling matches on the floor." Sebastian had slipped out onto the deck, his voice a casual rumble as his gaze took in the kids tackling each other to the sand.

Tamar stepped out behind him, carrying a platter of steamed vegetables. "You do know they actually started betting on those matches the other morning? It's escalating. Anarchy is descending. Like father, like son." Her mouth tipped into a playful, sultry smirk as she glanced over her shoulder at Lyrik who had followed her out, carrying another tray.

He shook his head. "Uh, no. Swear to God, I'm going to lock that kid up from thirteen to twenty. Won't even take the chance of him following in his daddy's footsteps. That's a no go."

Tamar giggled. "You do realize that is in like . . . six months? I think you might have to rethink these plans, Rockstar."

Lyrik curled an arm around her waist, tugging her back to his chest, his voice going deep. "Protect what's mine. However I have to do it."

She spun around, the fingers of her free hand crawling over his shirt up to the tat on his neck. "I think you've done a fine job of that. You've shown him how to be a good person. How to act. I don't think a padlock on his door is required."

"Yeah? Speak for yourself. Kallie is sure going to get one," Baz piped in.

"In your dreams, Daddy Bear." Baz's wife, Shea, stepped out. I recognized her from the tabloids.

She and Tamar seemed to be the two that always seemed to pop up in magazines and stories, Shea an old country singer who'd left her mark on the music scene years ago, and Tamar refusing to miss a single show when the band was on tour.

Self-proclaimed as Sunder's biggest fan.

"Don't you know when you try to hold your kids back is when they stage a revolt?" Shea's voice was pure southern persuasion.

"She turns thirteen, and you'll see who's staging a revolt." Baz's brows lifted to the sky. Clearly, he didn't agree.

Ash cracked up. "Thank fuck I had a boy. I would lose my damned mind if I had a girl."

Lyrik chuckled low. "Got one of both. Believe me, man, doesn't change a thing. Worry's gonna be there in one form or another. Worth every fuckin' gray, though."

A stake of agony pierced me, right at the center of my ugly, depraved soul. Wound bleeding hatred and vitriol.

My eyes squeezed closed like I could block out the assault of the past.

Then my lids were peeling open when awareness skimmed my skin.

Fuck.

Mia.

Mia who was looking at me like she was surprised to see that I was there while somehow not being surprised at all.

Her small son was tucked to her side, pointing his finger like mad at the mess of kids down on the beach, wanting to take part.

A literal handful as she struggled to keep ahold of him.

Hadn't seen her since last night.

Not since I was touching her and tasting her and making a litany of mistakes.

But with her, I wasn't sure how to stop it. How to stop the consuming intrigue that hit me every single time she got in my space.

No different today than it was yesterday except for now I had the distinct memory of knowing exactly how good she felt.

"Aww . . . look who is up from his nap. Come see Auntie, my handsome little man," Tamar cooed, moving to Mia and taking Greyson from her arms.

Mia rolled her eyes. "Up from his nap? He never went down. I swear, Greyson can smell fun, and if he thinks he's going to miss a minute of it, he's going to find his way back to it."

"Well, I wouldn't want to miss out on an afternoon at the beach, either. Can you blame him?" Tamar asked with her lips pressed against his chubby cheek.

He giggled and planted a sloppy kiss on her chin. "No blame

me, Auntie TT!" Something tugged at my chest. Kid was cute, that was for sure.

"Get ready, this deliciousness is done!" Ash began to pile the chicken breasts onto a platter. "Time to eat, my love bugs!" Ash shouted toward the beach. "Come and get it while it's hot."

Badass rockstar, all right.

Shea headed back inside to get the rest of the sides, and Mia volunteered to help.

Sparing me a moment.

A second to get it together.

Impossible because she was back just a minute later, organizing the sides on the sidebar where plates and utensils were already waiting.

"Beer is in the fridge," Lyrik told me, smacking me on the upper back as I stood there staring at his sister from behind, guy cutting me a glance as he passed telling me he was calling bullshit.

That he was fully aware that I was watching.

All eyes on her.

Couldn't turn away.

But he didn't get it.

Didn't get that looking any closer would be the destruction of me. Worst was it would most assuredly be the destruction of her.

I cleared my throat and followed him over to the outdoor kitchen fridge that was stocked with drinks. I grabbed a beer, popped the cap, and drained half of it in one gulp.

Hoping it might calm the nerves racing through my body.

Mia made her children's plates, balancing two of them while Tamar tried to get Greyson into a high chair at one of the patio tables. He cried and kicked his legs and shouted, "I big, I big. No, Auntie, no!"

The rest of the kids barreled back up the steps, herded by Austin and Edie.

Tamar finally wrangled Greyson into his seat and strapped him in. "There."

I roughed a hand over my face.

Feeling like I was sinking.

Drowning.

Washed away in a tsunami without even knowing it'd hit.

Didn't belong here.

Not for a second.

But Mia was trying to gather napkins and utensils for her kids while balancing their plates, and I was moving that way without thought, offering to take the plates from her as she attempted to tuck the silverware under her arm without dumping their food out onto the floor.

"Let me help you." My voice was a grumble. Some kind of fucked up plea.

Those eyes really met mine for the first time. Hurt and begging for more.

She hesitated.

"Please," I said.

She breathed out a tiny, pained sound, one that trickled across my flesh and hit me like a song.

A hypnotic melody that implored to be written.

"Thank you," she whispered as she handed over the plates.

"No problem."

No problem at all.

It was just a goddamned catastrophe.

I followed her over to the table where the kids had set up camp. Each of them climbed onto the cushioned chairs around the large table. Plates were set in front of the younger children, each of them exclaiming their thanks.

All except for Greyson who smashed a handful of his macaroni and cheese in my face the second I set it down on his high-chair tray.

Bullseye.

Apparently, I actually was the kid's target.

He shrieked with laughter and kicked his feet, his nose all scrunched up with his amusement. "Got you, Waif. I got you!"

I edged back, trying to wipe the mess from my cheek.

"Oh," Mia breathed when she whirled around and saw what her kid had done, her fist flying to her mouth before a smile was splitting behind it. "Oh, God."

I cocked my head, raking a gob of it off. "You think that's

funny, huh?"

"I do," Brendon popped off, throwing his hand in the air like we were asking for his opinion.

Smart ass.

I tossed him a scathing glare, the little punk.

Just like his dad. Calling bullshit.

Mia passed me a napkin, words falling from around her barely contained laughter, "I'm so sorry. I can't believe he did it again."

I wiped the stickiness away, fighting a chuckle building in my chest. "Kid hates me."

"No, way, Waif." His brown eyes widened and his brows shot to the sky. "I wike you." He grinned like he was posing for a picture. All teeth.

"Bite?" He scooped a big glob of it onto his spoon and held it up to me, clumps of it dripping off the huge mound and falling to the ground, way too eager for me to comply.

"Eat!" he demanded with the most massive, hopeful grin.

My eyes fell to Mia. Her expression was soft as she looked down at her kid in sheer adoration.

And shit. I was a damned fool. Such a fool because I was leaning down and taking the bite he offered, pretending like I was gobbling it up.

And it hurt and it slayed and it busted me wide open again.

Pulling back, I swallowed hard and pinned on the brightest smile I could find. Probably looked like the Joker.

Deranged.

Unhinged.

Crazed.

Greyson howled with laughter.

"My turn! Watch me!" He shoveled a heaping spoonful of it into his mouth. "I share, Momma."

He turned his face up toward her, looking for praise.

"That is very nice of you. But no more throwing food because that isn't nice." She tapped his nose with the last.

"I nice," he refuted, and God, I was going to lose my mind.

Already had, apparently, because Tamar had shown up at the table and set Adia's plate down in front of her. "Why don't you two make your plates. I'll get these guys set."

Mia's mouth pulled at one side and her eyes narrowed when something played across Tamar's red lips. A silent conversation transpired between the two of them that clearly had everything to do with me.

Awesome.

"Are you hungry?" Mia finally asked, shifting that gaze to me. There went my blood, traveling south, and not to my growling stomach.

"Starved."

She offered the smallest smile and an even smaller nod.

I thought maybe a truce.

A free pass.

She was going to let me off on the bullshit I'd pulled last night.

"We should eat, then. If we don't, Ash will never let us hear the end of it."

"Damn right, I won't," he hollered from across the deck.

At her side, I made a plate, fighting the rumble of something deep in my bones. I shoved it down.

I could do this.

I could stay here without fucking it all up.

Ruining it all.

I sat down beside her at the larger table, pretending like I didn't notice it was a circle of couples.

The love-fucked.

I took a hard glance at Mia. Tucking the feeling away. Wanting a piece of this for me.

Reminding myself again why that would forever be an impossibility.

Leif
Twenty-One Years Old

*S*trobe lights flashed in blinding rays of white light as I railed on the drums. Sweat flung from my drenched body. Soul crashing with the violent, raging rhythm.

The crowd surged and thrashed and toiled at the foot of the stage. Wild. Untamed. Minds absent, swept away in the reckless energy as they throbbed in the pit.

I fed off of it. Sucked it down. Muscles in my arms screaming with exertion as I pounded through the song.

The rest of the band came unhinged on the stage. Guitar and bass deafening. Miles screamed his aggression into the mic as his entire body slammed with the beat.

And for a few minutes, every single person in that club was free.

I tossed my sticks into the crowd. All the people standing at the foot of the stage were gasping for their breaths, as soaked as me, all the chaos they'd been holding onto released into the songs that we had played. I strode off the stage and went right for the room in the back.

Couches were set up all around. Lights cut low. Music blared from the speakers.

I accepted the bottle Miles offered as I walked in.

I plopped onto a couch. Did two fat lines that were already cut on the table, and I didn't complain at all when a girl I'd hooked up with last week got onto her knees and went to work on my fly.

Lyrik West and his crew rolled in.

I gestured to the table.

My offering.

As long as they had the dough, all were welcome to play with me.

The band was nothing but an easy cover.

Music might have been the one piece that I still possessed of my soul, but it was Keeton who owned me.

Lyrik cocked me a smirk as he took a seat and gave himself over to the oblivion.

I guessed it was the least I could do.

Leif
Twenty-Three Years Old

The front door of the auto-shop swished open, sending a slice of late afternoon light streaking into the reception area. Heaving out a sigh, I sat forward on the stool where I sat behind the counter, trying not to be annoyed as I tossed my phone to the grungy surface.

But this bullshit was stupid.

Sitting up here like I was some kind of mechanic's apprentice

or some shit.

I had barely glanced up at the figure that slipped inside before my throat was going thick with a tingly awareness. My head snapped up to find this girl who was all kinds of wary standing just inside.

Wearing the shortest shorts and a long tee that almost covered them, her blonde hair swept up in a messy knot on top of her head. Flipflops on her feet.

There was an oil streak on her gorgeous face.

An innocent face.

Shy and sweet. Cheeks full, almost as full as her pink lips.

Her green eyes were big and round as she took in the surroundings. "I . . . um . . . are you open?" she asked, her nerves skating through the air.

"Yeah."

She gestured out the door. "I got a flat. I tried to change it myself, but . . ." she trailed off, those eyes watching me as I pushed to standing.

My heart rate sped.

Sped with something brand new.

"You need my help?" I grunted out.

She smiled. "Yeah, I do."

We banged into my apartment. Door crashing on the wall as I went back for her. Diving in for a kiss that I didn't ever want to end. My arms curled around her tiny body. Lifting her from her feet. Spinning her and spinning her as we kissed and touched and clawed to get closer to the other.

Frantic.

Like if we lost this moment, we were going to lose everything.

We knocked into the entryway table as I yanked her shirt over her head, and a second later, I had her pressed to the door.

Kissing her like it was the last thing I was going to do.

Just as quickly, I pulled her away and lay her out on the couch.

Like I couldn't sit still.

Desperate to have her everywhere.

And I knew I was never going to be good enough for this girl when she shivered like she'd never been touched before when I ran my nose up the inside of her thigh, from her knee up to the hem of those super short shorts. When she whimpered as I dragged them down her legs. When she whispered, "Be careful with me," when I crawled over her.

I gathered her up, held her close, and I made a silent promise that I would always be.

That this was different.

Tender when I slowly pushed myself into the sweet relief of her body.

She gasped, and her head rocked back on the couch cushion, her chest pressing into mine. I swallowed the sound, relishing in the feel of her blunted fingernails sinking into my shoulders.

Her arms tight around my neck and her heart a thunder that raced to meet with mine.

I edged back, watching down on her as I fucked her.

But I knew well enough this was different.

This was different than all those girls.

Knew I wasn't ever going to be the same.

She nervously raked her teeth across her bottom lip, glancing up at me where she was curled up at my side with her head rested on my shoulder. Two of us under the covers in my bed. Her sweet body warm and alive next to mine.

Night pressed at the small window of my bedroom.

The sleazy sounds of Los Angeles howled through the darkness right outside the rundown building.

Sirens spinning. Gunshots in the distance. Shouts of hatred and abuse.

She just curled deeper into the safety of my arms while I pressed a kiss to her temple.

"Hi," I murmured.

A timid smile pulled at her mouth, and she gazed up at me, tentatively playing her fingers across the satisfied thrum in my chest. "I never imagined this was the way my day would turn out."

I squeezed her a little, the words I delivered close to a tease. "What, you didn't expect to get a flat tire?"

A slight giggle slipped from her mouth. "I think I hit a little more than a bump in the road."

I blew out a heavy sigh, shifted so I could spread my hand out over her cheek.

Sure I'd never spoken a louder truth in my entire life.

"Never could have anticipated crashing into you."

sixteen

Mia

*T*he house echoed a hushed stillness, the windows darkened to a wispy calm from within, walls seeping with a resonating silence.

The hour deep.

Only hours until dawn.

But I couldn't sleep. I guessed the worry and fear and dread were finally catching up to me. Wearing me thin.

It'd been four nights since the false alarm had rung through the house.

Tonight, I found I couldn't remain locked inside that room for any longer, so I'd slipped out to the pool with a bottle of wine in search of peace.

That peace lasted for all of ten minutes before I heard the heavy engine roar as it came up the street and parked in the garage at the back.

His footsteps echoed from the other side of the wall as he came up the sidewalk. The gate buzzed, swung open, and he was there.

Emitting his own gravity.

He was wearing tattered jeans and another thread-bare tee, this one white and stretched taut across his strong chest.

"Mia . . . what are you doing out here this late?" The words were grated, scraping across my flesh like the seductive rake of teeth.

A shiver rolled down my spine, and I clutched my wine glass to my chest as I sat forward a little, my legs dipping deeper into the cool waters like it could halt the flashfire that lit in my body. "I didn't realize I wasn't allowed to be. Both you and my brother seem to think I need to be permanently locked in my room. I might as well be Brendon and Kallie with the way you treat me."

Maybe it was a challenge. A gauntlet. A tease.

Anything to ease the tension that was banging between us.

He huffed a sound and looked to the side before bringing that penetrating gaze back to me. "Had I known you were going to be out here this late, I wouldn't have left."

Skeptical laugher rippled from my mouth, and I took a sip of my wine. "I thought you were here to play. I wasn't aware that my brother had hired you as a body guard."

"Maybe you'd be better off if he had. Seems it would have served a better purpose."

"I don't need a babysitter. I've seen plenty in my life. I'm not helpless."

His head shook, his hair tossing shadows against the brick walls where the yard lights glowed across his face. "Never implied you were, but you have more important things to be living for than I do."

There was something in his voice, the twist of a knife slashing his tongue that had me swiveling my attention fully to him. My eyes narrowed as I tried to make him out better through the lapping darkness. "Why would you say that?"

Blowing out a sigh, he glanced toward the wing of the house where my children slept. "I think we both know what's really important in life, don't we?"

My spirit clutched in an erratic way, and a thick, solid lump formed at the base of my throat.

"I know what's important to me," I answered on a haggard breath.

A smile tugged at his mouth. One that was utterly sad. Beautiful and dark and invading the space.

This man that was terrifyingly beautiful and devastatingly bad.

Written in the scars he wouldn't allow anyone to see.

"Do you want to join me?" I asked, lifting the bottle of wine I had sitting on the cool deck beside me.

Blatant enticement.

Apparently, I was wanting a few more of those scars for myself.

But I couldn't get over the other night. The way he'd touched me. Kissed me. The way for a few blinding moments, I'd felt utterly alive.

"I don't think that's a good idea, Mia."

"Friends," I told him. God. I was so full of shit. "We've been managing that, haven't we?"

He laughed a harsh sound. "If that's what you want to call it."

"I do."

He blew out an exasperated sound, his face downturned, hesitating, before he finally gave and started to move in my direction. He grabbed the end of a pool lounger and dragged it over to where I was, sitting down on the very end of it about a foot away.

He rested his forearms on his thighs.

His lean, cut body on edge.

I could almost feel his spirit fluttering in the stagnant air.

"Not exactly dressed in pool attire." He gestured to his boots and jeans before his gaze was sweeping me, my tank and short shorts, my bare legs exposed in the muted light in the water.

Hunger flashed in his eyes.

Desire and need.

Chills rolled. Goosebumps a ripple across my skin.

I cleared my throat and forced a light smile as I swiveled to face him, offering him my glass of wine. "I share as well as my son does."

Chuckling, Leif reached over and grabbed the full bottle instead. He tipped the entire thing up as he brought it to his mouth. His thick throat bobbed as he swallowed, his lips drenched in the sticky sweetness when he pulled the bottle away.

He used the back of his hand to wipe his mouth, eyeing me the whole time.

I gulped.

Why did he have to be so sexy?

He gave a new meaning to the Law of Attraction.

His own gravitational pull.

I felt like I was orbiting him.

Wanting more but terrified to get too close.

He angled his head to study me, and I took a shaky sip of my wine like it might stand as a good enough distraction to keep me from crawling on my hands and knees to him.

"How are you doing, Mia?" His voice was serious. Hard but full of care.

God. This man. He was going to be my undoing.

I laughed out a brittle sound and let my gaze wander across the yard. "Other than the fact I can't sleep? Jumping at every bump in the night?" Aside from the sorrow and the mourning? Aside from how damned badly I was aching to feel him?

"Great."

He expelled a low grunt of disbelief. "Great, huh?"

"Absolutely. Look at this place. How could I complain?"

Those eyes traced, warm brown-sugar again. "It seems you're missing something to me."

I exhaled a heavy sound, looking out at the gentle ripples of the water before I got brave enough to look back at him. "When you lose someone you care about most, there's bound to be something missing, isn't there?"

"Yeah." He said it without hesitation.

Hard and fast.

He left no question that it was from experience.

My eyes squeezed shut for a moment. "I just . . ."

I opened them to him waiting. Waiting on me. "I just can't make sense of it. Why? Why so much violence? A beautiful life wasted . . . and for what? I . . . I wish I would have given him the money. Wished I didn't push that panic button. He warned me not to move, and I did it, anyway."

Guilt crushed down on my chest. A thousand pounds of rocks. Burying me.

My words rushed out with the sorrow. "If I just would have listened to him, Lana would still be here today. He told me . . . he told me if I just gave him what he was after, he wouldn't hurt us. And I . . . I panicked, Leif."

My lips pursed in anguish. "One mistake. One I'm not ever going to have the chance to make up for."

His face pinched, and his teeth clamped down on his bottom lip as he shifted forward another inch. The muscles in his arms ticked.

I couldn't tell if it was rage or desire.

If he was holding himself back or letting himself go.

"You don't know that, Mia. You have no idea what a monster is going to do. When a man is nothing but cruel and vile. The length he will go. The thirst for blood."

My entire being cringed at the thought. "That is something I will never understand. Life is precious. It should be treasured and cherished. How could someone take it so casually and carelessly?"

His expression shifted.

Grief.

Regret.

Hatred.

My insides trembled.

God. Who was this man?

He fisted his big hands between his knees. "Sometimes people become monsters without knowing it's happening. Caught up in lawlessness before they realize who they have become."

I searched him, unsure of what he was saying. What he was implying. Only knowing the way that I saw him. "And then there are good people. Selfless people who will hurl themselves over a wall without knowing what they might be coming up against to protect someone else."

His laughter was rough.

A rebuttal.

"And sometimes people go running into danger in the hopes of making amends, knowing they could never pay a penalty so big, but knowing they will spend their entire lives trying, anyway."

"Is that what you're doing . . . making amends? For what?"

I could feel his disturbance vibrate the ground.

"I should go."

He started to stand.

My hand flew out and wrapped around his calf. Our gazes clashed as I looked up at him.

A shockwave of intensity

"Stay," I managed to say.

He heaved out the strain, cursing low before he slowly sat back down. My hand was still on his calf, refusing to let go.

"You don't want to get inside me, Mia. Know you think you do, but I promise you, that is not a place you want to be. You can't fix me." The words were gruff and low. A warning.

"And what if I were to like what I was to see?"

His dark chuckle curled in the space between us, and his hand was reaching out, tilting up my chin. "Like I said, you'd only see your own beauty reflected back. I am no good, Mia. You don't know me, and I promise, you don't want to."

My hand was shaking like crazy when I forced myself to let go of his leg. I reached to reclaim my wine glass, bringing it to my lips. I fought for normalcy. To find that uneasy casualness that we'd shared for the last few days, but that seemed impossible when he was sitting this close.

"So . . . how is playing with the band? Practice is going well?"

There.

As normal as could be.

He let go of a short laugh when he realized what I was doing.

A reprieve from the severity.

"It's good. Guys are crazy talented. It's an honor to play with them."

"That's funny because Lyrik said the same thing about you."

"Your brother is delusional."

"He said you pretty much rewrote a song that was giving him

fits."

"Fits? He said that?" Leif teased, lightness weaving into his tone and his face lifting into an easy smile.

God, that was pretty, too.

I peeked back. "Okay, fine, he might have said it was fucking with his head and he was about to commit homicide on the next poor, unsuspecting asshole that looked at him wrong. Same diff."

A smile played across his mouth. The man exuding a dark, dark confidence. I wanted to slip into the shadows of it.

"You rockstars are so dramatic." I rolled my eyes. Reminding myself why I'd convinced myself *rockstars* were so not my type all those years ago. I didn't have the time or the space for the pain.

But Leif's?

I wanted his.

To shoulder some of it.

Pray that in his aftermath he didn't leave me crushed.

"It was no big deal. He almost had it. Was just missing something. Great song, honestly."

I let my eyes trace him, like I could add up all the parts that made him whole. The pieces that formed who he was. "Honest?"

"Wow. Loaded question much?" he teased.

I grinned. "You don't look much like a country drummer to me."

He laughed a self-deprecating sound. "No . . . but sometimes it's stupid not to take opportunities when they're presented to you."

"Like Sunder offered you?"

"Yeah."

"You want my honest?" I asked.

"Shoot."

"It seems like a better fit."

His mouth quirked at the side, and the slight dimple showed in his cheek.

I had the urge to lick it.

"You better not let Zee hear you saying that."

Effortless laughter floated out. "He's like a brother to me. I'll be sure to use it the next time we get into a spat."

The hardness around Leif's eyes softened more. "You're all close." He glanced at the main house. "You want my honest?"

"Sure."

"I'm having a hard time figuring out who's actually related and the ones who just call each other family."

Affection moved through my chest. "That's the way we want it. You shouldn't be able to tell. Love and devotion shouldn't be hinged on whether you have the same blood running through your veins or not. I love all the kids like they're my own nieces and nephews. I'd never want them to know the difference."

"That's noble."

My head shook. "No, that's a blessing."

Air left his mouth, the man itching where he sat, jaw clenching tight. "It's rare to find a love like that."

"Another honest, while we're at it?"

"Shoot," I said, just like him.

The two of us getting caught up in the mood.

In the stillness.

In the peace that wrapped us like a sweet, sweet dream.

He might be dangerous, but I didn't think I'd ever felt more comfortable than right then.

"Have to tell you that you blow me away. Your kids are lucky to have a mom like you, Mia West. Or is that your last name?" he hedged, acting like it was just another casual question when I could see the muscles twitch and flex beneath all his hard, toned flesh.

I huffed a disparaging sound. "It is West. I've never been married. I guess I don't have the best luck when it comes to men."

"Kids' dad?"

Heaviness weighed down on my chest. "Things didn't work out."

Leif frowned. I might as well have been vague-booking.

Disquiet stormed through my being, that feeling way down in my bones. I set my wine glass aside and hugged my knees again. A lie should probably suffice, but I turned back to Leif with an ounce of the truth. "Sometimes we think we know someone and we don't know them at all. Lyrik thinks he bolted when he found out I was pregnant with Penny, but it was me who left him. It was hard, but some ties have to be cut before they strangle us."

A rush of aggression gusted through Leif. "He hurt you?"

"No. It was never like that. He was just . . . *trouble*. Involved in things that I didn't want for my life, so I had to cut him loose."

He threaded his fingers together, voice lowering when he pressed, "But he's Greyson's father?"

"Yeah. He'd turned his life around. Started his own business. Wanted to be a part of Penny's life. Support both of us. One thing led to another . . ." I trailed off.

Details not required.

"Because you still loved him." It wasn't even a question.

My nod was slow. "I thought I did. But I think it was more that I was hoping that we could work things out and be a family. That's what I'd always wanted, after all." I lifted my face to the night sky. "To create art and create a family. Those are my two most beautiful things."

"What went wrong?"

Disparaging laughter rippled out. "Everything, I guess. Things were always tumultuous between us. Super on or super off. Fighting constantly. In the end, there was too much distrust. Too many questions. Too much hurt. I realized I was fighting for something that hadn't been there for a long, long time, and I could fight for it forever, but it was never going to change the fact that he and I didn't belong together."

Leif stilled. Waiting.

Air puffed from my nose. "There was one night he didn't come home. It wasn't the first time it'd happened. I texted him probably a thousand times, and I realized that wasn't the life I wanted to live. Paranoid. Worried. Angry. So I packed our things and left. It didn't matter what the explanation or reason he was surely going to give, I couldn't continue to put me and my family through that constant turmoil."

"So, that was it?"

My shoulder hiked. "He's been trying to get me to come back ever since. I can't completely cut him out when he's still involved with the kids, and he was the one who'd helped to fund mine and Lana's art gallery to begin with."

Our pasts tied in a way that would never be undone.

"I'm sorry. Anyone dumb enough to mess up being with you? Don't think he deserves you, anyway."

He said it with a cocky smirk lined with the most callous truth.

I lay my head on my knees, peering over at him, just the outline of him in my periphery. It didn't matter. The man was the only thing I could see.

"I can't regret a second of it. I got my children out of it. To me, that will always be the greatest, most important thing."

Leif flinched. I wasn't sure if it was in agreement or pain. Maybe both.

Eyes narrowed, I focused on him. "Kids make you nervous."

Air puffed from his nose. Incredulous disgust. "Guys like me shouldn't get mixed up with kids."

"Why is that?"

His grin was wholly forced. "We've seen how much Greyson likes me. He thinks I'm a hole in one. It's better to stay out of the line of fire."

A giggle slipped free. "He's a handful, that's for sure."

"Maybe the kid is just a good judge of character. He'll scare off all the bad guys for you. Second he saw me, no doubt he was figuring out how to get me away from you."

His grin was brittle.

Amusement flashed while disappointment spun.

"Tell me not all the good men are gone."

Leif sighed. "Don't doubt he's out there, Mia . . . a guy who can handle it all. One who is good from the inside out. One who deserves you and those kids. Don't give up on that."

I could feel his reservations ripple through the space. "You gonna have more?"

My head slowly shook, and I tilted my gaze to the heavens. "I had a complication after I had Greyson and had to have a procedure."

I lifted my cupped hand toward the sky. "Having another would be like catching a falling star."

Impossible.

But I was the fool who would wish on it, anyway.

"I'm sorry." His voice was low.

"How could I be sad? I have the two most amazing children."

His jaw twitched with the crush of his teeth, and his eyes squeezed shut before he said, "You do." He scrubbed his palms on his jeans like he needed to break up the tension. "So . . . where do you go from here? Back to California? After the bastard is caught who took your friend?"

I looked that way. At the softness in those brown-sugar eyes, at the hardness that surrounded the creases, and I did my best not to think about the way his lips tasted the same.

Tender and biting.

"I'm not sure. I feel a little lost right now, honestly. Not sure where I belong or where I want to go. I always seem to find myself in these messes and don't know how to get myself out of them. I don't know if I have a backlog of bad karma coming at me or what."

"Or maybe you're just too sweet to see when you're mixing with the wrong people."

I knew what he was implying. Who he was referring to. Was I so blind to disagree? And why did I feel so damned compelled to dig deeper?

To seek and find and discover?

But I wanted to, to disappear inside his mind. Get lost in his cruel, brittle heart.

"Call me naïve, I guess."

"No, Mia, I'd call you kind." He edged in closer. The overwhelming force of his presence covered me whole.

Cloves and whiskey and hot, wicked sex.

His hand came out, the pad of his index finger scraping down my cheek and across my bottom lip. "Which is the reason I would gladly hurl myself over a wall to face the unknown. Why I would gladly rip apart any monster who would seek to do you wrong. Which is exactly why I stay away because the last thing I want to do is more harm. I will destroy you, Mia, just like I destroy every good thing I ever have."

"What if I don't let you get that close?"

He moved in, his lips an inch from mine. "Don't kid yourself,

Angel. I'm already there. You and I both know it."

Flames licked. Danced and jumped and burned in the naked space between us.

"How is it possible you already made it there?" I whispered.

"Maybe some things are meant to be, written before time, but when you get there? You've already fucked it up so bad that it's not yours anymore, and it gets lumped in with the things you can't have but feel like you can't live without. They become a piece that will forever go missing."

"And what if you're only meant to work harder for it?"

"That is nothing but a dangerous fantasy."

"Is that what you are, a dangerous fantasy?"

He leaned forward, his touch searing through me when he set his palm on my cheek. "No, baby, you're mine."

seventeen

Leif

D read whirred. A cyclone. A tornado.

A typhoon that twisted and blew and raged.

I raced through the middle of it, wind whipping at all sides, exhaustion weighting my feet as I struggled to break through the crush of the crowd that surrounded me like an army that had been sent to wall me in.

Arms like tendrils that curled and bound and struggled to hold me back.

Pain everywhere.

Body afire.

Soul consumed.

I broke through the mob, a roar rushing up my burning throat, eyes searching through the blinding rays of sunlight that streaked from the sky.

Blazing hot whips that scored my back.

Time ticked.

Another minute passed.

Running out of time.
I could fix it. Stop it. End it.
Offer myself. I burst through the door. Hands fought to hold me back.
"Maddie!" I screamed. "Maddie!"
I screamed and I screamed.
"Maddie!"

"Maddie!" I shot upright in bed as the name left my mouth, the shout of agony bouncing off the walls and echoing back.

Perpetual.

Eternal.

Gaining speed with each pass.

Sweat drenched my skin, heart hammering at my ribs, so hard something was bound to crack.

Sickness squeezed my insides to liquid, nausea climbing my throat and threatening to spill out onto the floor.

I gasped and choked, blinking frantically, trying to orient myself from the dream.

To bring myself back from the nightmare that would haunt me for all my days. The ghosts getting closer, demanding vindication. Screaming for retribution.

They howled and moaned in my mind, my soul at their mercy. *This.*

This was the debt I owed. I needed to remember that.

With the barest hints of dawn seeping through the windows of the bedroom, I tossed the covers from my body, and I pushed from the bed and walked straight into the attached bathroom. I shoved my underwear to the floor and turned on the showerhead to as hot as it would go. As soon as it began to steam, I stepped under the scorching spray. Praying for a second of reprieve.

I heaved out a sigh as I glanced down to my abdomen. At the scars. The only thing physical that remained.

If only they would have taken me.

But that would have been too easy. Not close to being cruel enough.

The wicked thirsted for blood.

And this morning, I could taste the fruition of it on my tongue.

"Shit." I banged around the little kitchen in the guest house, slamming the cabinet doors after rummaging through the contents and coming up empty.

No fucking coffee.

Now that was just cruel and unjust.

I blew out a heavy sigh, grabbing a tee that I'd tossed to the couch and pulling it over my head before I stepped out into the coolness of the breaking day.

For a minute, the humidity was held. A moment's sanctuary from the Savannah summer heat.

Barefoot, I tiptoed through the stilled hush of the morning, birds chirping through the light rustle of the trees that billowed from above.

If you listened closely enough, you could almost believe in peace.

I made it to the glass wood-framed doors at the back entrance of the main house, and I tapped in the code. The lock gave, and I quietly pushed open the door a fraction so I could slip into the sleeping house without being noticed.

I eased it shut behind me. Eyes on my feet, I roughed a hand through my still damp hair as I headed for the kitchen.

Two steps in, I froze when I realized I wasn't alone. "Penny. You scared me."

Somehow, I managed to keep the curse from ripping off my tongue.

The young girl stilled in surprise where she was turning on a burner on the stovetop.

Yeah, she was clear on the opposite side of the kitchen as me, a huge island in the middle of us, but there was no missing the flicker of fear in her eyes when she saw me.

It came right along with a million questions.

"I think it was the other way around." She searched me.

Wary.

Inquisitive.

Like she was asking me point-blank if she should be afraid.

I heaved out a strained sigh, and I shuffled over to the island, careful to keep a continent between us. I pulled out a stool and tucked myself into it so I was facing her. Figured if I was sitting, I wouldn't appear so much of a threat.

Knew I didn't exactly come across as a nice guy.

"You're up early." That made for good, casual conversation, right?

I mean, seriously, why did this kid make me shake? My knee was bouncing a million miles a minute under the island, heart still jackhammering in my chest, and I was having a hell of a time maintaining my faked grin.

"You're up early, too," she said in her soft voice, studying me as she went to the refrigerator and pulled out butter and a dozen eggs and took them back to the stovetop.

She was . . . cooking.

"Couldn't sleep," I told her, honestly.

Curiosity filled her dark eyes, and she glanced back at me as she took a knife to the butter and put a large dollop into the pan. "Me, neither," she whispered to the nothingness, away from me, but I could still hear.

Like I could taste her fear.

"So you decided to make breakfast?" I tried to keep it light.

"Don't you know breakfast is the most important meal of the day?" She kept her back to me, working away, her hair in a ponytail swishing down her back.

"Did your mom tell you that?"

"Didn't yours?" She peered at me for a beat before she turned back to the stove.

I blew out a sigh. "Well, I guess we could say my mom wasn't quite as cool as yours."

I could almost feel her blush, the way she was chewing at her bottom lip, barely turning enough that she could steal a peek at me. "She wasn't nice?"

A turbulence rose up from the depths.

Old, old wounds. Hardened and cracked.

I rubbed my fingers over my lips.

How the fuck was I supposed to handle this?

"She wasn't exactly nice, no."

A slash of sadness crumpled her face, her brows drawing tight in sympathy. "Did she hurt you?" she whispered, her expression a flood of worry.

I fought the cynical laughter scraping my throat, and I roughed my hand through my hair over and over again. "Not physically."

Not me, anyway.

Those dark eyes softened and deepened and saw too many things. Just like her mother. "I'm sorry. Moms are supposed to be our favorite people and it's stupid and wrong when they're not."

Something tugged at that ugly spot that throbbed from within. Still I was chewing at my bottom lip and giving her a tight nod. "Yeah, it sucks. But I think what matters here is that you have one of the good ones."

I thought it was fear I saw blast across her face before she quickly turned away and cracked three eggs into the skillet. They splattered and sizzled in the hot, melted butter. Scent of it rising into the air, binding with the sudden tension that rippled and shook.

"I don't want her to die, too." She muttered it so quietly that I could barely be sure that she'd actually said it.

But I felt it.

A slash across my soul.

"I won't let that happen." The promise was out before I could stop it.

Fuck.

Fuck. Fuck. Fuck.

What was I doing? Assigning myself responsibility? But I couldn't seem to make myself stop. Not when this kid clearly needed reassurance.

"She pretends like everything is okay, but sometimes I hear her crying at night," Penny continued. "I hate it when she cries, Mr. Godwin. I hate it, and I want to make it go away. That's why I couldn't sleep."

The last was barely a breath, her head tipped to the floor. The

pieces getting loose from her ponytail created a veil across her face.

Like she was ashamed to admit it.

Torment clutched me, hers and mine, her confession wrapping me in leather binds.

I pressed my hands to the stone of the island to keep myself from going to her. The surface cold against the fire that was raging in my veins. "You shouldn't worry, Penny. That's why you're here. So you're all safe. Your uncle and I are going to see to that."

I had no idea what I was even promising her, and I thought it was high-time I asked a few fucking questions.

Her chin trembled when she stared back at me. "Are you sure?"

Nothing will happen to you. Not ever. I promise you.

The pathetic oath roared through my mind. Decayed and rotten. Black venom oozed from the pits of this living hell that toiled inside.

I gulped around it.

"I promise. I won't let anything happen to her."

Won't let anything happen to you.

My spirit fired, and I swore, I caught a glimpse of Karma kicking her feet up on the ottoman in the den while sipping a cup of coffee, grinning maniacally behind the mug.

Someone needed to stab that bitch.

"Okay," Penny whispered.

She turned back to the eggs she was scrambling, and four slices of toast popped up from the toaster. She busied herself, putting butter and jam on the toast and plating some eggs.

Shyness had taken her whole when she turned around with the plate clutched in two hands, her shoulders to her ears as she crossed the floor. Carefully, she slid the plate over to me. "That's for you. Because your mom didn't do a good job of taking care of you."

Emotion clutched me. Heart and soul. I looked down at the food. "You don't have to feed me, Penny." The words grated free.

"But what if I want to?"

Warily, I gave her a rigid nod. "Thank you."

A tiny smile pulled at her mouth. "You're welcome." She turned away and headed back for the counter. "Coffee?" she asked from over her shoulder.

Disbelief left me on a shot of low laughter.

"Tell me you don't drink coffee."

Her head shook as her body swayed. Her demeanor a thousand pounds lighter. "Of course not, silly, I made it for my mom. *Because* she takes such good care of me."

I got it, what she was saying. But in the end, I couldn't blame my mother for who I had become. For what she'd gotten involved in that had been passed on to me.

It was all on me.

A second later, Penny was back with a steaming cup of coffee, sliding it over beside my plate. She grabbed a container of creamer and some sugar and did the same.

God, this kid.

Mia threaded in her.

Goodness and purity.

"You're the best, Penny. This is exactly what I came in here looking for this morning."

Redness flushed her face. "Really?"

"Yep. And you should probably call me Leif. The only person who calls me Mr. Godwin is . . . well . . . no one."

A timid smile flitted over her face. "Okay, Leif."

I gave her a nod and took a sip of the coffee. Warning spreading wide. Knowing I was digging myself deeper. Losing sight. Burying myself in something that wasn't mine to keep.

But I had to think maybe . . . maybe . . . this was another debt that I owed.

Another loss. Another penalty.

But if it gave this child a second's relief?

Then I would gladly pay the price.

Leif

Bursts of laughter and shouts of voices seeped through the walls. Sunlight crawled in through the edges of the windows and made its way through the cracks.

I was sitting on the floor, hunkered down like I was in some kind of war zone, hoping beyond hope that would be enough to keep me camouflaged, my back leaned against the couch with my acoustic guitar balanced across my lap.

Chicken-scratch notebook open on the floor beside me.

There were nothing but a disorder of words on the page.

Pencil slashed and sliced like knife marks in the thick journal paper.

Nothing quite making sense because there was no sense to be made for the mayhem going down in the depths of me.

Suppressing a scream, I dropped my pencil onto the notebook

and roughed both hands through my hair, blowing out a sigh toward the ceiling.

Swore, the family gathering happening right outside was more like pandemonium.

A storm gathering strength in the distance.

I was doing my best to remove myself from the situation and put some distance between me and the disorder.

I stared at the scratches of words.

Incoherent.

Senseless.

And basically the only thing I could hear for the last two weeks.

> *You came out of nowhere.*
> *A trainwreck.*
> *Paradise.*
> *Moved.*
> *Desolate.*
> *Would give it all up.*
> *If it would keep you from falling apart.*

Another shriek of laughter echoed from outside right before there was a huge splash of water as someone cannonballed into the pool, voice shouting, "Watch this!"

Penny.

That one was Penny.

I knew it. Felt the tenor of her voice reverberating through the floors. Could almost see her timid smile splitting her face as the pool swallowed her up, sent her floating, flooded her with joy.

Everyone was out there. The whole *family* spending their Saturday afternoon out at the pool, loving and living together, the exact way Mia had explained them to be five days ago.

Which was precisely the reason I was hiding out in the guest house this afternoon.

Quietly strumming at my guitar while not so quietly counting down the days until I could get the hell out of here. This sentence had become more than I could bear. More than I could handle.

The awareness I had every time I got in their space.

Swore I could feel hot blades being dragged across my flesh every time Mia sent one of her earth-shattering smiles my way. Every time she tried to act casual and like there wasn't this burning thing between us.

A fireball.

A lightning storm.

Flashes of light. So bright, they were blinding.

I curled my left hand around the neck of the guitar, tucking it close to me, and I strummed a few chords, lightly humming under my breath. I kept both low enough that no one could hear me.

Lyrics began to flow with the melody I was weaving. Words I couldn't seem to evict from my mind.

Moved.
Desolate.
Would give it all up.
If it would keep you from coming apart.
Are you falling?
Are you flying?
Tell me baby,
Is it worth dying,
For everything you've been living for?

My heart raced harder as the chorus came to life, pulse running wild as the key lifted and rose and dove toward the ground.

Hope and grief.

Belief and despair.

My spirit shuddered.

I had to wonder if you couldn't have one without the other.

A fierce pounding started up at the door.

Huffing out a breath, I flipped the notebook closed, set my guitar on the couch, and climbed onto my feet.

I scraped the hair back that had fallen in my face, my mind still running somewhere a million miles away, somewhere in the heavens, riding with the stars, and still right there with that girl who was outside.

Exactly where I wasn't supposed to be.

Warily, I turned the lock and pulled the door open an inch. Just enough to peer into the spray of the late afternoon sunlight that tried to flood into the guest house.

Brendon was there, smirking his little smirk, black eyes patting me down through the tiny crack in the door. Like the barrier between us might as well not be there.

He lifted his chin. "'sup?"

Kid was nothing but preteen swagger, wearing swim trunks low on his hips, outright confidence in his body, all while being about as scrawny and gangly as a stick figure.

I held the chuckle rolling around in my chest. "Not much, man. Just hanging out. Relaxing. What's up with you?"

"Swimming."

"I see that."

He was drenched, hair dripping, kid making a 10-foot deep puddle in front of my door.

Maybe if I was lucky enough, I could drown in it.

"So?" he prodded.

"So what?" I asked, leaning against the doorjamb and peering out.

"Are you comin' or what?"

"And where is it I'm supposed to be going?"

Huffing, he rolled his eyes like I was dense. "Um . . . outside . . . with the rest of us? Or are you going to be the loser who stays inside all day, afraid of a little sun?"

Wow.

"Loser, huh? Are you actually trying to offend me or is this some kind of messed up guilt trip?"

He lifted his hands out to the sides. "Guilt trip, obviously." His gaze narrowed. "Is it working?"

"Barely."

"So what's it going to take?" he asked. "We're about to have a dive off. Figured you'd want to be in for the title. Winner gets five bucks."

Rough laughter rumbled out. "Sorry to disappoint, but I'm not much of a swimmer, Brendon. Besides, it's hot as balls out there."

"My balls are just fine. You scared, Leif?" He narrowed his

eyes. Challenge thrown.

Scared?

Absolutely.

But he definitely didn't need to know that.

"Nope. Just . . . not my thing."

"Food your thing? Because Momma Blue is bringing out her famous lasagna in about five minutes. Missing out on that? Now that right there is just a bad judgment call. Ignorance. Stupidity. Whatever you want to call it. One thing for sure, you don't want to be lumped into that category, do you? That would just be embarrassing."

Good God, this kid was a blood hound.

Apparently, he wasn't going to stop until mine was spilled out onto the floor. No doubt, he'd sniffed out the fact my stomach was currently prowling up and down my spine.

He cracked a grin. "No one can resist Momma Blue's lasagna. Besides, saying you don't want any would be rude. Even I know that."

"You're worse than your dad with the guilt trips, you know."

He lifted both hands with a smile. "Hey, I already told you that's what this was."

"And who sent you on this little mission?"

This was where he hesitated, warring, like he owed a loyalty and didn't want to give anything away. He took a long look over his shoulder at Penny who was sitting on the pool steps with her feet in the water, peeking over at us with all that quiet timidness.

Too knowing.

Too wise.

Emotion clamored and clawed, trying to get free.

I attempted to shove it down.

Brendon looked back at me. "Penny is super shy, but she doesn't like it that you're in here by yourself. And it doesn't make much sense to me, either, for you to be in here when you could be out here with all of us. I mean, seriously, we are pretty much the most awesome people you are ever gonna meet. Life doesn't get better than this. Like . . . single best day of your life," he drew out. "Do you really wanna miss out on that? Get your butt out here, drummer dude."

I glanced around him at the slip of land that I could make out. Kallie was standing about ten feet behind Brendon and off to the left side, carefully peering my way, shifting her weight from foot to foot. Like she'd been sent on the mission, too, but had thought better of the danger of it and was hovering on the periphery.

Just out of reach of the lion's den.

"Come on, Leif. Suck it up. I could hear you playing in there, and whatever it was, it kinda sucked." The razzing played all over Brendon's mouth. "Might as well give it up for the day."

He quirked a brow.

Little punk.

I laughed in disbelief.

Was I really being handled by a twelve-year-old?

He crossed his arms over his chest.

Clearly.

"Fine. Let me put on some shoes."

Turning on my heel, I started back for the bedroom.

"How about some swim trunks while you're at it?" he hollered from behind me.

I threw up a hand of dismissal. Kid was lucky I didn't give him the finger.

He might be a bulldog. But he was five-foot nothing and sure as shit not badgering me into that.

nineteen

Mia

I was leaned over loading the dishwasher when I froze. Every nerve ending in my body alight.

Hypersensitive.

The man had become my mayhem.

A chaos that sprang into the hot, hot air.

I barely peeked back at the doorway where he came in carrying a stack of dirty dishes from the lasagna we'd just had for dinner. "Need some help?"

He approached. Caution in every step.

I just wished I had a little bit of that caution for myself.

Nope.

The only thing I could sense was the need that sprouted like invasive roots. Unnatural and rampant and overgrowing everything.

I swallowed hard as I took him in.

The man wore jeans when it was almost a hundred out. Black ones this time that were ripped at the knees, another one of those tees stretched so thin across the rippling strength of his chest that the threads threatened to bust.

Desire streaked.

Torrid and red-hot.

"You can just set them on the counter. I'm almost finished here."

He came closer. "I can help, Mia. According to Brendon, I don't have anything better to do." He attempted a joke that stalled out in the tension in the air.

Every cell in my body shivered.

I tried to pretend as if he didn't affect me at all.

That I wasn't tangled up in a knot of this man.

My nights had become filled with thoughts and dreams of him. What it would be like to really be touched by him. To be loved by him.

"I haven't been doing a whole lot myself, if I'm being honest."

He edged up beside me, barely knocking into my shoulder with his, a coy smile on his mouth. "I always want your honest."

The air rushed from my lungs, and I let go of a choppy laugh as I scrubbed down a pot, slanting a look at the man who was undoing everything. "I don't think I believe you. It seems to me you like hiding from the truth."

He chuckled, and he was shoving his hands into the sudsy water, rinsing the plates that he'd carried in. "Easier that way, isn't it?"

My head shook. "Easier? Maybe. Better? No."

"And what truth am I hiding from?" He seemed reluctant to ask it.

I knocked him back with my shoulder. "That you're a good guy."

His laughter was scraping. "You think because I'm doing a few dishes it makes me a good guy?"

"I think I have good intuition." I fought for easiness, and this time I knocked him with my hip. "Just like my son."

Could see the smile playing around his sexy mouth. God, it was getting harder and harder not to just . . . kiss him.

He shifted a fraction, the man so close to me his nose nearly brushed my cheek. Tingles flashed. "Bet my intuition is better, Angel, and I don't think you could handle what I would do to you."

"Yo!"

The dish I was holding slipped out of my hand and clanked into the sink when Brendon's shout batted from behind.

"We're all going to the park. Game time, baby. I'm about to show you all who's really a badass."

Leif shifted around, a smirk pulling to those lips, the man playing off casual way too easily when my heart was thundering out of my chest. "You better not let your parents hear you talking like that," Leif told him.

Penny popped her head in. "Mom, we want to go to the park! Come on!"

I glanced at Leif.

Timid but sure. "You should come," I said.

He cringed but those eyes were doing that tender thing again. "Not sure that's a good idea."

Maybe I was a fool, but I was beginning to think he was a very, very good idea.

Worth the risk.

Worth the pain.

Because he was so much more than the surface he showed. The best parts of him begging to be exposed. Pared away and revealed.

I grabbed a hand towel and dried my hands, cutting him a glance as I started for the kids.

A clear invitation.

"Yes, let's do it!" Brendon pumped a fist in the air when I headed their way, Penny smiling soft, my girl so sweet. I returned one to her, all my pride and love and affection, and I followed the two of them back out into the fading day.

My attention moved to my son who was still floating in the pool, his Auntie Tamar and Shea watching over him, the child smiling one of his adorable smiles, splashing like crazy as Adia came gliding through the water toward him riding on her battery-powered unicorn.

Laughing maniacally, she pushed the button that made a thin stream of water shoot out of the horn, hitting her cousin square in the face.

"You gots unicorned, Greyson," she sang as she rounded him like she was a barrel racer, leaning into the turn like she was trying to gain momentum.

"I get you! I get you!" he sang in return, kicking his feet as fast as he could under the water, spluttering and squeezing his eyes shut against the assault.

I guessed maybe he was getting some of his own medicine.

"All right, you two, out you go! Let's take this party to the park," Tamar said as she stood on the top step and helped Greyson out of his float.

"Yo, drummer dude. Let's roll," Brendon hollered from about five feet in front of me.

"Comin'." The low rumble caught up to me from behind, the sound of it skittering across my skin. My heart stalled out. My pulse completely missing for about five beats.

Anxious anticipation.

Dreaded desperation.

Because I'd felt it.

A shift.

As if maybe he couldn't go on denying this any more than I could.

My mouth was still tingling with the remnants of his kiss that I was afraid was never going to fade or evaporate. Fingers twitching with the need to touch.

"I call Leif," Brendon shouted.

"What?!" Ash demanded. "How could you, Brendon? And here I thought I was your favorite."

I bit back a laugh.

Boys.

Lyrik held open the gate as our entire family filed through and climbed down the back steps that led onto the sidewalk. We made

a right toward the main road that cut through the neighborhood.

All of Sunder were in the front.

Lyrik carried Adia, Ash carried Colton, and Austin carried Sadie, nothing but a train of hot daddies and their babies. If it were a busy road, I was pretty sure we would have been stopping traffic.

Connor raced up ahead with Brendon.

Willow, Shea, Tamar, Edie, and I had gathered in a small group, all of us chatting, Greyson spouting his gibberish as he shouted at the rest of the kids who raced ahead. "Go, Momma, go. *Wet's* get 'em."

"But we can't leave our Penny-Pie behind can we?" I told him, planting a kiss on his cheek.

Penny and Kallie had their arms linked at the elbows and their heads pressed together about ten feet behind us, confiding more of their secrets.

Sweet, sweet dreams.

Innocent hopes and grateful tomorrows.

Leif took up the rear, trailing the girls by about ten feet. Barely peeking at me. But it didn't matter—I could feel him, anyway.

"Hurry up, slow pokes," Brendon shouted from under the cover of the trees that extended over the sidewalk.

At the intersection, we paused to check that it was clear, and Shea shouted at the girls, "Be careful crossin'."

Kallie moaned. "Mom, we're eleven. Stop being so embarrassing."

I held the laughter that wanted to get loose.

When I made it to the other side, my gaze slipped back to Leif, his attention locked on the ground, agitation in his stride, like he thought it was his duty to question his reasoning for coming with us.

Those walls there, but shaky.

The man an outsider.

A beautiful, terrifying refugee who I hoped one day would find his home.

His place.

The same way as I was looking for mine.

My insides curled, nothing but foolishness when I thought I

wished that place could be me.

Kallie suddenly started to run toward us, bubbling with excitement.

Clearly, she and Penny had been hatching a plan. "Hey, Momma, is it okay if Penny comes to spend the night tonight after we get finished at the park? We want to make a fort in the back and sleep out under the stars."

Penny slowed her stride as she crossed the street. My sweet girl always got shy when the attention turned to her. Not wanting to be standing there or in the way if Shea said no.

In the distance, thunder rolled.

Just the quiet intonation of a building storm.

Summer getting ready to show off its bold, bold beauty.

Then all the peace in my heart dropped to the ground when I heard the sudden roar of an engine. An engine that came from out of nowhere.

From right up the street.

Straight from hell.

I didn't know.

I just knew I was too far away.

Too far.

Dread streaked down my spine.

Tires squealed as an accelerator was floored.

My heart stopped working and my knees went weak.

"Penny!" I screamed.

Penny's eyes went round as her head snapped to the right in shock. Terror took to her expression, my baby girl frozen in the middle of the crosswalk.

Like her feet were glued to the spot.

Horror clutched my soul in a bloody fist, knowing there was no chance I could get to her in time. Knowing there was no way for her to get out of the way.

"Penny!" I was still screaming. The plea echoing in my ears.

The car screamed. Almost as loud as me.

Her tiny body suddenly lurched forward.

Flailing.

Arms and legs and black, black hair.

Toppling and tumbling as the blur of a car raced through the small intersection, skidding and swerving.

Not slowing for the stop sign but speeding up as it blew through.

"No! Oh my God, Penny, no!"

I clutched Greyson tighter to my chest, my hand on the back of his head like I could shield him from witnessing this. Like I could shield myself.

Screams and shouts rolled. A clatter of feet that raced and rushed.

Lyrik flew passed, the rest of the guys on his tail. "Fuck. Oh God. Penny."

But all I could see was the pile on the ground.

My mind racing, blurred, trying to make sense of the scene.

My baby girl in a ball.

Curled against him.

The man steel where he was wrapped around her.

A shield.

A destructive force.

Everything finally gave, and I dropped to my knees.

Leif

*S*creams pierced my brain.

Spikes of agony.

Blades of desperation.

My pulse roared, deafening, the world spinning and spinning and spinning. Tipped on its axis. Falling into an endless abyss.

Adrenaline blurred the edges of my sight. Burned through my veins. Sloshing and destroying and stoking the rage.

Everything was a void. A black hole. All except for one singular focus.

The girl.

The little girl with the black hair who was balled against my chest. My arms steel bands around her, my body a fortress willing to take the blow to protect the treasure that was inside.

Covering her whole.

Pain splintered through my side, but I just curled myself tighter around her as the horror spread over us. The dust and debris and terror.

"Fuck. Oh God. Penny." Lyrik's voice cut through the dense, ominous air, but the only thing I could really hear were the screams that Mia had released.

Lyrik tried to pry my arm away.

I hung on tighter, clutching her in my hold, my mouth murmuring into the wisps of her hair that smelled like chlorine and sun and exhaust. "Are you hurt? Penny, are you hurt? Can you hear me?"

The fragile body tucked against me began to shake.

Vibrating.

Shivering.

Trembling.

Alive.

Relief tore through me with the force of a volcanic eruption, an explosion that I was certain would leave the deepest crater in the middle of me. Blowing something open that shouldn't have been released.

"Penny," I muttered, slowly shifting so all my weight wasn't on her while keeping her still to make sure I didn't injure her more. "Penny. Tell me if you're injured. Where it hurts. Please."

A sob ripped from her, a reverberation that ricocheted through my chest, her shaking body turning into an all-out earthquake. Her fingers curled into my shirt. Desperation as she cried out.

The sticky heat of blood seeped into my jeans.

Fear clamored. Hatred rushed.

"It's okay, Penny. I've got you. I've got you."

I eased onto my butt, still clinging to her, refusing to let her move a bone or a muscle or a cell. Arms aching with the need to keep her whole.

Real and intact.

Lyrik hovered over us, freaking the fuck out, a feeling I totally respected and got. "Penny. Are you okay? Tell me if you're hurt? Oh, God, oh God." He shot back upright. "Someone call an ambulance," he shouted, his roar of agony banging through the air.

Could feel the disordered energy whipping around us. Whirring and twisting and gaining speed.

But the only call I could feel was the woman.

The angel in the attic. I hugged her child, unable to let go even though I knew I had to.

That she wasn't mine.

That she never could be.

My face lifted just a fraction, just enough so that my gaze could crawl through the dust and debris to the woman who was on her hands and knees. Tamar had taken Greyson from her, trying to calm down the toddler who was wailing.

Or maybe it was the sound of his mother coming apart.

Torment clutched my spirit, my arms locked around Penny as I met the affliction in Mia's eyes. An affliction I knew too well. One that I could understand in a way that I wanted to scrape from my consciousness.

Mia crawled toward us, like she no longer had the capacity to stand, her spirit rushing out ahead of her.

Slamming me.

Soul first.

She was sobbing out loud by the time she made it to us, the woman a hurricane, a tornado that blew and screamed and howled. Her fingers searched, digging through the shield that I had made, her voice a desperate chant.

"Penny. Penny. Penny."

The little girl cried more, an outburst of fear at the sound of her mother's voice.

"Penny, oh my God, my baby girl. Penny." Mia crawled the rest of the way into the well of my lap, wrapping her arms around Penny just as tight. She buried her face in my arm, tears soaking my skin. "Penny."

A siren screamed from where it had pulled out from the station just a quarter of a mile up the street.

Took only a minute or two before the ground vibrated with the pound of heavy footsteps. Voices warbled as they broke through the atmosphere.

The child was pried from my arms, and I fumbled back, no longer able to breathe.

I sat in the middle of the street.

Knocked on my ass.

Watching the frantic scene.

Praying I hadn't been too late.

Please, God, don't let me have been too late.

I couldn't handle it this time. Not if I failed again.

Muttered, distorted voices filtered from the room and out into the darkened hall. Tufts of thready, yellowed light seeped out through the crack in the door, casting shadows onto the wall of glass behind me.

Night pressed in, as fierce as the storm that built overhead.

Foreboding clouds rumbled where they slowly crept over the house. Branches on the trees whipping like mad.

Angry. Crying their outrage.

I scrubbed my palms over my face, praying it would stand the chance to break up the disorder.

Tearing me to shreds.

Cutting me to pieces.

Tatters getting caught up in the destructive gusts of wind.

Memories too close and too clear and coming at me too fast.

"I will never let anyone hurt you. Do you understand? I will die first."

"Please, let's just . . . go. Get away from here."

I set both hands on her cheeks. "Soon, Maddie, soon."

Sickness clawed across my flesh, sprouting from the pebbles of pavement that had embedded in my skin.

Soft cries bled through the cracks of the door. Fear patent. Terror real.

Penny had just been released from the emergency room with no real injuries other than a few scrapes and bruises.

It was close.

Too fucking close.

I tried to suffocate the rage that blistered.

The monster freed.

I pulled my phone out of my pocket when it finally buzzed back, anxiety mauling me while I'd waited for Braxton to get back to me after I'd texted him an hour before.

Braxton: You sure you were singled out?

I huffed out the frustration, tapped a response.

Me: No. Not one-hundred-percent. But I think the chances are pretty damned likely, don't you?

Braxton: But why the kid? She doesn't have a thing to do with you. Doesn't add, man. Think it might've been random.

Fury raced. Didn't mean to be pissed at him, but this wasn't the time to sit back and see how things played out. My fingers were shaking with hatred as I responded.

Me: And you think these bastards would think twice about a kid who got in the way?

Braxton: Fuck man. I know. I know. I'm sorry.

Braxton: I pressed Ridge like I told you I would. He didn't know much. Only thing we got is your mom's been asking around again.

Anger squeezed my ribs with so much force I didn't know how I didn't implode.

Me: And?

Braxton: Said she's worried.

She was worried? That was fucking priceless.

Me: Worried they didn't finish the job the first time around?

Braxton: Word is, she and Keeton want to talk.

Me: You don't buy that bullshit, do you?

Braxton: Nope. Not gonna lie, don't trust any of it. You know I'm with you, man.

Me: Know it was him, Brax. It's time to prove it.

Or just fucking end it. Proof or not.

Me: Find out who knows I'm here. Turn up the pressure.

Braxton: On it. Will let you know as soon as I find out anything. Be safe.

My spine went rigid when the door suddenly flung open.

Lyrik jerked back the second he found me loitering outside the door to their suite.

The jagged rock in my throat wobbled, shards cutting into my skin.

I met his eye. "How is she?"

Lyrik sighed, looking down as he slanted his fingers through his black hair. He warred before he finally looked back up at me. "Terrified. Okay, but terrified. A little road rash, but I'm thinking her colliding with the road was a whole ton better than her getting hit by that car."

I gave him an uneven nod, my ribs getting battered by the clanging in my chest. "I should have—"

Barking laughter cut me off, low and cruel. "You should have what? Turned an eye?" He took a step forward. "Looked away? Or maybe just stood there and watched it go down?"

My head barely shook. "I . . ." I exhaled a sharp breath, my nostrils flaring. "That car . . . it swerved to hit her, not miss her."

Could feel the build of violence. The thirst for retribution becoming unbearable.

Rage erasing logic.

"I shouldn't have come here." At least I had that bit of sense remaining.

Lyrik scoffed. "You think this was somehow your fault? You think I'm not sick to my fucking stomach because I wasn't there? That I was too far ahead and out of reach of being there for my niece? You think I'm not questioning every goddamn misstep leading up to what happened tonight?"

He got so close he was nearly spitting the words in my face. "No matter if that was an accident or some bastard did that on purpose, which if he did, I promise you, he is going to pay. But either way, none of those things change the fact that *you* were there. Fact that you dove in front of a car to save a child you don't owe anything to. Fact that you saved Penny's life."

The last two words broke in his throat. Man suppressing a sob.

Grief wrenched through my being. I gritted my teeth, tried to keep my shit together. "Yeah, and what if it was me who put her in danger in the first place?"

Lyrik scraped the back of his hand over his mouth like he was trying to get rid of a bad, bitter taste, glancing away before he pegged me with a dark glare. "And what if someone is after Mia, man? After my *sister*? What if they followed her here?"

I blinked, spirit jolting with the rejection.

"What are you saying? Did something else happen?" I demanded, voice low, a barely controlled growl.

Aggression hardened his jaw. "Security confirmed it this evening. It wasn't some kids running the backyard to take a dip in the pool like I'd hoped. Someone tried to enter a code into the back door. I think they're watching. *Why* is what's fucking killing me. How can I stop it when I don't know what they want?"

Rage blistered. Searing my flesh. Inside and out. Blood molten.

He almost laughed, his head bobbing with the indictment. "That right there . . . that is why you *should* have come here. Need

someone else on her side, Leif. Need someone else here, looking out for her. Looking out for those kids."

Fury raced. "I don't—"

"Whatever you're going to say, *don't*. Just fucking stay. Don't know what's going on between the two of you, but whatever it is? Just fucking stay." Helplessly, he glanced over his shoulder at the door that remained open an inch. "She needs you, and I'm pretty sure I can't fix what she's missing."

"She doesn't need me."

Mia's soft voice floated out, quiet murmurings of reassurance and hope, the tiny cries of her daughter still seeping through.

Lyrik turned back to look at me, eyes pinning me to the spot. "Penny asked for you, Leif. What you do with that is up to you."

Without saying anything else, he turned and strode down the long hallway, disappearing at the end where the south-wing met the main house. I watched until he was gone, and I warily turned back to the muted movements that echoed from within.

Terrified of what those sounds were coming to mean.

Drawn to them all the same.

Unable to stop myself, I quietly knocked at the wood and poked my head through the door. "It's Leif."

Mia's strained voice called, "Come in."

I shuffled across the floor, my heart a boulder of dread as I eased up to the bedroom.

A muted glow was cast on the room by a lamp on a nightstand.

The mood both burdened and relieved.

At the side of the bed that ran along the right wall, Mia was on her knees. When she heard the creak of my footsteps, her attention swiveled to me.

Those sable eyes filled with too many things. Things I couldn't handle. Things I couldn't bear.

Guilt ripped through the center of me. But it didn't matter if my duty was screaming at me to turn my ass around and walk away, I inched forward, glancing at the crib on the opposite wall where Greyson was fast asleep, facedown with his butt in the air, wearing just a diaper.

Clinging to that tattered teddy bear he always dragged

everywhere.

Blowing out a sigh, I steeled myself as I let my attention drift back to them.

Penny's black hair was shiny and wet, the child freshly bathed like it could soak away the trauma of the day, strands spread out behind her on her pillow.

Her eyes were puffy and red, salty tears coating her cheeks.

Mia had showered, too, and she'd changed into a thin cotton nightgown. My teeth gritted, and I forced myself to look away, to stop the disgusting direction my thoughts went when this woman had nearly lost her child.

I was sick.

Twisted.

The devil.

And they were both looking at me like I could be their savior.

I roughed an agitated hand through my hair, hanging back by the door. "Hey, Penny. How are you feeling?"

Penny choked over a sob, the dampness in her eyes filling fast, deep, deep pools of onyx that were spilling over. "I'm so sorry, Leif. I didn't mean to."

A heavy exhale gushed out of my lungs, and I took a surging step forward before I could stop myself. "You don't have anything to be sorry for."

"I-I-I . . . I should have looked. It was my fault, and I wasn't paying attention because I just wanted to have a sleepover at Kallie's house. I . . . I put you in danger."

Her mother brushed her fingers through her daughter's hair, shushing her gently. A quiet sound of embrace and support.

A torrent of love that filled the room.

I beat back the panic, the feeling slithering over me, demons screaming in my ear.

"No," I managed to tell her through a shaking voice. "You couldn't have anticipated that, Penny. You didn't do anything wrong."

Her gaze moved over me, her bottom lip trembling. "You're hurt."

Damn it.

I should have taken the time to change but I couldn't force myself away long enough to do it. "It's nothing. Just a little roadrash." I attempted the joke, but it completely fell flat.

Mia cringed, like she couldn't stand it either, although she remained silent.

Like she was just . . . waiting on me. Trusting me to be there when she didn't have the first clue that would be her greatest mistake.

My attention jumped around, like I could find a safer focal point than looking at the sight of them.

The definition of beauty.

Goodness and light. Purity and faith.

My gaze landed on another one of those bears like Greyson had, this one a patchwork disaster of pinks that lay on the edge of her bed. I couldn't help it—a smile tugged at the corner of my mouth.

"What's that?" I asked her, desperately needing to change the subject before I went out of my mind.

Before I said or did something I couldn't take back.

Because I wanted it . . . I wanted this feeling so badly I thought I might die without it. This comfort that spun through the room like a cold winter's dream, blanketed and protected. Something safe and sacred. Something right.

Something that was actually worth living for.

But that was impossible. Only thing I would bring was destruction. My due a burden.

She snatched the ratty bear and held it to her chest, rocking just a little like touching it soothed some of the madness.

"Make it if you want it to matter," she whispered.

I was moving forward when I didn't have the right, too compelled to remain in the shadows when I ached to stand in the light.

Too bad the light only exposed the demons.

Called them out of hiding.

But maybe it was time they saw exactly who I was.

"Make it if you want it to matter?" I rumbled, repeating the sentiment like a question. A squeak climbed from Mia, and I realized she was holding back a sob.

That her entire being convulsed like she'd just been struck from out of nowhere.

Whiplash.

"My mommy made it," she whispered, peeking at her mother who gave up the fight on the tears, not that they'd been a stranger to her today. Her face blotched and red and scarred with the fear of losing what was most important.

"She did, did she?" The words were tight. Gravel.

Penny nodded emphatically against her pillow before she pushed up to sitting. "See."

She held it out.

Like she was beckoning me forward.

Bringing me to my knees.

I was there, on the carpet, kneeling down close to her.

I didn't dare reach out and touch it, just let my fingertips flutter in the air like I could feel the soft, worn fabric, the inconsistent patterns of pinks. Blush and rose. Strawberry and hot pink. The lanky bear was threaded together by a thick yarn, the lines almost purposefully haphazard.

"Your brother has one almost the same, except it's blue," I mused.

She nodded again, tears dry for the first time, like for a moment she'd been distracted from what might have been. "Yeah." She gazed down at it before looking back at me with eyes that were so much like her mother's. "Every new baby in our family gets one. It represents new life . . . there is one piece for all the people who make up the family. And this?"

She dragged her finger along one of the jagged seams of yarn.

"It represents the love that binds them all together, as imperfect as it might be."

She glanced at her mother for approval. Like she was wondering if she got the story right.

My stomach twisted. Jaw clenching tight.

"Look, Leif," she murmured with soft, childlike awe.

God, I needed to make an excuse and bolt.

But I inched forward, eyes following her small finger that ran over the material. "This is my grandma, and this one is for my grandpa. They were the ones who were there for my mom when she had me."

She was looking at her mother with those astute eyes again. Like she got it. Like she understood the sacrifice they all had made.

She fluttered her fingers over another patch of fabric. "This is my uncle Lyrik. And these over here are my mom's aunt and uncle."

She hesitated before she touched a spot where the fabric had frayed and partially come loose. "This one is my daddy."

Did it make me a fucking psycho that I wanted to jump to my feet and rant and rave and claim? Jealousy boiling my blood into venom and rage?

Why, yes.

Yes, it did.

My teeth grated. "It's beautiful, Penny. Every single piece."

She nodded more. "And one day, when I have a baby, I will make him or her one of these, just like my mommy did for me and my brother, just like my grandma did for her and my uncle."

"Because you make it if you want it to matter."

She nodded tight, and those knowing eyes lifted, filled with their innocence and wisdom, tangling with mine. "I might get to do that one day because of you, Leif."

Her mother whimpered.

I wanted to die.

"No, Penny."

Her lips pursed. "I thought . . . I thought I died already, Leif, because nothing hurt, and then I was so scared, and then I felt so safe when I realized it was you."

"Penny." Wanted to beg her to stop.

To spare me this grief.

To stop this reminder.

"I just wanted to say thank you. For being brave."

My eyes squeezed closed like it could stop the assault.

The images and the sorrow and the unending grief.

Like the day had become too much, Penny hiccupped a sigh and then yawned, the child flopping to her pillow in sheer exhaustion.

For a moment, I just sat there, watching the lines on her face fall into peace.

My pulse jumped when her lips moved. "Do you sing songs, drummer dude?"

I almost laughed at the nickname Brendon had given me, it sounding so strange coming from her tongue. "Yeah, Penny, I do. It's part of my job."

She snuggled deeper under her covers, her voice drifting like her own melody. "Good. Sing me a song."

A war went down inside me. A violent battle of what I'd done and what was to come.

I glanced at her mother who watched on with quiet belief.

Fuck.

What was the matter with me?

It was just a song.

I searched inside myself to find something that was fitting. Clearly none of mine would do.

I should have picked a random Carolina George song that Richard or Emily had penned. Something innocuous that meant nothing but I knew the words.

But I remembered . . . remembered the voice that had once sung to me.

The lyrics so contrary to what I knew.

But I thought maybe they had been meant for a child exactly like this.

Leaning forward, I took in a steeling breath and quietly began to rasp the words in a way I was quite sure they'd never been sung. A country ballad meant for a mother to her child.

I Hope You Dance by Lee Ann Womack.

The lyrics were low as I grated them from my tongue.

But I saw it—the way the song wrapped her in comfort.

A prayer that I meant.

A prayer that cut me apart.

And as I watched her drift to sleep from the sound of my voice, as I felt Mia's spirit twining with mine, I felt something inside me break away. Something burst and come flooding out.

Darkness.
Joy.
Grief.
Hope.
If only I were worthy to give them that.

twenty-one

Mia

*E*ven though he was singing painfully low, his voice still flooded the room. The words gruff and hard and bleeding melancholy.

The song scraped from his throat with pain and grief.

The most brutal agony.

Lost faith and misguided intentions.

It seemed impossible his voice could come out sounding that way, and still the tenor of it be riddled with the greatest amount of hope. As if faith had found holes in the bricks of his fortress and worked its way in.

What it'd become was the most shocking kind of beauty. Something that spun both my spirit and relaxed my strain.

My body slowly swayed.

Drawn into the sound.

A deadly lullaby because before you even knew what had

happened, you were enraptured.

Snared.

Hypnotized into believing that everything was going to be just fine.

Just like he'd done to my sweet, sweet girl. Exactly the way I wanted her to be. Soothed into a peaceful sleep where all the horrors of the day would be erased. Scrubbed from her memory and healed from her body.

We'd been lucky.

So very lucky that there was no way I could just consign it to chance.

Her wounds had been minor, but I knew what was left on her heart and mind was the sort of trauma that would leave a scar.

My gaze drifted to her, my heart in a clutch of agony and gratefulness.

I would never forget that moment—that single, bated second when I thought I'd lost her. That my child had been ripped away. Her life snuffed a century too soon.

Tremors rolled, and my stare traveled, drifting to the man whose voice had shifted to barely audible. Ragged, frayed words that whispered into her ears and filled her with calm. It was like he was offering everything he had to give, giving it away, any solace in his soul transferred to her.

Because there was no missing the outright misery that dented every line in his gorgeous face.

Eyes squeezed shut and his chest tremoring with the remnants of the song.

The tail-end of it drifted away as he begged for her to live with all she had.

To chase joy.

To always, always dance.

The lump in my throat grew to a fist, and I struggled to breathe around it, to clear the roughness when those eyes finally flickered over to meet with mine. "Did you ever want to be a dad?"

I shouldn't have asked it. I was breaking about every rule that had ever been made.

Jumping right over respectful lines and clear-cut boundaries.

But this? This wasn't a question for me. Wasn't loaded because I was a single mother and wanted to somehow fit with him.

It was found in the torture that covered him in shadows.

The expression that took hold of his face made me want to weep. His words hit the air like the slice of a knife. "Once, Mia. Once I did. But guys like me? We aren't made for the joys of this world. We aren't destined for the good things. We are bred for destruction."

My head shook in disaccord, unable to accept what he said. "I see your goodness, Leif Godwin. I see it shining out through all the darkness. I know it's there."

He laughed a gruff sound. "You're just seeing what you want to see."

My teeth clamped down on my bottom lip, my hand shaking like mad when I reached out and brushed back the longer pieces of hair from his forehead. "I see someone who is brave. I see someone who is fearless. I see someone who *saved my daughter.*"

A tremor raked through him at that, and I let my fingertips wander, gliding down the strong angle of his cheek. The man so beautiful he was making it hard to focus on what I needed to say without getting distracted by what I wanted. "But I also see someone who is hurting."

He snatched me by the wrist.

I gasped.

"Pain is just a reminder of your sins." His confession was nothing but a growl.

I searched his face.

"Of what you've done," he rumbled.

My chest quivered at the rake of his harsh words. Blow after blow.

"Of what is to come."

"And what is it that is to come? What are you waiting for, Leif?"

"Something I would never implicate you in." His face pinched in misery. "I . . . I should go."

I gave him a tight nod, not even surprised by the rejection because I could physically feel his pain.

He pushed to his feet. He hesitated as he stared down at my daughter. Everything ached when he reached out and brushed his fingertips through her hair, sheer affection on his face.

His jeans ripped and stained with his blood. Shredded from his surrender.

This man who would have died for my daughter.

He walked out the door without looking back.

That energy shivered and shook and cried out. Demanding to be heard.

My attention moved to Penny. My child fast asleep.

Safe.

Warm.

Loved.

We'd been through so much in our lives, but never once had I been so terrified as this. Faced with losing the one thing worth living for.

And Leif, he had returned that to me. Given us another chance.

He had sparked something in me from the second he'd crashed into my world.

Fire and ice.

I'd thought he'd been purposed, but never had I imagined he could have been purposed for this.

For something greater than I'd prepared myself for.

And I recognized it, so distinctly.

His pain.

The way he viewed himself, as if he'd been condemned to live *without*.

Alone.

Destitute.

As if he believed he truly didn't deserve or have the right.

I was on my feet before I knew they were under me, the weakness I'd been feeling all day swept away by the desperation to touch.

To feel him alive under me, too.

For him to understand the man I saw in him.

To return a little of the hope he'd restored in me.

I raced out of the suite and down the hall toward the massive bonus room, the one that opened to the wall of windows and overlooked the pool and yard.

The storm bared down. Gusts of wind that lashed through the trees. Sent them whipping and shivering and howling beneath the moon that burned through a thin break in the clouds.

The man was a shadow beneath, his shoulders hitched high as he strode across the yard toward his little home.

If he even had one.

The man lost.

A wanderer who raged as he searched through the earth for where he fit.

I wanted to carve out a place for him. Show him what it was like to belong. To be treasured and loved, the way he showed without asking for a thing in return.

I burst through the door he had exited, pummeled by a squall of wind.

A fierce fury that blasted through the air.

"What if I don't want you to go?" I shouted above it. "What if I want you to stay, right here, with me?"

In the distance, he froze, as if he had been impaled by the plea. Staked to the spot.

Slowly, he turned. Rain began to pelt from the sky.

"I keep telling you that you don't want me. That you don't have the first clue what you're asking for."

Brown eyes flashed beneath a streak of lightning. The man momentarily lit in a bright flash of light.

Afire.

Aflame.

Before he returned to shadows. To the darkness.

"You're wrong, Leif. I want you. I want all of you. I want your hurt and your fears and your sorrows. I want your beauty and your songs and your mind. You're wrong when you say it's my beauty reflected back at me when I look at you. Not when you're the epitome of it. I feel it, Leif. I see it."

His face pinched in pain. "I don't want to hurt you."

My hands clenched. "I know that. Why do you think I'm standing here?"

"I can't give you what you deserve, Mia."

"Then give me what I want."

A sound left him that was somewhere between a groan and a roar, the rain beginning to pound as he hovered and hesitated and tried to resist.

I saw the second he snapped.

The moment I whispered, "Please."

He crossed the space like some kind of warring avenger, on his way to plunder and annihilate.

To steal.

What he couldn't know was what he was steadily stealing was my heart.

By the time he got to me his hair was soaked, rivulets of water twisting down the hard contours of his striking, glorious face. His jaw set in stone and his body a rigid, powerful force.

Clothes drenched.

We collided in a flash of hands and tongues and nipping teeth.

He gripped me by the hips and jerked me to his hard, hard body as his mouth slanted over mine.

The kiss frantic.

Possessive.

A growl climbed his throat and spilled into mine as our tongues twisted and fought, those hands tugging me closer, against all his heat.

Flames leapt.

Climbed for the sky.

One touch, and I was melting.

Liquid silver in his hands.

"Leif." I clamored to get him closer, my fingers slipping through the slick strands of his brown hair.

He groaned and pushed me up hard against the door, controlling the mind-bending kiss.

I knew after this, I was never going to be the same.

"Fuck, Mia. Fuck. What have you done to me? I can't . . . I can't."

I could feel his brow drawing tight, his frantic kiss fueled by guilt, his heart pounding with greed.

"Yes, you can. I want you. I want you. Please let me show you who I see when I look at you." My nails dug into his shoulders, tearing at his shirt.

The thin, short nightdress I was wearing was soaked, sticking to my skin, my aching breasts straining against the material where I pressed myself against his body.

A rumble of need curled up his throat. "I will ruin you." ·

"I want you to," I begged.

I was already there.

My wreckage strewn at his feet.

He hoisted me up, and I wrapped my legs around his waist while he kissed me mad.

Savagely.

Fiercely.

No restraint.

His hands kneaded my bottom and his cock rubbed between my thighs.

I clung to his hair, probably tugging too hard as he entered the code, opened the door, and carried me into the lapping shadows of the massive room.

The storm battered the long bank of windows. When the door closed behind us, it cut the volume to a howling, moaning whisper.

Thunder rolled. A low warning of what was to come.

He carried me all the way across the room, winding between the half-painted pictures that waited on easels. Ones I still couldn't find the inspiration to complete. When he got to the far side, he set me down on top of a sideboard table, keeping my legs wrapped around his waist.

The fabric of our clothing stuck together.

Our hard pants rose into the air.

My heart struggled, leaping around in a desperate bid to meet with his, not sure if I would ever really be able to fully reach him.

Knowing it was okay if I didn't.

That maybe he needed this one singular night as much as I did.

That we needed to share *this*.

He angled back for a breath, those brown-sugar eyes looking at me with terror. As if I could possibly be the one to hurt him.

Like taking me would cost him everything.

As if he wasn't the one who had already scarred me.

Written himself on my spirit and my soul.

A man I could never forget even if he walked out right then.

I needed to show him. Needed him to know.

I kept him in the grips of my gaze as I slipped off the stained wood and slowly sank onto my knees.

A shiver of reservation rocked through him, though his body bowed forward with need.

With lust.

With this energy that filled the space until it was the only thing we could breathe.

With trembling hands, I reached up and slowly undid the buckle of his belt, watching up at him while he watched down on me.

Tension winding.

Flickers and sparks in the space.

The man gravity.

That severity whipped around him, as intense as the storm.

Pulling me into his darkness.

I licked my lips as I got the belt free and tugged at the button of his jeans.

Leif grunted, his big hand coming down, the pad of his thumb sliding across my bottom lip.

Chills streaked. Desire making me shake.

"You don't have anything to prove, Mia. You don't have to do this."

"You think this is obligation? Because I think I owe you something?" I jerked his belt from the loops. "This has been coming since the second I saw you. Since the second you had me pinned to that floor of the attic because I couldn't walk away."

I pulled down his zipper. The sound of it curled into the room.

A promise.

Reprieve.

His stomach tremored under the skin-tight tee, and his jeans stuck to his flesh as I went to pull them down, damp and heavy, just like every aching part of me.

My belly quivered and desire went racing like a stampede.

All reason trampled underfoot.

Breath punching from my lungs when his penis bobbed free.

Hard and long and thick. The head engorged and fat.

His jaw clenched tight, and he traced his thumb up and down the angle of my cheek. "Beauty."

Didn't he get that was what he had become to me?

The gorgeous stranger in the attic.

A dark storm.

A white light.

He watched me as he kicked his shoes off, and I tugged his jeans the rest of the way down. Leif shifted to free the wet fabric from his ankles. My gaze moved directly for the wound up high on his thigh, the skin pitted and torn and scraped.

I leaned in and kissed across the marred flesh.

"Fuck, Mia," Leif grunted in shock, a hand fisting in my hair like he wanted to stop me. I grabbed him by the back of both thighs, letting my lips lightly brush the injury.

"Mia . . . what the fuck do you think you're doing?"

"Adoring you. The person you are. The sacrifice you made." My hands shook harder. "You could have been killed, Leif. I . . ."

I trailed off, unable to finish the statement, knowing it would reveal too much. That he would see he had already gotten to me.

He wasn't even mine and losing him would destroy me.

Those eyes flashed. Desperation and desire.

He tugged at the hold he had in my hair, urging me up onto my feet.

"Angel," he mumbled.

In a flash, I was propped back onto the table, and he was taking me by the knees, spreading me so he could make room for himself. My nightgown bunched at my waist, and he pushed his bare cock to the sheer lace of my panties.

"Fuck. Can't get you off my mind, Mia. Tried, baby, I tried. But I close my eyes, and it's you I see."

I gasped. Moaned. Begged. My hands sought refuge under his shirt, pushing it up as I let my palms run the contoured lines of his abdomen. He tore it the rest of the way over his head.

One second later, the man was completely naked.

Glorious.

Magnificent.

Muscles hard and lean.

Rigid, brutal beauty.

His chest packed and the skin clean, a single tattoo of a palm tree marked on the underside of his bicep.

Scars littered the lower left side of his abdomen, a spray of four or five deep, discolored indentations.

I brushed my fingers over them. He flinched and I had the urge to kiss across them, too.

I did, leaning in and brushing my lips across the marred skin, not knowing what happened but sure whatever it was, it was wholly significant.

Part of what had shaped this broken, guarded man.

Rain pounded and the storm grew strength, and my chest was heaving while he stood there looking at me while I touched him.

Explored him.

Tenderly.

For a moment, he just watched.

Taken.

All that firm, toned flesh shivered beneath my touch.

Then he dove for me again.

Mouth capturing mine as his hands pushed under the material of my nightgown. His fingers found the edges of my panties, and he hissed when he dragged them down, the fabric eliciting a chill as it skimmed the length of my legs.

He dropped them to the floor.

"It isn't right, Mia. What I'm about to do to you. But I need it. Fuck, I need to feel something good. You, beautiful girl. I need to get inside of you."

His kiss was manic, a hand at the back of my head, angling me to take control.

He tasted of whiskey and sex and grief.

With the other hand, he gripped me by the hip and tucked me close.

Our bare skin grazed.

Shock streaked through my body.

Electric.

The barest brush, and I was already being burned alive.

My fingers searched, palms gliding over his chest. His muscle rippled beneath my touch. I kept going lower, dragging over his abdomen that twitched and shook until I held him in the palm of my hand.

My belly flipped as I stroked him.

"God. Mia. Yes."

The words wheezed from his throat, and his hand slipped from my head to my shoulder where he jerked the strap of my gown free, exposing one breast. He dipped down and swirled his tongue around my nipple.

I whimpered and gasped when he dragged his fingers through my center, the flesh drenched and throbbing.

He slipped two fingers inside of me, and I was already coming undone, his name a plea.

Bliss built. Too fast. Mind-numbing. I could no longer think.

"You want me, sweet girl?" The words might have been nice, but they came out a threat.

Raw hunger had taken to his gaze when he edged back to look at me, lust flexing every gorgeous muscle of his body.

"Yes."

"Tonight, I own you, Mia West."

My chest tightened, and my heart did that stupid, stupid thing.

Because falling for this man would only break me in the end.

He kissed me again, and I'd never been kissed this way.

In a way that was all consuming, desperate and dire. As if both of our lives depended on it.

I was terrified that maybe they did.

Our mouths at war.

Our hands an entreaty.

Our mingling breaths a covenant.

He dragged me to the very edge of the table, so close that my bottom was barely hanging on, and his hand clenched down on the side of my neck when he edged back to position the head of his cock between my trembling thighs.

He barely pressed in an inch.

I thought I might pass out right then.

He tightened his hold, fingers curling into my hair at the back of my head.

I could feel his manic heart going boom, boom, boom. In sync with the storm. In sync with my mind.

The man held me steady.

Riding a sharp blade of bliss that I knew was getting ready to cut me wide open.

Our foreheads touched.

I exhaled a shaky breath against his lips.

He rocked forward.

Hard.

Filling me full.

Thunder cracked, lightning a blanket of blinding white at the windows.

The room shook.

And I couldn't breathe.

The perfect intrusion was close to pained as my body fought to adjust to him. To his size and his presence and his aura.

Everything about him overwhelming.

Too big and bold.

I was consumed. Gone. And he hadn't even begun to move.

"Fuck…Mia." Leif's throat bobbed heavily, and he struggled for air, to hold himself together.

"You feel so good," he muttered with his forehead still pressed to mine. "Too good. God, what have I done? What have I done?"

Our bodies burned.

Fires and flames.

"Leif. Please. Let go."

On a groan, he did.

He gave.

Owning me, just like he'd promised.

His hips surged deep. Hard, fierce strokes that forced the air out of my lungs with each frenzied thrust.

The sound became a moan.

His name.

His name.

He angled back, taking me by both hips, staring me down as he fucked me straight into oblivion.

Nirvana.

An eclipse.

His darkness surrounding. Stars all around.

"Mia. Fuck me."

He seemed to get lost, too, spiraling, one hand coming to the back of my neck, dragging me to his kiss. The fingers of his other hand sank into the flesh of my hip, jerking me forward to meet each drive of his body.

He worked me into a sweat.

Worked me into a puddle.

Worked me into chaos.

Pieces of me coming apart.

Cracking.

Splintering.

I buried the scream in his neck when he broke me with bliss. As pleasure unfurled from that tiny pinpoint and scattered into eternity.

Where he sent me wandering in his mystery.

He yanked me from the table as my body was still rocking with waves, and he set me on unsteady feet and whirled me around.

My hands shot out to brace myself on the table, unprepared for the sudden shift. Immediately, he had me wound up again.

Grabbing my bottom in both hands, he filled me.

Hard and fast and possessive.

His face buried in my hair.

Two thrusts and I could feel it.

The erratic jerk of his body and the moan of his spirit as he took me flying with him again.

The chant wouldn't stop rolling from his tongue. "I'm sorry. I'm sorry. I'm sorry."

And God, I couldn't understand what he was apologizing for.

His body stilled, and he clutched me tight. He slipped his arms around my waist, and he leaned his chin over my shoulder and brought us cheek to cheek. "What have you done, Mia? What have you done?"

Leif
Twenty-Three Years Old

"What is this?" The sound of Maddie's voice stopped me in my tracks.

I'd been walking down the hall to the bedroom to grab my shoes so we could leave for dinner.

One second I was without a care.

Fucking happy for the first time.

Truly happy.

Not the fucked up, toxic kind, a fraudulent high that burned through my veins and left me in chains.

Next, alarm was sending a rash of nerves tumbling down my spine.

Barbs that lifted the hairs at the nape of my neck and shot my heart into overdrive.

Like any sudden movement might scare her away, I slowly turned around.

Maddie was standing in the middle of our living room with a fucking block in her hand. I gripped two fistfuls of hair.

"Baby," I wheezed.

Her face pinched in rejection.

Like she'd already heard the lie that was getting ready to come out of my mouth.

Same ones I'd been telling for the last six months.

Except for then, she didn't even have the suspicion, had no clue who I was.

Wanted to keep it that way because the last thing I wanted was for this amazing girl to know the real me.

"It's not what it looks like," I told her, hands coming out in front of me like I was trying to calm a scared animal.

Except it was exactly what it looked like.

Her chin trembled as she tried to hold back tears. "Then tell me what it is," she demanded, a sob hitching into a plea. "Tell me what this is."

"Baby."

I was across the room in a flash, ripping the coke from her hands and tossing it onto the couch, wrapping her up in my arms.

She went weak in my hold.

Sobbing into my shirt.

My innocent, harmless girl.

"You're a liar."

I nodded into her hair. "I am."

A motherfucking bastard.

But she didn't know I was shackled.

Fettered to the only life I'd known until she'd changed my perception of what life was supposed to be.

She clung to my shirt. "Why? How could you keep this from me?"

"Because I knew I never would have been right for you."

She pried herself back, peered up at me. "I . . . I don't understand. You have . . . you have a good job at the shop. Why would you—"

I pressed my fingers to her lips. Cutting her off. "It's just a front, Maddie. A cover for who we are."

Hurt spilled from her trusting eyes.

"Keeton?"

I gave her a tight nod.

"Braxton? The rest of the guys?"

Each question she demanded hit me like a gunshot. "Yeah," I managed through gritted teeth.

She dropped her head into her hands, and she started to tremble. She turned away like she couldn't stand to continue to look at me

"I can't . . . I can't believe this. It's all been a lie. All of it. Us. This house. Our relationship."

"No. I love you, Maddie. I fuckin' love you. It's the only true thing I have in my life."

I took her by the elbow.

Gently.

Tenderly.

With the little good that was in me because that little good belonged to her. "I never wanted you to look at me this way."

Emotion crested from her. Coming at me in waves. Warily, she turned back to look at me, tears coating her cheeks. "Then change it. Stop. Be the man I fell in love with. Because you know I can't stay here, otherwise."

I wound my arms around her. Hugged her tight. "Okay."

Keeton laughed. Nothing but mocking. He set his elbows on the table and threaded his fingers together. Eyes dimming with the evil that lived inside. "You think it works like that? That you can just walk? I think you're smarter than that."

Leif

*T*jerked awake. Disoriented. Body warmer than it'd ever been. A sense that everything in the world was right, which should have been my first clue that something was very, very wrong.

Tiny specks of light filtered in through the drapes that hung over her window.

Her window.

I slammed my eyes closed when I realized I wasn't waking up to the same twisted dream I'd been fighting for the last month.

Nope.

It was even more fucked up than I could have imagined.

I was actually wrapped around Mia West from behind.

In the motherfucking bare flesh.

That mass of black hair was bunched in my face, and her sweet spirit was dancing all around me. Tight, lust-inducing body tucked to the well of mine, like she'd been perfectly carved to fit in that space.

Panic welled to overflowing as my arms curled tighter around her.

She rustled, the tiniest moan coming from her mouth that had me conjuring scandalous ideas all over again.

As if I hadn't done enough.

Should have known if I stayed it would turn out this way. Should have trusted my gut when it'd first warned me to get up and go. That my staying here was only going to bring more calamity.

But no. I'd chosen to torture us both. Did I really think I could push us right up to a razor-sharp edge and neither of us were gonna get cut?

Slayed.

Misery pulsed.

I gulped around it.

It was worth it.

Worth the additional penalties that would be dealt.

Even if saving that little girl meant their names might not be avenged.

That selfish thought might as well have punched me in the face.

Fear and disbelief traipsed over me, a wild disorder, because I couldn't understand the spell this woman had cast over me. This girl who snuggled tighter into my hold like she thought it was a possibility that I might never have to let her go.

Since I was already gettin' selfish, I took a little more, held her tight and breathed her in and whispered that I wished I were better. That I might have something left that I could offer her.

But it was time to suck it up and accept the truth.

Devils and angels didn't mix.

I forced myself to unravel from her. As quietly as I could, I climbed off the side of her bed, snatched my jeans from the floor, and shrugged them on. I gathered the rest of my things from where they were scattered around.

Heaving out a sigh when I looked down at her, I gave myself one second more to look on her beauty as the sun peeked its way

through the drapes.

I slipped out Mia's bedroom door, only to pause to take a glance toward the room where her children still slept.

A pang slammed me. Somewhere deep. Something I couldn't allow myself to feel.

I ducked out the main door and made a beeline down the hall, barely slowing when I got to the multipurpose room at the back.

And fuck, had we found a new purpose for it last night.

The girl written on my skin, the taste of her emblazoned on my tongue. Knew I wasn't ever going to be the same.

The girl another regret.

Another sin.

Another due.

All of it on me.

I burst out the door and into the rising morning, ensuring the door was shut and locked behind me.

The ground was still damp and littered with leaves and branches from the violence of the storm last night. I rushed across the yard, bare feet on the concrete, my steps echoing their retreat.

A bastard who'd done his bidding.

I flew into the small guest house and went straight for the shower, like the scorching hot spray might burn away the brand she'd scored on me. No chance, but I still tried. Scrubbing at my body until it was raw.

By the time I stumbled out and dried and dressed, I could only feel her more.

Girl had gotten under my skin. Burrowed herself under my flesh. Would be just fine if those marks only went skin deep. But I knew . . . knew from the first night I'd met her that she had the power to seep into the cracks and the fissures. To embed herself where no other person could go.

Panic blazed, ignited by the suffocating guilt.

A shock of weakness slammed me, and I planted my hands on the dressing table to keep myself from falling, dropping my head between my shoulders with a heavy exhale. I squeezed my eyes closed like it might offer some relief. "Fuck . . . Maddie. I'm sorry. I'm so fucking sorry."

"Only you. Forever. No matter what."
"Do you promise?"
"I promise."

Her voice twisted through the room. A ghost. A specter.

Frantic, I moved for the closet in the bedroom and grabbed my backpack from the top shelf. I started shoving in a few things that I had to have, hands shaking like a bitch, before I moved into the bathroom to get my things in there. I knocked half the shit sitting on the counter onto the floor.

Not taking the time to pick it up, I left it and ran out into the living room to grab my notebook and my drumsticks, and I shoved them inside the bag.

I could send for the rest of my shit later.

I had to get out of there.

Right then.

No more playing these games.

Tiptoeing into a field of landmines where I'd already planted the bombs.

I knew full well where not to step, but my feet were treading there, anyway.

I tossed my backpack over my shoulder, grabbed my phone, and tapped out a message.

Me: Yo, Rhys. Change of plans. I'm heading back to Charleston. Let Emily and Richard know I'm going to be in town.

A few seconds later, my phone buzzed.

Rhys: What the fuck, man, waking me up at the ass crack of dawn to give me some shady-ass message. Only good reason for waking a man from his beauty rest is to tell him you won the lottery or there is a fight going down and you need a real man for backup. Doesn't sound like either of those to me. So what? You bailing on Sunder? Or did they

kick you? Drummin' not good enough?

Could tell he was trying to inject some humor into this shit. Guy always doing his own tiptoeing while slinging a load of bullshit.

Talking me down from the ledge I always teetered on. Like if he rambled enough of his nonsense, he would get a few true words from me. Guess he knew me better than I wanted him to.

Me: Just . . . changed my mind.

Rhys: Bullshit.

Me: Doesn't matter.

Rhys: Sounds like it does to me.

I squeezed the phone in my hand, tipping my face toward the ceiling and gritting my teeth like it might rid me of the shame.

Problem was, I wasn't entirely sure where it was coming from, which was completely fucked in itself.

Girl had messed with my mind.

My pulse screamed, roaring in my ears, and I had a pretty damned good idea that she was messing with my heart, too.

Me: Just deliver the message, would you?

Needed to get back to my band. To my music. To my one reprieve.

And relief was not something I was going to find with the words I was writing here.

I grabbed my keys from the high bar, rushed back through the guest-house door, and headed for the gate.

I shouldn't have looked back.

I knew it. But I'd never claimed not to be a goddamn fool, and I didn't think I was physically strong enough to ignore the fucking hook that had sank into my back.

My eyes raced, already moving, drawn to their destination.

Through the far windows in the main house in the kitchen, my eyes tangled with hers where I knew she was standing at the sink.

Sable eyes.

Fathomless.

Bottomless.

They speared me from all the way across the yard. She might as well have been standing right in front of me.

Hurt.

Sorrowed.

Rejection bleeding out.

Worst part was the acceptance that I found there. Like she'd already known I would let her down, exactly the way I'd promised her I was going to do.

Emotion wobbled at the corner of my mouth. A pathetic smile. A halfhearted apology.

Truth was, I was sorry.

I was fucking sorry, but it didn't change anything.

Forcing myself to turn, I let myself out the gate. I jabbed in the code on the pad to the side-door of the garage harder than necessary, keys getting stuck, like they were pissed off by this whole situation, too.

Rejecting what had to be done.

But it did.

Couldn't allow my judgement to get clouded any farther. Couldn't let myself sink any deeper.

Pushing the button to lift the third garage where my bike was parked, I went straight for it.

I flung my leg over the seat and settled myself onto the heavy metal, grabbed the handle bars, and squeezed them tight.

Trying to focus through the turmoil.

Through the betrayal of feelings that seethed inside.

"Fuck, fuck, fuck," I mumbled, pinching my eyes closed and trying to get myself together. I needed to reclaim my purpose.

What terrified me was that picture was getting vague. Distorted at the edges. Changing shape.

I forced myself to kick over the engine. The motor rumbled

low, power vibrating through my body. I pulled back the throttle, revving it, doing my best to convince myself to pop it into gear.

Nothing.

No will.

Go, Leif. You've got to get the hell out of here before you lose your cool.

Yeah, that didn't work because I climbed off my bike.

I stared at it before I turned to glare at the door that I'd just come through like it was going to swallow me up.

I couldn't believe that I'd been so reckless.

That I'd allowed myself to feel *this*.

That I was actually just going to walk away like a fucking coward. No care for the girl who'd given herself to me. Who'd offered me care and kindness.

Love just because she was willing to let a piece of herself go even at the risk of getting trampled.

"Fuck it."

Maybe staying here for a minute was exactly what she needed. Maybe Lyrik was right. Maybe they needed another set of eyes watching over them.

Offering a little good.

At least that was what I was telling myself when I jammed the button to close the garage, tossed open the door, and stormed back up the sidewalk.

I buzzed through the gate, legs carrying me faster than they should as I made my way along the edge of the pool toward the main house.

Truth was, I had no idea how to face what was waiting inside for me.

And still, I was unable to stop.

Damn the consequences.

Here I was, stepping into Eden. Just a quick deviation on my way to Hell.

I let my backpack slide from my shoulder and drop to the ground, never slowing, just picking up speed while that bitch Karma ran along beside me ranting in my ear.

She could fuck off right about then.

I punched in the code, threw open the door, and stepped into the great room.

No doubt, I appeared half deranged. Raging. Body shaking with a type of adrenaline that I didn't know how to shake.

Violence, I got.

But this?

It was an entirely different thing.

Kids were in the living room, but I moved right for Mia who was in the kitchen. She gasped and whirled around, and she leaned against the refrigerator door for support.

The girl the best thing that I had ever seen.

Wearing a silky robe that was doing stupid things to my head and desperate things to my dick.

I eased her way, and those sable eyes that had already told me goodbye filled with caution and confusion, and it was clear from the moisture still clouding them that I'd made her cry.

"I . . . I thought you left," she whispered over a harsh breath.

An entire gulf separated us. A sea that I didn't know how to cross.

I choked down the panic that had chased me in here. "I couldn't."

"But did you want to?" Hurt bled from her words. Her delicate throat trembled.

"Felt like I should stay." The words grated free, scraped from a block of stone.

She almost laughed, her head shaking.

"You *felt* like you should stay?"

It was an accusation.

"Yeah."

Sweat gathered at the nape of my neck when she turned away like she couldn't look at me.

Nerves going haywire.

I inched around the island.

That crazy energy banged.

My pulse got swept up in the force of it.

I stopped a foot behind her, not sure what the hell I really thought I was going to do. Tell her that I never wanted to leave. That I wanted to stay. That I'd be with her if I had the choice.

She swiveled back around.

"You don't owe me anything, Leif," she whispered below her breath to keep the conversation from the kids. "I knew what I was getting myself into last night. I was the one who chased after you."

She gave a couple bumbling nods. No question, she was trying to convince herself that was the way she actually felt.

My head shook, and I eased a fraction closer.

"You know better than that, Mia." Words came out gruff. "You said yourself that this has been coming. You and I were going to happen. One way or another."

If I stayed in the same place as her, we were going to collide.

Diverting her gaze to the floor, she chewed at her lip. "But you regret it."

Harsh, low laughter rumbled out, and I was moving forward, backing her to the counter without even giving a thought to what I was doing. My mouth hovered an inch over hers as I stared her down. "Yeah. I might regret it. But don't think for a second that I didn't want it, Mia. I've never wanted anyone the way that I want you. Not once. Not ever."

That in itself was a mortal sin.

Another lumped onto the growing pile.

Redness streaked across her chest and lit on her cheeks. The sweet scent of her made me want to do wicked, bad things.

"What does that mean?" she murmured, her voice raw and laced with misunderstanding.

I understood the affliction.

Only thing I knew was I couldn't stay away.

This girl had me hooked.

I planted my hands on the counter on either side of her, boxing her in. I leaned in closer, close enough that our noses brushed. "Means I couldn't leave."

And there we were.

Full circle.

Our bodies a mess of desire and our eyes a disaster of questions.

An annoyed groan echoed from behind us. "Would you kiss her already? I'm about to revoke your man card, Leif, and I don't even have one yet. That's just embarrassing."

My attention swung around to Brendon who was smirking all over the place. Kallie smacked her hand over her mouth to stop a laugh. And Penny . . . Penny blushed like she'd just witnessed something salacious.

I pitched my attention back to Mia.

Beautiful Mia with her carved cheeks and her full lips.

Yeah.

I wanted to. I wanted to kiss her.

So, I did. I kissed her soft. The girl so sweet where she sighed against my lips.

My forehead dropped to hers, and I whispered, words just for her, "I'm sorry, Mia. I told you I didn't want to hurt you. I meant that."

She barely nodded, unsure, and she seemed almost relieved when my phone buzzed.

I looked at the message.

Rhys: Keep your moody ass in Savannah. Put out a 9-1-1 and booked a show at The Hive. Tomorrow night. Maybe it will give you a second to come to your senses. Strap on your boots, the cavalry is coming, baby!

This guy. Couldn't stop my smile if I tried.

Me: Fine. I'll be here.

Rhys: Ah, too easy, brother. Seems to me you were experiencing some kind of cold feet. I can't wait to meet her.

Could almost see him waggling his brows from across state lines from beneath his trucker cap.

Me: Fuck you, man.

Rhys: Not my type, dude, not my type. But count me in

for another taste of those sweet Savannah ladies. Bring yours.

I looked up at the girl who was watching me.

Unable to resist, I snatched the first two fingers of her right hand and swung it between us, that simple connection feeling like the most powerful thing.

"Want you to come somewhere with me, Mia. Tomorrow night."

"Like . . . on a date?" she clarified, like she didn't believe what I was asking.

"If that's what you want to call it. My band's coming into town. Want you to be there."

Bewildered, she stared at me, completely caught off guard.

"Auntie! Say yes!" This squeaked from Kallie.

"Please. Say yes." Words grunted free, hand tightening around her fingers.

She warred. Think we both could feel us getting too deep.

"You should go, Mom." Penny's timid voice hit me from behind. It tugged directly at the string the kid had sewn in me.

Connection fierce.

Something I wasn't sure how to undo.

Worry moved through Mia's face when she glanced at her daughter before she looked back at me.

Scared.

Hopeful.

With all that bright, bright light.

She gave me a tight nod. "Okay."

And I felt it for the first time in three years.

Excitement.

Mia

"You're going on a date with him?" Tamar nabbed me by the wrist, screeching as she flung my arm around.

Waving a hand in her direction to quiet her, I tiptoed over to the door and peeked out.

Coast clear.

Breathing out in relief, I clicked the door shut and turned back to my sister-in-law who was standing there with one of her signature smirks.

Nothing but a red-lipped Cheshire. If we weren't careful, every canary in Savannah was going to go extinct.

"Are you trying to announce it to the whole dang house?"

This time she waved a flippant hand at me. "Um . . . newsflash, Mia, the whole house already knows. How do you think I do?"

"You're a snoop?"

A low giggle rolled off her tongue. "Okay, now we both know that's true, but this I heard straight from your brother's sexy mouth, which he heard from Baz, who heard from Shea, who heard from Kallie. Apparently, Brendon and Penny were in agreement to keep your secret, but when I pressed them, they gave. Five bucks each."

The explanation came from her casually.

Nothing but nonchalance.

Disbelief widened my eyes. "You bribed our kids?"

She shrugged. "Who said money can't buy happiness?"

"You are terrible."

She laughed. "That's why you love me. And besides, it wasn't like you didn't have a whole audience when the man asked you out. That took some balls."

Or he was just a sadist.

Because how was I supposed to say no?

I mean, not that I wanted to. Which probably made me the biggest fool of all.

I heaved out a sigh and sank down onto the side of the bed. It didn't matter that I was almost thirty, my nerves still rattled. "And what did my brother have to say about all of this? He sure didn't seem all that keen when Leif first got here."

Tamar's expression softened. "That's because your brother is going to wait around until someone's true character is exposed. Guilty until proven innocent." She grinned.

I shook my head, words a disparaging tease. "Oh, and Leif is innocent now?"

"Actions speak louder than words, don't they? And I'm pretty sure that action yesterday said everything that needed to be said."

It was instant. The assault of images that hit me.

Panic and horror.

That one second when I thought she might be gone.

My spirit curled in on itself, unable to fathom the thought.

My head shook, and I glanced at the floor like it might offer some kind of strength before I forced myself to meet the understanding on her face. "I wouldn't have made it, Tamar. If I would have lost—"

I choked over the last word, unable to get it out, tears blearing my eyes.

I never would have made it.

"Oh, sweetheart." Tamar erased the space between us, kneeling down in front of me, her blue eyes searching, her features written in worry and dread. "I know. I know. I couldn't imagine. None of us could."

My lips trembled, and I tried to make sense of it. "When I lost Lana . . . I was devastated. Crushed in a way that I couldn't quite understand."

I blinked, trying to see through the disorder. "But with everything that's been happening . . . it's like . . . it's like I haven't really been able to mourn her. Grieve her. But this?"

I couldn't hold back the tears. They ran hot down my cheeks, weaving across my lips.

Tamar brushed back the hair matted to my face. "But she's here. She's safe," she emphasized.

Comforting.

Encouraging.

"What if it wasn't an accident?" The worry was out before I could hold it back.

Pretending it had been was so much easier.

But my spirit wouldn't allow for it any longer.

I could feel the intention.

The cruelty.

The hate.

"What if someone is out to hurt my baby? I just have this . . ." I touched my chest, trying to find a way to put it into words. "This . . . horrible feeling. Right here. That something is so terribly wrong and I don't know how to stop it."

A tear slipped free of Tamar's eye. "We don't know any of that, Mia. And I know that's not a good answer, but the one thing I know is we are in this together. We are all going to be here, making sure you and your babies are safe, until we find out who is responsible. Do you hear me? You are not alone. Besides, I know of somebody who wants to get *real* close."

Only she could make me laugh in the middle of this, and I was

peeking at her, letting the confession bleed free.

"I slept with him last night."

She didn't look all that surprised. Still, she seemed cautious. Careful. "Was this . . . a trauma thing? You looking for comfort? Or something more?"

Emotion bottled in my throat, words barely slipping by. "For me? It was more. I think it was more with him since the first time I saw him."

A sigh pilfered through her nose. "You're falling for him."

My nod was shaky. Reluctant. Wondering if it made me a fool. "That obvious, huh?"

She grinned, playing softly with a strand of my hair. "It's hard to miss. The two of you are like a chemical reaction every time you get in the same room. Half the time, I think I need to duck for cover."

"I think maybe I should be the one ducking for cover." The confession scraped from my tongue.

Every question.

Every reservation.

She touched my chin.

"Why would you say that?"

Restlessness left me on a bolt of air. "That man is written in scars, Tamar. And all those wounds have him barricaded."

Blocked off.

No access to his dark, brooding heart.

I inhaled a shaky breath. "But that doesn't seem to matter because there is this part of me that feels like his heart is already mine when he's made it abundantly clear it can never be, and I'm pretty sure mine is already well on its way to getting crushed."

Brow twisting tight, she tipped my chin her direction. "Don't you know that we're all always halfway there? On the verge of getting our hearts shattered because we never know what tomorrow will bring? The question is, do you want to take the chance on something magnificent that might be waiting to come to be?"

"Does it make me a fool that I want to take that chance? In the middle of all this? Is it absolutely stupid and reckless for me to go after what I want?"

"No, Mia. No. It means you're still living. Still fighting for what you want. Still enjoying every day. Don't let whoever this sick asshole is steal that from you."

The playroom was chaos. Packed with every child in our family.

The entire place nothing but running and screaming and laughter and the loud pop music that Penny and Kallie were pumping through the speakers.

I didn't mind.

I sat back and smiled.

Relished in the small things. The perfect moments like these.

I startled when my phone rang where I had it clutched in my hand.

I cringed when I saw the name lighting up on the screen.

There it went—my one moment of peace shattered.

Tamar looked at me in concern, and I angled my head toward the door. "I've got to take this. I'm going to step out."

"No worries. We've got them."

With a nod, I rushed outside, nothing but wary as I accepted the call and put the phone to my ear.

"Nix, hi."

He breathed out a gush of relief at my voice. "Mia, what the hell happened? I could only make out a couple of words . . . something about Penny."

I started to pace, my attention turned toward the ground, my windpipe feeling like it was completely constricted as I forced out the words. "We had a close call yesterday."

"A close call? What exactly does that mean?" His words were slowed. Vicious stakes that impaled the air.

God, I had not been looking forward to this. I knew he was going to freak out.

I swiped the sweat that was already beading on my forehead,

long pieces of my hair getting matted to my skin. "We were taking a walk to the park. Some out of control driver nearly hit Penny in the crosswalk."

"Shit. Is she okay?" His demand was hard. Concerned. The miles separating us just making it worse.

"She wasn't hurt. She was shaken up pretty bad, though."

No doubt he could hear the warble in my voice. Could sense the absolute horror at what I'd felt.

Distress rippled through his harsh breath, protectiveness rising up. "How close was it, Mia? What are we talking about here?"

More of that dread laced up my chest. Too tight. Squeezing me in a vice of *what-if*. "It was close, Nix. Too close."

"But she managed to get out of the way?"

"Uh . . . um . . . yeah," I started to ramble, not sure how to explain, but just knowing Nix this wasn't exactly something I wanted to confide in him.

But this was his daughter we were talking about. I couldn't gloss over the details. "The drummer filling in for Zee was there. He was heading to play football with Lyrik and the rest of the guys. He was crossing the street behind her. He got her out of the way before she was hit."

Silent animosity echoed from the other end of the line.

Distrust.

Ancient hurt that was never going to heal.

"Who the fuck do you have hanging around my daughter, Mia?"

It was just so typical.

His jealousy.

His accusations.

Except he'd forgotten he didn't have a say over me anymore.

My own anger tremored through my muscles. "Tell me you're joking right now. This man saved your daughter's life, and you're questioning why he was there?"

He chuckled a demeaning sound. "Told you I didn't want you going to Savannah, Mia. I told you I wanted you to stay here. Where I can take care of you. Protect you."

"It was an accident, Nix."

"Bullshit."

The word reverberated through the air.

I think we both knew it was exactly that.

Bullshit.

My life was unraveling. My children unsafe.

He exhaled heavily, his tone softening. "Damn it, Mia. What the hell do you expect me to do? I'm stuck here in L.A. while you're all the way across the country."

I pressed my palm to my forehead. "I don't expect you to do anything. I just wanted to let you know what happened."

Silence pulsed through the line.

Weighted.

Drenched in apprehension.

"You should be here. All of you. It isn't safe. I need to be able to watch over you."

I released a helpless sigh. "Honestly, Nix, I'm not sure that I'm safe anywhere. I think it's best we stay here."

"God damn it, Mia." The gritted words were barely a whisper. "We're fine."

It was all hapless defense.

Issued without truth.

Because I wasn't so sure that we were or that we were ever going to be.

"Going to make sure you are. I promise you. Have shit I have to take care of here, and then I'm coming to get you and my kids, Mia."

Before I could refuse, the line went dead.

I dropped my head into my hands, trying to keep it together.

The last thing I could handle right then was Nix trying to get in the middle of my life. Take the reins the way he always did. Cause more trouble than he ever solved.

My spine stiffened when I felt the presence fall over me from behind.

Blinding and dark.

Perfect and disastrous.

Warily, I peeked at him from over my shoulder, my body slowly swiveling around. Reeled in by the tether that stretched

tight between us.

"Who was that?" Leif's entire demeanor was rigid. Opposing. His attention dropped to the phone I clutched in my hand.

I lifted my chin, refusing to skirt the truth. "The kids' father."

His nod was quick. Sharp as a blade. "Guessing you were filling him in on yesterday."

My lips pursed. "Yes."

"And?" Caution laced his tone, while that energy threatened to snap.

"He wants us to go back to Los Angeles to be close to him."

His jaw ticked, and I could hear his teeth grinding from across the space. "And?"

Agony crept in through the seams I was barely holding together.

"And what do you want me to say, Leif? That I want to stay? That I want to stay here where you are? Would you accept it or would you run?"

It was a dare.

A challenge.

A plea.

He inched closer.

Tension writhed in the dense humidity.

The man sucking me into his orbit.

"You think I'm a flight risk?"

I turned my focus to the gate, figuring it would be a whole lot easier than gazing on his striking face. "You were going to leave, Leif. You're the one who warned me nothing good could come of this. That you were going to ruin me." The words dropped to nothing. "And you . . . you were apologizing the whole time last night."

Rejection bottled in my throat, and that vacant space that he'd carved out in the middle of me howled to be filled.

"You think I didn't hear that, Leif? *Feel it?* I think it's been clear from the get go that you're going to break my heart."

His hand found my chin, tilting it back toward him. Those brown-sugared eyes flashed.

Grief.

Greed.

Fear.

"Wasn't apologizing to you, Mia."

Confusion knitted my brow, and the only thing it took was the stake of agony that burned up his expression to start a brawl in the middle of my chest.

I searched him, my tongue sweeping across my trembling bottom lip. "Then who were you apologizing to?"

God, did I even dare ask the question?

Sheer anguish dented every line on his gorgeous face, this man hemorrhaging from someplace I couldn't see, but it was anger that purged from his tongue. "It doesn't matter."

Disbelief left me on a haggard, brutalized laugh, and my hands moved to my chest like it might keep my heart from spilling out. "It doesn't matter? How can you even begin to say that, Leif? You push me away and then you refuse to let me go. I think I deserve to know why, don't you?"

"Mia . . . I . . . I can't."

"Leif . . . just . . . talk to me. Please. You can trust me. You've been holding me up. Let me hold you up, too."

"Mia."

It was refusal.

An appeal.

As if again he didn't know if he should hold me close or push me away.

"Leif, I'm standing right here, begging you to believe in me."

His head shook, and he took a step back.

A barrier built.

Disappointment hit me. Full force. My smile was forged, as fake as my surrender. "Okay. Fine. I get it."

Before I let myself get beat up anymore, I found the strength to turn and walk away.

If he wanted me, he was going to have to prove it.

I was halfway back to the door when he called my name.

A moan of affliction.

I stilled, unsure, but I turned when he muttered, "You want my honest?"

Kiss the Stars

"I do."

It was an oath.

A promise that I would hold whatever he offered.

He was in front of me in a second, a thunderbolt of grief, his hands squeezing my face in desperation when he released the confession, "I was apologizing to my wife, Mia. My dead wife. That's who I was apologizing to."

The words were jagged.

Sharp edges and crushed vestiges.

Nothing left to be repaired.

My eyes rounded with his revelation, mind rushing to process through his anguish.

Through what he had lost.

He started to step away. As if he couldn't stand in the declaration.

I let my phone slip free so I could grab him by the wrists. Slayed by the realization of where his desperation had come from last night. The ghosts that I had felt wailing in his spirit.

"God . . . Leif. I'm . . . I'm so sorry. So sorry." I blinked a million times, as if it might erase some of his pain. Like it could soothe mine as I struggled to fumble through the idea that she had been there with us.

Between us. On his mind and on his tongue.

That he'd felt dishonor in touching me. In being with me.

"You want more of my honest, Mia?" he almost spat, his face so close to mine, his torment frenetic in the blank space that separated us. A barrier that our souls tried to breach.

I wasn't sure that I could handle any more.

Tears flooded when he set those massive hands back on my cheeks, mine still manacles around his wrists.

"We move on from here? Then I need you to listen and listen good."

I barely managed a nod.

"I was apologizing to her because you are the first person who has made me *feel* since losing her, Mia, and the truth is, I'm not quite sure how to handle that. You're the first person who's made me question what I'm living for. The first person who's made me

243

think that maybe I might want something different."

He clutched me tighter. "Yeah, I've slept with other women, Mia. But you are the only one I've *been* with."

Sorrow spun.

For him.

For her.

For me.

"The only one I wanted." It was the confession of a sin.

The man on his knees.

I gulped down his misery.

"What happened to her?"

Grief clashed with the hardness of his expression. Stone and ice. He leaned in closer. "I told you that I'm really good at destroying everything I touch."

I heaved out a staggered breath, refusing to believe the cruelty that fell from his tongue.

"You might not have been in my life for long, Leif Godwin, but I *know* you. You would never hurt her."

His laughter was brutal. "Just because I didn't pull the trigger doesn't mean I wasn't responsible. Doesn't mean I'm not the devil."

God. I wanted to believe he was speaking figuratively. But by the expression on his face? I couldn't be sure. He curled his hand around the side of my neck, both possessive and tender. "And with you, Mia? You make it feel different. Make me want to be different. Be someone who is worthy of you. And that scares the shit out of me because I shouldn't want you. Because I'm wishing I could be the kind of man that I'm not ever going to be."

And I got it. I got it.

Saw so deep in his storm.

Like my fingertips had delved into the darkest depths of his spirit.

Touched upon the fear.

The reservations.

The hatred that seeped from his soul.

"Need to be here with you, Mia. Watch over you. Watch over your kids. Can't walk away until I know you're safe."

It was a harsh plea.

That maybe saving us would be his only salvation.

But what I heard the most?

He would never allow himself to love me.

Not the way that I wanted him to.

That would be like me chasing down a falling star and catching it in my hand.

Beautiful but gone in a flash. Disintegrated into nothing.

A dream turned to ash.

A shiver raced, and my stomach churned.

And I knew, right then, that I was already lost to him.

twenty-five

Mia

*T*ook one last glance at myself in the full-length mirror.

Considering I was going to a concert, I thought I would try to play the part. Tight, black, shredded skinny jeans, a thin, silky black tank with a strip of lace at the low neckline, and a pair of knee-high boots to match.

I'd done my makeup heavier than normal, and my hair was curled into fat waves.

All of it put together made me feel . . . sexy.

Maybe it would stand the chance to cover the fact I also felt crazy anxious.

My nerves splintered and fragmented.

When I'd gone to bed last night, I was sure this whole thing would have gone bust. Worried that Leif would retreat after allowing that glimpse of vulnerability. After opening a part of

himself up to me that I'd bet my life he shared with precious few others, if anyone at all.

The part of me that had begun to beat for him wrecked by what he'd gone through.

Praying he would allow me to hold it, while there was a huge piece of me that wasn't exactly sure how to handle that knowledge.

But no.

I glanced at my phone again, to the text that had been waiting for me since morning.

Leif: Be ready at 5. We're gonna ride.

I ran my damp palms down the front of my jeans.

Right.

Okay.

I was just supposed to climb onto the back of his bike. Act like nothing had happened after what had been revealed yesterday.

My heart wasn't just on the line.

It was on the chopping block.

I glanced at the clock.

Four fifty.

My pulse spiked.

This was it.

I grabbed my leather jacket from where I had it tossed on top of my bed, shrugged into it, and headed out the two doors into the long hall that led to the main part of the house. At the end of it, I made a right through the archway and stepped right into anarchy.

Every person in the family was there tonight.

The kids had tipped the couch on its side and piled a thousand pillows to the sky.

Their own personal stairway to heaven.

"I am King Zeus," Brendon roared from the top of it, lifting both hands like he was holding a thunderbolt, while all his loyal subjects scrambled around at the base of his throne.

"Mommy!" Greyson squealed when he saw me, bouncing on his knees and holding a pillow like it was some kind of treasure. "We building a fort! Do you wike it? See?"

"Wow." It wasn't so hard to exaggerate my enthusiasm when it was about the cutest thing I'd ever seen. "I love it."

I doubted so much that Tamar did.

I leaned over and kissed the top of his head, savoring in his sweet scent.

Penny met my eye. Cautious and knowing and sweet. "Mom, you look really pretty."

My smile wobbled, and I fidgeted with my hair. "That's nice of you, but I think I might have—"

The whistle and catcall coming from behind stalled the words, and I spun around with a glare. Eyes narrowing on the culprit.

"Holy Mia-Moly. You are some kinda sight, darlin'. Are you trying to knock the whole town dead?" Ash grinned from behind the counter, his thick, muscled arms planted on the island as he grinned across at me with his ridiculous dimples.

I rolled my eyes at Ash. "Hardly."

"He's right, Mia. You look HOT, mama," Edie said.

A blush gathered somewhere on my chest, the silky, lacy tank I was wearing under my jacket suddenly feeling too thin.

"You look stunning," Willow told me with one of her gentle smiles.

"I look ridiculous."

Ash pointed at me. "Oh, people are most definitely going to be staring at you tonight, but it's not because you look ridiculous."

Redness crept to my cheeks. I wasn't typically shy, but I was most definitely self-conscious of the fact I'd just spent the last three hours in front of the mirror getting ready.

Or really, the reason I'd done it.

So nervous. Wanting to look pretty for the man who had me in a fist.

Lyrik froze when he caught sight of me.

All kinds of protective.

Tamar smacked his chest. "You let one thing come out of that mouth, and I'm going to make you pay for it later."

She even made that sound sexy.

He grunted.

"You look amazing," she mouthed at me from across the

kitchen.

"I . . . um . . . are you sure you're going to be okay with the kids?"

Tamar laughed one of her sultry sounds. "Uh . . . if you're worried it's your children who are tearing down the house, look behind you. I think two more aren't gonna make a difference."

I worried my bottom lip, glancing behind me, back to her.

"Maybe I should stay."

"Let me think." She tilted pursed lips toward the ceiling for one second, tapping her chin, before she dropped her attention back to me. "Nope. You shouldn't. Go. Have a blast. We have them."

"Got them, Mia," Lyrik reassured me. "You don't have anything to be concerned about. All of us have them under our watch." My brother lifted his chin. "Tamar is right. You should go. Have a good time. You deserve a night just for yourself."

I gave him an unsure nod. "Okay."

"Just . . ." He glanced out the windows to the backyard. His muscles twitched. The meaning of his real concern clear. He moved toward me. Slowly. The words quieted and only for me. "Be careful. Don't take shit from anyone. But more than that? Go after what you want, Mia. What your heart tells you. Don't you dare feel guilty for chasing down what makes you happy. You got me?"

There was something in his statement that impaled me deep. My chest stretching tight in appreciation, those nerves going for another tumble.

"Thank you." The words trembled.

I moved in to give my brother a quick hug, but he didn't release me, instead muttered at my ear, "He hurts you, he can kiss his dick goodbye."

"Lyrik," I mumbled, subduing laughter, pushing away from him.

He chuckled and squeezed my hand. "Have fun, baby sister."

"I will."

I gave a timid wave to everyone, all those eyes on me, feeling exposed. I moved to my babies, hugged my sweet girl. "Have fun tonight."

"Don't worry, Mom. We're fine. I promise."

I kissed her forehead, loving the child that she was.

I had to chase down Greyson to get one of those hugs, the kid squirming all over the place, laughing like crazy as he played hard to get.

Finally, I pried myself away, and I sucked in a steeling breath as I released the latch way up high on the back door and stepped out into the stagnant heat of the late afternoon.

Sunlight blazed down through the bluest sky.

A wicked grin slid over his face when he saw me coming into view where he stood on the patio of the guest house.

Waiting.

Watching for me.

Need boiled my blood.

Instant.

Man wearing jeans and a tee and sex on his skin.

All that terrifying beauty rippling under the sun.

My stomach tipped to the side, want sloshing over.

He stepped down and headed my direction, radiating this natural arrogance that had me shaking at the knees.

He cocked a grin when he was two feet away, and he slowly roughed a hand through his hair, voice filling up with a lusty declaration. "You really are tryin' to kill me, aren't you, Mia?"

I fidgeted, messed with the hem of my leather jacket.

He eased forward.

Flames lapped.

He shocked me by looping an arm around my waist and pulling me flush. A tiny gasp sped up my throat. He buried his face in my hair, and I nearly died right then when his lips tugged gently at the lobe of my ear.

"Knew the second I saw you that you were the sexiest woman I'd ever laid eyes on, Mia West. But dressed like this? I changed my mind—it's you who is going to ruin me."

The blush took full bloom, and I was chewing at my bottom lip that was painted red when he edged back. He reached out and tugged it free, the pad of his thumb sending a crash of chills down my spine. "Don't mess with that lipstick. I plan on kissing it off later."

Those nerves skittered. Shivered and leapt.

Unprepared to find him like this.

Lighthearted for the first time.

Confusion knitted my brow. He just laughed, stepped back, and took my hand. "You ready to get out of here?"

"I'm not sure I could ever be ready for you," I admitted.

His expression softened, and he traced the angle of my jaw with the pad of his thumb.

Tenderly.

So at odds with the man I'd come to know.

"Know the affliction."

We stared for a beat.

Lost.

Hearts drumming out ahead of us.

He blew out a breath and snatched my hand. "Come on, let's go before I say fuck to this show and have you in my bed."

Turning on his heel, he started for the gate, leading me by the hand. Every so often, he glanced back at me with this look on his face.

One so different than I'd ever seen him wear before.

Like . . . like . . . he was almost happy.

Like he couldn't believe I was there.

Like the fact that I was meant everything.

I raced to keep up with him. My heeled boots clicked on the walkway, and I clung to his wrist with my free hand while my other was clutched in the massiveness of his. He punched the code for the gate, and he held it open for me to go ahead of him.

He'd already pulled his bike out of the garage, all that gleaming metal sitting there waiting to be tamed.

I inhaled a shaky breath.

"Are you nervous?" The warmth of him suddenly hit me from behind, his breath skating across the sensitive skin of my neck.

"Nope, not nervous," I squeaked.

Positively terrified.

Terrified this bad boy was going to strip me bare. Leave me

broken and mangled and beaten.

I was nothing but a willing participant.

He wound around me and grabbed the helmet he had hanging from one of the handlebars, turned back, and carefully situated it on my head.

Brown-sugar eyes never left mine as he fastened the strap.

My stomach quivered, and my knees knocked.

"Perfect," he murmured. He touched my chin. Gently.

Oh man, I wasn't quite sure how to keep up with him when he was like this.

Slinging his leg over the motorcycle, he balanced it, and his booted foot came down hard to kick it over.

God. How was that sexy, too?

This man oozed it.

Bled it.

The roar of the engine coming to life sent vibrations up the back of my legs and crawling across my flesh.

Taking over.

This low buzz that grew louder and louder.

Amplified when he pulled back the throttle and revved the powerful motor.

He sent me a cocky grin, angling his head for me to climb on. "You ever ridden before?" he asked.

"Once or twice."

"Most important thing is to relax and let your body follow my movements. Don't fight it. Enjoy it."

"That's easy for you to say."

He chuckled a low, grumbly sound, at one with the bike, and I was swinging my leg over and tucking myself close to the strength of his body.

I wrapped my arms around his waist.

Sensation raced, and my heart thundered at his back. No question, he could sense it, feel it, as if the man had a direct line connected to me.

"Hang on," he shouted.

It was becoming clear it was going to be impossible to let go.

He eased out onto the road, and the sun blazed down from

above, rays flashing through the leaves of the trees from overhead as he took the bike to the street.

Easily.

Fluently.

Fluidly.

Our bodies in sync.

I guessed we'd always been.

Like we recognized the other.

He slowed for the four-way stop, and I felt the hitch in his movements, as if he were seeing the scene play out all over again, too.

The horror.

The dread.

The what if.

I squeezed him tighter and tucked my chin over his shoulder. Let my gratefulness wash over him.

Seep and soak and simmer.

I was so thankful that he'd been there when we'd needed him most.

Power vibrated from the bike as he carefully maneuvered the Savannah streets. The venue wasn't that far from the house, and ten minutes later, we were pulling into the back lot behind a century-old building.

The structure was built of coarse, aged bricks, worn from the years the building had been used as a cotton warehouse, covered in soot and dust and old smoke damage from a fire in the 20s.

It was massive, four stories of exposed levels and lofts, years ago transformed into a trendy theatre and club.

I'd been here several times to watch Sunder play. It was one of those intimate venues where you could get up close to the performers.

Reach out and touch the stars.

Right there, lost in the vibe and passion and sensuality of your favorite musicians.

It wasn't all that hard to figure out who was going to be mine.

Leif rolled to a stop beside a black SUV. He reached down to grip me by the outside of the thigh. Squeezed in some sort of unheard reassurance. Or maybe it was a plea. As if he were asking me for understanding. Maybe support.

My attention drifted to the left to see a group of people standing around at the back door.

All eyes tuned in on us.

There was a woman who was probably about my age standing at the front of the group. Incredibly beautiful in a soft, innocent sort of way. Wearing a sundress and wedge heels and disbelief on her face, blonde waves tumbling over her shoulders.

A man was to her right, hands stuffed in his pockets, shaggy, brown hair curling around his face.

Tattoos littered his arms and outright confidence radiated from his body.

No doubt, that boy was too handsome for his own good.

But it was the burly bear of a man who was ambling toward us with a huge grin on his face that had a small smile pulling to the corner of my mouth.

Leif seemed reluctant to shut off the engine.

The second he did, a booming voice hit our ears.

"Holy shit, the Banger is here. I was wondering if I was goin' to have to come track you down and drag your scrawny ass over here."

Leif chuckled a laugh, shook his head with amusement. "That's Head Banger, to you," he shouted back while he offered me a hand to help me off.

More of that lightness filtered through the coming evening.

I wanted to slip into it.

Slip into the feel and the sound.

The guy walking toward us let his expression morph into counterfeit alarm. "It's worse than I thought. He let the heavy metal get to him. Knew letting him get with that band was gonna result in disaster. What did I tell you? Time to kick your city ass back into country gear, brother. We have a show to play. Place is gonna be packed. One day warnin' and tickets are sold out. Hells yeah. Told you this was our year. Let the awesomeness ensue. That is if you can keep up."

I tried to follow his crazy-train of thoughts as I undid the strap

of the helmet, not even sure who he was talking to except for the fact he never took his attention from Leif. I couldn't peel my eyes away, watching between the two of them as Leif climbed off his bike, amusement gliding into the atmosphere.

This.

This was what we'd needed after everything we'd been through.

"Would you leave him alone, Rhys? We haven't seen him in weeks and you're already tryin' to scare him off." This from the blonde who was making her way in our direction.

In feigned offense, he tossed her a glare. "Scare him off? This asshole missed the shit out of me." He whirled back to face Leif, his arms stretched out to the sides. "Didn't you, Banger?"

Leif held two fingers up. Just a pinch.

"Piss off, asshole, and tell me you love me. Know you want a kiss. Then after that, get to tellin' me who the hell this gorgeous girl is right here. You lucky bastard." He looked at me with his shit-eating grin. "You went and found yourself a rock 'n' roll princess."

Embarrassment blazed, and I bit down on my lip, glancing at my attire.

Yep.

Overboard.

I'd totally, totally gone overboard.

Leif stepped in front of me. "Watch yourself, man."

The guy's grin only grew. "Oh, so that's how it is?"

He basically tossed Leif out of the way and came barreling for me, wrapping me up in his mammoth arms, hugging me hard and flinging me around.

I screeched, caught off guard, but couldn't help but laugh as he continued bouncing me around.

"Rhys, put her down. You're going to suffocate the poor girl, and I haven't even gotten to meet her," the blonde said, her voice nothing but an amused reprimand.

"But I like her," he whined, and then he was grinning more, his voice lowered at my ear so only I could hear when he set me onto my feet. "Thank fuck you're here."

Confusion wound, and I looked at him, not sure what he was implying, wanting to ask him what he meant.

He glanced at Leif.

Emotion punched me in the chest.

And I knew it. I knew it to my soul.

Leif needed me, too.

Maybe as much as I'd grown to need him.

Leif sighed, as if he'd expected all of this, and he was shocking me again when he wound his arm around my waist and tucked me to his side.

Statement made.

Claiming me in front of them.

I had the urge to bury my face in his neck. Breathe in his warmth. Swim in the possibility.

And I knew I was getting ahead of myself, but then he spread his hand out against the small of my back and pressed a kiss to my temple.

That time, there was no stopping it.

Everything raced.

Attraction and electricity.

Leif cleared his throat. "Guys . . . this is Mia. Mia . . . this is the band."

He waved a hand at the girl out front. "Emily. Our lead singer. Lyricist and the most memorable, beautiful voice you'll ever hear."

The cute blonde waved with a shy smile. "Hi, Mia. I'm so happy to meet you. And for the record, don't get too excited. Leif might be exaggerating a tad."

Leif leaned toward my ear, though he said it loud enough that everyone could hear. "Not exaggerating."

"Hey, Emily," I said.

Leif lifted his chin toward the tall guy at her side. "Richard. Guitarist. Songwriter. Vocals. Also Emily's brother. Two of them started the band way back when they were kids."

Oh, yeah, there it was.

The resemblance.

"Good to meet you, Mia," Richard rumbled, eyes roving me, head to toe.

Not because he was checking me out.

Okay.

He was *checking me out*, but not because he was interested.

He was looking out for his friend. Wondering about my intentions. If I was there to cling to Leif's coattails on his way to stardom, get a free ride into the fame and the limelight and, if Lyrik's predictions were right, a huge fortune in their future.

Which the idea of it was kind of hysterical considering I'd sworn to myself I'd never date a musician.

And there I was. The girl hoping to catch the drummer's eye, but not for any of the reasons that Richard might have assumed.

"It's really great to meet you, too, Richard."

Leif pointed at the burly guy who'd just been tossing me around. "And this one here is Rhys. Our bassist. You'd do best to ignore him," he said, razzing his friend.

Rhys held up his hands in disbelief, his arms completely covered in gorgeous ink, swirls of words and dancing notes and brilliant, majestic landscapes.

It seemed completely at odds with the fact he screamed that he was one-hundred-percent a country boy.

All the way to the bones and the scuffed-up boots he wore on his feet.

"Hold the reins. Ignore me? And how is this girl gonna ignore all this? Come now, Leif. Let's not talk nonsense. And here you pretend to be the smart one."

He gestured to himself.

A slight giggle slipped out.

He was a big, huge goofball with an easy smile and a gruff voice.

He swung his attention to me. "Your boy here is just jealous he's in the background bangin' away at those drums and no one pays him a lick of attention. Except, it seems he went off and found himself a little attention, now, didn't he?"

He wagged his brows.

Leif's chuckle was free and warm, and he cleared his throat. The arm around me twitched, his fingers gliding under the back of my jacket and brushing across the satiny material.

Like he needed the connection.

And there went my train of thought.

Dipping right into his hands.

Drifting toward his gorgeous body.

"Mia is Lyrik West's younger sister."

Silence descended, a rumble of shock and eyebrows darting for the sky.

Lyrik West had that effect.

At least Richard could rest assured that I wasn't a starfucker.

The man roughed a hand through his hair and gave Leif the side eye.

Like maybe he thought he was crazy.

Chasing down a death wish.

My brother came with a reputation.

No doubt about that.

Cracking up, Rhys wagged a finger at me, but he was smirking at Leif as the ramble began to pour out, "You really did go and find yourself a rock 'n' princess, didn't you? Royalty, baby." His gaze shot my way. "Your brother is a motherfuckin' superstar. Someone stop me if I fangirl."

Richard smacked him on the back of the head. "Dude." He angled his head and repeated it with emphasis. "*Dude.*"

I didn't know if he was telling him to play it cool or reminding him that he was, in fact, a dude.

Rhys hiked his shoulders to his ears. "What? We're talkin' about *the* Lyrik West. And this is his baby sister. With *Leif.*"

There I went with that blush again.

Emily shoved Rhys in the shoulder. "Like Leif said, you'd do best to ignore this one."

Rhys shook his head. "Can a man get no love?"

She patted his chest. "Not if it's you."

I tried to hide my laughter, and Leif curled me closer, muttered my direction, "I probably should have warned you."

Amusement played across my mouth. "You do realize who I have to hang out with all the time? This is nothing."

Rhys pointed again, eyes wide as he looked between Leif and the rest of the band. "See. Is anyone else pickin' up on this shitfire craziness? She is talking about Sunder right now. Fangirl down."

The guy toppled back onto the pitted pavement.

Putting on a show.

Richard rubbed his forehead and started back toward the theater, glancing once at me. "Hey, Sunder Princess, we need a new bassist. You know anyone?"

Rhys popped up. "I'm comin', asshole. Don't make me take you down."

He ran up behind him and curled an arm around his neck. Richard tossed him off, laughing, and Rhys punched him in the shoulder.

"Don't mind my wild boys, Mia," Emily said. She reached for my hand and gave it a squeeze. "I'm really glad you're gonna be here tonight. We've been missin' Leif like crazy, so we figured we'd better make the trip up here to see what he's been up to. I'm glad he's been up to something good."

"Emily," Leif said, part warning, part exasperation.

"I'm just welcoming your friend, Leif. Southern hospitality and all." She winked at me and twisted her skirt with an exaggerated curtsy before she turned and headed after Rhys and Richard who were already climbing the back steps.

The door flung open right before they got there and a girl came rushing out, her brown ponytail swinging around her shoulders.

"Mells-Bells," Rhys shouted. "Where the hell have you been all my life?"

She rolled her eyes and tossed a thumb over her shoulder. "Working. Like you should be. Asses backstage. Soundcheck. Do I have to chase ya'll down every damn time?"

They fumbled in, mumbling apologies and hiding their smiles.

Leif hugged me closer. "So, that's Carolina George. Melanie is our assistant and Emily's best friend. Four of them make up the only family I have."

And I knew he was giving me a little more.

A piece of him.

I peeked at his gorgeous face. Heart manic. Excitement buzzing in my chest, affection riding in right behind it. "I can't wait to hear you play, Leif. So badly I can hardly stand it. Can't wait to see you in your element."

And maybe that was the most dangerous thing of all.

Mia

"How am I supposed to watch out for you if you're down on the floor?" His voice was a rumble of possessiveness.

"And how am I supposed to appreciate your talent from way back here?" I returned. "I want to see you up on the stage, Leif. Experience it. I am rock 'n' roll royalty, after all. I think I'm a pretty good judge." I let the tease wind into the air.

A temptation and a dare.

Okay, I didn't have a musical bone in my body.

But I was pretty sure I'd become adept at appreciating what he had to offer.

On a low chuckle, he curled his big hand around my hip and tugged me closer. "You might be wearin' a crown, but I'm thinking it's the angel kind."

A rush of dizziness spun through my head, all supplied by the need woven in his tone and the bottle of champagne I'd shared with Emily and Melanie right before it was time for them to go on.

He inched forward. His big body eclipsed mine where he nudged me into the shadows backstage.

I wanted to swoon and sing.

I brushed my fingertips across his sharp, sharp jaw. "Leif."

A plea I didn't quite understand.

He dropped his forehead to mine. "How's it possible it feels like this?"

"What does it feel like?" I barely managed to force out around the need that had grown thick in my throat.

He squeezed his eyes shut. "Right."

He jerked himself back and stepped away, roughing an anxious hand through his hair.

Too close.

Too exposed.

"If you're going down there, you'd better hurry. We're on in a couple of minutes."

"Okay." I started to head for the hall that led to the floor.

Before I got a foot away, Leif grabbed me by the hand, pulled me back, and spun me around.

His fingers drove into my hair.

He kissed me.

Kissed me long and slow and impossibly.

His tongue a lash of soft possession. Rigid, terrified devotion. He curled his hands around my head, twisting my hair up in a mess of need, the harsh rake of his breaths panted into my mouth.

I was gasping by the time he pulled back, clinging to his shirt, unable to stand.

A small smirk ticked up at one side of his delicious mouth, his thumb coming to brush across my swollen lips. "Told you I was going to kiss that lipstick off later."

I inched back. Inhaled a shaky breath. Grabbed the tube of it that was in my pocket and smeared it across the tingling flesh. "In case you want to give it another try later."

Then I moved around him, caressing my fingertips over the raging in his chest as I passed by, unable to stand there for a second longer without completely losing myself.

Could feel his groan clamoring after me. My mouth tugged at a grin, but I didn't look back, just swung my hips back and forth as I headed for the hall.

So maybe I wanted to play.

Watch the way his jaw clenched and his eyes darkened with a raw, desperate hunger.

Affect him a little the way he was affecting me.

The second I slipped around the corner, I beelined down the hall, practically running toward the door that let out to the floor. Too eager for my own good. I knew it. Knew I was teetering on a razor-sharp edge.

But right then, I was savoring this reprieve.

The grief would always be there, the fear of what was to come lingering at the back of my mind.

But Leif reminded me there was light in the darkness.

Hope in the destitution.

My fingers itched.

Colors flashed behind my eyes. Breath stolen with the compulsion to find a paintbrush.

It was Leif. It was Leif.

I pushed through the door, edging by the giant bouncer guarding the back, and shouldered my way through the crowd that vied to get a spot up close to the base of the stage.

Begging for attention. To feel a part of that energy that rippled through the air.

Something acute and extraordinary.

Potent and persuasive.

Like you were watching the sky. Waiting on something magnificent to happen.

I weaved my way through, unable to stop the magnet that pulled me forward.

It was Leif. It was Leif.

The lights flashed, and the crowd stirred, a crush of bodies that swelled toward the foot of the stage.

Pressed so tight you could hardly move.

But the vibe was different than a Sunder show.

Tonight, it was missing that raw, savage intensity that pulsed and throbbed and threatened to break loose. The mood hinged on chaos that was getting ready to crack.

Here, it was nothing but excited shouts that echoed from the walls, falling from the lofts that housed the specialty tickets and booths, whistles zinging and boots clattering on the hardwood floors.

The lights flashed again, dimming before a single teal spotlight blazed through the night.

Drumsticks lifted in the air, and Leif drummed them together over his head, a crack, crack, crack that reverberated through the atmosphere, that striking jaw clenched and his head bobbing with the beat.

My heart stampeded.

It was Leif. It was Leif.

The lights flashed again, dimming before springing to life in a bright ray of yellow to reveal Rhys taking his spot. He threw a fist in the air to a round of hoots and hollers and stamping feet.

Another strobe, this one red, and Richard was there, strapping his guitar over his shoulder.

A riot of voices lifted into the dense, heated air.

Blackness spread out over the mass.

A beat.

A breath.

Hushed anticipation.

A moment later, a strobe streaked through the mote-laden air, lighting Emily where she stood at the mic.

She curled her hand around the stand and leaned in. The drumbeat rose in a slow, ascending beat just as the bass began to thrum.

Richard moved forward and began to strum a melodic, mesmerizing chord.

Then Emily leaned in and she started to sing.

I thought the entire crowd was going to lose their minds.

Leif hadn't been exaggerating.

Emily's voice had to be one of the most unforgettable things that I would ever hear.

A silky, whiskey-laden lullaby.

Enthralling.

Spellbinding.

Their sound was so different than I'd expected.

This mesh of country and rock that whispered of seduction and rang with inspiration.

Lyrics riddled with pain and faith and family.

My body swayed and the music played and my broken heart raced out ahead to the beat of the drums.

Lifted.

Risen.

Taken.

Giving myself over to the rush of emotion, moisture gathered in my eyes, and I tipped my head back to the soaring ceiling where the strains and the melody danced. Vapors of ghosts and whispers of angels that swirled in the abyss that lifted above.

Shimmers of light that shined through the vast, endless black.

My eyes peeled open, drawn, following the tether I could feel stretching me thin until I was looking at the man who was watching me through the blinding flashes of light.

Like I was the only thing he could see.

It was Leif. It was Leif.

My falling star.

And I knew right then I would chase him down to eternity.

Leif

I let loose on the drums as the last song of the encore came to an end.

The song upbeat and fast.

Every person in the place was on their feet. Shouts riding through the hazy, stagnant air of the dank theater as they yelled and whistled and clapped.

Emily held the last note of the song. The miniscule girl a powerhouse.

People losing their damned minds over the performance.

It felt good.

Fuck, it felt good, being up there in the one place where I found joy.

The one bit of me that remained.

My eyes traveled, finding her in the mix of the rowdy bodies, the girl gazing back at me.

In awe.

Anxiety tightened my chest, all mixed up with the lust and greed that I felt at seeing her standing there watching me like I could be more than I was.

Our eyes tangled.

And I felt the spark.

The spark of something new and terrifying. Something that shouldn't be there.

But it was pushing up. Sprouting and taking root.

A new kind of joy.

I'd do best to pluck it out before it had the chance to grow.

But instead I was standing from behind my drum set, lifting the sticks in the air while the lights flashed at a raging beat and fans stamped their feet and screamed their approval.

Begging for one more song.

Emily glided over to the edge of the stage, and she reached down to graze her fingertips across the hands that were stretched her direction, begging to get closer.

Smiling, Richard tossed his pick out into the crowd.

Mayhem ensued, a sudden barrage of movement as arms flailed and bodies tumbled as they fought to be the one to catch that tiny treasure.

But it was Rhys ripping off his sweaty shirt the way he did after each show that had every damned girl in the place losing control. Putty in his hands.

All except for my girl.

Mine.

Mine.

Mine.

The chant of the claim echoed in my mind, and I attempted to beat it back. Contain the assault that blistered through me when I watched the gorgeous girl stand firm in the middle of the pandemonium.

Sable eyes on me. The long locks of her black hair curled in soft waves, bigger than she normally wore it, makeup done up thicker. Her lashes full and her lips fuller.

Girl looking like she'd just hit the runway or stepped off a stage herself.

Sexy as fuck.

Striking.

Gorgeous to the extreme.

"Thank you for coming out to see us tonight, Savannah!" Emily shouted into the mic, lifting her hand and waving. "We love you."

Another round of screams and shouts and stomps of feet.

"Stay awesome, Savannah," Richard issued into his mic before he pulled the strap of his guitar over his head and set it onto the stand, waving as he strode off the stage.

Rhys twirled his soaking shirt over his head and sent it sailing into the crowd, his tattooed chest and abs gleaming with sweat and causing the entire population of Savannah to drop to their knees.

Every single one of my bandmates commanded the stage.

Their talent overwhelming. But this business didn't merely require talent. It took charisma. Connecting with souls from on the stage like they were standing right there with you.

A rumble of ferocity burned deep inside.

I wanted it for them. Wanted it badly.

Problem was, I wasn't sure if I could remain. If I could stay and be a part of it without destroying their chance before they got started.

Everything was becoming blurred.

Distorted.

Everything except for the girl who was waiting at the foot of the stage.

All around her, people laughed and chugged beers and lingered for the coveted chance of getting an invite backstage, but she just stood there, watching me with those eyes that were doing crazy things to me.

I edged that way.

Severity crashed.

A lightning bolt that struck in the middle of us.

Shivers of it racing far and wide.

A crackle in the air.

A smirk ticked up at the corner of her sweet, sweet mouth that was painted in that lust-inducing red when she saw me moving her direction.

About fifty other chicks noticed, too, like they thought I was coming for them.

Not a chance.

I had one destination.

One mind.

I was moving for her when some fucker decided to take note of her, too. Not that you could miss the prettiest girl in the place.

Fact of it didn't give him a free pass.

Not when he moved in, whispering in her ear, country boy all dimples and charm and Georgia grins.

My heart hammered. Ribs squeezing tight.

Shit.

This was getting bad.

Goals out of sight.

Mia gave him a polite smile and a slight shake of her head, trying to dodge the advances she didn't want.

Asshole couldn't take a hint.

He took her by the arm like he had the right to touch on the beauty that was driving me out of my mind.

Without giving it a thought, I slid off the front of the stage. The crowd pulsed around me.

A living ring of bodies that pressed and contended to get closer.

I shoved through them. Needing to get to her. To squelch the derangement that was clouding my mind.

Didn't even give a shit that they were undoubtedly taking pictures.

Watching this go down.

Mine.

Mine.

Mine.

Fuck. Wanted to scream. Guilt billowed from the depths. This betrayal that was becoming my greatest sin. But I couldn't stop the possession that rose like a storm.

Dark and black and foreboding.

Prick tugged at her and tried to bury his face in her hair.

Bad call, motherfucker.

I grabbed him by the scruff of the neck.

Pussy nothing but a runt.

He started to whirl on me. No doubt, he was getting ready to throw blows.

If only I'd get so lucky.

Maybe it would take off some of the edge.

His punk eyes went wide when he saw he was about to get his ass beat by the guy in the back. "You . . . you're the drummer? Right?"

Everyone was staring like they'd just witnessed a fifteen-car pileup on the interstate.

Didn't give a shit.

Only thing I cared about was this girl who was looking at me in shock and surprise.

"Leif," she murmured in a bid to get my attention.

"That's right," I told him, unable to staunch the jealousy that spread through my being. The thought of someone else touching her. Loving her. Couldn't tolerate the image.

The thought or the assured possibility.

"Think you should probably head out, yeah?" I warned.

My gaze narrowed and my fingers twitched. Wanted to smash in his face for having the audacity to look at her. For even thinking about her.

Which was fucked up on so many levels.

He put both hands up, one with a beer dangling from his fingers. "Whoa, dude. Think we have some kind of misuderstandin', here. Meant no harm or disrespect. Didn't know this was your girl."

He backed away.

I stalked forward, same way as he'd done Mia.

"Yeah, well, I think *my girl* was making it plenty clear she wasn't interested, whether if she was with me or not."

He chuckled an anxious sound, attention darting over his shoulder like he was getting ready to bolt.

A hand landed on my arm.

Soft and sure and right. "I think he was just leaving, weren't you?" she prodded. Mia's voice wrapped around me.

A balm and a match.

Consolation and gasoline.

The guy's attention swung between the two of us. "Sorry. Seriously. We're cool, man. We're cool."

We so were not cool because I was burning the fuck up.

Losing it.

The collected focus I'd possessed for the last three years obliterated in a breath.

Her breath.

Her hand squeezed my arm, and she peered up at me through the drizzle of light that poured through the theater. Worry in her eyes and mischief twitching across those lips.

Something new rippled in the space between us.

Understanding.

Girl getting me on a level that no one else could.

Like maybe she could see through the grief and the pain.

My chest tightened.

No.

Not *through* it.

Like she was willing to wade through the middle of it with me.

"Hey, there, Drummer Dude," she said softly, grinning when she uttered the nickname Brendon had given me, all the kids taking suit considering there was no denying he was the alpha of the pack.

I heaved out a strained breath.

She grinned wider. Seduction and sweet. "Nothing like a little overreaction. Don't tell me you're jealous?" she teased, the mood a thousand miles from where we'd been yesterday.

A grunt of possession rippled through me, and I angled her way, erasing the space.

Body against hers.

Relief. Relief.

"He touched you," I grumbled.

A slight, disbelieving giggle rippled free. Laced with a deadly dose of temptation. "And I'd just told him to get lost. That I

271

wasn't interested."

She hiked up on her toes and placed that mouth next to my ear. "That I was taken."

A growl ripped up my throat and my arm was around her back and the fingers of my other hand were diving into the long locks of that black, black hair.

The girl wicked.

The girl pure.

The girl everything.

My mouth came down hard, devouring her lips the way she was devouring my soul. Kissing her mad. Relentlessly.

Right there in the middle of the crowd.

Could feel the laughter and the need rolling up her throat, a gush of lust that I swallowed down right as her hands were fisting in my shirt.

Flash. Flash. Flash.

A slew of cameras went off.

Shit.

We definitely didn't need this kind of audience.

A smirk hitched at the corner of my mouth as I tore myself away. I grabbed her hand while she stood there panting.

Shocked and turned on and the best fucking thing I'd ever seen.

"Come on."

I started to drag her through the mass.

"Where are we going?" she rasped from behind.

"Where I can get you alone."

People ducked out of the way as I pushed through. A few of them called my name, asking for an autograph or a picture. "Not tonight."

Like I had time for that.

One minute lost was one I wouldn't get to spend with her.

I knew the brutal truth of that.

I just needed to get her alone. Hold her and touch her and get lost in the perfect torture of her body.

I hauled ass for one of the side doors that led backstage, taking the one that led opposite of where I knew the rest of the band would have landed themselves.

There for the fans who'd purchased VIP tickets.

Interviews and all that bullshit required when you were trying to establish your celebrity.

Tonight, there was only one person that mattered to me. One person who I wanted to win over.

My spirit thrashed at the thought, but I just let it feed me, the frenzy that had taken over as I climbed the steps to the side door. The bouncer gave me a quick nod as he opened it and let us through, and Mia's excited laughter was racing down the hall ahead of us like it'd already discovered our destination as I dragged her through the darkened corridors in the deepest recesses of the building.

Tossing open doors, looking for a proper place.

Lights and motherfucking privacy.

I banged open a door to a storage room. "Not enough room for what I plan on doing to you," I grumbled, and she was laughing more as I continued our search.

A coat room.

Production equipment room.

Cleaning supply room.

I tossed open the next door. It knocked against the interior wall, revealing a deserted dressing room.

Hell fuckin' yes.

There was a long dressing table, three chairs in front of it, the mirror framed in lights. Racks with abandoned costumes lined the walls, wigs hanging from hooks, makeup and hair shit all over the place.

I yanked her inside and kicked the door shut.

"Leif." My name coasted from her tongue, all mixed up with a throaty roll of laughter. In two seconds, I had her pinned against the wall, hands riding down the soft curve of her hips and tucking her against my dick.

She moaned and giggled, opening to the demand of my kiss.

A groan warbled low in my throat. "You taste like a celebration, baby."

Sex and confetti and champagne.

Fingertips dug into my shoulders. "You taste like poison and possibility."

I was hypnotized.

Lustdrunk.

Lovestruck.

Didn't fuckin' know.

I just hoisted her up and exhaled in relief when she wrapped those legs around my waist.

Kissing her wild, I carried her across the dressing room. She yelped in surprise when I lifted her high, setting her onto her feet on the dressing table. Girl wore these sky-high boots and fitted jeans and a jacket that was leaving far too many things to the imagination.

To keep her balance, her hands shot up to grab the rail that supported a row of lights that hung from the rafters while I held onto her hips, staring up at her as she looked down at me.

Girl in a spotlight.

Right where she belonged.

Her cheeks high and carved, eyes sharp, rimmed in the darkest black. Lids dusted in some shimmery shit that made her look every bit the angel that I knew she was.

Lips plush and painted red.

A decadent bow that the devil wanted to rip to shreds.

"What are you doing?" she whispered as I let her go and eased myself back onto a chair in front of her.

"Wanna watch you."

Uninhibited.

Not the secret, covert glances I'd been stealing for the last month.

For tonight, I wanted her to be mine.

No question.

No reservations.

A nervous, sexy giggle slipped from her mouth, her hips swaying a bit as she held onto the railing above. "And what is it you want to see?"

"You . . . wanna see you dance for me. Shine for me. *Strip for me.*" Last came out a needy command.

A shiver rolled through her, head to toe.

"I . . . I'm not . . ."

"Best thing I've ever seen, Mia West. Every time I look at you, you steal the breath right outta me. Captured me the second I saw you. You have any idea? Any idea what the fuck you've done to me?"

She heaved out a whimper. Sable eyes flashed her own desire. Her own confusion and hopes and the things she shouldn't be seeing when she looked at me.

Seemed we were the same.

Hunting down what was only going to hurt us.

Threads of music seeped through the walls, floors vibrating with the heavy bass that rumbled and shook as the club came to life for the afterparty that followed every show.

One of the things that made this place so popular.

But it was Mia West who was going to make me never forget it.

She warred, then bit down on her bottom lip.

Her gaze tangled with mine.

Searching to see if she could trust me.

She shouldn't.

But I wanted her to.

Fuck, I wanted her to.

Inhaling a steadying breath, she released her hands from the railing.

"You owned me the second I saw you sitting in that chair in the attic, Leif Godwin. I hadn't even seen your face, and you had me."

She rolled her shoulders gently as she murmured it. A motion that undulated through her entire being, her hips beginning to sway to the beat that pulsated through the floor.

God damn.

My stomach fisted. Knots of greed. A tumble of lust.

Cock raging at the tight fabric of my jeans.

Tried to play it cool, but Mia unraveled every seam.

Slowly, she peeled off the leather jacket, letting it slip down her delicate arms, exposing all that snowy flesh that shimmered and glistened beneath the harsh dressing lights, girl moving in the slowest dance the whole time.

Heels shifting on the table surface as the jacket fell in a puddle at her feet. Underneath, she had on a thin, satiny black tank that showed off her toned shoulders, her tits peaking behind the fabric.

Flames curled and leapt.

The girl came on like the swelter of a blistering summer storm. Building in the distance. My mouth parched, waiting on the relief of the rainfall.

She reached up and gripped the railing, bending her knees as she shifted and swayed that delicious body.

Sensuous.

So damned sweet.

She angled to the side, presenting me the zipper to her heeled boot. I was all too happy to oblige. I dragged the zipper down, planting a kiss on her jean-covered calf as I slipped the boot from her foot. She swiveled around, allowing me the honor of doing the same to the other.

"Killing me, Mia," I muttered as I dropped the second to the floor, and something sly was playing around her mouth as she rocked her hips and shifted her shoulders and sucked me right into a delirious trance.

Dazed by the fucking wonder of this girl.

"That's what you get," she murmured, turning around and rolling her ass in my face, her fingers going to the button and zipper at the front of her jeans. The sound of her peeling it down hit the air before she nudged the waist of her jeans down just a peek. She looked back at me from over her shoulder. "That's what you get for making me feel this way."

"What is it I'm making you feel?"

Yeah, I was masochistic, too. Wanting to hear it. To know exactly what was brewing in that beautiful mind.

Easing around, Mia shimmied the pants down her hips, leaning forward a bit as she did. "Like I'm getting ready to witness the most brilliant, amazing thing. So bright it will eclipse everything. Like I'm so close to touching it, catching it. But I know it's gonna burn out, and I'm not going to know how to find my way through the darkness when it does."

Emotion fisted. Tangled with the need. "You're wrong, Mia. Burned out a long time ago." The words were grated. Shards of glass that scraped my raw throat.

"Then how's it that I feel you blazing through me?" Her confession was a petition. An appeal.

Guilt and greed warred inside me.

I sat forward in the chair, and I reached out and dragged her jeans the rest of the way free.

Nothing but gluttony.

She stepped out of them, girl in nothing but that flimsy tank and the skimpiest pair of black lace underwear that I'd ever seen.

Long, long legs on display.

A grunt broke loose.

Feral.

I gripped her by the outside of her thighs, running my nose from the inside of her knee.

Up, up, up.

Inhaling deep.

"Such a tease," I said.

Her head shook, and she knelt down. She might as well have been a viper getting ready to strike with how dangerous she was to me.

"It's not a tease, Leif. Not when it's the realest thing I've ever felt." Vulnerability seeped into her expression.

"Gonna show you just how *real* you make me feel, Mia."

Alive for the first time in years.

"That's going to require you on my lap." I let a smirk ride free, and I lifted her off the table, loving the way she exhaled a shaky, excited breath when I situated her to straddle me.

The girl the perfect friction where she instantly ground herself against my jeans. "Leif."

She needed it every bit as bad as me, and my hands slipped under her shirt as she pressed herself up onto her knees, her palms on the roaring vortex at the center of my chest that wanted to suck her into eternity.

Watching her, I inched her shirt up over her head. That river of black hair fell around her shoulders and down over her tits that were barely hidden by the strands.

"So pretty, baby. Got me so spun up, I don't know what to do with myself."

I fiddled with a lock, trying to get myself together. To tame the hunger that raged and begged and struggled to break free.

I dragged a knuckle across a rosy nipple that peeked out through the billowing waves.

She gasped, then writhed, grinding down on me hard as she wrapped both her hands around my head, girl's body pleading for more. "God, Leif."

"These tits," I murmured, caressing my lips across the tight bud. "So fuckin' perfect."

Shivers raced across her flesh, and her breaths turned shallow, and she was searching for a smile. For the lightness we'd been feeling earlier before the intensity had chased it away.

Obliterating reason and thought.

Just me and the girl.

My angel in the attic.

"They're tiny. Tell me you aren't a boob man," she attempted to play, but it was her eyes that gave her away.

Unguarded vulnerability.

Couldn't stop the admission from getting loose. "Think I'm a Mia man."

Her chest trembled. "Don't say things you don't mean. My heart can't take it."

I threaded my fingers in her hair at the side of her head. Forcing her to look down on me where she was hovering an inch above. "I mean it, Mia. If I could be. If I was different. Better. I'd be yours."

We stared for a bated beat.

Held.

Suspended.

Then we collided in a flurry of need.

A bomb going off at the base of a dam.

Everything we'd been holding back gushing free.

I pulled her to my mouth, kissing her deep and long before my lips were moving down to nip at her chin, sucking at the flesh of her throat that wobbled and bobbed, kissing down to her breast, sucking that sweet tip into the well of my mouth.

Mia moaned and jerked at my hair, and her head tossed back in a shock of need. I held her up as she arched back, devouring this girl's beautiful tits.

Moving from one to the other while she writhed and moaned.

"Leif. I don't know myself. Not anymore. Not with you. You make it different. Better. I want . . . I want . . ." She trailed off.

She didn't even need to say it.

I knew. I knew.

And I wished I could give her everything that she deserved. Love this goddess that I held in the palm of my hands.

She fought to touch me everywhere, hands getting under my shirt and dragging it over my head. My chest shuddered and shook, and she was diving in, going at my jaw, my neck, across my broken heart that she'd somehow managed to shatter even more, her lips and tongue kissing me in every spot she could find.

She was gasping, frantic, her fingers trembling as she went to work on the buttons of my jeans. I held her tight as I lifted my hips from the chair so I could shove them down, and she eased up a fraction so I could tear the lace from her body.

Her cunt bare and pretty, and my fingers were slicking through her drenched folds.

Lust surged, and I pressed two fingers deep into the well of her tight, sweet body.

She lifted and rolled, riding my hand. "Please. Yes. Leif. I can't."

A tumult of pleas fell from her mouth, and she dropped her forehead to mine, her head rocking while I wound her high.

"Want to touch you everywhere, Mia. Own you in every way. Mark you the way I've been dying to do."

Invade.

Infect.

"Scar me," she whimpered, a breath at my lips, like she was giving me permission to make good on all the warnings I'd given her the day we'd met.

Same ones I'd been giving her all along.

I grabbed my dick, stroking it once, positioning myself between her thighs.

She trembled, and I surged, guiding her down onto me in a swift, hard thrust.

Mia whimpered, and she buried her shock in my throat as I filled her full, her walls clutching all around me, so fucking good I nearly went off right then.

Both of us struggled for a breath, for air, to cling on to some sort of reality.

But if something true existed right then, it was us.

The devil and the savior I couldn't keep.

"Ride me, baby." I murmured the command, my hand at the back of her neck, holding her down close.

She exhaled, shivered in my hands, girl rising up to do me in.

Letting go.

Her body manic.

Her hands wild.

Girl touching me down to the vacant soul.

Teasing me with the idea that she might be the one able to hold it.

I shoved the thought down and existed in the moment.

Hands gliding up and down her glorious back, palms sliding over her lush, round ass. Gripping and taking, fingers sliding along her cleft.

Mia gasped, swishing her head as she fought to keep up.

To understand.

Girl meeting me thrust for desperate thrust.

Rocking over me like she meant it. Like this was it and there was no tomorrow.

Or maybe she was thinking if she held on tight enough, she might be able to do it forever.

Never let go.

And I wanted it.

To fucking fall.

To let go of the ropes from which I'd been dangling.

My stomach fisted and my body burned.

Fire taking us whole.

Torched.

She watched me with those eyes, and I held her at the small of her back so I could angle her just right, and I moved to strum my fingers over her clit.

She held on to me by one shoulder, the other running my abdomen.

Searching me.

Loving me.

"You, Leif. You."

I wanted to tell her not to do it.

To stop it before it was too late.

But she was there. The brightest burst of light that I felt fracturing to the depths of me.

A crack of lightning.

An earthquake.

Complete and utter devastation.

She trembled on my lap, crying out my name as bliss shredded her body.

The tight ball of pleasure that had gathered at the base of my spine split.

I gripped her by the waist, tucking her close as I came.

Body jolting. Mind splintering. Like I could feel who I was breaking in two.

Old ghosts found their way through the crack.

"Only you. Forever. No matter what."

"Do you promise?" she whispered, her smile soft, her trust real.

"I promise."

Vapors of the oath curled through me like an omen. A bad fucking dream.

Mia slumped down on top of me. Her chest jerked and heaved, like she was searching around for breath when she'd been the one who'd stolen it from me.

I burrowed my face in the erratic beat I could feel drumming in her neck, this shattered boom that sought refuge in the space between.

Searching for a new home.

"Fuck. Mia." I edged her back, stared up at the girl. "You are perfect."

Heat splashed her cheeks. It was something that was more than just shy. It was an overwhelming emotion that climbed and curled and fought to be recognized.

Mia touched my cheek. "I think you were the gift I have been asking for."

I couldn't answer her, just eased her off my cock, grinning smug when she glanced down at me and another shiver rolled through her body.

"Don't think I'm ever going to get enough, either. Wait until I get you home, Princess." My voice was gruff, things I was wanting to say barely contained.

She leaned in, a whisper at my ear, "I can't wait."

I grabbed her shirt. "Arms up."

Giggling, Mia eased back and lifted her arms, that sexy mouth twisting in a tease. "Yes, sir."

A grunt punched from my chest while I eased her shirt over her head, thumb and forefinger tweaking her chin when I said, "Watch yourself, Mia. Think you might be asking for more than you bargained for. I come with a greater cost than you think."

"That's funny because I was just thinking you're worth more than you know."

"Mia." It was a rasp. A warning and a goddamn prayer.

Severity stretched tight between us. Hearts connected. For one second, one-hundred-percent in sync.

Then a peal of laughter ripped from her when I looped my arm around her waist, lifting her against me while I shrugged my pants back up without letting her go, and she watched me like I was her king when I sat her onto the edge of the table, got on my knees, and helped her back into her jeans and boots.

But it was me who was kneeling in awe.

Adoring and worshipping the grace that was this girl.

By the time we slipped out of the dressing room, the roar of the club pounded through the old walls. A thunder of energy.

Everything bottled. An edge of desperation and decadence riding in the air as people cut loose. Let go of their chains. For a few moments free of the burdens of this world.

I'd always thought that was what music was all about.

A reprieve.

An expression.

Freedom from what was holding us down.

I dug into my pocket and shot off a text.

Me: Sorry to dip out. Got business to handle.

He replied before I even had the chance to shove my phone back into my pocket.

Rhys: Not sure how you're gonna handle that Sunder Princess. She's way too hot for you. Let me know if you want me to stand in for you.

Fucking Rhys.

Me: You wish, asshole.

He didn't even have to return the text to know the smug bastard was laughing, giving me a rise.

Her hand burning up in mine, I led Mia through the maze of narrow corridors, winding all the way along the back. We skipped the areas where the crowds had gathered, sneaking by the elevated voices.

The debauchery and revelry.

I had plenty of that myself.

Right there in the fact I wanted this girl for myself. Even if it were only for a little while.

A minute of relief.

We slipped out the back door and into the night.

Fucked with my head when she slipped onto the back of my bike like she'd done it a thousand times. Arms around my waist. Her cheek rested on my shoulder.

This girl feeling too right.

I took to the street, winding us back through the historic area of Savannah. The night thick and deep and hovering low.

Stars so close, we could almost reach out and touch them.

Mesmerizing.

Beautiful.

Wind whipped against our faces, and my heart ran so fast I was sure it was going to explode.

I took the last turn onto the street that led behind Lyrik and Tamar's house. I slowed when I saw the headlights facing back our direction. Parked on the other side of the garage up near the curb.

If I lived a normal life?

Wouldn't have given it a second thought.

It was just a fucking car.

Except unease clawed along my flesh. Sticky and hot. A rush of dread and anger and hostility.

My heart thudded in a ragged, restless beat.

Making the quick decision, I whipped my bike to the curb right in front of the gate, and I whirled my head around to look at her. "Get off, Mia. Get inside. Right now."

She hesitated.

"Go," I shouted.

Trembling, she jumped off the bike. Wary and confused, she fumbled up the steps to the gate, punching in the code and rushing inside, looking back at me in terror when she did.

Headlights still glared, but the car hadn't moved.

It just sat there . . . idling.

But I could feel it.

Something sinister that rode on the dense, suffocating air.

I inched my bike forward, coming closer and closer to the headlights still baring down, my eyes narrowing and trying to get a hold on the make and color.

And if I got lucky enough?

The bastard sitting behind the wheel.

But I could make nothing out, completely blinded when the driver suddenly gunned the accelerator and the car sped forward.

Adrenaline spiked, a vat dumped in my veins.

Instinct took over, and I wrenched the throttle back, angling the handlebars enough that I jumped the curb. The bike bounced as it hit the sidewalk, barely remaining in control.

Flash of a second later, the car blazed by. An inch away. Heat of it racing across my flesh, so close I could almost feel the hatred emanating from within.

Only thing it did was stoke my own.

Malice and disgust.

I flipped the bike around, body jolting as I jumped the curb, hitting the pavement hard. Didn't let it slow me, I gunned it, throttling it as fast as it would go.

World a blur as I raced to catch up to the asshole driving that car. Not knowing if it was me who was bringing my baggage, the landfill that was my life, or if it was the trouble she'd gotten herself into that was the real danger.

Made me feel deranged.

Recklessly determined to get to whoever was responsible.

To end it.

Fix it.

Eradicate it.

Whatever it took.

Aggression flamed. Hatred burned.

Blood turning to cold, bitter ice.

A war raging within.

For her.

For her.

Problem was, I didn't know who *she* was anymore.

My bike rocketed down the street at a dangerous speed, houses and trees whizzing by, and I was barely able to process what was right in front of me.

Nothing except for the taillights that I gained on.

I pushed myself harder. Faster.

Wind whipped, and my heart slammed against my ribs.

Madness whisking me into fury.

The car skidded before it made a sharp right.

Fuck.

I braked hard.

The roaring engine whined, and the rear-wheel locked up and sent the bike skidding into a fishtail.

I fought to gain traction. To get control.

Still, I took the turn too goddamn fast.

Too goddamn sharp.

Tires screeched as they slid on the pavement. Tried to see through the panic, and my foot came down in a bid to keep it from skidding into a full slide. One second before I hit the ground, I caught traction.

Righting it.

Barely managing to straighten it to upright before I gunned it again.

But the car I'd been chasing down was disappearing around a left turn about a quarter of a mile ahead.

I raced to get there, but by the time I made the same turn, the car was gone.

Vanished.

Nowhere.

Refusing to give up, I searched, taking the side streets slow like some kind of deranged motherfucker. Peering into windows of cars, like searching through rubble in a battlefield in the middle of the night.

Wanted to scream that I was coming up empty-handed.

That I'd failed again.

Finally had to concede that there was no chance I was going to stumble across them after I'd been riding aimlessly for the last hour and a cop running his beat had clocked me as suspicious.

Before I made a bigger mess of things, I turned and headed for home.

Home.

Bitter laughter rumbled out, knowing my brain had gone bad.

The taste of this betrayal sour on my tongue.

Venom in my blood.

But it didn't matter.

I parked my bike in the garage and went through the gate. Instantly, my gaze was pulled to the windows on her wing of the house. Dim lights illuminated the girl who was at one of the easels, a brush in hand.

Heaven.

Eden.

A perfect, tortuous Hell.

Drawn, I moved. No will left.

I punched in the code, and she didn't even flinch, like she'd felt my approach all along.

"Lost 'em," I grunted. Sheer defeat.

Sable eyes found me, the quivering at the corner of her mouth telling me everything. "I was worried."

"I know," I told her. What the fuck else was I going to say? Knew she'd already gone there. Both of us digging the same grave.

In the shadows, I eased up behind her, needing to seep into her warmth.

Nearly buckled at the knees when I caught sight of the picture she was painting.

Slayed.

Cleaved in two.

"It's you," she whispered, agony and affection written in her tone.

Knew she wasn't talking about the image she was actually painting. Knew it was the first time that she'd been able to pick up her brush to bring her art to life since she'd witnessed the trauma of losing her best friend.

But still, it sliced through me like a double-edged knife.

Brutal and beautiful.

I inched forward, that knife cutting me to the core, my breaths haggard as I peered over her shoulder at the painting.

In the image, I was on my knees, facing away but in profile, my expression somehow distorted yet clear.

I stared at the snowy ground where I knelt.

Broken.

The image ached of loneliness.

Of grief.

Of loss.

My fingers were drawing a face in the snow beneath me.

Mia lifted her arm again, her hand trembling with sorrow as she swept the brush across the obscured, shrouded face, detailing it more.

I knew without question that this was Mia's representation of the woman she saw as my wife. Like she'd plucked the misery from my soul and perfectly put it on a canvas.

Knowing me the way she couldn't.

Moisture gathered in my eyes.

I had to stop this.

End it.

Go back to the beginning.

Remember.

Problem was, the only thing I was doing was remembering.

Agony and pain.

And I couldn't stop.

Couldn't stop from giving her more.

I reached for Mia's hand, every muscle on my body edged with tension.

Sharp and bleeding.

I curled my hand over hers so that we were holding the brush together, and in haphazard strokes, I painted a second face in the snow beside the other.

The little girl the only thing I could see.

Haylee. Haylee. Haylee.

Mia gasped, and her free hand flew to her mouth to keep back a cry. "Oh, God. Leif."

I leaned in, my voice a scrape of anguish where I whispered in her ear, "I told you, I ruin everything I touch."

Leif
Twenty-Three Years Old

*M*addie bounced on her toes in our kitchen. Her feet bare. The girl adorable. Barely contained excitement radiated from her.

"What are you up to?" I asked, cocking a grin.

Because fuck.

She made me happy.

Made me smile.

My one truth in the middle of the lies.

"I have something to tell you."

That grin grew, and I spun the rest of the way around from where I faced the counter and leaned back against it. "And what's that?"

Her hands spread out over her belly and she bit down on her bottom lip like she was trying to temper the thrill. "We're going to have a baby."

Then she let it loose, squealing, and she was moving for me. "Leif, we're going to have a baby."

I pushed off the counter. Flying across the floor. Whisking her from her feet and swinging her around and around.

I hugged her.

So close.

Those arms were wrapped around me.

Nothing but love.

She sighed and pressed her face into my neck.

"I'm going to be a dad," I muttered low.

She nodded there.

Joy lit.

So intense.

I slowly eased her onto her feet, but I didn't let her go. Just hugged her and rocked her in the middle of our kitchen.

"I love you, so much," she whispered.

"Luckiest man alive," I murmured, barely able to speak with the clot of emotion that had gathered in my throat.

Luckiest man alive.

One who was barely treading water.

Fear burned up my throat. Sticky and tight.

I'd tried. Tried to cut ties. Only for Keeton to reel me back in. My obligation to him a millstone around my neck.

I didn't do much. Just the few jobs he required.

Problem was, Maddie didn't know. And I couldn't let her.

This betrayal, the lies, so heavy I didn't know how I continued to stand up straight.

She would hate me if she knew. Couldn't handle it, if she left me.

I needed her.

God. I needed her so bad.

I hugged her tighter.

Knowing the only thing I could do was shelter her from it.

Shield her from the depravity that I was trying to get out from under. Buying my way out.

Soon.

Soon we'd be free.

Until then? I would protect her and our child with everything I had.

Leif
Twenty-Four Years Old

A rattled cry filled the room.

My chest tightened and my eyes burned and my heart felt like it was going to bust out from behind my ribs.

The amount of love that filled me devastating.

Crushing.

This tiny, precious thing was set on Maddie's chest. My girl weeping from the exhaustion. From the joy. From the shock.

Her hair drenched with sweat and her face drenched with tears.

She pressed her lips to our baby's head while I pressed my lips to the top of hers.

Unable to believe this was my life.

That I'd been given this. Trusted with it.

"I love you. You did it. You did it," I mumbled, barely able to speak with the emotion that filled everything to overflowing.

I was talking to them both.

My only truth.

Maddie smiled this smile through her tears, running her shaking hands over every inch of our daughter.

"She's perfect. She's perfect."

I could barely nod.

Overwhelmed.

Overcome.

I kissed Maddie's temple. Set my hand on Haylee's back.

My hand close to eclipsing her entire body she was so small.

But her eyes? They were so big when they looked up at me.

In trust.

Devotion thrummed deep.

A massive demand that shouted in my ear.

This—this was my duty.

My reason.

My purpose.

I had to get free. For them. So I could be the man they needed me to be.

The second I walked through the door, she squealed. Clamored off the floor where she was playing with paper dolls.

She jumped to her feet.

Footsteps my perfect drumbeat.

A rhythm I felt to the deepest part of me.

She threw her arms into the air as she ran in my direction.

Blonde, shiny curls bounced around her little shoulders, and her smile was so big I didn't know how it fit on her face.

"Daddy!"

Love rushed at the sound of her sweet voice.

At her trust.

This adoration I had overwhelming. So much that sometimes it felt like too much.

I swept her off her feet.

She curled her arms around my neck. "I missed you. Don't ever leave me."

A smile edged my mouth. She told me that every time I left.

"I will always come back for you."

I prayed I was telling the truth.

I'd tried for years to get loose. Keeton would always reel me back in.

Threats.

Reasons.

His hold on me a noose.

But I couldn't keep doing this—walking out that door and not knowing if I'd return. If I'd be taken in a strike of violence, knowing what that would do to Maddie and my baby girl.

"It's over. I can't keep doing this." I stared down Keeton in the middle of the night. He'd called me in once again. Saying it was urgent. Holding this bullshit over my head. "I've got a family, and this isn't the life I want."

Never was to begin with.

In the middle of it before I'd known what had hit me.

Nothing but a sixteen-year-old kid bribed with a shiny new bike like I was a five-year-old being suckered into the back of a van with a piece of candy.

"Six months ago, you said I was done. And now you're demanding I come back? This is bullshit."

Keeton rocked back in his chair. "We need you right now. Things are shaky with Krane and his crew."

Yeah. They always were.

I gave him a harsh shake of my head. "And you know I can't fix that."

"Think you might be the only one who can."

"I'm done, Keeton. I mean it. You want to end me for walking? So be it. But I'm no longer your pawn."

His face flashed displeasure, hard because the asshole didn't like to be crossed.

I stood my ground. Think he knew I was serious this time.

"Fine, Leif. You want to be cut out? See this deal through, and you're free. Honorable discharge." He cracked a menacing grin.

He and I both knew there was nothing honorable about it.

I fought the disquiet that sparked.

The disbelief that Keeton would ever actually let me go.

I edged back and rapped a fist on the table.

"After this shipment? You forget I exist."

Mia

A light breeze whispered at the windows, the sound soothing and calm, washing over us where we lie in the middle of my bed.

Legs tangled under the covers and our hearts beating in sync.

Both of us were on our sides, facing each other, no words needed for the long minutes that passed as we fought to find our breaths.

I'd let him take me again because I'd known he'd needed it after what he'd revealed on the painting. If I were being truthful, I'd needed it, too.

The connection.

The physical promise that I was there.

Leif threaded his fingers through mine and brought the back of my hand to his lips.

He kissed me there.

Gently.

Reverently.

Tingles spread.

Emotion right behind it.

Those brown-sugared eyes searched mine. Tonight, they were so soft that I could feel them seeping through my flesh.

"Will you tell me about them?" I asked into the lapping shadows of my room, my voice quieted to make sure I didn't disturb the kids.

He flinched, but then, with our hands still twined, he reached up and brushed his knuckles down my jaw. "Not sure it's something you want to hear about."

Nervously, my tongue swept across my dried, swollen lips. "I want to know you, Leif."

"And I'm terrified for you to know that person, Mia. Terrified for you to know the real me."

I reached out and trembled my fingers across his lips. "I already see the real you, and I know there is no reason to be afraid."

He blinked, as if he wanted to shut me out. "That's you projecting again, Mia. Seeing what you want to see."

My head shook. "We all make mistakes."

He bit out a harsh laugh. "But some of us make mistakes that cost others their lives."

My heart skipped a beat of dread. Misery for this man. Maybe a little of my own. "Like I did with Lana?"

His head shook on the pillow. "No, Mia. That is different. Completely different. You didn't do anything to put her in danger in the first place."

I gulped around the lump that grew solid in my throat, not sure if I wanted to ask. Knowing I had to. "And you did?"

Grief struck through his features. Dark and forbidding. Disgust and hatred. "Told you I wasn't a good guy."

"And I've seen nothing but a good guy," I argued.

A swell of discomfort rolled through him. "Feel like I'm someone different when I'm around you. Think that might be what scares me most. Fact you make me feel like I could be someone different. Someone better."

"But you loved her? Loved them?"

Agony crawled through his body, a resounding, palpable wave that nearly took me under. "More than anything. They were my life, Mia. My everything. But the rest of who I was? He was a *bad* guy. He did horrible, bad things."

His lips pressed together. Blanching. Self-loathing pinching every line on his face.

Dark laughter rumbled from his lips. "You know, they say karma will one day bite you in the ass. Come back and make you pay." His brow twisted in vicious emphasis. "She got me double, Mia. That bitch took everything. All of it. But she made the ones who weren't guilty pay. And now . . . now I'm going to exact that same fate on the one she used to make it possible. And when I do? I doubt there's going to be anything left of me."

I should be scared. Terrified. Get up and climb out of this bed.

But I couldn't move. Couldn't do anything but stay there in the strong security of his arms. Sure he would never hurt me. That he was wrong on so many levels.

I blinked, searching his face, trying to keep up. To understand.

Something tender passed through his features, his own eyes confused. He touched my chin, tilting it up as he looked at me closer. "And then here you are, Mia . . . beautiful you . . . making me question everything. My purpose. My reason. But you've got to understand I can't let that go."

"B-b-but your music? The band?"

I couldn't make sense of what he was saying.

He cringed. "You want my honest?"

"Yes." I issued it without hesitation.

"Love them, Mia. They became the only family I have, even when I tried to stop it. Never wanted to use them, but when it comes down to it, that's what they were. A cover. An excuse. A distraction."

"I don't understand."

"That's because you can't."

"Or you don't want me to?"

"I told you that you couldn't get that deep, Mia. That I couldn't let you go there. It's not safe. And I'm not willing to let you get in the middle of what's coming."

I was suddenly frantic. A frenzy of words hurling from my mouth, desperate to find a way to meet with this man. To understand what he was really going through. "Who hurt them? Your wife? Your daughter?"

My fingernails scratching across his chest like I could claw my way inside.

Desperately, he squeezed my hand, words choked. "Please. Mia."

I didn't know what he was begging for. For me to stop asking questions. To stop making him *remember*. Or if he was pleading with me to make it better.

I touched him all over his beautiful, hardened face, hit by the realization of what he had done.

Of what he had put himself through the night he'd saved my Penny.

Of what he'd suffered.

And I couldn't . . . I couldn't. Tears streamed free, hot down my face. "I'm so sorry. I'm so sorry."

My hands were everywhere, and I was peppering soaked kisses to his face.

Adoring him with all the strength that I had.

It was Leif. It was Leif.

And I didn't know if it was my tears or his as we touched and adored and sought a way to heal.

When the haggard, stricken words fell from his lips and pled against mine. "She was three, Mia. She was three. A baby. A baby."

His agony cut and slayed.

And I tried to hold us both together.

To keep us from falling apart. But we were already sinking in his devastation.

With the fury that seeped from his pores.

Rage.

Hatred.

Violence.

Maybe it was the first time I truly saw them in him.

That dark, dark intensity fierce in the night.

True and real and terrifying.

His wounds deep.

Forever bleeding.

He set his hand on my cheek, his thumb rushing across my bottom lip. "Do you get it now, Mia? Do you get it? What I've been trying to tell you? Why this can't happen? I already lost what I'd been given to protect. And seeking retribution is all I have left."

The weight of his confession crushed down on my chest.

He blinked hard, his hold tightening on my face. "And then you look at me. You look at me, and I don't know how to walk away. Don't want to hurt you."

"Then don't."

"I can't make that promise."

"Can you try?" I was begging. I didn't care. Because I could feel it—what this had come to be. What he had come to mean.

"And what if I fail you, too?" The question was pure, gutted grief.

"What if you don't?"

I woke up, startled, dread slicking my skin as I shot up to the empty bed beside me. Sheets and blanket rumpled, a divot in the mattress from where he'd lain when we'd fallen asleep.

He was gone.

Agony lined my insides.

But little voices were flowing into my room, and I knew I didn't have the time to wallow. I forced myself from the bed, aching in a way I wasn't sure I knew how to handle.

Knowing he would be gone.

That he'd given too much.

But after last night? I had a new understanding of what he'd meant when he'd told me he had nothing left to give, even though I ached for him to find refuge in me.

In us.

And at the same time knowing seeing my children just might

hurt him too much.

I pulled open the door only to stop in my tracks.

Gasp leaving me at the sight.

Leif was in the living room with my children.

Greyson on his back and trying to tackle him to the floor, Penny giggling as she explained to him how to play the boardgame that was set out in the middle of them. Leif tried to balance Greyson on his back and listen to Penny at the same time, and both Brendon and Kallie were there, adding in their instructions.

Warm, brown-sugared eyes found mine, like he felt me before I'd even stepped into the room.

Heartache.

Affection.

The small room crowded.

Overflowing.

Abounding with something greater than I'd ever felt.

Love.

thirty

Leif

*I*t was getting harder and harder to separate.

Time. Space. Devotion.

Who the fuck I was supposed to be.

There I was, sitting propped up on her bed strumming at my guitar like that was where I belonged.

Wearing nothing but the jeans I'd pulled back on from where they'd been tossed onto the floor.

Discarded while I'd gotten greedy.

While I'd gotten lost in her sweet body again.

Another summer thunderstorm rumbled the walls, quick flashes of bright light blanketing the windows, the disorder almost a calm.

Every blip of light illuminating the girl who was curled up next to me.

That tight, sweet body exhausted and spent.

Her face sheer bliss where she slept.

Kudos to me.

Girl was radiating this joy that couldn't be missed. Emitting that light that pressed into the dark.

Had been this way for the last week. Neither of us able to get enough. Reaching for each other every chance we got.

Pure, straight-up gluttony.

No chance of gettin' full.

I glanced down at her, girl on her side, facing me. Waves of black hair strewn around her, and her heart beating this pace that sucked me straight into peace.

That feeling gripped my black, bitter soul.

Vacancy screamed.

Begging me to just let go.

Had the stark, striking need to play.

To get lost in her decadent harmony.

Girl a song.

Surrender.

I let my fingers play across the neck of my guitar as the other hand quietly strummed. My voice barely broke through the still of the night.

> *Moved.*
> *Desolate.*
> *Would give it all up,*
> *If it would keep you from coming apart.*
> *Are you falling?*
> *Are you flying?*
> *Tell me, baby,*
> *Is it worth dying,*
> *For everything you've been living for?*
> *Is it, is it worth dying, for everything we've been fighting for?*

I fumbled through the chorus, the words I'd been searching for catching in my throat.

Felt like I might as well have been touching her.

Adoring her.

Girl lying next to me a revelation. Something I never saw coming.

How did we get here?
Is it ecstasy?
Blasphemy?
Can you live in this bitter truth?
Is it rhapsody?
Heresy?
Lying here next to you?

Could barely get the lyrics to scrape free, their truth bottled deep, vying to be heard.

Recognized.

Accepted.

I jolted out of the stupor when my phone lit up on the nightstand. The ringer had been silenced, and the flash dragged my attention to it.

My chest tightened when I saw who was calling.

Unease.

Anticipation.

Being careful to keep quiet, I slipped off the bed, setting my guitar aside and grabbing my phone before I quietly slinked out of the suite and out into the hall like a motherfucking snake.

A cheater living a double life.

No surprise there.

But there was no room for an audience.

Not for this.

No chance I'd risk any one of them colliding with my past.

When I was out in the silence of the hall, I accepted the call, not knowing if I should be sagging in relief or sitting on edge.

"Brax." Kept my voice quiet. Hushed in the night.

"Yo, man. How's it?"

Perfect.

Amazing.

Torture.

"Good," I told him rather than dolling out the treachery.

"You got news?" I forced out the question, turning to stare out the bank of windows that ran the hall.

Pool was a dark, deep pit. Water a toil of energy.

Trees tall, dark shadows that thrashed in the night.

The yard nothing but desertion and rapid blips of light.

He blew out a weighted breath, confession laced with caution. Like he hated to be the bearer of motherfucking bad news. "Got news, but I'm not sure you're going to like it."

I waited.

He stalled.

"Just tell me, man."

Reluctance filled his admission. "Think it's your mom who knows, brother."

Bitterness surged.

Malice curled my hands into a fist, nearly crushing the phone. "You sure?"

He exhaled, his voice quieted in secrecy while a party raged somewhere in the distance behind him, fading as he paced away from the mayhem of that world. "Can't say for certain. But she cornered me earlier. Asked a bunch of pointed questions. Think she knows that I know where you are."

Worry and frustration coated his words. "You've been gettin' reckless, man. You want to stay hidden, yet you're strutting around in the limelight like you don't have a damned care. You knew it was gonna come down to this. But maybe this is exactly what it needed to come down to."

"What did she say?" I bit out.

That she wanted me dead, too? Reiterate her loyalty to Krane?

No fucking thank you.

He hesitated. Like he had something different to say. "She's claimin' she's worried about you. That she wants you to come back. That the two of you need to talk, lay it all out."

Loathing left me on a hard laugh. "She wants me, she can come and get me. Besides, what could she possibly have to say? What could she possibly do that would bring back my family?"

The betrayal sliced through me so deep that I was pretty sure my guts spilled out onto the floor. Mess on the ground nothing but a snarl of venom and discord.

Could feel the conflict halting his answer. "She said if I talked to you, to tell you that she would never have hurt them, and that she sure as hell would never hurt you. That she misses you."

"Bullshit."

"Is it though, man?" He sighed, paused, wary before he continued, "She said half a shipment has gone missing. Same as before, and she sure doesn't sound like she's on his side."

Rage slithered beneath the surface of my skin. Hatred lashing with every violent pulse.

"He's back at it, brother," Braxton said, voice grim.

"Then it's time to end him."

And if that meant my mother going down with him? So be it.

"We need to rethink how we do this. Think about it, Leif. It doesn't fuckin' add, your mother and Keeton. And my gut doesn't lie. She was telling the truth."

Rejection of his statement battered my insides.

As fierce as the wind that battered the window outside.

Her betrayal vile.

"Just . . . think about it, Leif, before you do something you can't take back."

Ruthless laughter tumbled off my tongue. "Too late for that."

"It's never too late if the deed isn't done. Don't mistake that." He huffed out a sigh. "You've been living for revenge for a long, long time. I get it. I want it. But don't let it fuckin' blind you."

"It's the only thing I've ever been able to see."

Until the only thing I could see was her. The angel in the attic.

Guilt spiraled.

Cut and slashed.

Unable to say anything else, I ended the call and pressed my hands to the flat-plate glass, phone pinned to the window. Sucking for a breath.

I glanced up just as lightning flashed.

Torrential rain poured from the sky and pummeled the ground.

Pool a riot of aggression that toiled and churned.

But it was the dark figure standing on the opposite side of it

staring back at me that ripped my heart from my chest.

Vengeance filled the bleeding void.

The memory of his face something I would never forget.

Lightning flashed again a second later.

Shadow was gone.

I blinked.

Narrowed my eyes as I focused to see through the blear of the rain.

Motherfucker.

Nothing.

Now I was seeing things.

Karma, that bitch, playing tricks.

And I knew, without a doubt, I had lost my mind.

That the threads I'd been clinging to had snapped.

I jumped when I felt the movement from behind, and I whirled around.

Penny stood in the doorway, her eyes squinted with sleep and her hair matted to a mess.

"Penny . . . what are you doing awake?" Words were gruff. Barely breaking free.

"I think I had a bad dream."

Heart still thundering somewhere outside of my body, I looked back over my shoulder, letting my eyes scan the yard.

Nothing.

Reluctantly, I turned away from the scene of my own nightmare, the ghosts so close to catching up. "Let's get you back into bed."

She nodded, and I tried not to feel like some kind of trespasser when I followed her into her room, not to feel like an intruder as I lifted her covers and resituated them over her when she lay back down.

And I tried with all of me not to feel like I belonged right there when I gently brushed my fingers through her hair, stared down at her cherub face, the small girl nothing but trust.

"I'm sorry that you had a bad dream."

"Do you have them, too?" she whispered into the night.

My nod was slow. "Sometimes, Penny. Sometimes I do."

Every fucking day and every fucking night.

"You make it better when you're here." Her eyes watched me like she knew—the child with the ability to see all the way down into who I was.

I just don't want to make it worse.

My soul screamed it. A prayer. A petition.

I ran the pad of my thumb across the dent in her brow. "You make it better for me, too."

A smile played around her mouth. "That's good. You make my mom happy, Leif, and I think she might make you happy, too."

What Braxton had revealed spiraled through my mind.

The debt that was left to pay.

What I owed.

The sin I'd committed.

Penny set those dark, dark eyes on me.

Full of trust.

Full of affection.

My spirit thrashed.

Because the only thing I wanted right then was to be good enough.

Mia

*T*here was a knock outside the main door.

Heavy.

Filled with implication.

I couldn't stop my grin. The speed of my heart that decided it was a fine time to take off at a sprint. The excitement that blazed as I tossed the shirt I was folding onto the bed.

I poked my head out into the living room. "It's open."

As if I would ever shut him out.

The door already rested open an inch, and he nudged it the rest of the way, the man filling up the doorway as he leaned against the jamb.

Looking like the most decadent sin.

Smirk riding on his lips while his jeans rode low on his waist. Though today he was wearing a button down, sleeves rolled up his masculine, sinewy arms.

I worried there was literal drool running down my chin.

That gaze raked me over like he was seeing the breaking day. "Trying to wreck me again, I see," he grumbled in that low voice.

Today it was a tease.

I never knew if I was going to get him gruff and hard or light and playful.

Didn't matter.

I'd take him either way.

He'd been mine for the last three weeks. No questions. No reservations.

Together.

Our days and nights shared in the most blissful of ways.

Testing and playing in those deep, dark waters.

The fear hanging over our heads had dissolved into vapor.

Back in L.A., an arrest had been made for a string of robberies. All of them had happened over the last month, and all of them within a ten-mile radius of the gallery. The detective was currently working to connect the man to the gallery's botched robbery and Lana's death.

Since there had been no more close calls or threats, we had to believe everything that had happened here had been coincidence. Our nerves frayed. Relating every single bump in the night to the trauma that we had sustained.

A sliver of unease rolled through my being.

Honestly, I still couldn't come to terms if it was right, if it was selfish and self-centered—finding this joy after Lana had been gone so soon.

The bigger part of me had to accept that beauty was born of the ashes.

That healing was found with those that most understood.

This man had suffered the greatest loss.

If he'd let me, I'd spend the rest of my life proving that love could come after tragedy.

I knew we weren't close to that.

So often, he would get sketched out and withdraw.

But each time, he just came closer.

My blindingly beautiful falling star.

A giggle slipped free as he stalked a foot into the room.

God, he made me feel like I was.

Free.

As if I'd found everything I'd been missing and hadn't known to look for.

"It's only fair, since you wrecked me the day that I met you," I told him.

I shimmied farther out into the room. Wearing a pair of cut offs that were short. A tank without a bra. No shoes on my feet.

A needy growl rumbled in his chest.

"Just what do you think you're up to, Sunder Princess?" A smirk flirted around his sexy mouth.

I turned, wiggling my butt just a bit, knowing that was all that it would take to get him to follow. I released a roll of light laughter as I talked to him from over my shoulder, "Um . . . laundry. You know, super princess-y duties."

Leif laughed.

Laughed that sound that was quickly becoming my drug. "So high and mighty, aren't you?"

I giggled more, a needy breath leaving me when he planted his hands on my hips from behind, his face pressed into my neck.

Tingles rushed.

I slowly spun around in his hold, hiking up on my toes and stealing a sweet peck of a kiss. "I sure hope you don't want me for my money."

He nuzzled in deeper, his nose running the angle of my jaw, words a whisper that quickened my heart into a frenzy. "We'll just have to live destitute together."

God, I wanted to hold him tight, confess it sounded like the perfect plan. That I would live every day with him however we were going to be. Just as long as we were together.

But I forced myself to ride on his lightness. To play along with his tease. I nipped his chin with my teeth. "What are you talking about, Drummer Dude? You are going to be a superstar."

Brown-sugar eyes danced, the man taking me by the hand and slowly spinning me around right in the middle of the room.

I nearly fell straight into a swoon.

"That what you want? A superstar?" he rumbled in his rough, magnetic way.

My face pinched in emphasis. "No Leif, I just want you."

And there went my cool. Melted on the floor where I was a puddle at his feet.

Greyson was burning up. Crying and crying, hair drenched with sweat. "I sick, Mommy. I sick."

"I know, sweet boy, I know," I whispered at his forehead, his fever running high. I sent up a silent prayer that the dose of medicine would quickly kick in.

I paced with him back and forth across the main room, mumbling words of comfort, shushing him and bouncing him and continually kissing his temple and his cheeks and his head.

"Is he going to be okay?" Penny's worried voice struck me from the side. My sweet girl always worried. On edge. I just hoped that as time stretched between us and the ordeal, she would gain confidence again. That the latent fears that seemed to constantly be at the ready to rise up would soon be snuffed.

"He's going to be just fine. I think it's just a fever."

He lifted his miserable little head to talk to his sister. "I gots fever, Pen-Pie."

"I'm sorry, baby brother."

"Is okay." He slumped back against my chest with a little whine, and I continued pacing, my arms aching like mad. Rocking this child at his age didn't come close to rocking an infant.

The door edged open, and my heart did that stupid, beautiful thing, racing out to meet him when he warily walked inside. "Hey . . . how's he doing?"

"I gots sick, Weif." He waved a pitiful hand.

I almost smiled with the love that overflowed.

My sweet, sweet boy.

I ran my hand through his hair, trying to give him comfort

while I glanced at Leif, offering him a soft smile to let him know that Greyson would be just fine.

He didn't need to worry.

That I was sorry our dinner date got cancelled but this was my life.

And my kids . . . my kids would always come first.

Would always be the most important.

The problem was, we hadn't even scratched the surface of how that might make him feel.

How the reality of it might bite and sting.

I kissed Greyson's head when he whimpered, trying to shift around his weight.

Leif moved forward and ran his hand down Greyson's back. "Here, let me."

I wavered. It wasn't like he hadn't picked him up before. Usually when they were wrestling or Greyson was taunting him in some fashion. But this? This felt . . . different.

Bigger.

Scarier.

Profound in some important way.

But it was Greyson who reached for him, climbing into his arms. "I gots you," he mumbled, like he was the one holding Leif and not the other way around.

I stood there, fidgeting, not quite sure what to do.

But Leif did.

He curled his arms around my son and hiked him higher on his chest. And he began to roam. Pacing and rocking. Cooing and singing.

Words I couldn't make out but sounded of the saddest melody.

It didn't take long before Greyson settled.

Before he found comfort in those strong arms.

Leif pressed kisses to the top of his head and rubbed his back and whispered magical things.

My chest squeezed.

Heart in a fist.

Hope in its clutch.

I tucked Penny into bed while Leif continued to soothe

Greyson into slumber in the main room.

I kissed my daughter's forehead, touched her chin. "Goodnight, my sweet Penny Pie."

I could feel her hesitating, wanting to say something but not sure how to speak.

I sank down onto my knees next to her. Giving her the time she was asking for.

She gazed up at me. "Are you happy, Mom?"

My mind flashed.

Every blessing.

Every joy.

I glanced out the door to where Leif was cradling Greyson.

My spirit sang.

Turning back to her, I tenderly brushed my fingers through her hair. "I am. Are you?"

She nodded fast. "I think . . . I think we should stay here forever."

Joy collided with the questions.

A whole new brand of *what-ifs*.

Ones that were racing out ahead of me. Waiting on us to catch up. Mixed with that was the worry that Leif's grief might cut too deep and be far too vast. Scariest was the way he talked about seeking vengeance as if it were a real plan.

I spread my hand out on her chest, over the quick beat of her innocent, knowing heart. My voice dipped in quiet significance, "I'm not sure where we'll end up at, Penny. Where our home is going to be. But just know wherever that is? We're going to find happiness there. We're going to live the life I always dreamed of giving you."

Belief tipped her mouth into a soft, half-smile. "You're already giving us that, Mom. I hope you know that."

Joy and pride flooded my eyes, and I leaned in, hugged her tight. "I love you so much, my miracle girl."

She nodded into my hair. "I love you to the moon and back."

Little did she know my love was way out, soaring with the stars.

Endless.

Boundless.

Eternal.

Footsteps creaked from the doorway, and I pushed myself to standing and swiped the tears under my eyes.

I did my best to put myself back together.

But my emotions were all over the place.

This feeling coming on stronger every day.

Brown-sugar eyes met mine.

Carefully.

Purposefully.

I'd once thought they were the only thing about him that hinted at softness. I should have known immediately they were a dark sea of compassion. An ocean of humanity. A bridge to his dark, brilliant soul.

"He's out," he grumbled so tenderly, so softly I nearly dropped to my knees right there. "Think his fever broke."

I could only nod, watch as he lay my son into his crib, as he ran his hand over his head, made sure he was safe and warm and comfortable.

It just got worse when he moved over to Penny, bent down, kissed her temple, and whispered a low, "Goodnight," even though she had already drifted to sleep.

Then he straightened.

Straightened to his full, imposing height.

His gaze captured me.

Froze me to the spot.

Bound me in his intensity.

I wanted to speak, but my tongue was stuck, and even if I could find my voice, I knew the words would never come out quite right.

So instead, I backed out of the room, still facing him. The man met me step for step. As if I had become the lure. The bait. What he couldn't resist.

He pulled the kids' door shut behind him, leaving it open an inch, and then he stalked toward me in a slow, purposed stride.

Jaw hard.

Eyes severe.

Heart beating so hard I could hear it going pound, pound, pound.

The drumbeat of us.

I eased deeper into my bedroom, and the man edged forward, the shape of him becoming an inky silhouette. My eyes barely adjusted, focused on him.

Face carved of that hardened stone. Brittle yet strong.

His head canted to the side, and something close to despair came from his mouth. "You got me, Mia. You fucking got me."

Confusion spun, but I was trapped in the web of his complicated mind. My head shook to let him know I didn't understand what he was saying.

He released a soft, seductive laugh. The man stepped forward, burning up my body when he placed his hand on my cheek and brushed the pad of his thumb over it.

Fire flashed.

His voice softened to a plea. "You got me."

His tongue darted out to sweep across his plush, full lips, his hand twitching on my face.

A slow intensity built in the air.

But this?

It was different than ever before.

Bigger and bolder and stronger.

Reaching out, I caressed my fingertips over the thrumming of his broken, beautiful heart. "You already had me."

His throat bobbed, and he moved down to grab the hem of my tank.

Slowly, he peeled the fabric over my head, those eyes never releasing me from their grip the whole time.

Goosebumps raced.

A flashfire across my flesh.

Leif edged in, that gaze on me, before he dipped down and kissed across my shoulder.

A moan rippled free, and my hands curled into his hair. "You have me."

Then he was kissing me everywhere.

Every exposed inch.

But where he normally consumed, he savored.

Featherlight brushes of his lips and tiny peeks of his tongue.

Relishing.

Adoring.

Different.

This perfection that wound me up so tight I could no longer see.

Desire crashed and pulsed and engulfed.

My love for him inundated the space.

Maybe he felt it, couldn't resist it, because he was mumbling these words that sounded liked confessions.

"Need you."

"Want you."

"You are everything."

"Perfect."

"What have you done?"

He flicked the button of my shorts, pushed them to the ground, and lay me out across my bed.

He stood at the end of the mattress.

Gazing down.

I arched and shivered.

Whimpered his name.

He shucked out of his clothes.

Bare.

Magnificent.

All I could see.

All I could imagine.

A future spread out in front of us.

My spirit flooded with him.

Overflowing when he crawled over me and wedged himself between my thighs.

When he took me.

When he filled me.

And I completely drowned when he pressed his mouth softly to mine and murmured his oath, "I love you, Mia West, and I'm never going to let you go."

We stared at each other where we lie in my bed. Fingers twined.

Hearts meshed.

My mind still dizzy with his confessions, and my body still swimming in his love.

Brown-sugar eyes deepened, a frown denting his brow.

"What is it?" I asked, voice quieted to a whisper.

He swept his fingertips along my hairline. "Not sure how to navigate this."

"Us?"

His nod was uncertain. "Yeah, us. This. Everything we've got goin' against us."

A smile fluttered across my lips. "I'm thinking we have more going for us than against us. We just have to stop fighting the current."

His mouth tipped up at the side, and he ran his knuckles down my cheek. "No use fighting it when I'm in too deep and there's no way for me to stand."

I skimmed my fingers down his jaw. "We just have to promise to hold each other up."

He cast me a soft, heartbreaking grin. "Hope floats?"

"It does." I chewed at my bottom lip, cautious but knowing we couldn't continue to live behind the walls. "Is that what you're feeling? Hope?"

He smoothed his palm down my bare shoulder and arm, chasing the shivers he elicited, gliding all the way down until he threaded our fingers together. He brought our hands up between us, fiddling with them like he needed a distraction while he searched for the truth inside.

"Scared to."

His expression moved through so many things.

His grief.

His regret.

The possibility.

His lips pursed for a beat. "It's hard for me to accept this isn't wrong. To believe I'm not stealing what should never be mine."

A swell of sadness coiled in my stomach.

"I know it's scary. I'm scared, too. And I know it's not the same. Not at all. But I think somehow . . . somehow, we were

purposed for this. For this second chance."

Crushing sorrow held him. A physical, living entity. He pulled our twined hands to my face, caressing my jaw over and over again. As if he were looking for comfort for himself and the only thing he knew how to do was give it to me.

Keeping his own joy under lock and key.

His jaw clenched. "Don't deserve your kids. Don't deserve you. And I just keep thinking I'm setting myself up to lose you. To lose them. But that doesn't change a thing because I still know I'll be fighting to keep you until the bitter end."

"I already told you, I'm here. We're here. You want my honest?" I asked.

Tearing down the walls.

Crossing the divide.

"Of course, Mia." For a beat, his eyes dropped closed, and then he was looking at me again. Pinning me with the ferocity of his gaze. "You have become the only truth I know."

I gulped around the magnitude.

And I offered him mine.

"I'm not sure I know how to go on without you, Leif Godwin. This love? It's one you made me feel for the very first time."

Releasing my hand, he reached to brush his fingers through my hair. "You are the light I stopped believing existed."

"And you are my completion."

We stared.

Prisoners of the confession.

Freed by them the same.

I hesitated, then asked, "How is this going to work? You have your band. Your dreams."

God, I'd never even allowed myself to hope to get this far, let alone thought of the logistics of making it work.

What I would do about California.

What I would do about Nixon.

"You wanna be with a mediocre drummer?" He let it come off like a tease.

I shifted, nudging him to roll him onto his back, and I climbed up to straddle him.

He grunted approval.

Those hands on my waist and my heart in his hands. "No, Leif, I want to be with an incredible drummer. A drummer who steals my breath. With a musician whose voice sings to my soul. With a wonderful man who has completely stolen my heart. Kissing you feels like kissing the stars."

A tremor rolled through his body. His features darkened in hatred.

A quick, stark shift to the atmosphere.

"Have to go back to L.A., Mia. Put an end to some old business."

Fear curled and lifted and rose.

Dread infected my blood.

"What does that mean?"

God. What if he was talking about putting himself in danger?

I wanted to press him.

For details.

For his intentions.

But he was silencing them when he reached up and gripped me by the side of the face. "It means I have to put to rest my past. It's the only way I can come back and live for you."

Disquiet clashed with a surge of love.

He let his palm glide down my jaw, my throat, until he was splaying his big hand over my chest. A touch that snuffed out the worry.

"Stay here with me, Mia. In the south. Let's make this our home. Be with me."

I leaned forward, kissed his mouth. "You are the only place I want to be."

Leif

"**D**ude, you killed it! Knew you were gonna rock this shit out of bounds. We rewrote the rules on this album. Pure perfection." Ash punched me in the shoulder, all grins.

Pride pulled tight at my chest.

Not something I was used to feeling. But it was there.

"Turned out pretty good," I told him, barely able to contain my smile.

"Pretty good? That shit is brilliant. Best album of the year, baby. Bet my house, we're going to be getting called up to an entirely different kind of stage. Willow and I are about to redecorate—with Grammy's."

Lyrik chuckled from where he leaned against the massive row of sound equipment.

"For the first time in my life, I think I'm gonna agree with Ash here," he razzed, smirking at his friend. "Album is beast."

Ash's brows lifted to the sky. "Agreeing for the first time? Now that's damn ridiculous considering I've been telling you bitches that Sunder is the best band in the land since I was about sixteen. You just gettin' on the train now?"

Austin clapped Lyrik on the back, his smile slow. "He finally started believing when he hit the hundred-million mark. Asshole needed more proof."

"Chump change, baby. Just wait until *Redeemed* drops. We aren't going to be able to leave our houses," Ash trumpeted.

Baz rocked back in the office chair, nothing but smug. "You're making me really regret the fact I jumped."

Austin shook his head. "Yeah, my big bro here is reaping the rewards and he doesn't even have to tour."

Baz shrugged. "Older. Smarter. Whatever. Besides, I'd probably break a goddamn hip if I got up on that stage and tried to perform."

Ash's expression morphed into disgusted disbelief. "What nonsense do you speak of?" He held out his arms. "This boy right here is barely hitting his prime."

"You just keep telling yourself that."

"Oh, I plan to."

Was hard to process the lightness in my chest. One I couldn't remember ever being there before.

Excitement.

Proud to have been here but anxious to leave.

I stuffed my notebook into my backpack, zipped it up. "Think I'm gonna head out. It's truly been an honor working with you guys."

Ash cracked a grin. All teeth. "What, you think you have somewhere more important to be?"

Tried to keep the smile from breaking out for fear it was gonna be downright giddy. "Might."

"Oh, yeah, and just where is that?" There was Ash, pushing all the buttons.

"All right, all right, let the poor guy be. He had to suffer through working with you the last two months," Baz said, standing

from his chair. "Besides, Shea and I are planning a little celebration at our house tomorrow night to toast another Sunder victory. Hope you all will be there."

He looked directly at me.

On the spot.

Was going to have to get used to this shit.

But she was worth it.

They were worth it.

I gave a tight nod. "That should work."

"Cool. See you then."

"Later," I said, heading out of the studio and toward the stairway that led to the main floor. I climbed to the top, only to stall out when I heard Lyrik calling to me from behind. "Hey, Leif, hold up a minute."

I turned around to face him as he stepped onto the landing. His black hair a disaster, tattoos bristling with his blunt energy. "Just wanted to tell you how much I appreciate you dropping everything for us these last two months. Knew you were going to be good, but I had no idea what you were going to bring to this album."

Didn't want to stand there getting puffed up and cocky, but his words were hard to ignore.

"Meant a lot . . . that you trusted me."

Guess I was speaking of so much more than just the music.

His nod was tight. "And what's the plan now? You headin' back to South Carolina?" There was no missing what he was getting at.

I blew out a sigh, wondering how it was that I didn't instantly feel defensive. "I love her, Lyrik, and believe me, that is not a sentiment that I take lightly."

Something unsettled moved through his expression. "So . . . how's it gonna be? They should be locking down the case soon, which means she'll be good to go back to L.A."

Knew all of this was between Mia and me, but I figured if it wasn't for Lyrik, we wouldn't have collided, anyway.

We wouldn't be here, in this place, planning a future together.

Huh.

I guessed that bitch Karma had overstayed her welcome.

"Asked her to stay. With me. Know it's going to take some patience to figure this out, that we're goin' to have to make sacrifices, but I don't think you're much of a stranger to that."

"No, brother. I'm not. It's fuckin' hard. But believe me, it's worth it. Music is like any other job. You do it, you do it well, and then you get your ass home to your girl. Don't fucking get distracted or start making pit stops on your way home, if you get my meaning."

I scraped out a rough laugh. "Loud and clear."

Not that I needed to be reminded.

He rubbed his palm over his mouth and down his chin, looked me square. "Take care of them." He reached out and squeezed me on the shoulder. "And fuck, man, let her take care of you, too."

Without saying anything else, he turned and bounded back downstairs.

I exhaled. For the first time, it didn't feel so heavy.

I walked out the door and into the blazing sun that was just beginning to dive to the west, the late afternoon hot and humid and filled with possibility.

That riot continued to go down in the middle of me.

Torn between love and loyalty.

One in the same.

"Only you. Forever. No matter what."
"Do you promise?"
"I promise."

I dropped my head, gulping around the memories, knowing that oath was no longer true.

Not sure if it made me a bastard.

A cheater and a liar.

Hating what I'd done. A blight that would lie on me forever.

"I'm sorry, Maddie. I'm so damned sorry."

It was a silent prayer, held in the wind, kept in the whisper that whipped through the trees.

Then I pulled out my phone and tapped out a message that I'd been contemplating all week.

Me: What happens if I let it go?

Phone rang.
"Braxton."
"What the fuck is going on, Leif?"
I stalled. Hesitated. Hadn't given him many details. Even though I trusted him with my life, it was always safer to keep names separated. Identities. Yeah, he knew I was in Savannah, but I hadn't given him the details of where I was staying or who I was playing with.

He would have lost his shit if he knew.

It was reckless, but I'd been from the beginning. But sometimes you had to wander lost before you found out where you belonged.

"Just don't know what good it'll do at this point."

He breathed out a skeptical sound. "Be straight with me, Leif. What the fuck is going on?"

"Met someone."

He sighed. Warring, too. "That's good, Leif. That's good. But it doesn't change the fact that you're hiding out on the other side of the country. Running for your life. Makes it more dangerous, honestly."

Distress pulsed. A warning that crashed through the fortress of bliss.

"Then how do I end it?" It was low and hard. A bitter plea.

"Might not be your concern any longer, anyway."

Hatred flashed.

His face burned in my mind.

All of it wrapped up with the need for this to just go away.

So I could stay here with Mia.

Devoted.

Not caught in this web between who I was and who I wanted to be.

"Pretty sure that greedy bastard has already dug his own grave," Brax continued. "Karma is coming for his punk ass.

Another shipment was scraped. Evidence is finally pointing to him."

Might have been the first time I was happy to hear that Karma had shown her face.

This was the exact thing Brax and I had been trying to gather for years. Enough evidence dumped at that bastard's door that there would be no question. Let his own mistakes eat him alive.

It wouldn't even have been a set up considering we were only pointing Krane to the truth.

"You haven't had anyone following you again?" he clarified.

"No."

Had never been so relieved to find out an arrest had been made. They still hadn't charged the guy with Lana's death, but the detective said he was close to piecing it together.

Could almost see Braxton nodding. "Listen, found out it was your mom who sent those two guys. All it took was a couple of beers for them to spill. She wasn't after you, Leif. She wanted them to deliver information but you had them running scared before they got the chance."

I blew out a sigh, not sure that I could believe it.

Accept it.

She'd done too many wrongs for me to buy that.

But still . . . if I was letting this go, I had to let it all go, and I found I was having a hard time hanging onto the anger when I wasn't even sure she'd been involved.

"Think you should sit tight for a few weeks. See how this thing goes down here in L.A. Hoping it will take care of itself. And that's how it ends, Leif. Then you live your life. Leave California behind. Be with your girl and play with your band. It's your time."

Maddie and Haylee's faces gusted through my mind.

Beautiful.

Innocent.

Sweet.

Grief clutched me by the throat.

Could I do it? Let it go? There was nothing I could do to bring them back, and I was starting to realize I'd been chasing down a feeling that was never going to come.

When it came to them, I wasn't ever gonna feel satisfaction or relief.

"Okay," I told him. "I'll hang tight. Let me know when you get word."

"You know I will." He paused before he said, "Happy for you, Leif. Honestly never thought you'd get there. Makes me fucking happy that you did."

"Thanks, man."

I ended the call.

Not sure if I felt like scum or if I was doing the right thing.

I'd made the mistake of bringing Maddie down with me. A prisoner to the life I was chained to without her even knowing what I was involved in.

Didn't want to be the fool who did the same thing to Mia.

Mia.

My angel in the attic.

My spirit clutched, girl calling to me from across the miles, and I got on my bike, kicked it over, and let the vibration move through me as I headed back to the West Mansion, knowing things were about to change and they were going to change for the better.

I took the twenty-minute ride back into Savannah, and even though I slowed the bike to take the narrow, neighborhood streets, anticipation wound me high.

Couldn't wait to get back to her.

See her face.

Start making plans.

I pulled into the garage, quick to park before I made a beeline for the gate.

I punched in the code and stepped into Eden.

Hell was going to have to wait.

I dropped my bag in the guest house before I turned in the direction of Mia's wing. That long row of windows lit up like glitter as the sun streaked down from the sky at a low angle.

My heart thudded. My stomach knotted.

I buzzed into the house, and the smell of fresh paint filled my nostrils.

I moved toward the hall, sight catching on the wet canvas

where I knew she'd stood with a brush in her hand.

A man on one side of a cavern. A woman and two children on the other. Their faces distorted in that mystical, haunting way, but there was no mistaking the fact they were breaching the distance.

Finding a way.

Anxious, I sped up, rapping my knuckles once on the partially opened door and poking my head inside.

Penny was on the couch, phone in hand. She looked up when she heard me and grinned.

Another cracked, brittle piece of my heart sloughed off.

"Leif, you're back. Did you get all finished? Uncle Lyrik said this album is the bomb. Do you want to go for pizza tonight? Mom said it was fine and then maybe we can ask Kallie, too!"

Her ramble of words were sweet and hopeful and gracious.

Like she was asking me for permission.

Like she'd welcomed me as a part of her life.

A child. A child. A child.

My spirit trembled and shook. Haylee's face flashed behind my eyes.

I missed her. Fuck, I would miss her every day of my life.

The wound that was my daughter would never heal.

But I had to believe Mia had crashed into my life with a purpose.

Proof had to be what possessed me when I looked at her children.

I crossed the space, leaning over Penny, and I pressed a kiss to her forehead. Relished in the gift. Something I was never supposed to have again, but I'd be a fool to question what I was given. "I would love to have pizza."

She rocked her head back, beaming up at me.

Love rushed.

I edged back, blinked, my entire world rocked.

Never imagined when I got pushed off that cliff that when I landed there would be an entire family waiting at the bottom to catch me.

"Where's your mom?"

She gestured with her chin. "In her room, reading."

"Okay. I'm going to go tell her hi."

"Okay."

I straightened, not sure what to do with the jealousy that bashed me in the chest when her phone lit-up with a Facetime call that read *Dad*.

No doubt, Mia and I had tons of sorting to do. There was no chance she could one-hundred-percent leave L.A. behind. Doubted that I could, either.

"Oh, there's my dad. He said he was going to call me right back."

My nod was tight, as tight as my throat when I swallowed. "No worries. Take your time. We'll leave when you're finished."

There.

That was civil, right?

The right way to handle this bullshit?

Spinning on my heel, I moved for Mia's door.

"Hi, Dad!" Penny said in her sweet way.

"Penny-Girl."

It should have been nothing.

The voice.

But every hair on my body stood on end when I heard it.

Paranoid.

My brain fried.

Waiting for the motherfucking shoe to drop.

That was it.

Still, I froze, cocked my head, and turned my ear. Dread lifted in a sticky sweat that coated my flesh. Mind distorted like a bad trip.

"When are you coming home?" It was a grumble. Petulant.

Selfishness to the extreme.

Vicious and cruel.

No.

This couldn't be happening.

It . . . it wasn't possible.

I was losing it.

Coming unhinged.

Sins I'd committed coming back to taunt me.

"I, um . . . I'm not sure," Penny answered, uneasy, because the prick was putting her on the spot.

"You need to tell your mom it's time for you to get back here. Done with her excuses."

Nausea boiled. Rising up fast. Filling my throat and coating my tongue in hatred.

I wasn't even aware that my goddamn feet had moved.

I was standing off to the side of Penny without even really knowing how I'd gotten there.

Not even fucking surprised at the same time.

Because I should have known.

Should have known I couldn't take and take and take and get away with what I'd done.

Like I could be absolved of the guilt.

Because angels and devils didn't mix.

But there I was, staring at the vilest one.

His face on the screen.

Nixon Shoewalter.

Our eyes clashed through the phone.

Hatred gnashed my teeth.

Knocked me from the side.

Blunt force trauma to the back of the head.

"What the fuck?" he hissed below his breath.

I stumbled back.

Stricken by what this meant.

Fuck.

I grabbed my head in my hands.

World a tilt-a-whirl.

Gaining speed.

Disorienting.

Devastating.

"Leif . . . what's wrong? Are you okay? You look like you're going to throw up," Penny rushed, jumping off the couch, waving that phone around like a bomb.

The atomic kind.

One that decimated everything.

I should have known I couldn't have this.

That I was just setting myself up to lose.

Only it was exponentially worse than even I could have imagined.

"I . . . I have to go," I managed to wheeze.

Heart manic.

Sight blurred.

Couldn't find my footing with her waving that phone in my face. Might as well have been a hot poker that was going to stab me in the heart.

I stumbled back, banging into the wall. A picture knocked to the floor. Glass shattered while the ground completely dropped out from under me.

I squeezed my eyes like it could stand the chance of bringing me back. Wake me up. Shake me out of this nightmare.

No. God. Please.

Agony mauled me like it was a fucking monster.

A wraith.

That bitch Karma was cackling off to the side as she commanded for him to finally do me in.

Like I actually thought I was going to escape her.

"Leif." Penny tried to grab my hand.

Couldn't even let her touch me.

I fumbled back from her like I was gonna get burned.

Who the fuck was I kidding?

I was dust.

Nothing but fiery, flickering out debris.

I finally made it to the door.

The voice I would never forget shouted from the phone, "You motherfucker. You got to my family. You are dead."

I tore down the hall and burst out into the fading light.

Shock shifting to rage.

Because he was wrong.

It was his debt that was coming due.

Leif
Three Years Ago

I crept in through the back door into the kitchen. Cringed when Maddie lifted her head from where she was waiting for me at the small table. Streaks of mascara ran down her eyes, hair a mess, distrust on her face. "Where were you?"

Guilt spiraled.

Shivered and shook.

I blew out a sigh and tossed my keys to the counter. "Out."

Wanted to keep her from it.

Protect her from the truth.

I was so damned close.

I just needed a few more days.

She laughed a disbelieving sound, and she pushed to her feet, her head shaking with hurt. "You're a liar."

In defeat, I pressed my hands to the counter and dropped my head, talking to the granite because I wasn't brave enough to look at her. "I'm trying not to be."

Soggy laughter ripped from her throat. "We have a daughter, Leif."

Slowly, I spun around.

Love gripped me by the chest. What this was doing to my girl.

She wasn't a fool. She was just blameless.

Incorruptible. Which was exactly the way I wanted it to be.

"I have an out, Maddie. After this last job, I'm done. Keeton is cutting me loose."

"You were supposed to be done three years ago," she begged.

"It's rare that I do anything for him. Just when he absolutely needs me."

"You think that makes it okay?" It was a shout. A whimper. Her outright disappointment. "Is this the life you want your daughter to live? Is this what you want her to see when she looks at you? Is this the legacy you want to leave behind?"

The force of her words should have blasted me back.

Instead, they propelled me forward.

Desperate to touch her. To get her in my arms. I wrapped them around her.

Tight.

Let her pound her anger out on my chest.

Murmured the whole time, "I'm sorry. I'm fucking sorry. I tried to get free. I tried, baby. I tried."

"Why should I believe you?" she choked out where she sobbed into my shirt.

"Because I love you. Because Haylee is my life. Because I'm doing everything I have to so I can get free of this. It's over this weekend, and then I'm taking all of us away. Far fucking away. Where none of this can touch us again."

"Do you love me, Leif? Really, truly love me? Tell me this isn't a lie. That I'm not wasting my life believing in you."

She looked up at me with the burden of what I'd done to her swimming in those green eyes.

Grief. Hurt. With the hope she'd sparked in me the day she'd stumbled into the shop.

I cupped her face, and I gave her my only perfect truth.

"Only you. Forever. No matter what."

"Do you promise?"

"I promise."

Braxton and I rode. Headlights of our bikes spraying through the dark, deep, bitter night.

Nixon was on his bike leading us into the darkness.

Couldn't stand the prick. One of Krane's crew who'd been sent to make sure we were square on our end.

Oversee.

Watch.

He was nothing but a pompous ass who didn't give a fuck about anyone. Had only worked with him a couple times. Barely knew him. It didn't take a whole lot to get the gist.

At least I had Brax at my side. The one guy in this disaster that I could trust.

It was close to dawn.

In the most wicked hour when no one remained awake except for the demons that roamed the earth.

The truck followed close behind, and we veered off the desolate two-lane road onto a dirt path carved through the desert, city lights making Los Angeles look like it sat within a dusky snowglobe in the far distance.

Our bikes bounced on the rough terrain. I gritted my teeth, fighting the feeling of unease that kept sweeping through me.

Disquiet a zephyr that hissed and moaned.

We came to a stop where three Mercedes SUVs were parked facing out.

Krane's men stepped out.

Soldier's carrying huge fucking guns.

Sweat gathered at my temples, and I swallowed down the fear. I hated this shit. Hated it with every fiber of who I was.

I was done.

So damn done.

Climbing off my bike, I gave a signal for our guys to get out. They followed instructions, quick to move the product from the hidden compartments in the truck, and Krane himself handed over the money.

We were nothing but middle men.

Moving product from one fucking monster to the other.

The devil in between.

I took it.

"Good?"

He patted my shoulder like a prick. "Good."

Dawn broke at the horizon. A blazing burn of golds that outlined the mountains and shot rays of pinks and oranges into the coming day.

It felt like earning a medal.

An award for making it to the end.

A race I hadn't wanted to run.

But I knew way down deep that I'd been easy to sucker in.

Greed a concept that had been ingrained in me long ago. Going without made you that way.

Hungry.

Jealous.

Thinking it was just fine if you reached out and took what you wanted no matter who you hurt.

You deserved it, right?

But I'd seen enough to know I'd rather starve than be a part of this sleazy, disgusting world.

Had seen homes shattered.

Families split.

Had seen men slaughtered.

Their blood spilled on the ground because that greed just kept going round and round.

Done.

I was so done.

I eased over a sloping hill, and the city came into sharp, plain view. My heart raced toward the good. Toward what was right. Swore in that second that I would never lie to Maddie again.

Phone kept going nuts in my pocket, so I pulled off to the side of the two-lane road, pulled it out, flinching when I saw the name on the screen.

"Keeton," I said, gruff when I answered it.

Done.

Done.

Done.

He had to fucking know. I wasn't going to get pushed around any longer.

"What the fuck happened last night?" he growled.

That knot of unease tightened. "Don't know what you're talking about."

He didn't even laugh. It was venom in his voice. "Krane claims ten-percent of the delivery was scraped."

That unease bloomed into a discord.

A jarring of dread.

I swallowed hard. "Weighed it myself."

"I know." It was an accusation.

Fuck.

I roughed a hand through my hair that was suddenly dripping with sweat.

Money I had in my pack weighing a million pounds.

"It was there, Keeton. All of it. Before we packed it into the truck. Nixon was there. He oversaw the entire thing."

"Seems like the perfect opportunity for you to take a little parting gift."

"Fuck, Keeton. Last thing I want to do is get indebted to you or anyone else. Wouldn't touch it. Want out. Not to dig myself deeper."

"Someone did it, or Krane is lying."

"And you trust that piece of shit?" I spat.

Guy was a savage.

Didn't give a shit about anything or anyone who got in his way. "He's a businessman."

Agitation blistered across my skin. A red-hot knife of fear. "Wasn't me, Keeton. I swear to you."

"Yeah? Well someone is lying to me."

He ended the call without saying anything, and panic had me on my bike, racing back toward the city.

We were leaving.

Getting the hell out of this town.

Wasn't even going to take the time to pack.

I was dropping this shit at Keeton's door and was gone.

Phone went crazy again, and I tried to ignore it, pushing my bike faster around the curves in the road, about five minutes from hitting the freeway.

Finally gave in when it would stop only to start ringing again.

I pulled off, ripped my phone free, almost breathing out in relief when I saw it was Brax. "You hear this bullshit?" I asked the second I put it to my ear.

Braxton had connections on every side. Always in the know.

He didn't say anything for a beat. Morbid energy held.

That dread slicked and shivered and sent my pulse slugging with fear. "Someone pegged this on Nix. Can't locate him, but I got word that Morgue was sent. Krane doesn't want repayment. He wants blood."

Morgue.

Wasn't a person.

Just a reference to any man who was sent for a hit.

Vomit lifted. Thick in my throat.

"Goddamn it," I hissed. Sickness clawing. "That idiot."

A disturbance burned through the line. "Word is, Nix has got a girl who's pregnant. Another kid who's seven or eight. Think he's heading their way. Krane is pissed. Wants to set an example."

"Fuck." It was a shout. Disgust. Horror. I knew I hated that prick. Knew he couldn't be trusted.

"Where are you?" I asked. "One of us has to check this out. Make sure his family is safe."

"About forty-five from the shop."

I sighed. Struggled. Battled with this feeling that rose up in me. I couldn't just . . . turn my back.

Ignore this.

"You have an address?"

"Think I can get one. How far away are you?"

"About twenty minutes from the shop."

Which meant no matter where in the city Nix's family lived, I was going to be closer. He didn't say anything. We both knew this had become my duty.

Krane was brutal. Didn't matter if I hated that fucker Nix or not.

Couldn't sit aside and let this happen.

"Text it to me. I'm on my way."

"Be careful, brother. Know you want to help, but don't get in the line of fire."

"His kids don't deserve what he has coming to him. I will warn them. Head off anything that might be coming their way. Until Nix can get there to get them out or this blows over."

I ended the call and hopped back onto my bike, and when I hit the highway, I hit it at a way too high rate of speed for the load I was carrying. Darting around cars. Cutting lanes.

I didn't care. I had to get there.

Stand in if someone came for his family. Doubted he really gave a shit.

But I did.

I fucking did.

Guilt clotted my throat.

What I'd put Maddie through.

The worry.

The fear.

Dragging them into a life that they didn't deserve.

This was a motherfucking *bad* life.

I only stopped to get the address when it came through.

Was barely breathing by the time I made it down into the city streets. Stop-light after stop-light. I was almost there when my phone started going manic again.

There was no ignoring it.

This feeling that consumed.

Vile and distorted.

Gripping me everywhere. I took a turn into a neighborhood that was nicer than what I expected, eased off to the curb, and pressed my phone to my ear when I saw it was Braxton.

He was shouting before I even got it there. "Nix went to Krane. Said it was you. Said he had proof that it was you. You need to get home."

I didn't even respond before I was flying down the street.

Taking every turn too fast.

Too reckless.

Too careless.

But that was what I'd always been.

Careless. Thinking I could keep two separate lives. Protect my family and please my piece of shit stepfather.

I turned the last corner onto our street.

And that was the moment every lie that I'd ever told caught up to me.

Mia

*A*gitated voices flooded my room, drawing my attention from my book. One second later, something banged against the wall before I was startled upright to the sound of glass shattering on the floor.

My pulse spiked, and I scrambled to get off the bed to find out what was happening.

The door flew open before I had the chance to go out.

Penny was there, shaking in the doorway. Worry written on her face.

"Penny. Sweetheart . . . what's going on? Are you okay?" I rushed, my attention darting everywhere. Trying to find out what was happening.

She struggled for an explanation. "I . . . I don't know. Leif got here and I asked him if he wanted to go for pizza and then Dad

called and then Leif ran out. He seemed really, really upset, Mom. And Dad was saying really mean things and then he just hung up."

Unease billowed.

Leif had to have heard Nixon on Penny's call.

Shit.

Moisture welled in her eyes, and apprehension blew up like a balloon inside of me. I hadn't been looking forward to talking with Nixon about Leif, or vice versa, really.

"It's okay, sweetheart. It's okay." I peered over her shoulder. "Do you know where Leif went?"

Her lips pressed thin. "I don't know. He wouldn't talk to me. But I'm worried about him. When I looked at him, I got this feeling . . ."

My knowing child shivered and touched her stomach that I knew was twisted in knots.

Empathy and compassion and warmth.

I ran my fingers down her cheek. "Take a deep breath. It's going to be okay. Your brother is with Auntie Tamar in the main house. Why don't you go in there with them? I'll go talk to Leif. I'm sure everything is fine."

Her nod was shaky, and I dropped a kiss to the top of her head and followed her out into the hall. She went to the left, and I went to the right, my steps quickened as I rushed for the door.

Trying not to panic.

But with every step, the air shifted.

This feeling taking me over.

The energy he'd left behind thick and ugly and distressed.

I pushed the door open to stagnant, muggy heat, and I tried to talk myself down from the ledge. Convince myself not to freak out as I crossed the yard to the guest house.

It wasn't like I'd had some delusion that Leif and Nixon were going to be friends. Or even civil. Their personalities had already promised they were going to clash.

But this was the last way I'd wanted them to meet.

I bounded the two steps to the small porch, not even knocking before I tossed open the door.

I nearly got knocked onto my butt with the frenetic energy that blazed back.

Heavy footsteps pounded from the bedroom at the back, the walls trembling and the air screaming with pain.

Warily, I inched that way, my breaths coming short and my pulse ratcheting in anxiety. By the time I made it to the bedroom doorway, my head was dizzy, and my heart careened in a manic beat when I found Leif there.

As hard as he'd ever been.

Every muscle in his body stone.

Jaw grit.

Hatred in his movements as he frantically stuffed his things into a bag.

Horror etched every cell in my body.

"Wha-what are you doing?"

He didn't even flinch. Already well aware I was there.

"Leaving."

It didn't matter that his intention was already plain as day, the word jolted me back.

Like I'd been impaled by an arrow.

All the way through.

"What? Why? What happened?" I stumbled into the room. Knees weak. Trying to hold it together.

He zipped up the bag. He refused to look at me as he slung the backpack over his shoulder. "Just time to go."

He shouldered around me.

Was he kidding me?

Anger surged. A crashing wave that slammed against the heartbreak that sliced through my chest.

I reached for him, my hand curling around his wrist. Fire streaked up my arm. This man who I was connected to in some intrinsic way. "Don't you dare walk out on me, Leif Godwin."

He jolted like he was shocked, his voice haggard, refusing to look at me. "Don't make this any harder than it has to be, Mia."

"Any harder than it has to be?" My head shook. Frantic. Disoriented. "I trusted you. Put my faith in you. Took all your reservations because I could see that you were haunted by your demons. I took on that pain, Leif, and I let it break me."

I touched my aching heart. That place that he held in the palm of his hand.

I angled around, trying to get him to look at me. To listen. To *hear* me. "And you know what, it was worth it. It was worth it because we met there. In the middle of it. In a place that was just for us. And from it, you promised we were going to build a life together. That we were going to make this thing work."

He whirled around, spite on his tongue as he released the foul-words into the bitter air. "Yeah, and I also promised you that I was going to ruin you."

"You're a liar."

His face blanched at my accusation.

White as a ghost.

Grief curled around me. Terrified of whatever was happening in his dark, bleak mind.

I pressed on, refusing to let him just walk out.

"You're a liar," I repeated, "if you say this doesn't mean something. You're going to stand there and pretend like you don't want me? That you don't feel me? Pretend like you don't know that we belong together?"

His sorrow darkened the atmosphere.

Finally, he looked at me.

Those brown-sugar eyes held nothing but torture.

His soul slaughtered.

"You're right, Mia. I am a liar. I've been lying to myself. Telling myself that I could possibly have this. That I could have you. That I might in some small way be deserving of those kids." He pointed aggressively in the direction of the guest wing. "Time to give up the ghost. Because guess what, those ghosts are here for me."

"What does that mean?"

"Means I can't fucking have you, Mia."

"No." My head shook, and a sob crawled up my throat. "No. I . . . I know you've experienced the worst kind of sorrow in your life, and I know the kids' father was on the phone and that's going to be hard to navigate, but—"

He had me pinned to the wall in a flash.

I gasped. Words silenced beneath the potency of this man.

Gloom covered me whole.

An eclipse.

But this darkness? It was vile and depraved.

He pressed his hands to the wall on either side of me as if he were trying to hold himself back, his nose pressed to my cheek as he grunted the anguished words, "You don't have the first clue, Mia. Don't have the first clue what I've done or what I'm getting ready to do. And I promise you, when I'm done? You're going to hate me."

He ripped himself back.

Torment and malice written in his expression.

Then he turned, nothing but a storm that thundered through the house as he moved for the front door.

Despair ravaged through the middle of me.

Violent.

Fierce.

Overwhelming.

I ran after him.

It didn't matter that it probably made me a fool.

That I was desperate.

Pleading.

We'd come too far, experienced too much, shared too much hope for me to let him just walk out.

Without an explanation.

Without a reason for the poison he was spilling on our lives.

I was a foot behind him when I rasped, "Then tell me you don't love me. Tell me that was a lie."

Leif whirled around.

I nearly hit my knees when his hands landed on my face in the same second his mouth crushed against mine.

He kissed me. Kissed me in a way that sheered through my heart. Cut all the way to my soul.

I could taste it. The guilt on his tongue and the surrender in his spirit.

He pried himself away, hands still holding me tight. "Doesn't matter how much I love you, Mia. It won't change who I am. And me pretending that it will? It's only going to hurt you more in the end. *And that's my honest.*"

Then Leif pulled his hands away as if he'd been burned by the shame, turned his back, and banged out the door.

"Leif . . . please, don't leave me."

He didn't turn back.

Didn't stop.

And that was the moment when Leif Godwin finally brought me to my knees.

Ruined.

Just like he'd promised.

"Hey." The bed sank down at my side as Tamar's worried voice filled my ears. Gentle fingers brushed through my hair where I was curled up in a ball.

My face buried in the pillow.

As if it might stand the chance of burying the heartbreak.

But I didn't think there was enough dirt on Earth to fill up the hole Leif Godwin had left.

My falling star that had burned out far too soon.

I guessed I'd been the fool who'd tried to catch him.

"How are you doing?" Tamar asked softly.

I sniffled. No use in pretending I hadn't been shattered in two. "Terrible. How are the kids?"

"Fine. They're watching a movie with Brendon and Adia, so I thought I would come and check on you. Did you sleep at all last night?"

I rolled a fraction, just enough so I could peek up at her through the mane that covered my face like a black mourning veil.

But that's what this felt like.

Like some piece of myself that had just come to life had died.

"Not really."

Sadness slipped from between her pursed lips. "I'm so sorry you're going through this, Mia. The last thing I'd expected was for him to leave like that once the album was finished."

Grief-stricken, I shook my head against the pillow. "Maybe I was the fool for believing that he wouldn't."

She hummed a disconcerted sound and kept playing with a lock of my hair. "I think he's scared. Scared out of his mind with what he feels for you."

I hugged myself tighter, guarding against the downpour of agony. "He's a coward. I mean . . . he . . . he couldn't handle my daughter talking to her dad?" I frantically blinked through the assertion.

Unable to make sense of it.

I kept rummaging around in the rubble like I could find an acceptable reason.

But there was no excuse for him leaving like this.

"He should have at least talked to me. Told me his fears. If he had to go, if he couldn't face them in order to be with us, then I would have understood. It would have broken me, but I would have let him go. But for him to leave while my daughter was waiting for him to take her for pizza? That's unforgiveable."

A disorder billowed.

The rumble of a quiet, building storm.

Something was off.

So off.

Tamar's words were soft. "Sometimes people never learn to see through their own darkness."

The knot in my throat wobbled, nothing but a ball of crushed up, broken glass, and through bleary eyes, I stared up at her.

"I wanted him to. I wanted him to find that in me. In us. So badly." The confession scraped from the wounds he'd left written on me. Bleeding and raw. "He suffers so terribly, and I know he's turning away from the hope of joy for fear of suffering it all over again. I'm not sure he knows anything but grief."

And there was the truth.

This man's pain greater than any person should endure.

"You saw the goodness in him, Mia. Your heart recognized what was hidden deep. But maybe he's not ready. Maybe he's not ready for the amazing things that the three of you are, and he's afraid of spoiling what you already have."

A grumble rolled from the other side of the room, and I peeked over through my mess of hair to see my brother toiling in the doorway.

"Mia . . ." Lyrik seemed to hesitate. "Need you to know something," he grumbled low.

My entire being flinched. I wasn't sure I could handle him telling me something horrible about Leif right then.

He eased into my room, ominous and powerful the way that he always was. "Know this is going to sound like I'm sticking up for him, but I think you should know that I talked to him after we wrapped the album yesterday afternoon."

My heart shivered.

Defenseless.

Terrified to listen but starving for any word.

Slowly, I forced myself to turn, to sit up, to face my brother and whatever he had to say.

"He was gettin' ready to leave the studio. Could tell he couldn't wait to get back to you. Ash was giving him shit about it, and he didn't even try to deny it. I followed him upstairs, asked him his intentions."

Sorrow lapped.

Why?

Why would he just leave me, then?

Lyrik wet his lips in agitation.

Misery moaned within me when he continued, "He told me straight up that he was in love with you, Mia. That the two of you were goin' to figure out how to make this thing work. Admitted it was going to be hard, but acknowledged you were worth it."

In his own helpless confusion, he hiked his shoulders while I choked over the sob that his words wrung out of me.

"Have to say, after talking to him, he didn't strike me as the guy who was just gonna bail." It felt like maybe his words were issued with some kind of warning.

I licked my dried, cracked lips. "He said it was time for him to go. That it didn't matter how much he loved me, he could never keep me."

Each word was lined with despair.

Lyrik scoffed a rough sound. "Yeah, well I'd buy the idea that he doesn't believe he's worthy of you. But the fact he took off because Penny was talkin' to Nix? Pretty sure the guy didn't figure out just last night that you have a baby daddy."

I fumbled over a shaky nod.

My stomach sick.

Nausea fierce.

Agony prowled my throat, so thick it choked me, and I was sure I was going to vomit.

No longer able to contain it.

To keep it inside.

I swallowed over the thick knot. "Something happened. Something bigger than I understand."

I knew it.

I felt it deep.

Throbbing wild and desperately.

"Maybe give him some time," Lyrik broached, a slow suggestion that threatened to wrap me in chains I could never be released from.

Sadness pilfered out on a surrendered sigh. "I can't have a man coming in and out of our lives when he pleases, Lyrik."

My brother's smile was grim. "Doubt he's very pleased right now, Mia."

I was pierced with an arrow of sorrow.

One in the perfect shape of Leif.

There was no question he was out there suffering even more than he had been before.

Tamar rubbed my arm, forcing her voice into some brightness that there was no chance I could feel. "Why don't you get in the shower and come and get something to eat?"

I started to nod, only to go still when I heard Penny's voice echoing down the hall. "Mom! Dad's here! Dad's here!"

Her voice was excited while my spirit stumbled through the dread.

Through the anger I felt that he seemed to be the catalyst that had sent Leif running.

It wasn't his fault.

Logically, I knew that. But I couldn't help the blame.

Gloom covering me like a dark, black shroud.

A shiver of disgust rolled.

Tamar edged off the bed and spun in the direction of the door. "What is he doing here?"

I shook my head. "Probably jealous I had a man here."

"God. I can't stand him." She let it hiss from below her breath. I wasn't even sure if she was directing it at me.

I guessed it was the first time I realized that neither could I.

Wholly.

Truly.

The man a mistake who had given me my greatest joy.

Because my pulse spiked, shivered, and slowed.

A wary thud pulsing in my chest.

Lyrik pushed from the wall with a heavy exhale from his nose. A bull getting ready to charge. He'd never exactly been a Nixon fan.

But none of it changed the fact that he was my children's father.

I scrubbed my palms over my face in an attempt to break up the disorder. To paste on something that bore a semblance of normal.

"Mom! Mom!"

The door banged open to the main room.

"Dad's here!"

Lyrik looked at me, jaw hard. "Your call, Mia."

His hands clenched into fists. No doubt, he would gladly toss Nixon's ass to the curb.

I shook my head. "It's fine."

It wasn't though.

Because I grimaced when my bedroom door flung open and Penny raced in.

Nixon followed her in, carrying Greyson.

Greyson who squirmed and whined in confusion, stretching his whole body for me when he saw me. "Mommy! I get you!"

I forced myself out of the bed and to standing, hating that I was wearing a tank and short sleep shorts.

347

I met Nixon's glare, his want, his questions. Drudging through the force of them, I edged by Tamar who stood rigid so I could take Greyson from him. The second I had him in my arms, Greyson clung to my neck, staring out, like he'd forgotten who Nixon was.

And maybe that was my fault.

Taking them away.

But it felt right.

Affirmed by the cruel stare that pinned me to the spot.

Tension filled the air.

Tight and dense and suffocating.

Something ugly and wrong that made me want to crawl out of my skin.

"Nixon," I said, dipping my chin. I couldn't even begin to hide my annoyance that he'd just shown up here.

I felt terrible that the smile slipped off Penny's face, my sweet girl uneasily looking between us, but I couldn't find it in myself to fake it.

"Mia." This from Lyrik who raged by the wall.

I didn't look at him, just muttered, "It's fine, Lyrik. You should probably give us a minute to talk."

I could feel the animosity coming off of my brother, the silent threat he emitted. Nixon just stared him down. Both of them volatile. Prone to violence.

"Do you want me to take the kids?" Tamar offered from right behind me.

"Yeah."

Nixon grunted. "Leave my kids here."

Lyrik took a step forward.

I put out my hand. "It's fine. Just go."

I could sense Tamar nod, her wariness, the little shock of vicious that she was radiating from her body as she wound passed, Lyrik hesitating, before he finally gave.

At least I knew I would always have them to take up my side.

The four of us were frozen in this lock-down until Lyrik and Tamar's footsteps retreated, both doors clicking shut.

I glanced at my daughter. "Penny, please take Greyson into the next room."

She seemed unsure, questioning it all, but she took Greyson from my arms. "Thank you, sweet girl."

She nodded, looking back once, before she stepped into the other room and closed the door.

"What are you doing here?" I demanded as soon as they were out of earshot.

The second I said it, Nixon let go of the anger he'd been restraining. "I told you I was coming to take you and my kids home."

I was struck with a bluster of rage. Something old. Something I'd tried to keep covered for the sake of my children. "And I think you should know by now that you don't have a say about what I do."

He angled forward. His ice-blue eyes hard, all the sharp, cut angles of his face harsh. "Well, I think I have a say in where my kids are living and who they are hanging around, don't you? Where is he?"

"Not here." I wasn't about to honor him with the details.

"Stay away from him, Mia. I'm warning you."

I could feel the force of the grief twisting my face. "That's what this is about? That's why you showed up here? Because I'm with someone else? Because I fell in love with someone else?" I spat the words. Knowing they were daggers.

I didn't care.

He didn't get to do this.

Fury blistered across his face, and he released a cruel bout of laughter. "You think you love him? You don't even know him."

I scoffed. Disgusted. Wondering how I'd ever let this jerk touch me. "You don't know anything about me, Nixon. Know nothing. You know nothing of what I feel or what I want or who *I know*. And you don't get to come barging in here pretending like you do."

"He's dangerous, Mia."

My face pinched. "What are you talking about?"

A disturbance rising up. A flicker of awareness that sent worry flooding through my senses.

Contempt rolled from his tongue. "Leif and I? We go way back. Asshole hates me, and the only reason he is here is to get back at me."

Shock rocked me to the soul.

An earthquake.

A fault line that split me in two.

"What did you just say?" I tried to make the words sound defiant, but they trembled in my throat.

Aftershocks.

He knew Leif?

That couldn't . . . that couldn't be possible.

No.

"I said he's dangerous, Mia, and you and the kids are coming with me."

Dizziness spun, and the nausea I'd been fighting all day hit me hard. I ran into the bathroom.

Dropped to my knees.

Purged the pain.

I clung to the edge of the toilet, trying to see through the tears that rushed down my face and blurred my sight.

Leif knew Nixon.

Leif knew Nixon.

Oh God.

Why . . . why would he do this to me? Why would he come here and rip me apart?

I will ruin you.

I will ruin you.

Is that what he meant? Had he done this on purpose? Cruel and unjust.

No. There was no way. He'd pushed me away a thousand times. But our connection had been too great. The man my gravity.

There was no faking that.

My mind spun, back to what Penny had said. The worry she'd worn when she'd explained Leif's reaction to Nixon.

They *knew* each other.

They did.

That's what had sent Leif running.

I moaned through the agony, and I could hear Nix in the other room, telling Penny to get her things.

Greyson was whimpering. Crying for me.

I had to get it together. Understand what Nixon meant. I refused to believe it—that Leif was actually dangerous.

That he would hurt us.

Leif's voice spun.

"But the rest of who I was? He was a bad guy. He did horrible, bad things."

"Just because I didn't pull the trigger doesn't mean I wasn't responsible. Doesn't mean I'm not the devil."

I puked some more. Unable to keep it down. To stop this eruption of grief. The poison that roiled inside of me.

The bathroom door banged open. Nix was there, a backpack on his shoulder. "Let's go."

"Nix, I—"

"Get up, Mia. We don't have time for this."

"I don't understand."

"I'll tell you in the car."

My mind raced, head spinning, disoriented. My hand shot out to the wall to keep me steady.

Everything weak.

Everything wrong.

"I'm not going anywhere with you. Tell me what's going on. I want to know what you mean. How do you know Leif?"

His rage crashed through the tiny room, and he was in my face. "I'm leaving right now, with my kids. Are you coming with me or not?"

He turned around and walked out the door, picking up Greyson who'd been coming my way, my son crying and crying. I was right behind him, grabbing at his shirt. "Put him down. You aren't taking him anywhere."

"Watch me, Mia."

I stumbled out into the main room, and Penny was there, her backpack on her shoulders. Confusion and fear in her eyes.

"Come on."

"Where are we going?" she asked, pushed up to the wall, trust wiped from her face.

He stretched his free hand toward her. "To get ice cream. You guys can play while me and your mom talk."

Greyson stopped crying at that. "Owkay."

God.

This was a disaster. A complete wreck.

"Just, come on, Mia. Put some shoes on. I just need to talk to you. That's it. I told you I would always do everything to protect you. I've been here. Fighting for you. You aren't going to trust me now? After that twisted fuck came here and messed with your head?"

I wanted to scream at him for talking like that in front of our kids.

Scream at him not to speak such blasphemy.

Beg him to take it back.

Make it untrue.

I needed answers.

A reason.

Nixon was the only one who could give them to me.

"Fine. We can go let the kids play and we'll talk. But that's it. I'm not ready to leave Savannah. Give me a minute to change."

I went back into my room, changed into jeans and a tee, and rinsed my mouth with mouthwash, tried to remain upright.

Not to go dropping back to my knees.

This pain too real.

Too intense.

I thought I could handle it. The scars Leif would leave behind. But I wasn't so sure of that, anymore.

I came back out, and Nixon went out the main door and turned to the right.

I gestured to the hall down the left. "I need to tell Tamar and Lyrik what's going on."

"You can text them from the car."

"Nixon."

He didn't even listen. The man on some kind of mission that I didn't want to be a part of.

Frustrated, I followed him out, and I texted my brother after I got into the rental SUV that he'd parked at the back street. For a moment, I questioned if I was being unreasonable, this anger I held, when I saw he'd thought far enough ahead to have a car seat in place for Greyson.

His son.

I glanced at him, at the rigid clutch of his jaw, and I tried to find that balance. That respect I'd had for him. For the fact he'd always tried to be here the best that he could be.

He pulled the car out onto the street, followed the directions I gave him for the fast food place that had a playground that the kids liked, while I tried to come to terms.

To remember this wasn't just about me.

My children were the most important.

I had to put them first.

"Take a left up here," I told him, except he was accelerating. Glancing in his rear-view mirror. He made a sharp right, and then a quick left.

Frantic, he made another, our speed increasing with each second.

My lungs squeezed, and I jerked to look out the side-mirror. A white car was behind us, weaving side to side. Trying to get to the side to box us in.

And the dread I'd been feeling all day spread and compounded. Became a horror that completely closed off my throat.

I pressed myself to the door and looked over at Nixon.

In disbelief and a plea. "What's happening?"

His teeth ground, his hands blanched on the steering wheel. "Fucked up, Mia. I fucked up. He was coming for you. I had to get you out of there."

"What?" I demanded, my voice held low like it could protect the kids. But it didn't matter. Because Penny knew. I could feel it—her terror invade the space.

"Nixon, what have you done?"

Leif
Three Years Ago

*P*anic.

Desperation.

They whipped my blood into a storm as I raced through the streets. Weaving through cars and running through red lights like no obstacle could stand in front of me.

The world a blur except for one singular focus.

My family.

My family.

I chanted their names as the miles burned from under me.

Like they could hear me.

Like Maddie would listen. Fucking answer her phone so I could tell her to get the hell out of the house, hide out until I could get to her.

Kiss the Stars

But it only rang a thousand times, phone clutched in my hand as I dialed it again and again as I blazed down the streets.

Reckless.

But that's what this life had been.

It was time for this to end.

I just had to get there.

Get there in time.

I careened around the last turn onto our street, pushing the bike so hard my knuckles felt like they were gonna bust open.

Muscles tight.

Lined with steel.

Terror screamed up my spine when I saw the red and blue lights strobing against the daylight. Cul-de-sac at the end filled with fire trucks and cop cars and ambulances.

This neighborhood that was supposed to be a safe place. An area where our daughter could run and play and grow.

Bile rushed, and my bike flew down the narrow street before I was ramming on the brakes, tires skidding. I didn't even let it come to a full stop before I lay it down and jumped off.

Couldn't even feel my feet as I raced for the house.

My spirit already inside.

Screaming and screaming.

No. Please. God. No.

A crowd had gathered. A circle of morbid curiosity that pressed and vied to get closer to the tragedy.

It was.

I could already feel it.

The evil that oozed from the walls. Shouted its wickedness. A claiming of the innocent.

It didn't matter my soul already knew.

That it screamed and roared with agony.

I shoved through the people who formed a tight circle, held back by the yellow tape.

All of them gasping and crying and speculating.

A vicious buzz that screamed in my ears.

No, no, no, no.

"Maddie!" I screamed, raging, pushing through.

Jagged breaths and ice-cold blood.

Hands sought to hold me back, but I broke through the tape as I screamed, "Maddie!"

Officers grabbed me by both arms to keep me from getting to the house.

I roared, breaking free, and I surged through the door while they shouted at me to stop. Guns drawn.

I couldn't. I couldn't.

I had to get to them.

I flew inside, and I slid, slipping on their blood. My body gave, and I fell.

Falling.

This hell unending.

On my hands and knees, I crawled across the floor. Going nowhere with the pile of men who held me back.

But I fought and I fought, because I couldn't stop, refused to give up.

I was weeping.

Guttural sounds ripping from my chest.

"Maddie. Haylee. Please."

I needed to hold them.

One more time.

"Haylee. Oh God. My baby."

"Get down, on your stomach."

The shouts banged the walls, but the only thing I could hear was my spirit that wept.

Wails shattering the air.

Mine gutted.

Hers forever silenced.

My baby.

I was nothing.

Nothing.

Boneless.

Empty.

Nothing but rage.

Men hauled me away in shackles and chains. The interrogation felt like it went on forever as I sat there with my clothes stained with their affliction.

The curse I'd put on their lives.

As if I could do this.

But I had, hadn't I?

The sins scored and seared and marred until I was nothing but rotted flesh.

Their goodness stripped away.

And the only thing left the vengeance that was to come.

Leif

"Haylee!" The cry rocking from my mouth jolted me to sitting, heart crashing like a beast in my chest.

Worst part?

Worst was the way my arms burned with the vacant weight of my little girl.

The way my soul screamed with the truth of what I'd done.

The way it'd done for the last three years.

I dropped my head into my hands, squeezing it like it might stand the chance of blotting it out.

This unending pain.

Wondering how the fuck I'd gotten here.

Loving a girl that part of me had hated.

The way I'd been tormented with a nameless, shapeless face.

And now she was the only face I could see.

Kiss the Stars

My guts twisted at the idea that bastard had ever even touched her. Last night, I'd had every intention of going for him. To just end it. But I couldn't bring myself to leave.

Mia. Mia.

My spirit groaned with her name. Body aching, already fucking addicted to her touch. Should have known I could never have them. That they were going to slip through my fingers like sand. Gone the second I'd hoped they were real.

My sins too great.

The evils I'd committed had accrued too much debt.

Now, I had to pay.

Rot in this motherfucking misery.

Hell.

That's what I got for thinking I could possibly live in Eden.

And there was Karma, sitting on the shitty couch across the room, buffing her fingernails while she smirked.

Well-played, bitch, well-played.

My attention jerked to the nightstand of the rundown hotel where I was staying when my phone lit up with a call. Looked like I'd missed about fifteen thousand of them.

I grabbed it, squinting through the grainy light of the room.

Stomach clenched when I didn't recognize the number.

Warily, I accepted it. "Hello?"

"Leif."

Sound of her voice made me feel like I'd gotten knocked with a sledgehammer to the back of the head.

My mother.

"Don't hang up," she demanded in her hard way.

I roughed out bitter laughter. Was so not in the mood. "Give me one reason not to."

"I'll give you three. Mia and her kids."

Her words pierced me all the way through.

"What about them?" Tried to make it come off strong, but my voice fucking cracked.

"Listen to me, Leif, we don't have much time. I have reason to believe they're in danger."

"And how the fuck do you know anything about them?"

359

Aggression pulsed with the appeal.

She huffed out a rugged sound. "You think I haven't been watching you all these years? Following you? You're my son."

She said it like it meant something.

But I didn't have fucking time to argue with her about the virtue of good parenting right then, did I?

"Listen to me, Leif." Her tone didn't help things. "Braxton came to me last night. He told me you called him distraught because you found out Nixon is the father of your girlfriend's children."

Mine. Mine. Mine.

Couldn't stop it from infiltrating my mind.

Anxiety spreading wide, I slipped from the bed and started pulling on my clothes that I'd dumped on the floor while I had the phone pressed between my ear and shoulder.

"Tell me why you think they're in danger." The words were gravel.

"Nixon had invested in this Mia girl's gallery. He was moving product through it. Some stolen art and guns. I don't know if she knew or not, but from what Braxton said about her, I'm guessing she didn't. Nixon was already in deep with Krane, but because they're blood, he kept letting him slide. Giving him the benefit of the doubt. But Krane isn't a fool. His suspicions deepened when shipments coming from the gallery started coming up missing. A woman at that gallery was killed as a warning."

Apprehension flooded my system.

Blood thudding hard when I realized it was all tied.

Lana.

Nixon was responsible for Lana.

Sweat slicked my skin.

Awareness riding free.

Terror taking over.

I shoved my feet into my shoes while she continued talking.

"Apparently, they've had the girl followed, too. A warning that they were watching. Keeton went to Krane two days ago, Leif. Gave him the evidence he had that Nixon is the one who's been guilty all along. When I found out what Braxton knew about your

connection, I put a tail on Nixon. Nixon left for Georgia last night, Leif, coming after her, and one of Krane's men flew there after him."

Horror slicked beneath my skin.

"What?" I forced through the clotted disorder.

"I know you don't believe me or trust me. I get it. I was a horrible mother. I know that I was. Since the day you were born. Selfish and stupid. And when I met Keeton . . . I thought I'd finally found a solution for who I was. For all the ways I'd failed you. Someone to take care of us. And he did in his own way."

My teeth clenched, unable to process all of this.

She continued without stopping. "I know you think Keeton blamed you for skimming off that deal. Think he believed it was you. Thought we didn't care."

I ground my teeth in spite. Barely able to keep it together.

"He didn't, Leif. He never condoned what happened, and he never would have gone after you. But once you were gone, he had to act like he was in line with Krane . . . for the sake of Petrus. For the sake of the family. For the sake of Braxton. He had to protect everyone who was involved. If we went after Nixon? You know there would have been more bloodshed. He had to make the choice."

I could hear the weight of her swallow. "We decided it was best to let you think we were against you. Safer for you to stay far away from L.A. Until we had enough to take out Nixon without it putting the rest of the crew in danger. Believe me or not. It's up to you. But it is the truth."

A jagged breath ripped from my lungs.

This was what I'd wanted all along, wasn't it? To see Nixon go down?

Burn at the motherfucking stake?

An end to the scourge that he was.

But the only thing I cared about right then was Mia.

Mia and Penny and Greyson.

Possession rushed. A protectiveness that blotted out everything but them.

"I sent Braxton to take up your side. His flight landed an hour ago. Go. Protect her."

She ended the call without saying anything else.

Instantly, I dialed Mia.

My soul chanted it. *Mia. Mia. Mia.*

It went to voicemail.

I tried again with the same result.

Dread curled, blood drenched in violence, mind spiraling that direction.

I dialed Lyrik while I grabbed the gun I'd shoved into the nightstand drawer. Checking that it was loaded.

He answered on the first ring.

Like maybe he'd been waiting on me to call.

"Lyrik."

Worry silently shouted back before he grunted out the words, "Where the fuck are you?"

"Mia's not answering," I said instead.

"Yeah, that's because her prick of an ex-boyfriend showed here a couple hours ago and the guy who was supposed to be sticking by her side took off like a pussy."

Shit. Fuck. I blinked, trying to see through the barrage of fear that impaled me.

"Things get too heavy for you?" he taunted.

Yeah, way too fucking heavy.

"Where are they? Need to know, right now."

Thought he must have felt the violence that was skating from my tongue because he lowered his voice like he was trying to keep the conversation from the rest of the house. "What's going on?"

"Nixon isn't who you think he is."

"Yeah, well I think he's a piece of shit, so . . ."

"He was using the gallery as a cover, Lyrik. Running shit through the back. Lana was killed as a warning. Need to make sure Mia is safe. Think they've been sending a message this whole time."

A message that was meant for Nixon but somehow had ended up as one for me.

My purpose.

My reason.

This goal.

"Fuck." Something banged in the background. "Motherfucker."

His voice dropped in contempt. "They left with him two hours ago, Leif. Got some bullshit message that they were taking the kids for ice cream. Knew it. Knew it way down deep that something was amiss. That fucker is dead."

Sickness clawed. Fact she was with him. The kids. The kids.

The world spun for a beat.

I gritted my teeth. "Where? Where did they go?"

"I don't know where they went. Fuck." Could feel Lyrik coming apart, too.

"Dad." Brendon's distanced voice broke into our chaos.

"Not right now, Brendon."

"Dad, listen. I know you're upset about Aunt Mia leaving. I know where they're at. Where Penny is. I have her on my locator on Snap."

"Where?" I demanded.

Silence stretched on for too fucking long, and when Lyrik spoke again, the entire world dropped out from under me.

No footing.

"Not at an ice cream parlor."

His voice was grim. Hatred riding in behind the despair.

"Where?"

"North. Some sketch neighborhood."

"Drop me the location."

"Coming with you."

"No, Lyrik."

"This is my sister and niece and nephew you're talking about."

I swallowed around the ball of barbed wire in my throat. "These people . . . they're cruel . . . evil," I told him, knowing he now knew the truth about me.

I was one of them.

"You think I'm a stranger to that? Coming with you. Where are you?"

"About five minutes from your house."

Hadn't been able to stay with Mia, but I couldn't bring myself to get very far, either.

"Meet me at Whitaker and Taylor in ten."

He didn't give me a chance to refuse before he hung up.

But we didn't have time to fuck around. Despair hit me at the thought that we might already be too late.

I purged the thought and shoved my gun into the back of my jeans, tore open the door, and stepped outside, furiously blinking through the blazing daylight.

Trying to keep control.

Focus.

Knowing the time had come, but it looked entirely different than I'd ever anticipated.

My gaze moved.

Drawn to the parking lot below.

Braxton was there, leaning against a car. Skin dark and eyes fierce and loyalty firm. He tossed his cigarette to the ground and straightened.

I lifted my chin.

He grinned.

"It's time," I told him.

"Yeah, brother. I know. Let's roll."

I bounded down the steps of the crappy hotel and climbed onto my bike. Braxton got behind the wheel of the car he'd rented, falling in line behind me. My bike grumbled and groaned, reigned like a pack of vicious dogs that were fighting to be unleashed.

I took the couple turns through the shadowed Savannah streets.

Lyrik rolled out beside me at the intersection where he'd told us to meet. Tattooed arms stretched out, hands fisted on the handlebars. He gave me a look. I gave him one in return.

He throttled it, flying down the road.

Braxton and I followed suit.

Leif

*I*t was a sleazy street.

Same damn story but a different town.

Rundown houses on every side. Chain link fences fronting the overgrown yards. Sparse trees and dead weeds growing up all over the place.

A few were nicer. People trying to make something out of this life.

Our motorcycles rumbled through the stagnant heatwaves as we took another turn deeper into the neighborhood, our pace slowed and controlled while our spirits raged.

Could feel it.

Coming off of Lyrik.

Coming off of me.

Do or die.

And I had no idea what I was going to come up on. Come up against.

If it'd be the same scene that had destroyed me three years before.

If this would be my end.

But I would give it all to them. No questions or reservations.

Lyrik put his left hand down, gesturing for us to slow. We eased off to the right of the narrow neighborhood road.

Engines chugging and rumbling before we killed them.

Silence rolled.

Evil howling through the sticky stillness.

We both climbed off our bikes, and Braxton stepped out of the car. Could only imagine what we looked like.

Nothing but bloodshed and brutality.

Someone was probably peering out their blinds right that second, calling the cops, which part of me had already wanted to do, but I knew full well this had to be handled a certain way.

Only chance we had was taking this motherfucker by surprise.

We edged down the street. Three of us shoulder to shoulder, stalking toward disaster.

Each step riddled with my deepest fear.

We moved farther down the road. Past one house. Then another.

Every second felt like eternity.

Torture.

Wanted to fucking blaze a path of carnage.

But I held it. Bottled it. Let it feed the determination that lined every muscle in my body.

Lyrik slowed a little more, on guard, silently angling his head to the right at the house that sat on the corner of two streets.

It faced out to the road to the right, blips of the backyard visible through the broken-down planks of rotted wood that was meant to serve as a fence.

Knee-high weeds filled most of the lot. A dilapidated shed was at the very back, roof caved in at one side. But it was the tiny glimpse of a new but plain white SUV parked haphazardly off to the side that sent a dagger of aggression through my soul.

My entire being lurched forward a step, but it was Lyrik who was putting out his hand against my chest, a silent, "Stay cool," mouthed from his lips.

Cool.

Not possible.

It wasn't like he was any closer to managing it, either.

His entire body vibrated with madness.

It only amplified tenfold when there was a sudden wail echoing from the house. Distorted and blunted.

Muted.

But there all the same. I nearly cracked because there was no length that I wouldn't go.

This time it was Brax who stepped in. He gestured with his chin to Lyrik, letting his line of sight glide to the back fence. Lyrik nodded, slinking that way, gaze darting everywhere before he scaled over the top. Landing silent on the other side.

Nothing but stealth.

Braxton edged through the side of the front yard. I followed, sound of my boots barely crunching under me, my pulse so loud I was sure that was what was going to be what gave us away.

We pressed our backs up to the side of the wall, searching that we were clear before we started to slip around to the front.

Breaths shallow and ragged as we waded through the disturbance.

Terror seeped through the crumbling walls, and there was another mumbled cry.

Greyson.

Greyson.

My heart clutched. Fisted and throbbed and nearly bolted from my chest.

Braxton felt it, sensed me getting ready to slip, and he cut me a look, his gun steady in his hands as he pressed close to the wall while mine was shaking.

Finger on the trigger.

Swinging his head around a fraction, he peered through a crack in the window.

Could tell from the way his spine went rigid that we had a

confirmation. They were inside.

My guts twisted and my spirit screamed, taking over. Nothing left but this determined desperation.

He gave a sign for me to round to the other side so we would be surrounding them.

I eased that way, shaking and shaking.

I slipped around the other side of the house, peeked up through a window into a vacant, destroyed kitchen. Cupboard doors hanging from their hinges, garbage strewn, broken dishes left behind like the evidence of the hopelessness that leaked from inside.

The broken window had been left open a crack.

I nudged it farther, and I hiked myself up and slipped inside.

I landed on my feet, cringing when the impact made a small thud.

But that chaos raging from inside was louder.

Bleak and tortured.

I kept my footsteps as quiet as I could, inching for the open archway that led out to the living room.

Whimpers bled into my ears, the taste of terror on my tongue.

Nearly dropped to my knees when I pressed my back to the wall and peered out.

Memories flooded my mind.

Blinding.

Gutting.

Horrid and vile.

Morgue.

The same one who'd killed my family. The same one who'd let go of a spray of bullets when I'd gone after him and Nixon the first time. Motherfucker had been the one to *postpone* my intentions. Hitting me five times on my side. I'd almost died. Probably would have if it hadn't been for the unrelenting need for retribution.

It was the same man as I'd seen out in Lyrik's yard that night.

Same one who was looming over Nixon and Mia right then.

Wickedness blazed back.

Evil hovering in the room.

I could barely see her, her back to me where she was tied to a chair facing away. Her hair mangled and her head slumped forward.

But I could feel her.

The girl the storm inside of me.

Light. Light. Light.

Nixon was to her right, hands tied in front of him as he spouted his bullshit. His reasons why he wasn't guilty. Putting the blame on someone else.

Fuck.

I'd thirsted to put a bullet in that motherfucker's head for so long. The wrath that had consumed. My entire reason his end.

But the only thing I could discern right then was getting Mia free.

Safe.

Nothing else mattered.

I caught Braxton's eye where he was kneeled down low, hidden by a short wall that created a foyer at the front door.

He rested his hand on his thigh, giving me a countdown. Three, two . . .

I tightened my hold on the grip of my gun, trying to keep my ragged breaths steady. To keep quiet.

Ready to strike.

I counted down to one in my head when the little voice filled the space, "Uncle, I got you."

Greyson.

Shit.

Could hear rustling get louder from the back of the house, the quickened pace of energy, and I knew Lyrik was trying to shush him, keep him quiet, get them out, and the only thing I could think was thank God, thank God he got to the kids.

But Morgue jerked up his head and started that direction.

Neither Braxton or I waited for that final count.

We both swung around, guns drawn, the bastard pinned between the middle of us.

He calculated, looking for his shot.

A door banged at the back of the house, and that ferocity

shifted, something perfect and relieved.

Lyrik had gotten the kids free.

I knew it.

I knew it.

And I was trying not to look at Mia while I kept the gun steady. Not to focus on the blood that dripped from the corner of her mouth or the fear and relief that burned from her swollen, beaten eyes.

But rage.

It burned.

So intense.

So ugly.

My finger twitched on the trigger.

"Put your gun down, Morgue. This job is over." Braxton's hard voice sliced through the agitated air. The guy shifted his head just a fraction to look at Brax.

Brax who edged out farther from behind the wall.

Two of us closing him in.

That was the second that pussy deadbeat jumped from the chair, knocking it over, running with his hands tied in front of him toward the window to the opposite side of where I stood.

Running in front of Mia, leaving her sitting there as he dove for the window.

Morgue spun.

Shots rang out.

Piercing.

Shocking.

Nixon's body jerked as he was struck in the back multiple times.

And I was running.

Running for Mia as his aim shifted, my arm outstretched with the gun pointed at him.

Faster than I could make sense of it and anticipating what was going to go down all the same.

Because I knew full well if Nixon was gone, he wouldn't be leaving Mia around as evidence.

Bullets flew, tearing up the living room.

And I was pulling the trigger as I dove in front of her, and Mia's scream was filling my ears.

Lights flashed through my eyes.

The blackest blacks and the starkest whites.

A haze.

Heaven.

Hell.

I flew into her, knocking her chair over.

Toppling us over.

Didn't give a thought to the pain in the front of my shoulder, the darkness that kept rushing in to steal my consciousness.

Blood flooding across my shirt.

Only thing I cared about was getting her untied.

Freed from her bindings.

But Mia.

She slumped to the floor.

A shattered groan left me, and I frantically rolled her onto her back, holding her face, screaming and screaming as those sable eyes fluttered and her breaths rasped. "No, Mia. Don't close your eyes. Don't close your eyes. Don't leave me. Don't leave me."

Sirens wailed.

Coming closer and closer.

"I've got to go, man." Braxton hesitated for a second, looking to the door, before he bolted as the sirens grew closer, leaving two bodies at his feet behind.

But none of that mattered.

Just her.

Mia.

My angel in the attic.

The purpose I'd never anticipated.

My reason I'd never seen.

Not until the second she'd crashed into me.

"I'm fine," I grunted through the shock of pain, shoving my

arm back through my bloodied shirt.

The doctor frowned. "I'd recommend that we admit you overnight. You suffered a significant amount of blood loss and you need a round of antibiotics to prevent an infection."

Yeah, and I'd recommend that he step out of my way.

"Going to have to pass."

He huffed in disbelief. "You were shot."

It'd barely grazed me, and I had already spent hours being barraged by questions from officers. Last one finally left two minutes ago.

Two dead.

Two injured, one in critical condition.

Two children unharmed.

Unscathed.

Relief. Relief.

That overwhelming feeling was gnarled by the anxiety that crawled and infested and decayed.

"You can write me a prescription if you want. But I'm out."

I slipped off the bed, wincing like a bitch.

He shook his head. "You're in pain."

He had no idea.

"You can find me on the fifth floor if you need me," I grumbled, going for the door.

Arm in a sling, shirt covered in blood, but it was my soul that was doing the bleeding.

I went for the elevator, punching the up button about fifteen times.

Dread whirled around me.

A vortex of apprehension.

That storm I'd felt coming since the second that girl had stumbled into my life.

When the elevator doors opened, I stepped into it and rode it to the fifth floor.

Even though the hall was lit, I could feel darkness pressing into the hospital, ominous clouds that gathered at the edges of my sight and mind.

Regular visiting hours were long since over, but there were

people who still mingled about, whispering outside doors, worry radiating from their hearts.

Nurses hustled, and a few rooms were still lit.

Feet heavy, laden with fear, I made it to the end of the hall where two double doors led into the intensive care unit. There was a counter to check in. The visiting hours later in this area, though I didn't think there was anyone stupid enough to try to stop me from getting through those doors.

The man fronting the counter pushed the button and the double doors automatically swung open. I moved inside, footsteps slowed while my heart raced the fastest that it ever had.

Hope and horror.

Hope and horror.

Two emotions shoved so close together inside me, I wasn't sure I could differentiate one from the other.

My breaths came shorter and shorter as I took a turn down the hall to the right.

Like I was going against the current. Against the grain.

I could barely move by the time I made it to her room number.

Lyrik was there, standing outside the door, his back pressed to the wall, his head rocked back toward the ceiling.

Panic sloshed, and terror slogged through my veins.

I froze three feet away.

He pulled from the wall when he saw I was there, and I was crushing my teeth when I met his eyes.

Waiting for the worst.

For the debt to increase.

These sins greater than I could afford.

Lyrik roughed a hand through his hair, blowing out a shuddering sigh. "She's awake."

My hand darted out to the wall to keep me standing.

Fear exhaled on a haggard breath.

Respite.

Reprieve.

Still, I was asking, disbelief in the plea, "She's okay?"

He nodded. "She's going to be."

My spirit screamed and my soul shouted.

"The doctor is in there right now. First thing she did when she woke up was ask for you and the kids. I think she's as worried about you as you were about her."

Emotion shivered, and I blinked.

Uncertain.

Unworthy.

Could I just . . . walk in there?

Be with her?

"You're a fool if you're standing there questioning if she could love you right now. Question is, after everything, can you love her?"

I looked at the closed door.

Every nerve alive.

That connection booming through the air.

I gulped as I pushed it open.

Energy crashed.

Mine. Mine. Mine.

I was inundated with it.

Blinded.

Her goodness.

Her purity.

Her light.

Even though she was beat up, her smile was soft—an invitation—when she looked at me from where she was propped up on the bed, attached to a thousand monitors, all of them beating with life.

The air punched from my lungs.

Knees going weak.

The best thing that I'd ever seen.

"Hi," she whispered, voice thick.

"Hey."

The doctor shifted a fraction, the woman taking in my state, eyebrow arching in question.

"This is who I was telling you about. The man who saved me. Saved my children." Mia's voice was acute affection, a message delivered in her words.

Thank you.

And I didn't know how to stand under that.

Like these sins could be erased.

Moisture glistened in her eyes, and the girl looked at me the way she always had.

Like she saw something better.

Something right.

Something meant for her.

Love burst in my heart.

Wasn't sure how any of us remained upright under the eruption of it.

The doctor hummed, looking between us.

I edged for the bed.

Wary.

Eager.

Sorry.

Fucking sorry, and still suffering all that hope this girl had somehow made me believe in again.

I leaned in, dropped my forehead to hers, breathed her in. "You're okay."

She nodded, face getting soggy from the tears that slipped free.

"An artery in her thigh was nicked," the doctor explained. "Thankfully the paramedics arrived quickly, and it was easily repaired in surgery. It seems somebody else took the brunt of it." Her voice shifted in implication.

My eyes dropped closed, and I knew that was the only thing I wanted.

To be her shield.

Her protection.

This girl my own savior. One I didn't deserve but who was still waiting on me.

I let my lips press to hers.

Lightly, though I lingered.

"You're okay."

She nodded under my kiss. Tears slipped from the corner of her eyes.

"You're hurt," she whispered.

"It's nothing." I edged back and set my hand on her face. "I'm so sorry."

"No, Leif. You have nothing to apologize for. I told you I always recognized the man you are. The one who was waiting to be freed. He's the man I fell in love with. He is the one standing right here, in front of me. The one who saved us. He's the one I want."

"Don't want to be anywhere else, Mia. I . . ." I struggled with what to say. "My past . . . the guy . . . he was a bad guy. And I know you get what that really means now."

I knew we had an audience. But I didn't care. I was so over hiding behind the walls.

Behind the anger and the hate and the fear that had held me captive for the last three years.

I had to lay all of that at her feet.

"But if you can see past that—through it—I will live for you, Mia. Live for you with all that I have. I love Penny. I love Greyson."

My heart panged with the truth of it, their sweet faces flashing through my mind. God, I loved them so much.

"*And I love you.* I want to spend my life with you. Let me love you. Let me love your kids. I want to see your joy. Want to be a part of it. Want to see you paint. Let's make beauty together."

She brushed her thumb over my jaw. "Don't you get it . . . you are the beauty reflected back at me. You thought you were the darkness, but you were my light. I love you, Leif. Let me love you back."

I nodded at her, tightened my hold on her cheek. A promise. A pledge. "I will let you love me every day, just like I will be loving you."

Sable eyes gazed up at me, her lips trembling, pulling up at one side as the tears kept gliding down her face. "We caught a falling star, Leif."

Mia's eyes flitted to the doctor, mine following the path, my chest panging with uncertainty.

The woman gave a soft smile. "I was just giving Mia some of her test results. Her bloodwork showed a positive pregnancy. With her past medical history as well as her current situation, we need to consider this high risk. I ordered an ultrasound, and they should be in with a mobile unit soon. But as of right now, everything looks good."

Shock slowed my heart.

I couldn't process.

Couldn't speak.

Couldn't do anything but look down at Mia who was looking up at me with all that hope and love shining bright, and she whispered, "Are you happy?"

I knew it was worry in her question. Compassion. This girl who got me on a level that no one else could.

The one who would hold me through the pain.

Understand my grief. Not count it as a detriment or disloyalty.

The doctor slipped out when the ultrasound tech came in, and I watched as she squirted gel on Mia's belly, as she held a probe to it, as the tiny thing showed up on the screen.

As my world shifted and shook.

As my heart took on a new truth.

I'd once questioned fate.

Destiny.

The idea of living each day thinking every event, conversation, and person that passed through our lives had been set on that path long before we even knew what direction we were headed.

Carved in some proverbial stone eons before we were born.

All coming together for the greater good.

I'd scoffed.

Mocked it.

I looked down at Mia.

Recognized the girl.

My purpose.

My reason.

And I thought I saw Karma in my periphery smile before she turned and slipped out the door.

I squeezed Mia's hand, dropped my forehead back to hers. "You got me, Mia. You fucking got me. *And that is my honest.*"

She smiled.

Smiled her hope.

Her joy.

This girl filling me up with her love.

She cupped my cheek. "And I'm never going to let you go."

epilogue

Leif

We lay under the deepest night. A big blanket spread out on the lawn below us.

Stars strewn on forever.

Penny shrieked, pointed her finger. "There's one."

A streaking light blazed through the sky.

Arching and bright before it burned out.

The meteor shower in full force.

"I see it, Penny-Pie!" Greyson shouted, bouncing on his knees in excitement and pointing to where it had burned out. "It was a big one! Did you see it, Daddy? Did you see it?"

My chest squeezed.

So tight.

Sometimes I wondered how it was possible that I could continue to breathe under the magnitude of it.

The greatness of what had been given into my life.

Healing breathed into my soul.

I ruffled my fingers through his hair where he sat close to my side. "I saw it, buddy. It was a good one, wasn't it?"

Carson crawled over, planting his tiny hands on my chest, rocking on his knees. Slobber from his adorable smile dripping onto my shirt, the little guy getting his second tooth. "Hi, little buddy."

"I'm the big buddy, and he's the little buddy, right?" Greyson asked, poking his head in between us, his shoulders coming up to his ears as he peered at his baby brother.

"That's right. My buddies."

My boys.

My life.

My love.

Mia sat on the blanket with her knees hugged to her chest, that gorgeous face tipped toward the sky.

River of black hair cascading down her back.

She turned that tender gaze on us.

Sable eyes flashing with all her love.

Another meteorite went blazing through the sky.

Mia lifted her hand.

Cupped it beneath it.

Her eyes closed. "There. I caught it."

The softest smile edged that seductive mouth when she looked back at me, my wife, my perfection.

My completion.

"Don't ever let it go," I murmured, not even caring that I was staring, that Penny was blushing the way she always did.

"You should sing Mom her song, Dad. The one you wrote when you fell in love with her."

Yeah.

She called me *Dad*, too.

My little hopeless romantic who was growing up so fast.

She'd struggled with the loss of Nixon the most. Something I'd warred with, too. We'd kept the sordid details from her as best as we could, but she was old enough for the shadow of him to cloud her.

The wounds to scar and invade.

But we loved her with everything. Held her through her hurt. Filled her with our love and our belief.

I'd sat her down a couple months after and told her I was there for her, no matter what. She could think of me however she wanted to. As a friend or a protector or a parent. Told her she could call me anything she wanted. Well, except for Mr. Godwin, of course.

She'd asked if it was okay if she called me Dad. She said dads were just like moms. They were supposed to be our favorite people in the world. They were supposed to take care of you. And she said that was what I did.

And I was never going to stop—proving that devotion to her. To her mom. To her brothers.

"Aren't you all tired of hearing me play yet?"

They'd been following Carolina George around as much as they could since Carson was old enough to travel, watching from backstage in the places they were allowed, waiting for me at whatever hotel we were staying at if they couldn't.

At my side, the same as I would forever be for them.

Knew they couldn't always do it.

But we made it work.

Just like Mia and I promised we would.

But had to admit, I loved it when I was home, out in our backyard in the outskirts of Savannah where we could gaze up at the stars.

Penny giggled. "Never."

Mia looked at me with those eyes, mouthed, "Never."

I grumbled, but I really didn't mind, taking Carson with me as I stood to grab my guitar where it sat on a chair next to our snuffed-out fire.

We'd done marshmallows and hot dogs earlier.

A campout two steps from our quaint, perfect house.

I set Carson back on his bottom, and he clapped when I sat down and situated the guitar on my lap.

Was proud to play the drums with Carolina George as they

shot into fame. My extended family who I was crazy proud of. Drumsticks one of my closest friends.

But I didn't complain all that much when I strummed a guitar. The medium didn't matter. I just relished in the expression.

To me, that was what music was.

Beautiful. Brutal.

Everything you couldn't really say.

I strummed the chords and I let the lyrics spin into the cool breeze of the night.

I sang to my family, playing through the chords, the memories of the way I'd felt then.

Terrified.

Learning to hope again.

Remembering what it meant.

Penny rocked and gazed at the sky, while Greyson curled up at my side.

The song trailed off, and I was looking at Mia.

Lustdrunk.

Lovestruck.

My angel in the attic.

A savior I thought the devil could never keep.

But Mia?

She had found the good in me.

the end

Thank you for reading *Kiss the Stars*

I hope you loved Mia and Leif's story as much as I loved writing it!

Did you love the men and women of Sunder? Start where it all began with Shea and Sebastian in *A Stone in the Sea*

https://geni.us/ASITSAmzn

New to me and want more? I recommend starting with my favorite small town alphas!

Start with *Show Me the Way*

https://geni.us/SMTWAmzn

Text "aljackson" to 33222 to get your LIVE release mobile alert (US Only)
or
Sign up for my newsletter
https://geni.us/NewsFromALJackson

More from A.L. Jackson

ABOUT THE AUTHOR

A.L. Jackson is the New York Times & USA Today Bestselling author of contemporary romance. She writes emotional, sexy, heart-filled stories about boys who usually like to be a little bit bad.

Her bestselling series include THE REGRET SERIES, CLOSER TO YOU, BLEEDING STARS, FIGHT FOR ME, and CONFESSIONS OF THE HEART.

If she's not writing, you can find her hanging out by the pool with her family, sipping cocktails with her friends, or of course with her nose buried in a book.

Be sure not to miss new releases and sales from A.L. Jackson - Sign up to receive her newsletter http://smarturl.it/NewsFromALJackson or text "aljackson" to 33222 to receive short but sweet updates on all the important news.

Connect with A.L. Jackson online:

FB Page **https://geni.us/ALJacksonFB**
Newsletter **https://geni.us/NewsFromALJackson**
Angels **https://geni.us/AmysAngels**
Amazon **https://geni.us/ALJacksonAmzn**
Book Bub **https://geni.us/ALJacksonBookbub**
Text "aljackson" to 33222 to receive short but sweet updates on all the important news.

Made in United States
Orlando, FL
10 March 2023

30900610R00236